Praise fo

"Readers will root for both Ginny and Jacqueline in this heart-warming tale from Carlson."

Library Journal starred review

"Two career-focused women swap hospitality jobs, and chaos ensues in this latest jovial novel from Carlson. Her lighthearted take on an old trope charms."

Publishers Weekly

"A clean, wholesome, and fun read from start to finish, *Just for the Summer* by accomplished author and gifted storyteller Melody Carlson is especially and unreservedly recommended."

Midwest Book Review

"It's lighthearted but honest about work problems and challenges. Melody Carlson always spins a great yarn!"

WTBF

Praise for *Second Time Around*

"The uplifting latest from Carlson follows a fortysomething empty nester who moves from her stylish Victorian to a fixer-upper. This is perfect for fans of clean romance."

Publishers Weekly

"This read is the perfect book to cuddle up with during a stormy weekend."

Interviews and Reviews

Praise for *Looking for Leroy*

"No one writes clean, contemporary romance quite like Carlson, who delivers another winner with this novel."

Library Journal

"Carlson's latest inspirational novel is a sweet toast to second chances. Missed opportunities and misunderstandings abound in this heartwarming tale that's sure to appeal to Carlson's many fans."

Booklist

"Melody Carlson paints a vivid yet beautiful tale of finding old love and of forgiveness."

Urban Book Reviews

Welcome to the Honey B&B

Books by Melody Carlson

Courting Mr. Emerson
The Happy Camper
Looking for Leroy
Second Time Around
Just for the Summer
Welcome to the Honey B&B

Follow Your Heart Series

Once Upon a Summertime
All Summer Long
Under a Summer Sky

Holiday Novellas

Christmas at Harrington's
The Christmas Shoppe
The Joy of Christmas
The Treasure of Christmas
The Christmas Pony
A Simple Christmas Wish
The Christmas Cat
The Christmas Joy Ride
The Christmas Angel Project
The Christmas Blessing
A Christmas by the Sea
Christmas in Winter Hill
The Christmas Swap
Christmas in the Alps
The Christmas Quilt
A Royal Christmas
The Christmas Tree Farm

Welcome to the Honey B&B

MELODY CARLSON

Revell
a division of Baker Publishing Group
Grand Rapids, Michigan

Published by Revell
a division of Baker Publishing Group
Grand Rapids, Michigan
RevellBooks.com

Printed in the United States of America

Library of Congress Cataloging-in-Publication Data
Names: Carlson, Melody, author.
Title: Welcome to the Honey B&B / Melody Carlson.
Description: Grand Rapids, Michigan : Revell, a division of Baker Publishing Group, 2025.
Identifiers: LCCN 2024018899 | ISBN 9780800746025 (paperback) | ISBN 9780800746742 (casebound) | ISBN 9781493448647 (ebook)
Subjects: LCGFT: Christian fiction. | Novels.
Classification: LCC PS3553.A73257 W45 2024 | DDC 813/.54—dc23/eng/20240429
LC record available at https://lccn.loc.gov/2024018899

Cover illustration by Sybille Sterk / Arcangel
Cover design by Laura Klynstra

Baker Publishing Group publications use paper produced from sustainable forestry practices and postconsumer waste whenever possible.

25 26 27 28 29 30 31 7 6 5 4 3 2 1

1

Honey

Honey McKerry suppressed the urge to firmly lower the cast-iron skillet directly onto her husband's slightly balding noggin. Instead she blew out the breath she'd been holding during her attempt to count to ten, then slowly turned away, reminding herself for the hundredth time, *CT can't help it.* She set the heavy pan back on the stove and opened the upper cabinet, removing the overly familiar jars of peanut butter and honey. Jif Extra Crunchy and McKerry's homegrown honey—CT's favorite go-to sandwich, well, unless he changed his mind midstream, like he'd done just now.

"You're sure you don't want eggs, then?" She carefully placed the pair of freshly laid brown eggs back into the recycled egg carton. Her Plymouth Rock hens had really started producing when spring warmed up, but like so many things in her life since CT's illness had progressed, caring for chickens had become too much, so she'd given them to Marta and Anna next door. She repeated herself. "Sure you don't want eggs, CT?"

"No, no. My legs are okay," he replied confidently.

"I said *eggs*." She peered into his face to make sure he understood her. "Not legs." Although it wasn't a leap to speak of legs since his bothered him some. When he ignored her, she put her last carton of homegrown eggs back in the fridge. Maybe she'd fry up a couple for herself later, if she got hungry. She should've known when CT demanded scrambled eggs for breakfast, he would forget or change his mind. And by the time he'd dressed and made his way to the kitchen, a task that took nearly an hour, their morning egg conversation had floated off to the twilight zone.

"Oh, yeah." He nodded as he picked up the newspaper. "Eggs *are* good."

Sometimes she felt as confused as him. Maybe it was catching. She studied him before speaking. "So you don't want the peanut butter sandwich after all?"

"Yeah. Eggs and a sandwich. Like I said." He slid his chair toward the kitchen table, then opened the paper and pretended to read. She knew he was just looking at photos, maybe trying to make out a few headlines. But it had been almost a year since reading for retention became too much for him. For some reason she liked that he kept up the pretense. Maybe it made them both feel better . . . or at least gave her a moment of peace, knowing he was occupied.

She got the eggs back out. "You must be pretty hungry, CT."

He patted his flat stomach. "Oh, yeah. Ravished."

"Okay then." She smiled at his misused word. It just went with the territory. Eighteen months had passed since his diagnosis. She still remembered CT's response when the neurologist explained that he had FTD.

"Am I going to deliver flowers?" he'd asked with a twinkle in his dark brown eyes. They'd all laughed at his wit, but underneath Honey's cheery veneer, a cold chill had swept through her. She'd heard of FTD, and it wasn't good.

Oh, she wasn't blindsided by the diagnosis. Clearly, something had been going on for some time. But at the beginning of the testing, she'd never expected anything this life-altering and serious. At first the professionals blamed CT's forgetfulness on his hearing loss, then perhaps sleep apnea, and finally, after dealing with both issues, the doctors had suggested hydrocephalus, which was treatable. But after six months of acquiring new hearing aids, a frustrating month trying a CPAP machine, and various doctors and specialists and tests, CT's brain scans revealed frontotemporal dementia—or *disorder*, her preferred substitute for the *D* word. "Just like Bruce Willis," she would sometimes say to lighten things up. After all, CT had been a big *Die Hard* fan. But unfortunately, most of the time, the poor guy didn't really get it.

"Did you feed the cat?" she asked absently as she cracked an egg into the pan.

"No. Don't need a hat."

She rolled her eyes and picked up another egg. "Got your hearing aids in, CT?"

He reached up to check an ear, then sheepishly shook his head before returning to his faux reading. She knew she should nag him to go fetch them instead of simply getting them herself. While it was good for him to do what he could while he could, it was just so much quicker to do things for him. She put the last of the eggs in the pan, gave them a quick stir, then jogged up to the bedroom, where his hearing aid charger was supposed to be plugged in on his bedside table.

To her dismay, though not her surprise, the charger was AWOL again. Now it was off to the various other locales where he liked to *relocate* miscellaneous items. Never mind that she'd told him time and again that the bedroom was handiest. "The Lone Rearranger strikes again," she muttered as she checked his bathroom, which looked like it had been hit by a small tornado and smelled like a middle school boy's locker room. Next she looked in the den, where CT kept an odd assortment of unrelated bits and pieces and piles of books he'd once read and liked to imagine he would read again someday. She quickly sifted through a basket of charger cords, dead batteries, and a dysfunctional wristwatch and was about to hit the storage room under the stairs when she heard the smoke alarm going off.

The eggs!

She dashed back to the kitchen and turned off the flame beneath the now-blackened eggs, which were solidly adhered to the pan. She opened a window, then flipped on the exhaust fan, attempting to ignore her frantic husband as he hopped around, yowling and flapping his arms like a crazed chicken. "Make it stop!" he cried, covering his ears and wearing the anguished expression of a frightened four-year-old.

"Go outside." She took him by the arm and directed him toward the back porch. "Check on your bees." She nodded toward the stacked boxes of hives and led him outside. She wasn't a big fan of bees, but for some reason CT adored the buzzy little beings. He used to call his hives his *peaceful place*.

He nodded, clutching her hand and groaning with each step as he ambled down the porch stairs. On solid ground, he began to mumble. "My bees . . . yeah, bees don't burn down your house. Coming, bees, coming."

"Right." She watched him weaving slightly as he made his way to his beloved hives. Reassured he was okay, she went back inside. The kitchen was still smoky and the alarm still blaring. She got out her stepladder and, stretching high, reached for the smoke alarm, balancing precariously as she pressed the red button and waited for it to stop screaming at her. As she climbed down, she felt a bit shaky. This was something her big, strong husband used to do for her. A lump swelled in her throat, but she reminded herself this little event was not tear-worthy. Better to laugh . . . when she could.

Still, it was hard to let go of some things. Her can-do, capable husband used to handle so much for her. CT, at six foot six, was a man's man who could build almost anything, repair almost anything, hunt wild game. Like a country boy, he could survive. The man could plant and grow and dance a pretty good two-step. He even managed the bills and knew how to file tax returns, something she was still grappling over. But after their checking accounts got seriously messed up a few years back due to CT's disease, she'd taken over the business end of things and let him take over the simple things that hadn't overwhelmed him at first, like replacing light bulbs or smoke alarm batteries or taking out the trash.

But those days were gone now too. CT always forgot which day the garbage truck came. Sometimes she'd go racing out in her bathrobe, running the can down their driveway, waving to the truck driver to stop. Ladders messed with his balance. Tools were dangerous. And unexpected noises like a smoke alarm were unnerving. Even if he could've handled the noise and scaled the ladder, he'd probably forgotten how to make the smoke alarm stop blasting by now.

Honey sighed and scraped the burned eggs into her clean white sink, staring for a moment at the blackened ugliness as she washed it down the garbage disposal. Then realizing the skillet would require more attention, she decided CT would have to settle for a peanut butter sandwich after all. Along with a big glass of milk and a banana. He'd have forgotten about the eggs by now anyway. One benefit of FTD.

She carried his breakfast into the clean outside air and found him investigating something by the barn. Feeding the barn cat? She doubted it as she whistled for him, waving him over to the picnic table. She watched as he attempted to insert more spring in his step, but he still walked like a man two decades older than his years.

"That's what I want." He pointed to the sandwich. "Peanut butter 'n honey. Honey from my Honey." He grinned at her. "And from my bees too."

"How are your bees?" She watched him ease himself onto a bench.

"Happy. Happy bees . . . happy honey." He looked up with adoring eyes. "Bee honey is sweet. Not as sweet as my Honey."

She patted his shoulder. How many times had she heard that line? And yet she never really tired of it. "CT is sweet too."

"Is the house burned up?" His creased frown revealed he was dead serious.

"No, dear, the house is fine. The kitchen is fine."

"You be careful. Stove is hot. Dangerous."

She remembered when she used to tell him that very thing, back when he still thought he could cook. Now she just removed the knobs when she was done cooking. She was tempted to point out that she'd been on his errand, off looking for his missing hearing aid charger, when the stove got dangerous, but why bother?

"Where's your sandwich?" he asked as she turned away.

"I'm going back for it," she said, even though she had no intention of having peanut butter and honey. It was easier to play along than explain. By the time she brought back her coffee to sit with him, he wouldn't remember. Then as she went up the porch steps, her phone rang from her pocket. Planning to ignore it, she peeked at the caller ID to see it was Jewel. And since her daughter rarely called, she answered.

"Hey, Jewel," she said pleasantly. "How's my favorite girl?"

"I'm your *only* girl, Mom. But I guess I'm okay."

Honey heard the terseness in her daughter's tone. "So, what's up?"

"It's Cooper. I'm getting worried."

"Well, Cooper is almost fourteen. It's natural to be a little concerned. But she's always been a good girl." Honey poured herself a cup of coffee and sat down at the kitchen table, tracing a finger over the wood grain. This old oak table once belonged to her grandmother, right here on this very same farm.

"I'm worried about the new friends Cooper's been making."

"Oh, new friends?" Honey felt a spark of concern. She'd worked in a middle school for twenty years, long enough to know that new friends could be good . . . or bad.

"You know how kids are, Mom. How influential peers can be at this age."

"Yeah." Honey sipped her coffee.

"Especially to a girl with low self-esteem."

"Since when has Cooper had low self-esteem?"

"Since her best friend Molly dumped her and started talking smack about her."

"Oh, that's too bad." Middle school girls could be so cruel.

"So Coop started hanging with these *new* friends, and I don't like to judge anyone, but they seem pretty rough. I think their parents totally ignore them."

"That's not good."

"And school lets out on Thursday." Jewel's tone was desperate.

"And you're worried about her being unsupervised for the

summer?" Honey brightened. "Why don't you send her up here to visit? I could actually use a hand."

"With Dad?"

"Well, him . . . and farm work and lots of things." Honey looked out the window to where the lavender field was just starting to green up, but the weeds were greening up too. And then there were the pumpkins that hadn't been planted yet . . . She doubted CT would be up to it this year. "I'm positive we could keep her busy."

"And out of trouble." Jewel let out a relieved sigh.

"And your dad would love having her around."

"Tell me the truth, Mom. How is Dad?"

Honey stood, phone in one hand and coffee mug in the other, and went to look out the back window. CT was still sitting peacefully at the picnic table, peeling his banana. "He's okay. Well, for him, anyway."

"But the illness. How is he handling it?"

"Oh . . . the same as before. He forgets things. Overreacts to things. Tires out pretty easily. Not much has changed since the last time we talked. Only perhaps . . ." She bit her lip. "A little worse." Okay, that was an understatement. But why worry Jewel? She had her hands full single parenting a teenager and running a struggling business in a less than stellar economy. "How's the art gallery doing?"

"About the same as the last time we talked," Jewel parroted her. "Not so great."

"Maybe with summer coming it'll pick up?"

"Look, Mom, I have an idea." Jewel's tone was suddenly lighter. "What if Cooper and I *both* come back to Oregon? We can help with the farm and spend some time with Dad while he can still remember our names."

Honey felt slightly defensive, as well as uncertain. She'd welcome help but knew Jewel could be a handful at times. And while the farmhouse had enough bedrooms, the shared spaces would be a challenge. How would it feel to share her kitchen with a stubborn young woman with strong opinions on almost everything?

Who knew where that might lead? Add to that mix a teenage girl recently uprooted from her friends—it sounded like a recipe for disaster.

"Oh, I don't know, sweetheart." Honey tried to think of a tactful rejection. "That's a big change for you and Cooper. It's too much to ask of—"

"It's not too much. In fact, it's settled. My friend Jess has been begging to buy my gallery since Christmas, and I'd almost made up my mind to sell to him. It was a fun project, but I'm done now."

"Really?" Honey wasn't so sure. "You love that gallery."

"That was then. This is now. Honestly, Mom, I think we've come up with the perfect plan. Cooper and I will help you with Dad. And I'll have more time for my art, something I've missed lately. Plus, it'll get Coop away from her new friends. It's decided. I'm going to call Jess right now and—"

"You need to give this careful consideration, Jewel," Honey interrupted. "That's a huge life decision. Don't be too hasty and—"

"I'm not being hasty. It's been silently percolating in me for a while now. I just didn't have time to really wrap my head around it. But we're coming, Mom. You can count on us. I gotta go. I need to work out a deal with Jess and a dozen other things. Talk to you later. Love you." And before Honey could protest, Jewel hung up.

Honey just shook her head as she went to finish cleaning up her eggs. Frowning at the messy skillet, she pulled out a Brillo pad and began to scrub. Jewel was too impulsive. Dropping out of college just one semester before graduating. Then her hasty marriage to wealthy Rodney Benedict, a man with four failed marriages behind him. What a mismatch that turned out to be. Then her ill-timed pregnancy, hoping it would save her unraveling marriage. Even if marrying Rodney had been a mistake, Cooper was a treasure.

Then without thinking it through carefully, Jewel had invested her entire divorce settlement into that art gallery—just a few months before the COVID pandemic hit. Although, in Jewel's defense, Honey thought that had turned out all right. So why did she want to abandon it now?

Honey ground the steel wool into the cast iron with a vengeance. Sure, not all Jewel's impulsive choices had foreseeable results, but leave it to that girl to jump out of the frying pan and straight into the fire. Honey just hoped her impetuously headstrong daughter would come to her senses before letting history repeat itself . . . again.

2

Jewel

As Jewel walked through her downtown gallery, the thought of being free from this place and the responsibilities that came with it, not to mention being completely debt free with money in the bank, was surprisingly exhilarating. As she closed the front door to block out a siren blaring nearby, her idea to move back to the farm felt like a dream about to come true.

For everyone. It would be a creative reboot for her. A time to do what she loved most, focus on her art. And it would allow her to be a better mother to Cooper. She was tired of being pulled in too many directions. Like she often said to herself, "I'm only one woman." But she'd been a divided woman. Part-time artist, part-time business owner, part-time mother. With consequently very little time for a personal life.

And what about her parents? They were such good people. In their mid-sixties and about to enjoy the "good life" when her dad was diagnosed with this insidious disease. She knew she'd been a neglectful daughter. But her parents had always had their own lives to live. And they had each other. Sometimes she envied them that.

But their lives were changing. And this was her opportunity to rebuild relationships with them. Perhaps for only a small window of time with her dad. She bit her lip as she straightened an abstract landscape on the wall. It should be easy being around Mom. They'd always gotten along fairly well. Sure, there was room for improvement in their relationship. And sometimes she felt she didn't really know her mother. But she knew she was basically an understanding person. Mom's work in the middle school had exposed her to all kinds of people, and she was gracious and accepting by nature. But Jewel was no fool when it came to Dad.

She and her father had a rich and colorful history of family feuds. Power struggles that began when she was about Cooper's age and had decided to dress like a goth. She couldn't help but chuckle to remember that relatively short period of rebellion as she thought of her own daughter. Maybe the apple really hadn't fallen far from the tree. But, unlike herself, Jewel's hyper-traditional farmer dad had thrown a fit over her black-outlined eyes and dark clothing. He didn't understand her need to express herself.

Really, her dad was sweet, but he could be so stubborn and stuck in his ways. Not to mention judgmental and harsh over some things. Especially when it came to his only child. He'd wanted her to remain that sweet, wholesome farm girl forever. When she gave up the goth fad in favor of her first boyfriend, her dad had still held her at arm's length.

But the last couple times she and Dad had talked on the phone, he seemed different. Almost mellow. To be fair, he mostly talked about his bees and honey making, going on and on about how many jars he'd collected, and circling around, repeating himself . . . unless she interrupted. She'd try to be a patient listener, but she'd never been overly fond of bees or honey. Still, she was glad he had a hobby he loved so much.

She continued to scribble relocation chores onto her ever-growing to-do list. Some people couldn't understand how a creative dreamer like her also liked to get things done, but she'd always been like that. And first on her list was to call Jess. Like her, Jess was an artist, but unlike her, his colorful glasswork pieces were starting to take hold with her clients. So much so, this gallery had become Jess's largest venue for displaying and selling his works. For months he'd been cajoling her with the taunt he would own the place one day. A realistic possibility since his art was definitely her bestseller. She could imagine him rubbing his hands together over her news of selling and moving. She glanced around her handsome gallery. Yes, she'd invested both creativity and finances into this place, nearly starving in the lean years. But hopefully the payoff would be worth it now.

Assuming Jess was in his studio and ignoring his phone, she prepared to leave a message, but then he answered. After some chitchat, she described her Oregon plan and suddenly they were squabbling over the price of her gallery. She knew he wanted it. Badly. Finally she invited him to send her a properly written offer, which she would consider. But she reminded him, with her upgrades and the prime location, her gallery wouldn't be hard to sell. She wanted a fair price.

"Don't you want a friend to own it? Someone who will love and respect it like you did? Otherwise it's like handing over your child to strangers." His tone was on the verge of pleading, and she felt confident he was in.

"Well, there are days I would hand my flesh-and-blood child over to strangers," she teased. "But if your offer works for me, this place is yours. Just don't lowball me, Jess." Then she hung up. Jess knew she was impulsive, but she hoped he wouldn't assume she would cave to get out of here. After all, she'd invested a lot into this gallery. She ran a hand over a live edge display table, wondering if she should include this piece in the sale or take it with her. *Take it!* Her gallery was doing well, and Jess needed to respect that this was not a fire sale. She wasn't washed up, and she could remain in San Jose indefinitely if she wanted to. The trouble was she didn't want to. Not anymore. She'd had enough of city life.

She paused from loading flattened cardboard boxes into the back of her SUV, a task about midway down her to-do list, in order to call her best friend Monica. She excitedly told Monica the happy news. "And I'll have to beg out on that dinner date with you and the girls. I plan to be gone by then."

"Oh my gosh! You're kidding?" Monica was clearly shocked. "I've never heard you mention a word about country living before. Seriously? And with your parents? On a farm? Is this really you, Jewel, or am I being punked?"

Jewel laughed. "I grew up in the country and now I'm going back. Maybe it's a DNA thing. You know, it's in my blood."

"Could've fooled me. I thought you were pretty citified, girlfriend. And what about Cooper?"

"Change will be good for her. For both of us."

Monica laughed like she didn't believe a word of it. "And your gallery?"

"Jess might take it off my hands. If we can agree on a deal."

"Yeah, of course. He must be over the moon. Hey . . . what about your condo?"

"I shouldn't have any trouble selling it. I was about to call Hayley to—"

"No," Monica said quickly. "Don't call Hayley. I mean she's a good Realtor, but wait, okay?"

"Okay?" Jewel closed the back of her SUV, then returned to the gallery through the back door, pausing to straighten up some packing materials.

"Sell it to me."

Jewel nearly dropped the items she'd gathered. "Seriously?"

"You know how I adore your place. The building, the location, the view, even your decor. Please let me buy it. You know I'm sick of renting a room from my brother and his wife. Plus, she's pregnant now. I've been looking for something for over a year."

"Yeah, but can you afford the mortgage?" Jewel always got the impression her flight attendant friend was strapped for money. Jewel made more than Monica, and her monthly home payments frightened even her sometimes.

"I think so. I've been saving for a down payment for ages, and I got that inheritance from my grandma. I think a fair market price, not to mention less Realtor fees, might fit into my loan approval numbers. You can at least let me try before you call Hayley."

"Okay, I'll wait." Jewel made another note. "But I'll do some price checking on comparables and get back to you, okay?" As she hung up, she couldn't help but do a happy dance. This was all working out better than expected. Like it really was meant to be. And why not? Cooper needed a change, and Jewel's parents needed her. And truth be told, she probably needed them too. Maybe it really would take a village to raise a child.

When Terra came to work her usual afternoon shift in the gallery, Jewel decided to act like nothing whatsoever was in the works. Terra naturally leaned toward negativity and would probably assume her job was at risk. Better to just play it cool with this young woman and hope that Jess would keep her on, if he took over.

"I have to leave early today," Jewel told Terra. "I want to get home before Cooper for a change." She laughed as she grabbed her bag from beneath the counter. "Gotta keep my eye on that girl these days."

Terra just nodded with a serene expression. Cool and calm and collected. Well, until something went wrong. Then watch out. "Have a good evening. Call me if you need anything."

When she got home, Jewel went straight to work. She was a minimalist by nature, so clutter, at least on the surface, was never her problem. But if you dug deeply enough into closets and cupboards, she looked like more of a hoarder. But she'd recently read a good rule. If you keep it out of sight and rarely use it, get rid of it. And so that's what she started doing. Old wedding gifts, clothes she hadn't worn in years, shoes that were ridiculous—all were tossed into boxes to be donated. And just a couple boxes were set aside to keep.

By the late afternoon, Jewel had stacked quite a few packed boxes inside the front door. The ones on the left to give away and the ones on the right to take to Oregon. She hadn't heard back anything for sure from Jess or Monica, but it all still just felt right. Like the universe was truly lining everything up for her. And then she heard the key turning in the front door. Cooper was home from school.

"What's up?" Cooper demanded as soon as she stepped inside.

She closed the door and dumped her backpack next to the give-away stack. "Spring cleaning?" She gave Jewel a dubious look. "You better not have touched anything in my room."

"Don't worry. I'll leave that to you."

"So what's going on, Mom? Why aren't you at the gallery?" Cooper's attention was more on her phone than on her mother as she talked. "I thought you worked until six on Tuesdays. Something wrong?"

Jewel studied her daughter with suspicion. "Why? Did you have plans? Is my presence here messing things up for you?"

Cooper shrugged. "No . . . of course not." But she scowled as she typed something into her phone, holding it at an angle that prevented Jewel from seeing the screen. Probably a warning text to her new friends. Maybe they were on their way up here. Was her daughter canceling some dubious plan? All the more reason to get out of town. ASAP.

Cooper slid her phone into the back pocket of her torn jeans, then, cocking her head to one side, pursed her lips. "Something's up. I can feel it. What's the deal?"

"Come sit down." Jewel led the way to the breakfast bar with Cooper trailing her like a suspicious animal.

"You're kinda freaking me out. Is this serious?" Cooper perched on the edge of the stool and tugged at the edge of her black rocker T-shirt, something Jewel had tried to discourage her from wearing to school. Honestly, she doubted Coop even knew who the Grateful Dead were. Did she realize they were from her grandparents' era?

Jewel sat down across from Cooper, trying not to stare at the lime-green tips on her otherwise sleek brunette hair. Jewel would've loved to have thick, dark hair like her daughter's as a teen. Instead she'd been stuck with mousy brown. "Here's the deal, Coop. I talked to Grandma today. I think she needs help with Grandpa."

Cooper frowned. "Is he getting really bad?"

"I don't know all the details, but I can tell your grandma is getting overwhelmed."

"I wish they lived closer." Cooper's dark brown eyes looked genuinely sympathetic.

"So do I." Jewel felt bolstered by this response. Maybe this would go over better than expected. "But they don't. And since we can't bring them to San Jose, we are going to join them in Oregon."

"For a visit?" Cooper's tone turned wary.

"Not exactly." She braced herself. "We, uh, we're going to move up there."

"*Move?*" Cooper leaped from the stool with wide eyes. "Like permanently?"

Jewel simply nodded, holding on to the edge of the granite countertop as her daughter flew into a tirade. "I can't believe you'd do this to me, Mom. Have you lost your mind? No way am I moving up to Oregon! I've been on the farm before, and it's, like, in the middle of nowhere. No way can you force me to go. My life is here. In San Jose. My school is here. My friends are here. You can't just rip me out of—"

"I can, Cooper." Jewel stood. "I'm your mom."

Cooper glared at her. "Well, I have a dad too. What will he say about your hauling me up there? I heard you can't take kids out of the state when you have shared custody. My dad won't—"

"I've already let him know." Jewel picked up her to-do list and pointed to the third item and the check mark next to it: *Inform Rodney about the move*. "Your dad is fine with it. In fact, he thought it was a good idea."

Cooper slammed her fist onto the countertop before letting loose with some expletives Jewel had never heard come out of her little girl's mouth before. Then Cooper stomped off to her bedroom and slammed the door behind her.

"Well, that was fun," Jewel muttered as she opened the fridge. Maybe she could distract herself by fixing dinner, except that it was slim pickings in there as usual. She closed the fridge so firmly that the bottles inside rattled. Not that she didn't enjoy cooking, she just never had the time. Even if she did whip up something amazing, Coop wouldn't be willing to eat with her now anyway.

As Jewel reached for her phone, she doubted that even Coop's favorite sushi would coax her out of her room. Not for a couple of hours at least. But sushi made for good leftovers. She let out a long, loud sigh as she called to place her order. Single parenting a teenage girl was not for wimps.

Shortly after their takeout arrived, Jewel heard Cooper come out of her bedroom. Had the sushi plan worked after all? Jewel didn't look behind her as she set the bags on the counter.

"Mom?" Cooper's voice had a slightly positive tinge to it, or was Jewel just being optimistic?

"Yeah?" She turned to her with a bright smile. "Got sushi."

"Uh-huh." Cooper eyed the bags, then turned to her mom. "What about Tony?"

"Tony?" Jewel folded her arms in front of her. Tony was her on-again, off-again boyfriend. Too handsome and charming for his own good and a bit of a narcissist. And yet Jewel had never fully given up on him. Even so, Tony hadn't even made it onto her to-do list today. Was it oversight or intention? She wasn't sure. Maybe she didn't care.

"I thought you were pretty serious about him." Cooper stepped closer, looking intently into Jewel's eyes, almost as if she were reaching for a lifeline. "And I know he loves you."

Jewel couldn't help but laugh. "Tony loves Tony, Cooper. Sometimes I fit into his world, but never permanently."

"It's only because you're always so busy." Cooper was not giving up. "Work always distracts you." She raised a forefinger in victory. "And what about the gallery? It's been, like, your whole life. Are you just going to walk away from that?"

"Not exactly. I'm selling it. Probably to Jess." Despite her daughter's motives, she had to respect the girl for trying, for using her head and persuasion skills. Not that it would do any good. Jewel opened a white carton and sniffed. "Yummy."

"But the gallery is your everything, Mom. You can't just give it up. Seriously, sometimes it's like you love that gallery more than you love me." Cooper made her best "poor me" face. And maybe she was right about Jewel's priorities.

"I'm sorry you felt like that, but honestly, it's not true. You're far more important than any gallery, Cooper." Jewel reached out for her, but Cooper pulled away with angry eyes.

"I can't believe you! You're just plain selfish. I hate you!" And once again, Cooper stomped off to her room, slamming the door so hard, Jewel braced herself for a call from their neighbor, old Mrs. Curmudgeon-Cunningham. So, okay, this wasn't going quite as smoothly as Jewel had hoped. She opened another carton, letting out more fragrant aromas of sushi, but her appetite was gone. She put it all in the fridge and picked up her to-do list and stared blankly at it. Her plan was going to work. It had to work. Cooper just needed time to adjust to the idea.

Jewel sat down on her sofa, reading the item on her list that read "get bids from moving companies." She wondered if moving everything was really such a good idea. All her furnishings fit so perfectly here in the condo. She ran a hand over the creamy white upholstery of her contemporary-styled sofa. And where would she store these pieces on the farm? In the barn where mice and moths could attack? Maybe Monica would like to work out a deal with her. Or maybe Jewel was biting off more than she could chew. It wouldn't be the first time.

3

Honey

At times, CT seemed almost normal. In those moments, Honey sometimes suffered memory lapses of her own. As a result, she'd spilled the beans that their daughter and granddaughter were coming to Oregon. Her goal had been to cheer him up, but now CT asked, multiple times per day, when they would get here. He always assumed it should be "right now" and spent far too much time gazing out on the driveway. It was ironic how he could forget whether he'd eaten lunch or not, but for whatever reason he did not forget the girls were coming. Maybe he was reading her thoughts. It made no sense, but sometimes it seemed he could do that.

"Are they coming today?" CT asked as she cleared the breakfast table.

"No, CT. Not today. I'll let you know when I know for sure."

"I know . . . you know . . . but will they be here?" He gave her a puzzled smile, a reminder she'd overexplained. Keep it simple.

"Not today."

"Oh." His smile faded. "What day is it?"

She told him, and then to distract him from further disappointment, Honey decided to bring up the subject of pumpkins . . . again. "We need to plant pumpkins." She reached for his empty plate. Truthfully, she didn't particularly care if they got planted or not, but she knew how much CT would enjoy the lush green plants once they started to grow, and even more so in the fall when the field would be spotted with bright orange orbs, and they could invite the grade school kids out to pick them. That had always been fun.

"I can do it," he told her. It was the identical response he always gave, and she suspected the outcome would be the same too. He would soon forget and get involved in some other "task" that didn't need doing. Like yesterday when he'd moved all her gardening tools from her gardening shed, which was handily located right next to the garden. He'd tucked every single tool into the back of the barn. Even her wheelbarrow and garden cart. It had taken her almost an hour to locate her missing tools. And it had taken more than a little self-control not to throw a hissy fit. Instead she'd retrieved her tools, locked her shed, and attempted to keep things light when she reminded him that the Lone Rearranger had struck again. Unfortunately he didn't think that was as funny as she did. And by the time she was done re-rearranging, she no longer had any interest in weeding her garden. It could wait. But today was a new day. And if CT got focused on seeding pumpkins, she might have an uninterrupted hour.

"I'll help you get started," she told him as she rinsed the last plate.

"Started?" he echoed.

"On pumpkin planting."

"Oh, yeah."

"Today. I'll help you."

His brows arched. "Okay? You'll help?"

"As soon as I'm done here." She put a soap tablet in the dishwasher. "You go put on your boots."

CT nodded, slowly pushing himself up from his chair. He seemed to be moving extra slow today, and Honey realized she'd need to help him not overdo things. They'd just get the process started in the cool of the morning.

Of course, the cool of the morning was evaporating by the time CT got his boots on. And, although the temperature was already in the seventies, he emerged from the house wearing his winter parka and knit cap and was just putting on his heavy work gloves.

"I don't think you'll need those." She tugged on his coat sleeve.

"Oh?" He looked up at the clear sky. "Guess not."

With her help, he removed his winter wear, and she laid everything on the porch bench. "Come on," she urged. "I got the seeds ready for you." She handed him the gallon bucket of seeds, then picked up his old planting stick. "Remember when you devised this clever plan?" she asked.

"Clever? Plan?"

"Your pumpkin stick?" She waved the four-foot pole in the air. It had only been a year since he'd managed to do this task without too much coaching. But how quickly things could change with FTD.

"Pumpkin stick?" His frown revealed the memory lapse. "Does it grow pumpkins?"

She wasn't sure if he was joking or serious. "Come on, I'll show you." She led him over to the field she'd already tilled with the old tractor, doing it piecemeal when CT had been preoccupied with his bees. Otherwise he'd want to run the tractor himself, and she'd already witnessed how dangerous it could get when CT mixed the brakes and throttle on his John Deere. Fortunately he hadn't been hurt when the machine bucked him to the ground a few months ago. But it could've been catastrophic. After that, she'd quietly sold the more powerful John Deere to their neighbor and hid the old tractor key, along with CT's ¾ ton diesel pickup key, in the back of her underwear drawer.

Honey stepped into the pumpkin field, laid the stick on the ground, then held it straight, poking a hole into the dirt with the pointed end. She reached for a seed from the bucket, popped it into the ground, then, using her foot, tamped down the dirt around it. Then she measured with the stick to the next hole and repeated the process. "Remember?"

CT's face brightened as he reached for the stick. "I know how to do that."

Relieved by his enthusiasm, she stood a few feet off, observing him clumsily measure and plant a seed, and then another. The old CT might've laughed at this inept farmer, whose rows were as wavy as the sea. But nothing about this seemed funny to her. She bit her tongue to keep from telling him his line was way off. Really, what did it matter?

"You got this?" she finally asked. He simply nodded, eyes downward as he stomped the ground. Moving methodically, he measured and poked the next hole into the dirt, beginning a slow chant. "Poke-n-plantin' pumpkins. Poke-n-plantin' pumpkins." Seeing her amusement, he attempted to give his stick a spin and shuffled his feet like he was Gene Kelly, but he nearly tripped himself.

"Soft-shoe is tricky in work boots." She laughed, and his eyes twinkled as he went back to measuring and poking. "But thanks for the floor show, CT." Relieved at this small success, she told him she'd be in her garden. "Just holler if you need anything." He just nodded, still chanting cheerfully to himself as he stomped a circle around a freshly planted seed. Honey strolled over to her nearby vegetable garden, feeling happy contentment. It was possible to live with FTD. She just had to plan her activities more carefully and be patient. Not for the first time, she was grateful they lived on a farm. Oh, sure, it came with its challenges. But CT loved being outdoors, and although they only had ten acres now, it was enough room to roam and to keep him happy.

She glanced beyond the pumpkin field, over to the parcel of land that CT had sold to the Oroscos more than three years ago. At first she'd been upset about the agreement her husband struck with their friend Miguel. After all, this farm had originally belonged to *her* family. Not CT's. For nearly a hundred years too. She'd inherited the house and barn and land from her grandparents, and she'd dreamed it would stay in the family. But Jewel had never shown the slightest interest in farming, and a hundred acres was far too much for her and CT to manage. Still, it was her family's land, and Honey felt she should've been consulted in its sale.

About seven years ago, while she was still working at the middle school, they'd started leasing half their acreage to Miguel Orosco. Miguel had retired from the Air Force in his thirties and was strong and eager to be a farmer, and CT had been something of a mentor to him. Then a couple years later, when CT was on the barn roof installing a silly weathervane that Honey had found at an estate sale, he'd slipped and fallen and broken his leg. After that, Miguel took over all the cultivating—and did a great job with it too.

While still recovering from his broken leg, CT had struck a deal to sell instead of lease the land. Again, without her knowledge or consent. Honey didn't dispute that the enterprising younger man was the perfect choice to relieve them of that acreage, but she didn't appreciate being excluded from the agreement.

She glanced to the east as she reached for her hoe. Squinting into the late-morning sunlight, she spotted the double-wide manufactured home that Miguel had put in shortly after purchasing the land. At first it was shockingly bright white in the sunlight and felt intrusive to her. But not long afterward, Miguel had painted it a peaceful dark taupe, which helped it blend into the landscape. And now she had to admit the Orosco farm was attractive, and probably better maintained than the McKerrys'. She peered at the poplars Miguel had planted a few years ago, surprised to see they were green and leafy and nearly as tall as their house now. Pretty.

Although it was a comfort to have good neighbors, she had regrettably voiced her opinion to CT a bit too harshly and loudly. Things weren't going well at school, and she'd been in a mood and had probably just been up for an old-fashioned vent. Eventually, she got over it and in time she even expressed her gratitude for having the Oroscos as permanent neighbors. But for some reason, probably the onset of FTD, her husband had gotten stuck on it. Of all the things he could forget, he couldn't seem to forget that the Oroscos owned the land that used to be theirs. And after his leg healed up, he missed that land. And sometimes he got pretty worked up over it.

She hoed into the garden bed she was preparing for tomatoes, loosening a stubborn weed, but continued mulling over the way CT's brain worked. Or didn't. Sometimes he got stuck on things that seemed like pure fiction to her. She couldn't understand how he could mix up facts the way he did. Like the Oroscos. Even though that land purchase happened before CT's diagnosis, she'd already observed that things had been off with her husband. In hindsight, she felt certain that was why CT had offered the land to Miguel for such a low price. That was about the same time she'd noticed their checkbook was a mixed-up mess and around the time CT started struggling to pull out the right amount for cash for a simple purchase. It was like money suddenly made no sense to him. So practically giving away their land was meaningless to him.

Although Honey was upset at the time, she was okay with it now. Oh, maybe she regretted that she hadn't paid more attention, but she'd been distracted with her job at the middle school. Amid the post-COVID school politics, budget cuts, and general lack of teachers, there was plenty to preoccupy her mind. And although the figure CT had quoted was too low, Honey liked Miguel. He was a hard worker and had a young daughter to raise and a mother to support. And so she'd begrudgingly accepted the idea, imagining CT would be relieved to have less responsibility and thinking they'd be free to travel some as soon as she retired. Think again.

She bent down to tug on a stubborn milkweed, pulling so hard she tumbled backward onto her hind end. Sitting there in the dirt, with the weed dripping its sticky white juices all over her hand, she felt a smidgeon of guilt. Monarchs liked these milkweeds. She should've left it. But not in her garden. There was plenty of milkweed on the backside of the barn to accommodate butterflies. And since CT was oblivious to weeds these days, they would probably go undisturbed too. A blessing for the butterflies.

She glanced over to see her husband still happily planting pumpkin seeds. "Just be thankful for small favors," she reminded herself as she gingerly got to her feet. In moments like this, she could feel her sixty-plus years in her joints. But determined not to give in, she reminded herself that today was a good day and returned to weeding. Now, instead of fretting over the past, she focused on the fact that her daughter and granddaughter were coming soon. Perhaps even next week, Jewel had told her yesterday. Although Honey didn't plan to tell CT this . . . yet. She would let him know when their arrival was imminent. Not a moment sooner.

Honey noticed her unused gloves on the garden bench as she reached for a spade. Too late for that now since her hands were already a dirty, sticky mess. A small price for having undisturbed time in her vegetable garden. She loved being out here. Especially this time of year. Already, her peas, lettuce, kale, and spinach were solidly up, and some carrots and radishes were bravely sprouting as well. The tomato seedlings in her little greenhouse were ready for transplant too. Maybe Cooper could help with that. Honey was actually relieved that Jewel hadn't come up here as quickly as she'd originally hoped. Honey had wanted to get the spare rooms cleaned up some before they got here, but it seemed every time she went upstairs, she'd barely get started on one of the rooms when CT would holler up the stairs, calling her back down for something *urgent.* Urgent to him, anyway. It usually turned out to be some mundane chore, like helping him locate his phone—right by his chair—or a lost shoe. Or last week when he'd called her down to straighten out "the doggone TV remote" that didn't work, only to discover he was using an old cordless phone. Where he unearthed the useless thing, she couldn't say, but she'd dropped the defunct item in the trash.

Finally, she decided to just let Jewel and Cooper declutter, clean, and arrange their own rooms. After all, they were coming to help, right? And there was so much "help" needed inside the house, she often felt downright slovenly. Her job and summer farm work had always provided a good excuse for letting a few things go before. She'd always managed to catch up. But that was before CT began requiring so much of her time.

Some of her friends claimed a lot of things went undone as they aged. But no one seemed to mind particularly. Still, Honey had a hard time letting go. She liked sprucing up a room, getting ready for guests. She'd always been active and physical, and even she used to believe she and CT were young for their age. Before frontotemporal dementia, or BFTD as she sometimes called it, the two of them had managed to run the farm, maintain a social life, and still enjoy hiking, hunting, and fishing together when they could get away from the farm. And they'd been conjuring up even bigger plans for her post-retirement.

She glanced over to the dust-coated silver camp trailer parked next to the barn. They'd purchased the Airstream after selling off that acreage to Miguel. It had been her concession gift from CT, and she'd carefully selected all the interior amenities in the classic '38 RV. Her hope had been to visit all the national parks and cover the back end with bumper stickers that showed off everywhere they'd camped. But on their first short experimental trip to Crater Lake, CT had been surprisingly absentminded, forgetting how to do the simplest of tasks. On their second trip, to the Oregon Coast, he got confused while emptying the sewer tanks, creating a horrible, smelly, not to mention embarrassing, mess at the dump station. With only two bumper stickers on the Airstream, they hadn't taken it out since. And now she was certain they never would again since she'd listed it in the local paper and had already had several calls with strong interest. She expected it'd be gone by the weekend.

Honey looked over to the pumpkin field to see no one there. Not too surprising for CT. He probably headed inside for a bathroom break. He took them frequently. Just part of FTD. She continued weeding for a few minutes, glancing up now and then, but finally concern got the best of her. She wasn't even sure why. Probably just experience. She leaned her hoe against the shed and walked over to the pumpkin field. Seeing the overturned bucket and spilled pumpkin seeds, her concern spiked. And then she heard a voice in the distance, shouting something unintelligible. Using her hand to screen her eyes from the sun, she spotted two men facing each other on opposite sides of the east fence. The one with his arms raised, waving a stick and yelling, was CT.

She braced herself as she jogged over to see what was wrong. She was pretty sure the other man was Miguel. When she got there, Miguel looked frustrated and . . . something else. Was it hurt? Or anger? But his hands were planted in his jeans pockets and his lips tightly sealed. Honey imagined he was biting his tongue.

"You stole my farm," CT growled at him. "Now you got my tractor." He pointed to Miguel's John Deere. "That's mine. You give it back, you thief. Right now." He shook his pumpkin stick in the air threateningly.

"Whoa, CT." She grabbed his arm and took the stick. "That's not true."

"It is true." CT glared at her. "Miguel stole the farm. Now he stole my tractor."

She pointed to his chest. "No. You, CT, *you* sold him part of our farm. He paid for it fair and square. That eighty acres is his land."

"No. It's mine." He pointed to the tractor. "That's mine too."

"It used to be yours, CT. But we sold it to Miguel. Remember? Last winter."

"You're lying. Miguel *stole* my tractor. I know my tractor. I can see it."

Honey felt the sting of CT's words as she tried to give Miguel a sympathetic glance. She turned back to CT, placing a firm hand on his arm. "It *was* your tractor. Now it belongs to Miguel."

"You're lying. Miguel's a thief. A dirty thief. He took it from me. Last night. I heard him in my barn. He took it."

"No, CT. Miguel is our good neighbor. He helps us. He is not a thief."

"You're lying. Both of you." CT shook her hand free from his arm. "I'm gonna get my gun."

"CT!" Honey raised her voice. "You will do no such thing."

"I'm gonna get my gun," he yelled louder before storming off.

Honey just stood there, waiting for him to get out of earshot, which wasn't far due to his hearing loss. Then she turned to Miguel. "I'm so sorry for this."

Miguel sighed. "It's okay, Mrs. McKerry. I understand."

"It is *not* okay. But as you know, CT can't help it. His brain is messing with him again."

"I know. I'm sorry to see it." Miguel's dark brows drew together. "Will he really get his gun?"

She shook her head. "Don't worry about that. I already sold his guns. You know, right after that time he mistook Miller's best bird dog for a coyote. Good thing he missed."

"Yeah. That was close." Miguel nodded. "You were smart to remove the guns."

"Of course, he won't remember that, well, until he gets in the house."

"I'm sorry about the tractor. Maybe I shouldn't have bought it from you."

She waved a hand. "No, no. If it wasn't that, it'd be something else. Please, don't worry about it."

"I worry about you." He looked into her eyes. "How are *you* doing?"

"Oh, you know. I'm okay."

"I know it's hard being a caregiver. I took care of Beth before she died. Even with Mama's help, it was a rough road. And there's only one of you."

"Well, my daughter and granddaughter are coming," she told him. "That should help."

"I'm glad to hear it."

"I better go check on CT. God knows what he'll be up to next." She grimaced to imagine him wielding a kitchen knife. That had never happened before, but you never knew . . . She remembered today's little surprise and, hoping to lighten things up, decided to share it. "You know what, Miguel?" She chuckled. "CT brushed his teeth with Preparation H this morning."

Miguel laughed. "Might be good for his gums."

"Maybe, but it took him three cups of coffee to get the taste out of his mouth."

"Think the caffeine added to his temper?"

"Maybe. Anyway, please, don't be concerned. He'll have forgotten this whole business by suppertime."

"Sure hope so." Miguel waved before returning to his tractor and firing up the engine.

Honey walked back to the house, less confident than she was trying to appear. Despite his memory problems of names and dates and daily tasks, CT sure didn't forget everything. Like the fact he used to own and operate vehicles or had an admirable firearm collection. Pickups and guns occupied a deep place inside him. Probably part of being a man's man. Even when she'd tried to hide or throw away his rifle magazines, hoping subscriptions would soon expire and quit appearing in their mailbox, CT always seemed to find them. And if a pickup commercial played on TV, CT was all eyes and ears and sometimes tears. Yes, some things were hard to let go. For her too.

4

Jewel

Driving north on I-5, Jewel marveled at how smoothly cutting her ties in San Jose had gone. It had been much less complicated than she'd expected. Selling her gallery to Jess was fairly simple. A down payment would give her an income up in Oregon. And although she didn't have a ton of equity in her condo, it was satisfying to sell to Monica. All in all, things had wrapped up nicely. Very liberating. Like shedding a bulky winter coat and stepping out into a sweet summer day. For the first time in a long time, Jewel felt nearly happy. And when she'd packed her art supplies, which were safely tucked in the back of her SUV, she felt she finally had the right energy to get serious about painting again.

The only wrench in the works had been her daughter. Cooper seemed determined to thwart Jewel every step of the way. After several protest tantrums and attempts at sabotage, Cooper had totally disappeared about two weeks ago. But thanks to the tracking device on Cooper's phone, Jewel quickly located her runaway. She'd moved into her friend Cassie's house, thinking it could be a permanent setup. Although Cassie's mom had been sympathetic, she had problems of her own and wasn't eager to adopt another teenager.

After that, Cooper had doubled down with the silent treatment. Then she'd refused to pack up her room. It wasn't until

Jewel informed her daughter that the movers would deal with her things—in whatever way they felt was best—that Cooper cooperated.

Then about a week ago, Cooper attempted a dramatic phone call to her dad, using all her charm in an attempt to talk him into full-time custody. She begged him to take her in, even offering to change schools if necessary since Rodney lived on the other side of town. Jewel hated playing eavesdropper, but it was hard not to hear her daughter's heart-tugging pleas.

Thanks to the newest wife's pregnancy and Rodney's plans to accept a job in San Diego in August, Cooper's Oscar-worthy performance was futile. Jewel actually felt sorry for Cooper afterward and didn't nag her about packing or mention Oregon for a couple days. She also didn't mention how disturbing it was that Cooper's final grades had been in the toilet. Although it did give Jewel additional incentive. A fresh start was in Cooper's best interest too.

Finally, though, they were on their way to Oregon, trailing the moving van packed with all their earthly possessions. Jewel checked her rearview mirror, imagining Cooper's Doc Marten heel marks leaving long black tracks on the freeway behind them. Of course, that was ridiculous, but the back seat had grown so quiet, she needed reassurance that Cooper was still in the SUV. When they'd first started out, the audio from Cooper's video games had been obnoxious, but Jewel hadn't bothered to ask her to turn it down or to use her headphones. Why poke a hornets' nest?

Naturally, her stubborn daughter refused to sit up front like a civilized person. Instead, she camped in the back with her bedding and her phone and the junk food Jewel had allowed her to purchase when they got gas in San Jose. Cooper's thumbs were furiously pounding out what Jewel supposed was a rant to her friends, who were most likely just crawling out of bed now. Jewel just hoped those misfits weren't concocting some sort of roadside rescue mission at their next fuel stop.

Relatively assured they were out of harm's way and that Cooper looked moderately comfortable, Jewel tried to relax. She usually enjoyed a long drive. And the farther north they went, the better the countryside looked. Oak trees were greened up, and recent rains made it look like the rolling fields were coming to life. It would only get better up in Oregon. Someday Cooper might thank her mother for doing this. Or not. It was hard to say. Maybe it didn't matter. Some teens were determined to be miserable no matter what.

Jewel remembered how strong-willed and outspoken she'd been as a teen and yet somehow her parents endured her. But there had been two of them. And despite Jewel's attempts to divide and conquer, for the most part, her parents presented a united front. Hopefully they'd partner with her for Cooper too. At least Mom anyway since she was familiar with young teens.

Jewel wasn't sure how Dad would be. Although she felt his illness had softened him, she wasn't too sure. And based on a few things Mom had shared about his recent feuds with their neighbor, Jewel realized Dad might be more of a challenge than she expected. But she wouldn't let him bully her daughter. Not if she could help it.

It was around two when they finally crossed into Oregon. The fuel light came on, and Jewel knew it was time to find a station. The back seat was quiet again. Cooper was either asleep or faking it. Though if she really had been making an escape plan, which Jewel knew was ridiculous, she doubted her friends could've made it up to Grants Pass. All the same, the thought of Coop making a run for it was a little unnerving. And besides gas, Jewel needed a pit stop too. Just the same, she drove past the exit for a big truck stop. Despite its low prices and fast-food options, it looked like an opportune location for a teenage girl to pull a vanishing act.

"You hungry?" Jewel asked as she drove into a smaller gas station just off the freeway.

Cooper's sleepy grunt, along with the crinkle of an empty Doritos bag and several candy wrappers, seemed to suggest she wasn't interested in food. Fine.

Jewel noticed the Dr Pepper bottle. "Potty break?" she said cheerfully.

Cooper rolled her eyes, then opened a door and slowly emerged. Brushing chip crumbs off her tattered jeans, she tugged her long hair into a messy pony and headed toward the building.

Jewel hurriedly ran her card and got the gas pumping, then followed Cooper inside. She headed straight for the restroom and Jewel, feeling paranoid, tried to appear inconspicuous as she checked under an occupied stall to see her daughter's scuffed-up Doc Martens.

They both finished at the same time, but no words were exchanged as they locked eyes in the mirror while washing their hands. *Don't rock the boat*, Jewel reminded herself when she wanted to tell her daughter to open the door with her foot to avoid touching the germy surface. Then, instead of grabbing a snack like she wanted, she followed Cooper back to the SUV. Setting the gas nozzle in the pump, she was grateful for her half-full water bottle and baggie of trail mix . . . and that her parents' farm was only three more hours. Plus, they were expecting her. Mom was a good cook. Hopefully she'd have something tasty waiting for them.

As she started the ignition, she reminded herself to be grateful she hadn't lost her daughter. Not yet, anyway. She shot her mom a quick ETA text, along with the warning she was transporting a hostile captive.

That's what it felt like. As if she were relocating a prisoner. Maybe she should've brought along handcuffs and shackles. As she drove toward the freeway entrance, she made a feeble attempt at small talk, but the silent treatment from the back seat wasn't encouraging, so she put a lid on it. *Just get there.* At the stoplight before the freeway, she texted her mom again, advising her that movers might arrive first and telling her to have them start unloading in the barn.

She hadn't kept much more than their beds, several favorite pieces of furniture, and her art, as well as their personal belongings. Yet, she'd been surprised at how it nearly filled the small moving van. And although she'd been relieved that Monica had decided to purchase her larger pieces, saying goodbye to her home was harder than expected this morning. Buying and furnishing her condo had made her feel independent and mature, especially after she'd escaped her codependent role in a marriage where she was often treated like a child. The condo was where she was finally able to do some real adulting. Saying goodbye to their home hadn't been as easy as she tried to make it appear—for Cooper's sake. And maybe it was wrong to pretend. Maybe she should spill the beans and admit all this to Cooper and initiate some vulnerable conversation. Transparent, honest communication.

"You know, Coop," she began carefully as she cruised down the center lane. "I'm feeling kinda blue about leaving San Jose too. Took me by surprise to feel that way."

"Yeah, right." Her daughter's tone dripped with sarcasm. "Boohoo for you."

She bristled but, determined to make a dent in her daughter's prickly armor, continued. "I'm serious, Coop. I *do* feel sad. I worked hard to build us a life down there. It wasn't easy after your dad and I split. I put a lot of energy into creating something I hoped would be good for both of us."

"Yeah, sure. Then you just throw it all away? Seemed to come pretty easy to you. Never mind how I feel about it."

"I'm sorry it's been so hard on you, but it'll get better. I promise you, it'll get better. And eventually, you're going to understand that my parents really need me right now. They need both of us."

Cooper made a growling noise, which was followed by dense silence and the hollow sound of tires on the road.

Still, Jewel wasn't ready to give up. "I hope you'll come around. In time, I know you will." She paused to change lanes and pass a semi. "Your grandparents are really looking forward to seeing you. Grandpa's having a hard time with his illness, and Grandma is in over her head." Jewel glanced at the rearview mirror to see Cooper hunched over, glued to her phone, headphones in place, totally oblivious. So much for conversation. Not for the first time, Jewel realized that single parenting teenagers was not for the meek of heart. She just hoped that burning her bridges in San Jose and moving back to her childhood home wasn't about to make it much worse.

5

Honey

Some June days felt like a slice of heaven. And this was one of them. Honey stepped out onto the back porch, just to breathe in the pungent fragrance of moist earth and tender plants sprouting from the ground. A cool breeze with the hint of warmth rippled through new green leaves on the apple trees. Like a much-needed mental health break, Honey tried to soak in as much as she could while she could.

Days like this begged to be spent outdoors. And yet, so much inside work demanded her attention today. It just wasn't fair. But she'd put off too many tasks last week. Or she'd been distracted too many times. It was hard to remember. But Jewel and Cooper would be here around five and she'd hoped to make a nice dinner for them. Not to mention she still needed to get fresh sheets on those beds upstairs. Never mind her earlier manic imaginings of line-dried sheets scented with lavender, sparkling windows, bouquets of flowers, baskets of fruit, fresh-smelling bathrooms . . . The kinds of things she used to have prepped for when guests arrived. Back when she was younger and more energetic. Not that they'd had that many guests in recent years. Besides that, Jewel and Cooper were family.

She returned to the laundry room off the porch to put the wet sheets into the dryer. She even tossed in a nature-scented dryer sheet, hoping it would make up for real sunshine. To be fair, at the rate she was going, Jewel and Cooper would be lucky if she even got these clean linens upstairs before they arrived. CT had been extra needy today. Almost like he could sense her attention was divided and wanted to push her. Sometimes he reminded her of a small child who got jealous and unreasonably demanding when his mother was too busy.

"Honey?" CT's voice called out for her as if to prove her point.

She slammed the dryer shut but left the porch's back door open, securing the screen to keep out any critters. Since losing their beloved Piper last winter, they'd been dogless. As a result, raccoons were getting way too familiar around the farm. Although it was usually after dark when they reared their heads. And last night, they smelled a skunk. Country living at its finest. Their feisty barn cat Whiskers was a good mouser but couldn't keep the bigger varmints away. She picked up the laundry basket of clean towels and walked through the kitchen, where breakfast dishes were still piled in the sink.

"Honey!" CT called out again, this time with an urgency that suggested real pain. Had he hurt himself again? She'd just bandaged up his knee after he'd landed on it tripping down the rickety porch stairs . . . not for the first time either. She was starting to hate those stairs.

"Coming," she yelled out to CT. "Where are you?"

"Here," he called back as if that explained everything. She went from room to room, finally locating him in the downstairs bathroom.

"Yes?" She poked her head in through the open door.

With a childlike expression, he held up an empty toilet paper roll. "Where do you keep this?"

She pointed to the basket where she kept toilet paper in plain sight, then seeing it was down to one roll, opened a cabinet door, extracted a package, and refilled the basket with a couple extras. "Here ya go, CT. Right where it always is." She heard the impatience in her tone as she handed him a full roll and picked up her laundry basket.

"I'm dumb." CT's countenance fell. "I forgot."

"You're not dumb." She set down the laundry basket again and, despising her impatience, opened her arms to hug him. As always, he welcomed the hug, holding her close.

"I love you, Honey." He buried his nose in her hair. "You smell good."

She laughed. "I'm sure I don't. But glad you think so." She looked up into his face. "I love you too, CT. Sorry if I was impatient, but there's a lot to get done with Jewel and Cooper coming."

"Coming? Here?" His brow was puzzled. "To this house?"

"Yes. Sometime this afternoon." She stopped herself from saying "like I already told you a dozen times." Instead, she added, "And I've a lot to get done before they get here."

"I can help."

"Yes." She pulled fresh towels from the laundry basket, folding and stacking them next to the sink to take upstairs for her soon-to-arrive guests. Hopefully CT wouldn't dirty them all before the girls arrived. "Maybe you could clean up the breakfast dishes. That would help."

"Did we eat breakfast?" he asked.

"Yes." She checked her watch. "And it's probably time for lunch. Could you make yourself a peanut butter sandwich?"

"I can do that." He nodded happily.

"And have some milk too?" She knew this was a risky task, but he could still handle it most of the time.

"Yes."

"That would be helpful." She picked up the basket of towels. "I need to take these upstairs."

She hurried upstairs, hoping she'd just bought herself some uninterrupted time. She was just hanging towels in the bathroom when she heard CT hollering like something else was seriously wrong. She knew it was probably nothing . . . and yet. With knives and fragile glassware—and had she remembered to remove the stove knobs this morning?—the kitchen could be a dangerous place. She ran downstairs, calling out that she was coming. "What is it?"

CT was staring down at the floor with a horrified expression. His favorite honeypot with a bear on the front was now a shattered, sticky mess on the kitchen's hardwood floor. CT looked brokenhearted.

"Oh, CT." She tried to disguise her frustration as sympathy but didn't think it was convincing. Not to her, anyway. "It's okay. You go get yourself some more honey while I clean this goop up."

"More honey?" He looked confused. "From the hives?"

"No. We keep jars in the pantry. Remember?"

"Jars?" Although he was the one who filled the jars and put them there, he still seemed bewildered. He'd obviously forgotten.

"Jars of honey. In the pantry. On the back porch." She pointed that way. "That big red cabinet. Remember?"

He nodded with a cloudy expression, like someone trying to see some faraway place.

"You go get some honey, okay?" If nothing else, it would occupy him for a few minutes while she wiped up the mess.

"Okay."

As she dampened a dish towel, she listened to his trudging steps scuffle toward the back door. Cleaning up shards of pottery and thick honey was a slow, sticky process. She was just finishing up the worst of it when CT returned. But the floor tiles still felt tacky. It would have to wait until she mopped the whole floor . . . later.

"Found 'em," CT announced, victoriously displaying two gleaming amber jars of honey. "We got lots of honey, Honey."

"Great." She rinsed off her sticky hands.

"Do you know how many honeys there are?"

"Not exactly." She dried her hands on a fresh towel, then took the jars from him. "Do you know how many?"

His smile was crooked. "A lot."

She pointed him to the kitchen table. "Now you sit down, and I'll fix your peanut butter and honey sandwich, okay?"

He smiled. "My Honey is a honey."

By the time she made CT's lunch and was just starting to clean up the breakfast dishes, the dryer buzzer signaled that the sheets were done. Honey felt done too. She sat down across the table from CT with a weary sigh.

"Want a sandwich?" He held up a half.

She sighed. "No, but thanks." She reached for a banana and set it by his plate. "I don't think you had your banana today."

He nodded as he slowly chewed.

Honey knew she should have a banana too, but she just didn't feel hungry. Mostly she felt tired. But thinking CT should be safely occupied for a bit, she decided to get the clean sheets out of the dryer and take them upstairs. As she trudged up with the full basket, she sniffed the linens. It wasn't a bad smell, but nothing like clean pure sunshine. Her favorite place to line dry sheets in the summertime was a clothesline CT had helped her string over the lavender field a few years ago, but at the moment, as much as she enjoyed that aroma, it felt like too much work. Maybe the girls would want to help her with that sometime this summer.

She was just fitting the bottom sheet onto the second bed when she realized she was slightly out of breath and lightheaded. She sat down on the edge of the bed and took in some deep breaths. Maybe she *was* overdoing it. Why not let the girls finish up in here? After all, they were young and strong. And she still needed to get some potatoes on the stove if she was going to make potato salad for dinner.

Honey wanted to make their first meal here special, and Jewel had been raving about her potato salad. Of course, it was more work than plain mashed potatoes, which CT would prefer, but the salad would make for good leftovers tomorrow. Besides that, she needed to get her roast into the oven soon, if she wanted it to be done on time. She wished she'd learned how to use that Instant Pot Jewel had sent them last Christmas. But life was so full of distractions, and she just hadn't gotten around to reading the instructions. Maybe Jewel could show her. Her daughter swore by the thing, claimed it was a big time-saver. And, boy, she could sure use more time.

By the time she got back to the kitchen, CT was removing a plate from the dishwasher and setting it in the cabinet above.

Honey frowned, biting her lower lip and wanting to scream. "So . . . did you empty *all* the dishes?"

"Yep." He looked pleased with himself. "Helping you."

"But those dishes were still dirty." She opened a cabinet door and studied the shelf of drinking glasses. The dirty ones were mixed in with the clean.

"Oops?" CT frowned. "Dumb me."

"No, you're not dumb." She turned to him. "But you do look tired."

"Yeah. Hard work."

She still had to remind herself how he tired easily. "Why don't you go sit for a while? Get rested up before the girls get here."

"What girls?" His brow creased.

"Jewel and Cooper. Remember? They'll be here soon."

His expression was fuzzy, but he nodded.

"Go get in your chair." She gently nudged him toward the living room. "Put your feet up. There'll be plenty to do later."

"Yeah. Good thinking, Honey." He pecked her on the cheek. "You do good thinking for me and for you too."

She forced a smile, then walked across her still-sticky kitchen floor to sift the dirty dishes from the clean ones and reload the dishwasher. She felt bone-weary as she got the potatoes ready to cook. Maybe potato salad was a bad idea after all.

But Honey continued to push herself, putting one foot in front of the next. Step-by-step, she got the roast ready and into the oven. She chopped onions and pickles and made dressing for the potato salad. Then she revived the green salad she'd made the night before and added more tomatoes, cucumbers, avocado, and lettuce. It wouldn't be long before she could add veggies from her own garden. That would be nice.

Then, tired of the stickiness, she got out her mop and bucket and gave the old wood floor a good mopping, making the oak planks almost golden again. Finally she put the mop things away and went into the living room, where CT was quietly snoring. She sat down and attempted to catch her breath. She'd certainly been working hard, but she never used to get winded so easily.

Was she just getting old? Or was something else going on? She hadn't been to a doctor since her GP retired back during COVID. Maybe it was time to find a new doctor and schedule a checkup. Well, if she could find the time. Where did one go to find time anyway?

6

Jewel

"Can you believe how green everything is up here in Oregon? Such a beautiful place. But that's because of all the rain they get. Of course, they do suffer from drought occasionally." Jewel had been chirping away at her daughter since they left the interstate for this less traveled highway. But Cooper's silent treatment was ongoing. Still Jewel persisted. She'd either drive her daughter crazy with chitchat or start answering herself. "Did you ever see so many sheep? And check out those little lambs. Aren't they adorable?"

She checked her rearview mirror to see that Cooper had put her headphones on again. Well, so much for aggravating her into a response. At least they were almost there now. As she drove through the small town of Sweet Springs, where little had changed since Jewel was a girl, she didn't bother pointing out places of interest. She knew Cooper would probably just sneer anyway. And Jewel was fed up with trying to placate her. If Cooper wanted to act like a big baby, she'd let her.

She turned down the long driveway to her parents' house, peering toward the barn to see if the movers had arrived yet, but there was no sign of the red-and-white truck. Just as well. Now she could supervise the unloading. She parked in front of the farmhouse and without another word to the lump in the back seat, hopped out before running up to the front door and knocking loudly. When no one answered, she let herself in. "Hello?" she called out. "It's me. We're here!"

She could smell something good cooking, but no one answered her greeting. She called out again then went into the kitchen to see what looked like dinner in process. But then she noticed salad splattered across the kitchen floor and an upturned bowl in the corner. "Mom!" she called out. "Where are you?" She raced all through the house but saw no sign of either of them. Jerking out her phone, she tried her mom's cell, but it went straight to voicemail. She left a quick message, then ran outside and found her mom's car parked nearby. She started to yell even louder. "Mom! Dad! Where are you?"

She was just calling her mom's phone again when Cooper got out of the car and approached with a curious expression. Still irritated at her daughter, Jewel ignored her as she checked around the garden then headed for the barn, calling out louder yet. She looked inside the barn and all around but, again, saw no sign of either of her parents. "What is going on here?" she asked herself. Had something happened with Dad? Perhaps he hurt himself again. Something beyond skinned-up knees? Maybe he needed medical attention.

She was just coming out of the barn, calling out again, when Cooper came over to her. "What's up with you?" she asked. "Why are you screaming your head off?"

"Nothing's up with me. Your grandparents are missing."

"So what?" Cooper shrugged.

"So what?" Jewel snapped.

"They probably went someplace. Why go into conniptions?"

"My mom's car is still here! Salad is spilled all over the kitchen floor. Something is wrong!" Jewel wanted to shake Cooper. But her phone rang with an unknown number. She answered without thinking about it. "Yes?" Jewel growled into the phone.

"Is this Jewel McKerry?" a man's voice asked.

"Yes. Who is this?"

"This is Miguel Orosco. I'm your parents' neighbor."

"Oh, yes. Okay. Do you by any chance know where my parents are?" she asked eagerly.

"Yes. Here at St. John's. In Sweet Springs."

"The hospital?"

"Yes. ER."

"Oh no," she exclaimed. "Is it my dad? Is he okay?"

"Actually, it's your mom."

"My mom?" She felt her heart pounding. "Is she okay?"

"I, uh, I think so. I'm not sure. She's being seen by the doctor. I'm out here in the waiting room with your dad. Your mom gave me your number when we checked her into the hospital. I would've called sooner, but your dad was, well, he was pretty upset."

"Oh dear. I can imagine." She already had her keys out. "I'm on my way."

"Good. That should help. Your dad doesn't exactly trust me."

"Sorry about that. I'll see you soon." She was already getting into her car when she realized Cooper was sitting on the porch steps.

"Your grandma's in the hospital," Jewel called to her. "We need to go check on her."

Cooper ambled over to the SUV with a mildly interested expression. "What about the mover dudes? Shouldn't they be here soon?"

"Yeah. That's right." Jewel grimaced. "Can you stay here and show them where to put stuff?" She pointed to the barn. "In there, for the most part. Kind of in back, out of the way. Can you do that for me?"

Cooper shrugged. "I guess."

"You got your phone," Jewel reminded her. "Call me if you need anything."

"Okay." Cooper's eyes flickered with just a trace of empathy. "I hope Grandma's okay."

"Me too. I gotta go, Coop." Jewel forced a smile. "Thanks for taking care of the movers. I'll call you when I find out what's going on."

Cooper gave her another apathetic shrug. So much for empathy. As Jewel started the engine, she remembered a time when she would've asked Cooper to pray over a situation like this. Not today. Cooper would probably just make a sarcastic remark or laugh. And Jewel didn't need that right now.

As she drove to the hospital, she prayed. "Please, Lord, let Mom be all right. Be with her and, please, help her with whatever is wrong." Turning into downtown Sweet Springs, she wondered what exactly was wrong with her mom. An accident? Why had she dropped the salad on the floor? Had she cut herself? But Jewel hadn't seen any blood or a knife. What had happened?

As Jewel parked near the entrance of the ER, she thought one good thing about small towns was their hospitals were never too busy. Hopefully small hospitals gave good medical attention. She hurried inside and quickly spotted her dad, waving his hands with an angst-ridden expression at a dark-haired man who appeared to be trying to calm him down. A doctor perhaps? But when she got closer, she saw the man had on dirty jeans and a torn plaid shirt. Probably the neighbor Miguel.

"Dad," she said as she approached them, remembering how her mom coached her to use short simple sentences a few days ago. He looked at her but didn't seem to recognize his own daughter. In fact, she barely recognized him. He looked so much older.

"It's me, Jewel." She reached for his hand but still saw no flicker of recognition in his eyes. Just anxiety and maybe fear. When he was upset, her mom had warned, he required extra patience.

"I'm Miguel," the stranger told her as Dad jerked his hand out of Jewel's grasp.

"Thank you for calling me," she told Miguel, then turned back to her father. "It's me, Jewel. Your daughter. I was out at the farm when Miguel called—"

"Miguel!" her dad spit out the name, shaking his finger at the man. "He hurt Honey."

Miguel glumly shook his head. "No, sir, I did not hurt Mrs. McKerry." He spoke to her dad but looked at Jewel, as if hoping she understood.

"Yes. You. Did." He glared daggers at Miguel.

"Dad!" Jewel chastened her father. "Miguel is your neighbor."

"He's bad. He hurt Honey. And he's a thief."

"Dad," she tried again, softening her tone even more. "Remember me? Your daughter? *Jewel.* I wouldn't lie to you." She placed a firm hand on his forearm, feeling him trembling beneath his flannel shirt. Was it anxiety or his illness? Or both?

"Jewel?" He squinted as if to see her better. "Yeah . . . I think I know . . . you."

"Let's go sit down." She gently guided him to the waiting room, but he was still upset, mumbling about Miguel and what a bad, bad man he was. She hoped her dad's behavior wasn't frightening the woman and small girl sitting by the fish tank. They already looked agitated and probably didn't need him going off right next to them. She glanced back at Miguel with an apologetic expression. "Talk later?" she mouthed to him. To her relief he nodded, albeit somberly, seeming to understand the difficulty of the situation.

"Let's sit there." She pointed to a pair of chairs by the window. It took a bit of coaxing and some physical assistance to get him to ease his tall frame down onto a chair, but then he leaned forward and, cupping his head in his hands, began to sob. She put her hand on his shoulder, trying to speak words of comfort, but wasn't sure they made any difference.

She looked up to where Miguel was maintaining a safe distance. Clearly he was stressed too. They were all out of their comfort zones. What should she do? And what was wrong with Mom? And what about Cooper? She'd only been in town about an hour and already she was in over her head. And so, for the second time today, she prayed. Silently. And suddenly, like her difficult daughter, she questioned whether this move to Oregon was really the right choice. What had she gotten herself into?

CT

This carpet is green with speckles. That's not right. When did Honey get green, speckled carpet? Did she get this when I was in the field? That's the color . . . new hay green. Why would Honey want new hay green in here? Where is Honey? Where am I? This plastic chair is so hard, and there's a window with cars out there. Whose cars? Who's here? Where am I? *Where is Honey?* Did I say that or just think I said it?

This place smells funny. It isn't home. Where am I? Why is my face wet? Did someone splash me? Is it raining?

This window between me and the cars is dirty. Finger smears all up and down. Probably from that little girl. She looks like a finger-smearing girl. Or maybe she smeared her nose there. Her mom should wipe her nose. Why doesn't she wipe her nose? Is that what I smell? The little girl needs a bath. Why doesn't that woman take her away and give her a bath? "Where's Honey?" Did I say that or just think it? I can't remember.

I feel someone beside me. She nudges me. "What did you say?" she asks me. Who is she? And how did she get here? "Do I know you?" I ask.

"Yes. I'm Jewel. Your daughter, Daddy. Remember me?"

I feel the fog lifting. Just a corner of it. "Jewel?" I ask her. "My Jewel?"

She smiles, and the fog lifts higher. "Yes. Your Jewel. How are you doing?"

I don't know what to say. "Not good," I think I say.

"I'm sorry." Her eyes are brown, or maybe green. There's a name for that. Are they like my eyes? Is she really my little girl? She is too old.

"Jewel?" I stare at her. "Where's Honey?"

"I think she's with the doctor."

"Where are we?"

"At the hospital."

"Am I sick?"

Her mouth does something funny. What does that mean?

"Am I sick?" I say the words louder to make sure she hears me.

"Not exactly, Dad."

She calls me Dad again. Is she really my little girl? Is she tricking me?

"Where's Honey? Where's my wife?" I push myself to my feet. "Why can't I see her? I need my Honey."

The woman stands up, reaching for my arm like she thinks I'll fall over. Like she thinks I'm a crazy old man. I'm not. Doesn't she know I don't need her doggone help? "Where's Honey?" I shout.

"Shh, Dad. You're getting too—"

"Don't *shh* me." I jerk my arm from this bossy woman. Who does she think she is? "I want Honey." I see the other woman pull the snot-nosed girl closer. Does she think I eat small children? Now a woman in pajama clothes comes up to me. She is round like a pumpkin with pictures of cats all over her pajama shirt.

"Can I help you?" Pumpkin Cat Woman asks.

"I don't know," I say. "Can you?"

"I work here," she says. "You seem worried."

"I want Honey."

"Are you hungry? Diabetic?" She looks at the woman who says she's my daughter. "Do you need assistance?"

"I need Honey!" I can hear the two women talking quietly. I can't hear their words, but they are talking about me. I know it.

Pumpkin Cat Woman takes my arm. "I can get you honey," she says. "Come with me." Now she leads me somewhere. A hallway. Another place. A room with a couch and two chairs. Not my living room. Same green, speckled carpet. Not my carpet. "Sit down here," she says. "I'll get you some honey."

I sit down, but I think Pumpkin Cat Woman is balmy. I don't want *some* honey. I want my Honey. I want Honey to take me home. I want my bees. Pumpkin Cat Woman leaves, but the woman who says she's my daughter stays right by the door. She's looking at her phone, but I think she's guarding the door like a century. Is that what they're called? Century, sensory, sentry? That's it. Sentry. *Where's Honey?*

I bend over, holding onto my head with my hands so I can keep it from spinning away. It spins away sometimes. Goes off on its own without asking me first. I can't stop it. I can't start it. I can't find it. Honey says it's not my fault. It's tricking me. But why does this happen to me? What did I do to deserve this? *Where is Honey?*

"Doing okay?" the door sentry asks.

I make my fierce face. I think I do. Honey says I can scare people. Can I scare the door sentry?

"Dad?" She steps inside the door. "Are you okay?"

"No! I am not okay. Where is my wife? I want to go home!"

"Your wife is being seen by the doctor. She's in—"

"She does not need the doctor. She needs me. Now."

"Mom is sick," Sentry Woman tells me. "She needs medical attention."

"Sick?" I try to remember what that word means. I think I heard that I am sick. Honey is not sick. Honey is Honey. "Honey isn't sick."

"Yes. She is, Dad. She needs help." Sentry Woman's arms are folded in front of her like a locked gate. I don't think she'll let me leave. Maybe if she turns away, I can sneak out.

I rub the sides of my head, trying to make it work. "Miguel!" I remember now. "He hurt her. He knocked her down. In the kitchen. He hit Honey."

Now Pumpkin Cat is back. She carries a paper cup. "Tea and honey." She hands it to me.

"Honey?" I sniff the cup. Doesn't smell like honey.

"Have a sip. It might make you feel better." Pumpkin Cat turns to talk to the door sentry quietly so I can't hear. Now Sentry Woman leaves and Pumpkin Cat guards the door. She is big. I don't think I can sneak past her.

I try a sip from the white cup. It tastes like paper. Not honey. I set the cup on the green, speckled carpet. Not home. I need to go home. The fog is thicker. I forget . . . where I am . . . where is home . . . where is Honey? My face is all wet again. I think the roof is leaking. I need to get on my feet. I need to escape this green, speckled carpet place, away from Pumpkin Cat, away from the snotty-nosed girl. But Pumpkin Cat blocks the door. I am lost. The fog is swallowing me. Eating me alive. *I need my Honey.*

Honey

Despite the buzzing and pinging of medical machines, glaringly bright lights, and a stiff bed and hard pillow, not to mention the rather noisy conversations carrying on outside her room, Honey hadn't felt this relaxed in ages. She was wired up with all kinds of devices and had an IV stuck into her arm, but she didn't even care. Well, maybe a little. Her fall was bad timing. Not that she'd planned it. It wasn't until she was in here in the ER, being interviewed by a kind female doctor named Jamie that Honey even pieced together what had actually happened. Or what she thought happened. She was still a bit fuzzy on some details.

Best she could recall, the roast was in the oven, the potato salad was assembled, and she'd just added a few more veggies to the green salad. With about an hour to spare before Jewel and Cooper arrived, she was thinking about taking a little break and reading the newspaper. Humming to herself, she'd spun around to put the salad in the fridge and lost her balance. Then she tumbled forward and whacked her head on something. The oak table or the hardwood floor? She wasn't even sure.

And she honestly wasn't even sure how long she'd lain there amid lettuce and tomato and cucumbers. But when she'd tried to stand, she'd felt dizzy . . . and sick, like she was about to take another tumble. She called out to CT, although in retrospect she wasn't sure what he would've done besides wring his hands and get upset. Then she'd remembered her cell phone in her back pocket and called the closest neighbors—the Oroscos. Miguel had answered and, sitting among chopped vegetables, she groggily explained her need for help then hung up and, still a bit dazed, tried to get her bearings before just lying down.

The next thing she knew, Miguel was there, helping her into a kitchen chair and insisting on driving her to ER. He got her into the back seat of his pickup and somehow rounded up CT, who was yelling at Miguel like he'd come to steal the family jewels. Miguel managed to get CT into the back of his pickup by showing him the knot on his wife's forehead. Surprisingly that had shut the man right up. He just stared at her with that confused expression and rubbed her hand mechanically.

But as they rode toward town, CT grew more agitated. Honey exerted more energy soothing her husband than concerning herself with her own condition. In fact, by the time she was in the ER waiting room, she wondered if all this fuss was necessary since she felt better. But then she'd gotten sick in front of the reception desk, and it wasn't long before someone wheeled her into the ER for treatment.

After some examining, she was taken to a darkened room where they used a machine to scan her brain. She was surprised at how relaxed she'd been through the whole thing. It actually felt good to lay still, the only noise the rhythmic clicking of the machine. And now the young Dr. Jamie was back in the little room where Honey had been resting peacefully. "How are you feeling?"

"I feel fine," Honey said brightly. "I think I can go home now." She started to swing her legs around, then realized she was still connected to wires and things.

"Not so fast." Jamie put a hand on her shoulder. "I have a few more things to ask you."

"I thought I answered all the questions." Honey leaned back, closing her eyes against the now-throbbing pain in her head.

"Tell me about your fall," the doctor said, not for the first time.

With eyes still shut, Honey replayed what she'd said earlier.

"And do you recall if you were unconscious or not after you fell?"

"Like I said earlier, I honestly don't remember. But I think maybe I was unconscious. It seemed like I was on the kitchen floor for a while."

"And do you remember exactly what made you fall? Did you faint? Or did you trip on something?"

Honey opened her eyes. "Good question."

"Try to remember."

"Okay. I was carrying a bowl of green salad from the counter by the sink over to the fridge and, yes, come to think of it, I did trip."

"What caused you to trip? Do you recall?"

A light bulb went off inside her shaken brain. "Yes. I think I remember now. CT had been in the kitchen earlier. He'd been working in his pumpkin patch but had come in for a drink of water. I filled a water bottle for him, then scolded him for getting mud all over my clean kitchen floor. I'd just mopped it."

"Yes. And then what happened?"

"He must've left his hoe in the kitchen. I bet he leaned it against the counter or maybe the table. I'm not sure. But now I do recall seeing the hoe on the floor when I was down there in that salad mess. CT must've forgotten it. He's very forgetful."

"Uh-huh." Jamie nodded. "Well, that makes sense. So you didn't faint, then?"

"No, I don't think so."

Jamie was looking at something on a computer screen. "We got results from your scans, and everything looks okay."

"So my brain's not too scrambled up?" Honey tried to sound light.

"Well, you definitely have a concussion. And you really need to take it easy for a while."

"How long is a while?"

"Hard to say. But I recommend at least a week of doing nothing. And I mean absolutely nothing. But do schedule an appointment with your GP ASAP."

Honey winced. "My GP?"

"Don't you have one?"

"Not exactly." She explained about her old GP retiring.

"Well, get one. If necessary, I'll refer you to one. Because we made another little discovery regarding your health."

Honey felt a wave of concern. She'd been so tired lately . . . with an occasional fluttering in her chest. But she was only in her mid-sixties and in generally good health. "My heart?"

"No. Not yet, anyway. Your blood pressure is extremely high. That could affect your heart as well as put you in danger of stroke."

"But I've always had low blood pressure."

"Well, you don't today. It could be related to your head injury, but I don't think so. You've been here a couple hours, and it's still very elevated."

"Oh."

"I ordered blood pressure meds from the hospital pharmacy. The nurse will bring them to you soon. Then we'll keep you here until your blood pressure goes down enough that I feel it's safe for you to go home."

"Okay." Honey sighed. This was more than just a bump on the head.

"Thanks for answering my questions, Mrs. McKerry. I just wanted to make sure you didn't faint and fall."

"Right."

"By the way, Mr. McKerry is demanding to see you."

"Oh, please, don't let him in here. It will only upset him more." Honey reminded the doctor of CT's FTD.

Jamie nodded. "We'll keep him out there."

"I just hope he's not alone."

"Your daughter's with him. If you give me permission, I'll explain your condition to her."

Honey wanted to say, "No, don't tell anyone," but that sounded childish. "I guess that's fine, but I'm not sure I want my granddaughter to hear everything. I mean, she's got a lot to deal with. She's only thirteen."

"I didn't see anyone besides your daughter with your husband."

"Okay, then tell my daughter, but don't worry my husband about it." Honey reminded herself that if Jewel had come to help, she probably needed to know what she was up against. Although it might make her hightail it back to San Jose. But maybe that would be for the best. Honey wasn't sure. Not about anything.

"You just rest. And don't worry." Jamie's tone felt as soothing as a cool glass of water. "You're going to be just fine."

"Thanks." She considered asking if Jewel could come in here to visit but realized that would probably leave CT alone . . . and that would not be good. And so she just leaned back and closed her eyes and tried to relax. High blood pressure? A concussion? What next?

8

Jewel

Nothing was going like Jewel had imagined. She'd only been here a few hours and she was already on the verge of a full-blown panic attack. What had she done by recklessly selling everything and moving up here? How was Cooper going to react to all the chaos? Her grandpa was losing it, and her grandma was seriously ill. Sure, they needed help more than ever now, but this was way outside of Jewel's wheelhouse. Nothing about her life—being an independent artist, owning an up-and-coming art gallery, not even single parenting—had prepared her for this. She'd made a great big horrific mistake.

She twisted the handle of her boho bag as she sat across from her dad in the small waiting room. The one reserved for their "special" cases. Fortunately the hospital staff seemed to understand this situation. Or else they just wanted to contain CT and keep him from upsetting more people. But Jewel was getting fed up with him. She knew he was ill, but this was ridiculous. She loved him, but she had to control herself from shaking him and telling him to snap out of it.

Was he really this far gone? Or was he trying to get attention from his drama king act? Naturally, he was stressed. But so was she. Still, she wondered how long it would be before he would have to go into some kind of assisted living. Her mother had sworn she would never do that. "CT wants to live out his last days on the farm. To die with his boots on," she had said more than once. Well, that was a fine platitude when life wasn't a great big mess, but Mom might feel different about things now.

Jewel used to be a smoker back in her rebellious twenties. She knew it was a stupid habit, but more than ever she wanted a cigarette right now. She could imagine inhaling that soothing breath of tobacco smoke, holding it inside, then slowly releasing it and blowing away her troubles. Instead she recrossed her legs, folded her arms tightly in front of her, and stared helplessly at her fractured father. Hunched over, mumbling to himself about the color of the carpet, still wearing his work clothes, in need of a shave. An onlooker probably assumed he was a drifter from the streets.

She'd tried to comfort him several times, but he'd simply shrugged her off as if she were a stranger about to steal his wallet. She'd offered him food, but he'd just waved her away. Even when she tried to assure him that Mom was okay, it didn't seem to register. He was too far gone. And at this rate, she wouldn't be surprised if he wound up in a hospital bed himself. Maybe in the psych ward. And maybe that was a good idea. If someone could sedate him, just knock him out until it was time to take Mom home, he might actually appreciate it. She knew she would.

She reached for her phone and texted Cooper again, asking for an update on the movers and making sure she remembered to turn off the oven before the roast became a burnt offering. Cooper reassured her that the movers had come and gone and claimed to have everything under control. That is, unless Cooper was texting from the back of the moving van after informing the movers to transport all their belongings—and her—back to San Jose. She wouldn't put it past her disgruntled daughter. Especially if Coop fully understood what they were up against now that Grandma was incapacitated. Jewel glanced back at her confused dad and realized she desperately wanted to run in the opposite direction too. Was it too late to pull the plug on this?

"Hey there." A male's hushed voice came from the doorframe.

She looked over her shoulder to see Miguel lurking in the shadows, probably trying not to upset Dad. Who knew what might happen if Dad spotted his archenemy lurking nearby. She'd never seen her dad so angry before. As if Miguel was personally responsible for all the woes of the world. Jewel quietly rose and went over to Miguel.

"I thought you went home," she whispered, although her dad seemed oblivious.

"I did. I had to move some cows. But I decided to come back and check on you guys. How's it going?" He tipped his head toward her dad. "How's he doing?"

"He's a hot mess. I honestly don't know what I'll do with him if Mom has to spend the night here. I'm not sure I can get him to go home with me. He doesn't seem to trust me. I'm not sure he even knows who I am."

"Do you think they'll keep your mom overnight?"

"The doctor told me it's a possibility." She stepped outside of the doorway. "She said it's not only the concussion. Mom has extremely high blood pressure. 224 over 119."

"Yikes. That's super high. My mom has high blood pressure too, but it's never been that high."

"Poor Mom." She peeked back at Dad, but he was still staring at the carpet.

"How's your mom's head? Did they read her CAT scans yet?"

"Yes. They didn't see any internal bleeding. So that's good." Jewel noticed a woman coming their way.

The woman smiled, showed them a hospital badge, and introduced herself. "I'm Marge Stewart, a guest volunteer. I was told you might need some help with Mr. McKerry."

"Help?" Jewel studied the gray-haired woman.

"My husband had Alzheimer's." Marge's eyes were kind, but her smile reflected sadness. "I know how difficult it can be in a situation like this. I'm happy to sit with him awhile, if you two want to go get a coffee or just have a break."

Jewel brightened. "That'd be nice."

Marge peeked into the room. "He seems upset," she said quietly.

Then without another word, the older woman went in and sat by him, but not too close. She spoke slowly and gently, and after a bit, he looked up. Marge continued to chat with him, almost as if he was an old friend. She waved them away and, grateful for even a brief escape, Jewel took it.

"Do you know where I can find a cup of coffee?" she asked Miguel.

"I do." He pointed down a hallway. "Right this way." As they walked, he explained that his dad had been in this hospital for a couple of weeks. "So I got to know the place pretty well."

"How is he now?" she asked, mostly to be polite.

"He passed away."

"Oh, I'm sorry." She glanced at Miguel.

"It was several years ago. I'd just gotten home from the service." He indicated a turn ahead.

"Oh? What branch of military?"

"Air Force. I'd just retired and almost signed up for more, but I'm glad I didn't now. It was good to be around for my mom's sake. She was pretty lost without him. And it was time for me to be home for my wife and child too."

She peered curiously at him, trying to guess his age. "How long were you in the Air Force?"

"Nearly twenty years." He pointed to a cafeteria sign. "There she blows."

"Thanks." She stopped by the entrance to the cafeteria. "Care to join me for a coffee?"

"Sure. But I'll warn you, it's not exactly Starbucks."

She smiled. "That's okay. I was never a Starbucks girl anyway." As they went inside, she did some mental math. Twenty years in the Air Force plus eight at home, would make him at least forty-six. A few years older than her. But why did it matter? Sure, he was handsome and, according to her mom—*not her Dad*—Miguel was a good guy. But a guy with a wife and child. After they got their coffees and sat down, he asked her how long she planned to stay in Oregon.

"The plan was to stay indefinitely," she admitted. "But to be honest, I'm getting a little worried now."

"Afraid it's going to be too much?" His brow creased as he stirred cream into his coffee. "Your dad's memory issues and now your mom's troubles? Feeling overwhelmed?"

She barely nodded. "I knew Mom needed help with Dad . . . I just didn't expect this."

"She didn't either."

Suddenly Jewel remembered something. "I'm not sure how to ask you this," she began carefully, "but my dad said some bad things about you. And Mom told me he's got some kind of grudge against you. But Dad acts like you were responsible for Mom's injury. In fact, he seems certain of it."

"I know." Miguel leaned back in his chair. "He got it into his head that I did something to your mom. That I hurt her. But I didn't. I replayed the whole incident in my head on my way home, trying to figure out what made him think that."

"You mean, besides the fact he's got dementia? Did you come up with an explanation?"

"Maybe. Here's what happened. Your mom called me after she fell and hit her head. She sounded a little incoherent, so I rushed right over. Your dad didn't seem to be around when I got there. She was in the kitchen, and it looked like she'd tripped over a hoe, which seemed odd. When I helped her out to my truck, I had the hoe in one hand. I tossed it down when I saw your dad, but he might've got it into his head that I'd clobbered your mom with it."

"It sounds crazy, but crazy makes sense with Dad."

Miguel sadly shook his head. "Your dad already thinks I stole his land and his tractor. Now he thinks I injured his wife. I'm sure glad your mom got rid of the guns or I'd be seriously worried for my and my family's safety."

"I'm so sorry about that. I hope your family's not too scared of him."

He smiled crookedly. "It's not all that bad. Although I do worry about my mom sometimes. She can get worked up. But my daughter just takes it in stride. That's Anna for you. She's a real rock."

"How old is Anna?"

"Just turned fourteen."

"Fourteen and she's a rock? Wow, my daughter Cooper's thirteen and anything but. I'm having parental envy."

"Yeah, I've heard some horror stories about girls their age. It can get ugly."

"That's for sure. I've been at serious odds with Cooper for a while, but today was the worst. She wore me out. I was really looking forward to seeing Mom. And now this." Jewel set down her coffee. "I can't imagine the hissy fit Cooper will throw when she learns we'll be playing nursemaid to both her grandparents now. There'll be no living with her."

"Don't feel too bad. I've heard most teen girls grow out of this stuff. I'm just really lucky Anna skipped all that. Don't know what I'd do without her."

Jewel was pea green with envy now. This guy had it all. He wasn't single parenting. He had a wife and live-in grandma to help. No wonder Anna was perfect. "I hope Anna's mom knows how lucky she is."

"She did." He spun his Styrofoam cup on the table. "Beth passed away several years ago. Cancer."

Jewel pursed her lips as her jealousy melted away. "Oh dear. I'm so sorry. You lost your dad and your wife."

"Yeah. Life sure has its ups and downs."

"So it's just you and your mom and daughter now?" she asked, feeling nosy. What was it to her if he had a new wife or more children?

He nodded. "We've been through a lot, but we get along okay." He looked intently at her. "I think you will too. Just give yourself time . . . and grace."

"Grace?"

"Don't be too hard on yourself. Or on your daughter."

"Or my dad?"

He firmly nodded. "Most definitely."

"Sounds like you've been pretty gracious to him, Miguel. Mom has told me how rough Dad's been on you. I'm sorry."

"That's life. I just wish there was a way to mend things with him. The problem is the troubles are in his mind, so it's a real challenge to navigate."

"Believe me, after a couple hours with him, I know." She heard her phone ping with a text and looked to see it was from Cooper. She read it and smiled. "Well, a bit of good news. My daughter turned off the roast before it turned to toast, and unless she's pulling a fast one, she's still at the farm."

"You thought she'd go someplace else?"

Jewel attempted a weak laugh. "I was a little worried she'd stow away with the moving van and return to San Jose. That's how resistant she's been to this move."

"Well, for your parents' sake, I'm glad you and your daughter came. They really do need help. I try to do what I can, but your father makes it difficult."

"I'm starting to understand. It's too bad Dad does that."

"Maybe having you and Cooper around will help mellow him." Miguel finished his coffee. "And if Cooper needs a friend to show her around town, or whatever, I'm sure Anna would be happy to assist."

"Anna sounds so wonderful, you might not want her to be around my brat."

Miguel laughed. "I probably made Anna sound too good. Remember, I'm her dad, I'm a little biased."

"She sounds like a sweet girl." Jewel finished her coffee. "I guess I should get back to my dad."

"Yep, and unless you need me here, I should probably get home. There's a lot of work to do around the farm this time of year."

"I'll tell Cooper about Anna."

"And let me know how it goes with your mom. Or if we can be of any help."

"I'll do that. Hopefully they'll let her go home soon."

9

CT

All these people! Running around like chickens. Headless chickens. And one of them has green hair! Who are these girls? Why are they here? Isn't this *my* house? I think it is, but it's not the same. I think this is my chair. It feels like my chair. But everything is different. Why do people keep changing everything around? Who are these people, anyway?

"Dad?" the tall woman says to me.

"What?" I glare at her. Why does she keep calling me Dad? She's not my little girl. She's a big girl!

"Mom is resting in her room." The big girl places a hand on my shoulder. "Are you ready to have some dinner now?"

"No." I shake my head so hard it makes my brains rattle, but I want her to understand. "Not hungry!"

"You need to eat something."

"Not hungry."

"Grandma made roast beef," the one with green hair says. I think she's a child, but she's tall too.

I shake my finger at her. "Why is your hair green?"

"Because I like it like this."

"Who *are* you?" I ask her.

"I'm Cooper," she speaks loud and slow. Does she think I can't hear?

"Cooper?" I stare at her. "That's *my* name. Cooper . . ." I try to remember the other part of my name.

She smiles and nods. "Yes. I know. You are Cooper *Thomas*. I'm Cooper *Janelle*."

"No, I'm CT," I correct her.

"Okay, then I'm CJ." She sits in the chair across from me. The chair where Honey should sit. Where is Honey? "Mom named me Cooper after you."

"Mom?" I try to put the puzzle together. "Is Honey *your* mom?"

"No." She shakes her head. "Honey is my grandma. You are my grandpa."

"And I am your daughter. *Jewel*." The other woman holds a plate of food right under my nose. Stinky food. "Please eat something, Dad."

I lift my hand to block the plate. "Not hungry."

"You need nourishment, Dad."

"*Dad?*" I look for the one with my name, but she is gone now so I look back at this one. "Who are you?"

"I'm Jewel."

"That's your name? Jewel? Like a ring?"

"Yes. You named me after your mother."

"*Mother?*" What is she saying? "You mean Honey?"

"No, I meant *your* mother. Honey is *my* mother." She keeps holding the plate right in front of me. Does she think I want to eat that? It smells like garbage, and I know it will make my stomach hurt. Bad food does that.

"Take that away. To the garbage!" I raise my voice to make sure she can hear.

"*Daaad*." She steps back.

"Am I *your* dad?" I ask.

"Yes. I'm your daughter, Jewel. Remember?"

"I don't know. I don't know. Sometimes I can't remember things." I rub my head . . . maybe I can make my brain work better. My brain doesn't work right sometimes. I don't know why that is. It used to work all the time. It used to be the way I wanted it to work. Now it just does whatever . . .

"Grandma says give him a peanut butter and honey sandwich," the green-haired girl tells the woman. They think I can't hear, but I can. "With a glass of milk."

"Yes." I bob my head up and down. "Peanut butter and honey. That's it."

"Okay." The girl takes the plate away, and I can breathe again.

"Jewel?" I try out the word. "Is that really your name?"

She smiles. "Yes. That's right. Jewel."

"Okay." I lean back in my chair and close my eyes. "I'm tired." I want to sleep so they will go away and stop bothering me.

"You're probably worn out." Her voice sounds nicer now. "You had a busy day."

"Yes. I was in the hospital." I don't remember why I was there, but I'm sure it was something bad. Did I fall down? I reach up to touch my head. Is that why I can't remember things? Because I hit my head? Yes, that's what happened. Or else I am having a dream. When I wake up, I will be better and things will make sense again. I think they used to make sense. But I can't really remember that now.

Honey

Honey knew she needed to rest yet felt it was impossible. She could hear Jewel and Cooper in the living room, trying to coax CT to eat something. He'd already rejected the roast and, despite Jewel's best try, according to CT, the peanut butter sandwich she'd fixed for him was "not done right." Honey had forgotten to mention that he liked his bread toasted, so now he was complaining that it was too soggy, telling them he'd choke on it and die. And chances were, he might choke too. Another element of FTD was somatic illnesses, and if CT thought something would make him sick, it surely would. She needed to explain this to Jewel.

After the events of the day, CT was really scrambled. He still didn't recognize his daughter and granddaughter. Never mind the fact that Honey had spent this morning prepping him for their arrival. It was all lost in the mix. He was completely befuddled. As frustrating as it was to her, there was nothing she could do about it. If she had earplugs, she could ignore him and block it all out. Forget for a moment that her dearly beloved was nutty as a fruitcake. Of course, thinking that only made her feel guilty. People weren't supposed to talk like that. But she'd only thought it.

She definitely felt sorry for CT. He didn't like his condition any more than she did. Under normal circumstances he would've rejoiced over his daughter and granddaughter's visit. Instead, he was holding them at arm's length. The world was such a confusing place for him. And today had not helped.

She leaned back into her bed pillows, still longing for escape and knowing there was none. She might get a tiny reprieve while she recovered from her concussion, but CT would expect her to be up and at 'em soon. He would never understand the doctor's insistence that she "rest" for a few days. Well, at least she had help.

"Hey, Grandma." Cooper stuck her head through the cracked-open door. "You asleep?"

"No." Honey pushed herself back into a sitting position. "Come in, Cooper."

"Mom said to bring you some tea." Cooper held out a glass.

"Thanks, sweetie, that sounds good." Honey patted the edge of the bed. "Can you sit and visit for a bit?"

"Sure, if you want." Cooper handed her the glass and sat down. "You feeling better?"

"I guess so." Honey shrugged, determined to play this down. "To be honest, I didn't feel all that bad. Mostly a bad headache." She tugged a lock of Cooper's hair. "This is a pretty shade of green."

The girl smiled. "You really like it? I did it myself."

"I think it displays real creativity and individuality." Honey felt a throb and reached up to touch her swollen forehead.

Cooper narrowed her eyes. "That's a big lump, Grandma."

Honey attempted a smile. "Think it'll knock some sense into me?"

She shrugged. "You really need more sense?"

"I think I do."

"How's that?" Cooper leaned forward.

"Well, I did some pondering in the hospital. I think God is trying to tell me something."

"Seriously? That's pretty harsh. God whacking you on the head just to tell you something?"

"Not exactly, but I think God is using it."

"How so?"

"He is reminding me that I can't do it all."

"Well, no one can do it all."

"That's for sure. But I think I probably try to . . . or, at least, I did. Maybe this bump on the head will help me remember I can't."

"Yeah. Mom sometimes acts like that too. Like she can do it all. It's aggravating."

"Might be hereditary." Honey poked Cooper's arm. "So watch out, sweetie pie."

Cooper laughed. "Don't worry about me. I don't even *want* to do it all." She ran a finger along a quilt square, tracing the seams on the patchwork piece. "Did you make this quilt, Grandma?"

"As a matter of fact, I did." Honey surveyed the pale shades of fabric, faded from too many times on the clothesline. "Back when your mama was a girl, I got into quilting one winter. This was my first big project. Don't look too closely though. It's full of mistakes."

"Looks pretty good to me."

"Thanks." Honey sighed. "Do you know how to sew?"

"No. But I'd like to learn."

Honey brightened. "Maybe I can give you lessons. When I'm better."

"Cool."

Honey reached for Cooper's hand. "I know you weren't too excited to come to the farm," she said cautiously, "but I want you to know how glad I am that you're here. Thank you for coming. It means the world to me."

Cooper's countenance dimmed. "Not to Grandpa."

"Well, that's only because he's so confused. He's not usually this bad. But stress does that, and today's been pretty hard on him."

"I guess it was hard on all of us."

Honey studied Cooper's face. "How's your mom holding up?"

This girl was hard to read. "Okay, I guess. Anyway, she's good at faking it."

"Faking it?" Honey took a sip of tea.

"Yeah. Mom always acts like everything is just fine. She hates to admit when she's made a mistake. She can be seriously lost, and she's like 'we're fine, we'll get there.'"

"So you think she's made a mistake?"

"Yeah." Cooper winced. "No offense, but I'm pretty sure she knows it was a mistake to sell everything and come here."

Honey didn't know what to say. She was probably right.

"Not that we can do much about it now." Cooper stood and walked over to Honey's dresser, where Honey's framed photos were displayed. "Is this you and Grandpa?" She held up their wedding photo.

"It is." Honey sighed as she stared at the photo. Such a young couple. Her long dark hair was topped by a wreath of teacup roses and baby's breath. She'd crafted it herself and arranged the flowers in the church. She'd even sewn her bridesmaids' simple dresses. CT had worn a plain brown corduroy sports jacket—and no tie. Her grandma had made their wedding cake. It was a shoestring wedding, for sure, but the marriage lasted longer than that of some of their friends who'd gone all out.

"You were so young and pretty." Cooper set the photo back.

"Well, we were both young. I was only twenty and your grandpa just twenty-two. Of course, we thought we were all grown-up." Honey laughed. "Funny how that works."

"Is this Mom?" Cooper held up the photo of a little girl and a yellow lab puppy.

"Yep. She was about seven. And Goldie was just a pup."

Now Cooper picked up a more recent photo. "Where were you and Grandpa in this one? It looks kinda tropical."

"That was years ago on our thirty-fifth wedding anniversary.

Our one and only big trip. It was always hard to get your grandpa to leave the farm, but he reluctantly agreed to go to Maui with me for spring break that year."

"Oh, yeah, I remember now. Mom still has a box of shells you sent her. I used to play with them when I was little."

Honey smiled. "It turned out to be a fun trip. But even then . . . I could tell your grandpa was acting different. I think that's the first time I really noticed how forgetful he was getting. And he wasn't that old." Suddenly Honey regretted being so transparent with her granddaughter. Why burden the child with these old people problems?

Cooper put the photo back, then turned toward Honey with a surprisingly compassionate expression. "Is it hard on you? I mean, watching Grandpa like this? Does it hurt a lot?"

Honey felt a lump growing in her throat, but she didn't want to cry in front of Cooper. "Well, yes, to be honest, it does hurt some. But it is what it is, right?" She lifted her chin and forced a smile.

Cooper came back and sat on the bed again. This time, she took Honey's hand. "I'm so sorry, Grandma."

This unexpected act of kindness cracked something deep inside of Honey's chest. "Th-thank you," she muttered, struggling to hold back tears. "I guess it's been a lonely road."

"Well, we're here now." Cooper squeezed her hand. "You're not alone."

"I really appreciate that." Honey leaned her head back, closing her eyes and taking in a calming breath.

"And you can talk to me, Grandma. I'm a good listener. All my friends always tell me that. I think it's because it's just been Mom and me, and she's always talked to me a lot. I mean about grown-up things. So don't worry, I can take it."

Honey opened her eyes and stared at her granddaughter. She wasn't sure how she felt about Jewel talking to Cooper about "grown-up things." Had Cooper been forced to grow up too quickly? Had she been allowed to really be a child?

"I'm probably talking too much." Cooper released her hand and stood. "I know you're supposed to rest."

"Yes." Honey barely nodded, but the motion made her head ache. "You're right. I do need to rest. Thanks for the tea . . . and sympathy." She attempted another smile. "You're a dear girl, Cooper."

"Love you, Grandma." Then Cooper quietly exited the room and Honey allowed her tears to fall freely. It had been a lonely road. And despite having her daughter and granddaughter here, Honey knew it would get lonelier as CT's illness progressed. After forty-six years together, a lifetime was a lot to lose.

10

Jewel

Nothing had prepared Jewel for the parental scolding she'd just received from her mother. She and Cooper had been at the farm only three days, and already her mother was lecturing her on how to raise her own child. Although Jewel managed to bite her tongue while her mom told her to "just let Cooper be a child," she was fuming as she stormed across the pumpkin patch. Not that it mattered since nothing had sprouted there yet. But she suspected her dad would want to tan her hide if he was watching. Not that he could catch her since he walked like an old man of about 104. Oh, why had she come here in the first place?

Wanting to get as far from the house as possible, she found herself walking the fence line and, not unlike her dad, she felt aggravated that the original farm property had been divided like this. What had her parents been thinking, selling it off so easily? Of course, it wasn't really her business since she did recall denying any interest in farming. She'd laughed it off at the time. Now she had regrets. But it was too late and what was the use getting agitated over it? She kicked a dirt clod.

"Hello there."

Jewel looked up to see Miguel approaching. Today he had on denim overalls, a faded gray T-shirt, and a beat-up cowboy hat.

All he needed was a straw in his teeth and a pitchfork and he could pose for Grant Wood's *American Gothic*.

"Hey there," she said back without enthusiasm.

"I could be wrong, but you look like you might be having a bad day." Miguel came over to the barbed wire fence, leaned on a post, and studied her.

"As a matter of fact, I am." She shoved her balled fists into her jeans pockets, suppressing the urge to growl.

"Trouble at home?"

"I guess it's what you get with three generations under the same roof." She peered curiously at him. "You wouldn't know anything about that." She frowned. "Being that your mother and daughter are perfect."

Miguel threw back his head and laughed. "What on earth gave you that idea?"

"Well, you told me how wonderful Anna is, and I assume your mother is lovely too."

"I love Mama and Anna, but just for the record, life isn't always a bowl of cherries at my house." He glanced over his shoulder. "I just got bawled out for getting Mama's clean floor dirty. I didn't bother to point out that it was *my* clean floor and I can get it dirty if I want." He gave a crooked smile. "That would just be throwing gasoline on the fire."

"Well, I guess I feel a tiny bit better."

"And Anna was just nagging me to take her to town. My mother is busy in her garden, and Anna is determined she needs a new pair of shoes right now." He put emphasis on the last two words. "When I refused to take her, she gave me the icy treatment."

"Okay." Jewel nodded. "I feel even better now."

"Maybe you just need a break." He bent down to lift one of the barbed wires higher. "Care to come over? Mama just made sweet tea."

She glanced over her shoulder, doubting anyone would miss her. And if they did, it might be for the best. "Sure." She ducked through the opening but caught her shirt on a barb.

"Here, let me help." Miguel unhooked her, then gave her a hand to stand up straight. "Welcome to my farm."

"This used to be my farm," she said a bit sharply.

Miguel looked slightly offended.

"Sorry." She forced a smile as they walked through an alfalfa field. "I guess my foul mood has affected my manners."

"Well, I'm used to your dad going after me. Hope it's not going to become a family thing."

"Don't worry. I had my chance to be a farmer years ago and I turned my nose up at it."

He looked at her from the corner of his eye. "Having second thoughts?"

"I don't know. I mean, sure. I guess. But not necessarily about farming."

"What about, then?"

"About moving back home," she confessed for the first time.

"That's not surprising. It's a big change for you. Going from city girl to country girl. That's a lot."

She nodded. "Yeah." As they got closer to his house, she could see all the improvements he'd made to the property. "This is really pretty over here," she said when they reached the shade of the poplar trees. "So green and cool."

"Let's go sit over there." He pointed to a patio with outdoor furniture and lots of planted pots. There was even a small pond and fountain.

"Wow, this is like a little oasis." She flopped down on a wooden chair with a pillow cushion on it.

"I'll go get the tea."

After he went inside, she looked around. Someone had clearly put some time and effort into creating this sweet spot.

"Hola," a woman's voice said from behind her. "Who are you?"

Jewel turned to see a small woman with gray hair poking out from under a big straw hat. She was cautiously approaching with a bewildered expression. In her hands was a watering can. Jewel stood and smiled. "I'm Jewel McKerry. My parents own the property over there."

"Oh, sí. Your mama has told me about you."

Jewel nodded. "You must be Mrs. Orosco."

"Sí, you call me Marta." She set down the watering can and peeled off garden gloves. "It is warm today." She fanned herself and sat down.

"Are you the one responsible for this beautiful garden?" Jewel waved to the flowering pots.

"Oh, sí. I love my flowers."

"They're beautiful." Jewel sat back down as Miguel came out with two glasses of iced tea.

"Just in time, mijo." Marta eagerly reached for a glass. "I am so thirsty."

He handed the second glass to Jewel. "I'll go back for another."

"He is a good boy," Marta said as she sipped.

"But he forgets to take off his dirty boots?" Jewel teased.

"He told you about that?" Marta waved a hand. "I like clean floors."

"So does my mother."

"How is your mama? Is her head better now?"

"Yes. She claims she's fine, but I'm trying to keep her from doing too much."

Marta frowned. "But you are here?"

"I needed a break. My daughter's there to help Mom if needed."

"Oh, sí. Miguel says you have a girl about Anna's age, no?"

"A tiny bit younger."

"Anna . . . she says she is bored." Marta shook her head. "Bored? How do you get bored with so much to do? But she is young. Like a filly. She wants to run around."

"That sounds pretty normal. Cooper is always telling me she's bored."

"Our Anna should meet your Cooper. They can be bored together." Marta laughed.

Miguel came back out with his tea and took the chair next to Jewel. "So you ladies are getting acquainted?"

"Comparing notes on teenage girls," Jewel said.

"Anna should go see this Cooper girl," Marta told him. "They could make a friendship together."

"Easier said than done," Jewel warned. "My daughter can be quite cantankerous."

Marta frowned. "Cantankerous?"

"She can be a real pain," Jewel explained. "I love her, but sometimes . . ."

She waved a hand. "Oh, that is the way with mamas and daughters."

"Tell me about it." Jewel rolled her eyes. "My own mother was just telling me how to raise my own daughter."

Marta's eyes twinkled with amusement, but she said nothing.

"I know, I shouldn't complain about my mom." Jewel felt a twinge of guilt. "She has so much on her plate already. But I was aggravated."

"I know. Your poor mama has full hands with your papa. It is too bad, his condition."

Jewel's stomach knotted. "Yes, I hadn't realized how bad it had gotten until we got here."

"I want to take food to them. To help out. But your papa does not like my cooking." Marta's brow creased. "He says it's no good."

"Mama's an excellent cook," Miguel said in defense.

"I have no doubt," Jewel told them. "My dad doesn't seem to eat anything but peanut butter and honey sandwiches."

"He does get very good honey from his bees." Marta took another sip of tea.

Jewel nodded. "So we just eat what we want, and if Dad doesn't like it, someone makes him a sandwich."

Marta brightened. "I could bring food for you and your mama and daughter."

"That would be wonderful," Jewel said. "I've been trying to do the cooking and, well, I've never been too impressive in the kitchen."

"I heard you used to be a good artist," Miguel said. "Do you still paint?"

"I want to." Jewel sighed. "There hasn't been much time since we arrived, but I hope to set up an area in the barn where I can paint undisturbed."

"An artist?" Marta looked impressed. "That is wonderful."

Jewel waved her hand toward the flowerpots and the gorgeous patio. "It looks like you're the artist here, Marta."

"Gracias!"

"You have a definite gift for creating a beautiful space."

Her smile widened. "I want to make it like my mama's patio. Back in Texas. But it is different here. Not so warm and dry. But flowers like it." Marta stood, then picked up her gloves and watering can. "I must finish my work before it's too hot."

As she puttered away, Miguel grinned at Jewel. "Not to mention it's close to her siesta time," he added quietly.

Jewel finished the last of her iced tea. "This was good. Thank you for inviting me over. It was just the break I needed." She stood and looked around again. "It really is beautiful here, Miguel. You're lucky to have this place."

"Blessed," he said, standing. "God has been good to me."

She wondered at this. God had let his wife and father die—*that* was good? But not wanting to rain on his parade, she simply nodded. "Well, thank you for sharing your piece of paradise with me."

"Anytime." He walked her back out into the sunshine where it really was starting to get hot.

"I better hurry back. No telling what my dad might've gotten into while I was gone. Yesterday, he decided to take apart the lawn mower. I doubt it will ever work again."

"You can borrow mine." He continued walking with her.

"Thanks. You don't need to walk me home. I know the way," she teased.

"But you might want help slipping through the barbed wire."

She suddenly remembered getting caught. "Thanks."

"Maybe I'll put a gate there."

"Oh, that's not necessary."

Miguel shrugged. "What if our girls decide to become friends? It would make it easier for them to visit."

"Oh, yeah, right." But she wondered if he really meant more

than just the girls. And why did that send a little thrill through her? "Just don't let my dad see you making a gate. Who knows what he'll think about that?"

"I'll disguise myself and do it by the light of the moon." He winked. "No one will ever know how it got there."

She laughed as they reached the fence. "Well, that just might work."

He lifted the wire and, this time, she slipped through without getting caught. She thanked him again, then turned back to her parents' house, thinking how fortunate they all were to have such nice neighbors. Too bad her dad didn't agree!

11

Honey

The old farmhouse had four bedrooms, yet it suddenly felt small to Honey. As much as she loved having Jewel and Cooper around to help out, she realized they needed more room. And if they felt this crowded in the summer when it was possible to be outdoors, what would it be like on a cold winter day?

That wasn't her only concern though. The stairs were getting trickier for CT to navigate. And even though she'd relocated their bedroom to the first floor more than a year ago, CT still felt the need to go up to the second floor and poke around. And once he was up there, he had no respect for Jewel's and Cooper's personal space or belongings. Sometimes they would go to their rooms and find things not only rearranged but missing as well. Why CT wanted the odds and ends, or where he put them, remained a mystery. But there was no denying he was the one responsible.

It was all very irritating, but today felt like the last straw when CT stumbled down the stairs. His arms had been loaded with a few clothing items that he claimed were his, although they were not, and as a result, he hadn't been using the banister.

"Are you hurt?" Honey asked as she helped him to his feet.

He just nodded, allowing her to lead him to his chair in the living room, where she examined his scrapes and bruises. She was just bandaging his knee when Jewel came in from working in the garden.

"What happened?"

"Dad was exploring upstairs again." Honey nodded to the pile of stolen clothes still heaped at the foot of the stairs. "You might want to put those things back." She lowered her voice. "And install locks on your doors."

Jewel shook her head. "He could've been killed on those stairs."

"Yes." CT nodded like that was a real possibility.

"Plus, I saw him stumble on the back porch stairs yesterday," Jewel said. "This isn't good."

"I know." Honey rolled his pant leg back down over the bandage. "But what can we do?" She shook a finger at her husband. "I keep telling you to stay off those stairs, but do you listen?"

He gave her his hangdog look.

"I know." She kissed his grizzled cheek, instantly realizing he hadn't shaved lately. "You forgot."

"Yes." He nodded. "I forgot. I won't do it again."

"Right." But she knew his words meant nothing. Oh, sure, he hoped he wouldn't do it again, just like so many other things, but he would. His brain would trick him into believing there was a reason to go upstairs. And Jewel was right, a bad fall could kill him. As she took her first aid kit back to the kitchen, she wondered which was the worse way to die—from a bad fall or from slowly losing your mind and winding up bedridden in diapers with someone wiping your chin? She knew which route she'd choose for herself.

"Mom," Jewel said as Honey came into the kitchen. "We have to *do* something."

"Do *what*?" she asked with irritation. Jewel and Cooper had only been here a week and they were already trying to change things. She needed and appreciated their help, but she and CT were used to being on their own. It wasn't easy adjusting to a bigger family. But at least CT had started to remember their names . . . some of the time.

"About this situation. With Dad." Jewel sounded determined

to have a conversation that Honey would rather avoid. Really, they could talk until they were blue in the face, but what good would it do? She returned the first aid kit to its cabinet, then turned her back to Jewel, trying to think of a way to change the subject.

Honey stared blankly at the calendar on her fridge. The picture of the lighthouse made her long to visit the coast. Not that it was likely to happen. Suddenly she noticed today's date. "I almost forgot. I have a doctor's appointment this afternoon with"—she squinted at the tiny appointment note—"Dr. Gretchen Bauman. I guess she'll be my new GP. The ER doctor recommended her."

"Yes. I saw that," Jewel said. "It's at two. Cooper can stay with Dad, and I'll drive you there."

"Thank you." Honey moved toward the door.

"But I want you to stay and listen. I have an idea, and I want you to hear it." Jewel was relentless about whatever was on her mind.

"An idea?" Honey braced herself for some harebrained plan.

"When I took the baking dish back to Marta yesterday—you know, the one she sent the tamales over in—"

"Oh, yes. Those were so good. I meant to write her a thank-you note."

"Well, I thanked her for all of us. Anyway, she gave me a tour of their house. You know, it's a manufactured home."

Honey took a deep breath. "Yes, I'm aware of that."

"So, anyway, Marta explained how Miguel originally placed the home there as a hardship dwelling."

"A what?"

"The manufactured house was meant to be a hardship home for his parents. Because of their age and health issues, he got it permitted as a temporary residence. His real plan was to use his GI loan to build a stick-built house over by the creek. For him and Beth and Anna."

"Well, their house doesn't look temporary to me."

"No, it isn't now. But what I'm saying is it was okay with the county to have it placed there."

"Yes? And your point?"

"My point is you can have two homes on farm property if one is considered a temporary hardship dwelling."

"Temporary? Like a camp trailer?"

"No, a manufactured house, like the Oroscos have, doesn't feel temporary at all. In fact, it's really nice."

"Good. I'm happy for them. Such nice people."

"So I don't know why we don't get something like that placed on your property here. A single-level home with good accessibility for Dad and—"

"I'll tell you why, Jewel." Honey pursed her lips. "Your father and I cannot afford it."

"But *I* can afford it, Mom."

Honey held up her hands. "I would never let you do that."

"But with Cooper and me living here, it's too crowded." She thrust her arm in the direction of the living room. "And Dad is falling down the stairs."

"I know it's not ideal, but we can make do."

"But don't you see, if you and Dad had a nice manufactured home to live in, Coop and I could stay right here in the farmhouse. We could fix the place up." Jewel held up a forefinger. "Which brings me to the rest of my idea. Can you imagine how great this place would be as a B&B? It'd be such a great way to make money."

Despite her reservations, Honey considered this. "You know, I used to imagine doing something like that. Back when we were younger."

"It's such a pretty location, out here in the country. I have artist friends who would love to visit and paint here. And I got to thinking we could even offer artists retreats and all kinds of things."

"Oh, Jewel, that's a big dream. It sounds interesting, but it also sounds impossible."

"But my mom always told me to dream the impossible dream," Jewel reminded her.

Honey smiled. "Yes, I was younger then. When you have more energy, impossible things seem more possible."

"Well, I'm still young." Jewel stood up tall. "And I have energy and ideas. Better yet, I have the funds. The proceeds from selling my condo and gallery are just sitting in the bank. Can't I invest them here?"

"But that's an investment that won't pay you back."

"The B&B could pay me back. Plus, Cooper and I would have a place to live." Jewel pointed out the kitchen window. "And I can imagine creating a studio for myself and maybe even a small gallery out there in the barn. Right now it's not being used for much of anything. And that old building has such cool architectural lines, it could be gorgeous."

"You really are a dreamer." Honey slowly shook her head, trying to absorb all that Jewel had just thrown at her. It was overwhelming. And tiring.

"Can't you just let me dream?" Jewel locked eyes with her. "The risk would be on me, not you."

"I don't know."

"I would take care of all the details. All you'd need to do is trust me."

"I don't know," she said again. "I'm not sure what to say."

"Imagine living with Dad in a low-maintenance home. You two could be very comfortable and safe. No stairs to fall down. A bathroom that's easy for Dad. Wouldn't it be wonderful?"

"Sure, if you could wave your magic wand and make that happen. I suppose it would be nice."

"Okay then, just let me try, Mom."

Honey shrugged. "I'm too weary to argue with you, Jewel. Go ahead. See what you can do. But I'll warn you. Your first obstacle will probably be county codes. Two houses on one property? It just doesn't sound doable to me. I'd be surprised if they agree."

"Well, I learned how to comply with San Jose codes while renovating my gallery. I'll bet they're way stricter than Sweet Springs. Plus, thanks to that, I know how to jump through hoops."

Honey could hear CT moaning in the living room, calling out for her to come help. "I need to go." She opened the cabinet of medical supplies again. "He probably needs some Advil for his bumps and bruises."

Jewel pulled out her phone like she was getting ready to call the county that second. "Just know that I'm on it, Mom. Unless you say no way, I plan to give this a good try. You're sure you're okay with this?"

"That's fine. Go ahead and do what you can, dear." Honey patted her idealistic daughter's shoulder in what probably felt like a condescending way, then hurried to check on CT before he got really worked up. She did appreciate Jewel's youthful enthusiasm and energy, but this wild idea for a second home and a B&B really did sound like an impossible dream. Still, why not let her have at it? Her daughter would probably discover the whole thing wasn't practical or doable or even possible. But at least it would give her something to dream about. Maybe that was what mattered most. Honey wished she had room for dreams.

Jewel

It took several days to hear back from the county, but she was relieved when they finally agreed to the placement of their temporary hardship home to help care for her dad. Jewel had doggedly pursued this goal by visiting the local manufactured home company on the same day she'd gotten the green light from the county. According to the internet, there was a company located just outside of Sweet Springs. When she got there, she saw the big sign for Hanford Homes and soon discovered the owner was none other than an old high school beau, Aaron Hanford.

"I had no idea this was your business," she said. She studied him closely from behind her sunglasses. Aaron definitely appeared older but was still fairly attractive in a middle-aged way. He had a bit of a paunch and thinning hair, but he maintained the same swagger and confidence she remembered from high school. Just a bit warmer and friendlier.

"So tell me. What on earth are you doing back in little old Sweet Springs?" he asked as he strolled with her through the lot, pointing out various model homes that were bigger and more expensive than what she had in mind.

"I was about to ask you the same thing," she confessed. "I thought you moved out east."

"I did for a while. But when my dad retired a couple years ago, he offered me this business and, well, it seemed a good opportunity."

"I heard you got married," she ventured. "Any kids?"

"Yeah. Two teen boys. But they live back in New Hampshire with their mom."

"Oh? Divorced?"

He held up two fingers and shrugged. "Twice."

"I'm sorry."

"How about you?"

She held up one finger. "Once."

He smiled. "Well, that happens. Just gotta make the most of it, right?"

"I guess. But New Hampshire isn't close. Don't you miss your sons?"

His smile faded. "Yeah, sometimes I really do. But it was my choice to move back. And in order to afford child support, plus alimony for my second wife . . . well, I needed the kind of job that pays the bills."

"Like selling these?" She pointed to the big manufactured home in front of them. It was nice enough but more house than her parents needed.

"Yeah. And I do a little contracting too. It all works pretty nicely together." He pointed at her. "But you still haven't told me what you're doing here. Or why you're looking at manufactured housing. Is it for you? Are you here to stay?"

She explained her recent move home and her parents' need for help. "The county gave me the green light for a hardship house, and I want to find something to make life easier for them. It needs to be affordable and not too big since they have less land now."

"Yeah, I heard they sold the farm." He scowled. "To the Oroscos."

She didn't miss his disdain. "Only part of it. Do you know the Oroscos?"

"My baby sister married Miguel Orosco. Man, was that ever a mistake."

Jewel blinked. "Your sister?"

"Yeah. Do you remember Beth? She was five years younger than me."

Jewel barely recalled a little sister. "I'm so sorry for your loss, Aaron. Miguel told me his wife passed away, but I didn't realize she was your sister."

"Well, I blame Miguel for it."

"You blame him? For her cancer?"

He let out a long, exasperated sigh. "Long story. Another time." He put on a phony smile. "So what kind of house are you looking for?"

Still trying to wrap her head around Aaron's sister being married to Miguel, she attempted to get her bearings. "Well, like I said, my parents need something simple, small, and low maintenance. And accessibility is critical. My dad's health will continue to deteriorate. At some point he'll need wheelchair assistance and a hospital bed."

"I'm sorry to hear that." He pointed down the row of houses. "I might have something to interest you."

As they walked to the other end of the lot, he asked again how long she would be in town.

"I'm hoping to renovate the old farmhouse and turn it into a B&B. It's old and needs lots of repairs and upgrades, but it has personality and potential. And it's really pretty out there."

"Sounds like you need a contractor."

She glanced at him. "Yeah, do you ever handle remodels like that?"

"Sure. I just finished restoring the Phillips' house up on the hill in town. Turned it into a real showplace. You should see it."

"Well, we don't need a showplace. And I'll be on a budget."

"Aren't we all?"

"A *small* budget."

He laughed as he pointed to a house painted a garish shade of yellow that almost hurt her eyes in the bright sunlight.

She struggled to think of something to say as they approached it. "That's a real eye-catching color," she commented wryly as he unlocked the turquoise blue door. "I hope the interior colors aren't as wild as this. It might be hard to see past them."

"Don't worry. This got painted to please a customer with wild taste, but the folks lost financing before we had a chance to change anything inside." He opened the door with a flourish. "Voilà."

She went inside and was immediately relieved to see the neutral color scheme. "This isn't bad." She instantly regretted her words. After all, he was a salesman. She needed to act less interested. But she was pleased that it was bigger inside than she expected. And it had vaulted ceilings.

"It's just under a thousand square feet but has three bedrooms and two baths and, as you can see, an open floor plan." He crossed the main living space. "And check out the width of the doorways. You could easily maneuver a walker or wheelchair."

She walked around, looking it all over. "It looks like it could work. Well, except for that exterior paint color." She grimaced. "But I assume we'll get our choice of colors when we place our order. Right?"

"You could order one from the factory. Or you could take this one."

"Really? I thought all of these were models just for looking."

"Well, this one has been sitting here for a while. I wouldn't mind moving it. Especially to an old friend." He grinned. "Like you."

"And it could be painted."

"Of course."

"I bet Cooper and I could do it ourselves."

"Cooper?" His brows creased.

"My thirteen-year-old daughter."

He looked relieved. "Oh, yeah, a thirteen-year-old should be able to paint. Work's a good way to keep a kid outta trouble too."

He chuckled like he knew a thing or two about raising teens. Although Jewel had her doubts. How much could an absentee father really know about parenting? Cooper's dad was sure clueless.

She stepped closer to Aaron, her mind fixed back on the house and a possible deal. "So, Aaron, will you give an *old friend* a good price on this eyesore?"

"Eyesore?" He waved his hand toward the kitchen. "Did you notice the quality of these appliances? No scrimping here."

She shrugged, trying to maintain her nonchalance. "I'll admit it looks okay in here, but the exterior . . ."

"Needs paint." His smarmy expression reminded her of a used car salesman. "Why don't we head to my office, and we can talk about it." He fanned himself with a hand. "It's pretty toasty in here." He nodded up to the overhead ceiling fan. "And just so you know, besides those, there's a heat pump with forced air and AC. Your parents would be comfortable year-round."

"Good to know. Okay, let me take one more stroll through. I want to take some pics and seriously think about it." Keeping her poker face on, she took photos of the main room, then headed back to the master suite. She mentally measured the space, imagining the potential to comfortably hold a hospital bed and recliner for Dad, with room left over to maneuver a wheelchair or walker or whatever might be needed. Recently Mom had been talking about how the farmhouse bedrooms were too small and were unable to accommodate what was surely in their future.

She took more pics of the roomy main bathroom, noting that its wide-open shower would be perfect. Mom could use the other two bedrooms and have a full bath all to herself. And it would be so great for them to have everything on one level! It really was ideal. Now if only it fit within her budget. She mentally crossed her fingers as they went back outside. Cringing at the brightness of the exterior—had they used crosswalk paint?—she realized it was actually a happy mistake that could work in her favor.

The heat was beating down on them as they crossed the asphalt back to the building that housed Aaron's office. As promised, it was much cooler in there, and his young assistant met them with bottles of chilled water. Jewel tried not to eavesdrop as the pretty girl told Aaron about a difficult customer who'd just called.

"Well, you call Dale right back and tell him this is a limited-time offer," he said a bit sharply. "And that he's not the only fish on the line." Aaron laughed. "Well, don't use my words, but you know what to do, Alyssa." He winked at the girl, then grinned at Jewel. "Right this way." He led her into his private office and seated himself behind an oversized desk in front of a bookcase full of sales catalogues. Aaron suddenly turned all business, throwing dates and numbers and plans at her so quickly, she felt her head spinning. She asked questions and wrote notes on her phone until she fully understood what he was offering.

"This all sounds pretty good," she admitted. "But to be honest, I'm a little overwhelmed at the moment. I only intended to look today. To get ideas. This is a lot to take in."

"Of course it is. But you know what they say, Jewel. Strike while the iron's hot."

"I never really understood that idiom."

He laughed. "Well, opportunity is knocking. Don't be afraid to open the door. I can guarantee you that you won't find a better deal in the state."

"Right." She nodded, wondering if that was really true, or if it was just a sales pitch. All the same, it was tempting. She was eager to get her parents settled and get started on the B&B. But she hadn't shopped around. "I do appreciate your willingness to get the house in place as soon as possible, but—"

"I sure can't do this for everyone, Jewel," he interrupted. "You know, offer a great price and prompt placement. Normally, a customer has to wait a good long while to get exactly what they want. But you're a special case. You don't know how glad I am to offer this deal to an old friend. It's meant to be, but it's up to you. If you don't want it, I'm sure I can find someone who does. Now that I've decided to move that one, it'll just be a matter of time. I should've got someone in here to paint it last spring. It would have sold in a heartbeat."

She hated the idea of losing out on the "ugly" yellow house with the great price. "Okay, Aaron, you're right." She swallowed hard. "I guess I want it."

He grinned and shook her hand. He excused himself to get his assistant to print out the sales contract, then came back to his office to make congenial conversation. It was mostly small talk, but the more they visited, the more Jewel grew concerned. Not for agreeing so quickly on this purchase since it really did seem a fair price for everything but because she was worried she gave Aaron the wrong impression . . . that she had personal interest in him. Had she been overly warm and friendly? Just to secure a good deal?

"So you really think you'll be ready for placement as soon as I promised to get you scheduled in?" he asked as she signed the papers. "We do have a gap in the schedule that week. I'd like to fill it."

"I don't see why not." She signed the last line, then dug her checkbook out of her bag. Was she really doing this?

Aaron checked a desk calendar and then looked at his phone. "Well, I can come out tomorrow afternoon to do a quick survey of the land. You know, to make sure you've picked the best location. Then I'll send my surveyor, engineer, and technician to mark things out."

"Wow, that's great. Thanks."

He explained a few more county fees that, as her contractor, he would handle. Finally, they both stood and shook hands again. "It's a pleasure doing business with you, Jewel. And a pleasure to see you again." He held on to her hand just a few seconds longer than necessary.

"Thank you for all your help." She extracted her hand from his with a nervous smile. "I can't believe how smoothly this seems to be going."

"I'm glad. But there's always a hiccup or two along the way. Fortunately, we know how to work through them." He walked her to the office entrance. "I have meetings all day tomorrow, so I can't be out to your place until later. Probably closer to six." His brows arched hopefully. "And I'll be ravenous by then."

She got the hint. "Well, I'm not sure what we'll have for dinner tomorrow, but you're welcome to join us. Although I'll warn you, I've been doing the cooking and I'm no expert in the kitchen."

"Thanks, but I thought I'd invite you to join me. There's this new restaurant in town. I've been hoping to give it a go."

Wanting to stay in his good graces and not sour the deal, she agreed. Reluctantly. But she questioned her decision while walking through the Hanford Homes parking lot. Had she led him on? Been disingenuous? Although Aaron Hanford was probably a nice guy, did she really want to get involved with him . . . again? She remembered how little respect she'd had for him after they dated briefly in high school. At the end of the relationship, she'd actually accused him of being a full-blown narcissist. But that was ages ago. They'd both been young and immature.

And Aaron seemed quite amiable nowadays. Well-spoken and kind. She could tell he'd done and seen a lot since high school. Really, what was the harm of getting to know him better? Still, she couldn't quite put her finger on it, but something about him made her uneasy. Was he just a bit too opportunistic? Or was it his salesmanship? Perhaps she was being overly judgmental. After all, he was really helping her out with this house. Why not give him a chance?

12

Honey

Jewel sauntered in through the front door with an expression that reminded Honey of the cat who'd swallowed the canary. "Hello there, people," Jewel crooned at them.

Honey tossed back a casual greeting as she set CT's lunch on the TV tray. She knew Jewel had gone to the county seat for something today, but something more was definitely going on here.

Cooper, who was watching an old western with CT to keep him from wandering around outside in the heat, didn't even look up, but Honey's curiosity was stirred.

"What's up?" she quietly asked her daughter, nodding toward the kitchen before CT overheard anything and got interested in something he might not understand. "Want something cool to drink?"

"Yeah, I could use some iced tea," Jewel said, following her.

Honey closed the kitchen door, then sat at the table. Already she felt winded from doing practically nothing. But maybe that's what happened while recuperating from a head injury and high blood pressure. Dr. Gretchen had warned her not to overdo it at their appointment the other day.

"You look tired, Mom. What have you been up to?"

"Nothing much."

"Looks like you fixed Dad lunch," she said while she grabbed the pitcher of tea from the fridge. "I thought you were going to let Coop do that."

"Well, she was sitting with him. I really appreciate that. Let me get a few things done in peace."

"Such as?" Jewel poured a glass of tea.

"Just a load of laundry and then a few things out in the garden."

"And you cleaned the kitchen and made Dad lunch and—"

"I don't need a lecture, Jewel." Honey raised a hand to stop her. "I'm sitting now. Dr. Gretchen pretty much said the same thing. I just sort of forgot and got carried away."

"Is Dad rubbing off on you?" Jewel teased, setting the tea in front of her.

"Funny." Honey narrowed her eyes at her daughter. "It's hard feeling better and wanting to get back to my routines."

"Well, maybe your routines need to slow down."

Honey just nodded. "I'll keep that in mind if you tell me what you're up to. I know you've got something up your sleeve."

Jewel brought her own tea to the table and sat down, then immediately started pouring out an incredible story of purchasing a manufactured home.

"What?" Honey sputtered, nearly choking on her tea. "Are you kidding?"

"No, Mom. Wait till you see it."

"But, Jewel, we barely talked about this. What on earth were you thinking?"

"I was thinking it was a great deal. And it's perfect for you and Dad."

"Without even talking to us?"

"I did talk to you, Mom. You said go for it. Remember? Was I supposed to talk to Dad too? Can you imagine how that would go?"

"No . . ." Honey rubbed her forehead. CT was the one with memory trouble, but maybe Jewel was right, maybe it was catching . . . or else her concussion was messing with her mind. "Did I really tell you to go ahead with it?"

"You pretty much agreed to trust me."

"I vaguely remember now." Honey rubbed a finger over the condensation on the side of her glass.

"I'm sorry to catch you unaware, but trust me, this new house will be perfect. For both of you. For all of us. It was all really amazing. Like a miracle." She began describing a house that actually did sound like an improvement from their current living conditions. Then she pulled out her phone and showed Honey some photos. She had to admit, it did look like a nice "temporary" home. And definitely not a camp trailer.

"But it must be expensive, Jewel. Your dad and I don't have that kind of—"

"I already told you that I'm buying it, Mom. And it allows me to make this house into a B&B. You know, like I said. I'll make some improvements here, and Cooper and I will stay—"

"I don't know . . . that's a lot for your dad to adjust to." Honey tried to imagine how CT would react to being uprooted from the home they'd lived in for most of their married life, ever since they took over the farm for her grandparents. Beyond that, how would she react? She loved this old house. Her grandparents had practically raised her while her parents were following her dad's military career. Not that her opinions mattered much these days. Everything in her life seemed centered on CT and his pressing needs. But to be fair, her life ran smoother when CT was happy. But was he ever truly happy? Not really. Still. "But your dad's used to this house, Jewel. He might not like the change."

"Does he like falling down the stairs?" Jewel challenged. "Or having a bedroom that will become increasingly more difficult to navigate as he loses mobility?"

"Well, no, but you're talking about a huge transition."

"Look, Mom." Jewel set her glass down with a clunk. "The time is coming when Dad won't really know where he is. Just yesterday he asked me if this was his house. He was totally lost, and you know he'll get more and more so."

Honey felt tears prick her eyes. She'd been so good about holding them in before. But lately . . . well, they just seemed to pour out at the drop of a hat. And hearing Jewel's prediction that CT would just get more and more lost . . . well, it was heartbreaking. Poor CT.

"I don't want to make you sad." Jewel reached for her hand. "I'm sorry, Mom. If you want me to pull the plug on this house, I probably can. I'll call Aaron and tell him that I—"

"No, no . . . don't do that." Honey reached for a paper napkin, then used it to wipe her eyes. "It's actually a very good plan. I should be grateful to you for caring enough to figure things out for us."

"Really?" Jewel looked misty-eyed now. "You think it could work?"

"Well, it's hard to know whether anything will work when it concerns your father. The best laid plans of mice and men. But it does sound like an easier way to live. I'll admit that every time I hear footsteps upstairs, I worry that your dad's snuck up there again and that he is going to come tumbling down. I'm sure that doesn't help my blood pressure a bit."

"No, it's bad on both of you. And I really think you'll love this little house, Mom. It's so nice. Small but open. With vaulted ceilings and a heat pump with AC. We could make it so comfortable for you guys. So much simpler than all this." She waved a hand at Honey's somewhat-cluttered kitchen. "So much safer for Dad."

As Jewel went on about the house, showing Honey more photos on her phone, Honey felt herself being steadily pulled in. Deeper and deeper. And Jewel was right about CT. In time he wouldn't know where he was. He probably wouldn't even care. Having one floor would make life simpler. Although it did seem too good to be true, and she knew what that usually meant.

But then Honey looked around her beloved old country kitchen. Sure, it was worn and cluttered and not what anyone would call "low maintenance." But she would miss it. Just like so many other things she missed about the life she used to know and love. And now the tears flowed again. Not for CT this time . . . for herself.

13

Jewel

The sun beat down on Jewel's back as she bent to repair a drip line spout that had somehow disconnected, creating a pool on the far edge of the lavender field. Seeing deer tracks nearby, she thought she knew who the culprit had been. Although, unlike Dad, Jewel still liked the deer that made themselves at home on the farm. Dad wanted them dead.

"Dang deer," he proclaimed loudly from behind her. Startled, she stood and turned to see him, hands on hips, glaring at the ground. Not for the first time, she wondered if he'd been reading her thoughts. For a guy who couldn't remember what day it was or where he'd set his hearing aid charger, he was surprisingly tuned in sometimes. Just one more mystifying aspect of his illness.

She brushed dirt from her hands. "We don't know it was deer." She shrugged. "Might've been a digger."

"Nah. It's the deer. They eat my pumpkins too. Gonna get my gun and get rid of 'em."

She just nodded. It was pointless to remind him that Mom had removed all his guns from the house. "What are you doing out here?" she asked. "I thought you were working on your bees."

"Too hot." He adjusted the brim of his hat.

"Too hot for bees?"

"Too hot for me."

"Then you should get into the shade. Or inside the house."

"The house is shade." He frowned as if trying to make sense of his own words. "Sun?"

"Come on, Dad. Before we both get heatstroke." She linked her arm in his and walked him back along the fence line toward the house. "How are your bees?"

"Buzzin'." He grinned. "Makin' honey."

"Cooper wants to help you with them."

"Cooper?"

"You know, the one with green hair."

"Where's Cooper?"

"Helping Mom in the kitchen."

"My mom?"

Jewel glanced at him. "Honey, your wife."

"Oh, yeah." He nodded like he got this, but she assumed he was just playing along.

"How are you feeling?" she asked.

"Feeling?" He pursed his lips. "Okay."

She decided to push him a little. "What does okay feel like?" Maybe it was futile, but she still felt if she could get him to think, it might help stave off this devastating, brain-invading disease.

"Okay." He nodded vigorously. "Okay is okay."

"Right. So do you know what today is?" Cooper had gone over the date with him at breakfast this morning.

"Today," he answered.

"Right." She couldn't help but smile. Her dad's best defense was attempting to be clever. And since it worked sometimes, why should she question it?

"It's sure hot today."

"Hotter than . . ." He frowned as if trying to remember the rest of what he wanted to say.

"Hotter than a revenuer's pistol?"

"Yeah. Hotter than that."

A movement on the other side of the fence caught her eye, and she recognized Miguel walking toward them. She grimaced, realizing this could turn into a mess. She made a cautious wave, hoping he might rethink this encounter, but he continued toward them.

"Hey, neighbors," he called out.

Dad growled. "What does *he* want?"

"Just saying hello," she told him, smiling toward Miguel. "Hey there."

"I was about to call your mom," he said to Jewel, "but then I saw you out here and thought I'd talk to you in person."

"You stay over there." Dad aimed a finger gun at Miguel.

"Yes, sir." Miguel held his hands up. "My mother wants to invite your family to our house for a barbecue on Saturday night."

"Nope." Dad glared at him. "Won't go."

"I'd be glad to go," Jewel said. "And I'm sure Mom and Cooper would too." She looked at her dad. "I guess you can just stay home alone on Saturday night."

Dad looked stymied.

"What can we bring?" Jewel asked Miguel.

"I don't know. You'll have to ask my mother for the details."

"Okay."

"Too hot," Dad mumbled, tugging her arm. "House."

"Yes, you go on and get inside." She extracted her arm from his. "I'll be along in a few minutes."

Dad looked like his feet were planted there. He wore the expression of a lost five-year-old.

"The house is over there." She pointed him in the right direction. "Just head for the barn and keep going, Dad." She gave him a gentle shove. "Get something cool to drink."

He nodded and began plodding toward the barn. When he was out of earshot, she turned back to Miguel. "Sorry about that. You know how he can be."

"It's okay. But do you really think you should leave him home alone on Saturday?"

"No." She smirked. "But I have a feeling he might change his mind if he sees us all going over to your place. Anyway, it'll be a good test."

"Yeah. It'd sure be nice to repair our broken bridges. If that's possible."

"I'm willing to give it a good try."

"How's your mom doing?"

"Much better. The challenge now is to keep her from doing too much."

"She's a real go-getter."

"Believe me, I know." She sighed. "Cooper and I try to step in when we can."

He nodded slowly. "And how is Cooper adjusting?"

"Pretty well. She seems to get along really well with my mom. Better than I do."

"That's probably typical. My Anna and Mama are like that."

"Yeah, I try not to feel left out." Jewel looked over to where her dad was almost to the barn now. "Dad's moving pretty fast, at least for him."

Miguel nodded. "Yeah, he can really move sometimes—like if he's heading over to chastise me about something." He chuckled. "But other times it looks like the poor guy can barely walk."

"FTD is weird like that. I've been reading everything I can find about it. And all I keep coming up with is it's a very strange disease." She held up her hands in a defeated way. "Pretty frustrating for everyone around him."

"Yeah, I've noticed. So how are you doing, Jewel?" He looked intently into her eyes, signaling this wasn't just a polite inquiry but an invitation to an honest answer.

"I don't know. I mean, it feels kind of like a balancing act, or a tightrope walk. Every member of our family can be tricky. Dad because of his illness. But Mom can get pretty defensive if I try to help too much. She's always reminding me she's not helpless."

He looked amused. "I get that from Mama too. Like walking a fine line."

She nodded. "And Cooper, well, I never know what she's going to do. Most of the time she seems mad at me. Then once in a while she says or does something nice. Sometimes, between the three of them, it feels like I'm going to lose my marbles."

Miguel laughed. "I can imagine."

She told him about the manufactured home she'd purchased yesterday, pointing out where she wanted it to be placed. "Close enough to the house that it's easy to pop back and forth but far enough away to give us a feeling of space."

"That's great. When do you think it'll be here? Ours took about six months, but I've heard things have slowed down even more since then."

She explained about Hanford Homes and how Aaron offered to help get everything settled. She noticed that his smile faded at the mention of the Hanford name. "But it's nice on the inside. And Cooper and I can paint it."

"Wow, that's fast. Good for you."

"Yeah." She peered curiously at him. "I knew Aaron Hanford in school, but I didn't realize you married his little sister. I mean, I never really knew her, but Aaron mentioned it."

"Yeah, Beth was a Hanford." He shoved his hands in his pockets with a somber expression. "Aaron didn't really approve of our marriage."

"That's too bad."

"Yeah. For Anna's sake, I wish things were different." Miguel pointed over her shoulder. "Looks like your dad might need some help."

She turned to see her dad striding purposely toward them, wielding a pitchfork like a weapon. "Oh, great." She exchanged looks with Miguel. "Looks like he's on a rampage now."

"I'll clear out," Miguel told her. "That should help."

"Thanks." She gave a meek smile. "And sorry."

His dark eyes were sympathetic. "No problem. I understand."

She turned from him and hurried toward her dad. "Whatcha doing there?" She pointed to the pitchfork. "No hay to pitch today."

"Scared him off." He shook the tool in a victorious way. "Land grabber."

"Daaad!" She put warning in her tone. "That's not true. And it's unkind. Miguel bought that land from you."

He let a foul word fly, something he never would've done before, but something she knew FTD was responsible for adding to the mess.

"It's too hot out here." She took his arm and began to guide him away. "Let's go get some tea."

"Tea." He sounded a little breathless now.

"You're tired, Dad." She felt his steps slowing. "We need to get you inside."

Using the pitchfork like a cane, he hobbled with her back to the house. But when they reached the porch steps, he dropped the pitchfork and started to fall. "Easy does it," she caught his weight, then helped him sit down on the lowest step. "Just rest here a minute," she told him. "At least it's shady. I'll get you something cool to drink."

"What happened to Grandpa?" Cooper asked as Jewel hurried inside.

"He got too hot and tired." Jewel filled a water glass.

"Looked more like he was gonna murder Miguel," Cooper said wryly.

"Yeah, that too."

"I talked Grandma into having a rest."

"Good job." Jewel looked into her daughter's eyes. "Have I told you lately how much I love and appreciate you?"

Cooper made a face. "Don't get all mushy, Mom."

"Can if I want," Jewel teased as she opened the back door.

"Yeah, whatever."

"Well, thanks anyway." Jewel went back outside and, sitting on the step beside her dad, handed him the water glass. "Drink this slowly." She watched as he took little sips before finally finishing it off. She took the glass and asked if he was ready to go inside.

"Yeah. My chair." He attempted to stand but didn't have the strength. Despite Jewel's attempts to get him on his feet, she couldn't, so she called for Cooper and after a few aborted tries, the two of them managed to get him on his feet and slowly and precariously up the porch steps.

Finally, he was situated in his chair and, after being reminded how to work the recliner mechanism, he stretched out and closed his eyes. Satisfied that he would stay there awhile, Jewel tiptoed back into the kitchen where Cooper was eating a banana.

"I think he wore himself out." Jewel loaded a few dishes into the dishwasher, then paused to tell Cooper about the Saturday night barbecue.

"I already know about that."

Jewel blinked. "How did you know?"

"Anna came by a little while ago. She brought me a video game she thought I'd like. She told me about the barbecue."

"It's nice that you and Anna are getting acquainted." Jewel closed the dishwasher. She'd been cautious not to appear overly excited about this new friendship, worried that her approval could turn her daughter the opposite direction. Neutrality was the safe route.

"Yeah, Anna's okay." Cooper shrugged. "Now if you don't mind, I'm gonna go try out that game."

"Sure, that's fine." Jewel removed a pitcher of tea from the fridge. "By the way, did you feed the cat?"

"Mom." She sounded exasperated. "Don't you know I always feed the cat?"

"Well, I thought Grandpa still did it . . . sometimes."

"Seriously?" She rolled her eyes. "If we left that to him, poor Whiskers would starve."

"Or live off the fat of the land," Jewel teased. "You know he's a mouser."

"He still deserves some good food. And water." Cooper's expression softened. "He likes me now, even lets me pet him."

Jewel raised her brows in mock surprise. "According to Grandma that's no small thing. He totally ignores me. I guess Grandpa was the only one he ever warmed up to." Jewel checked the thermometer on the kitchen window. "Gonna be hot today. It's already eighty-five."

"Tell me about it. I was helping Grandma in the garden and just about baked my brains out."

"I noticed someone set up a sun umbrella out there."

"Yeah, that was me. Some of Grandma's baby plants were getting sunburnt and she was worried. It was my idea to move it over there, but she really liked it. She even sits out there sometimes."

"Cool. I'm so glad you're helping Grandma. And Grandpa too. Thanks, Coop. I know it's not much fun being—"

"You don't have to keep saying that, Mom. I'm not an infant. I get it. Okay?"

Jewel stepped back, holding up her hands. "Yeah. Sure. Okay."

After another adolescent eye roll, Cooper grabbed a root beer and left. Jewel poured herself an iced tea and sat at the kitchen table, grateful for a moment of peace and quiet. Life with her parents on the farm kept such bipolar pace. At times she couldn't run fast enough or even pause to catch her breath or think. Then suddenly everything would come to a screeching halt, and she wouldn't quite know what to do with herself. It was confusing and disconcerting, and she was pretty sure it wasn't going to get better.

14

Jewel

The second floor of the farmhouse was a furnace by five o'clock, but after a quick shower, Jewel felt ready to meet up with Aaron. Maybe she'd ask him for a recommendation for a contractor who could install a heat pump with AC into this old house. Otherwise, she could hardly expect B&B guests to stay in these second-floor rooms.

At the sound of a vehicle coming down the driveway, she looked out to see a big black pickup driving in, with a trail of dust behind it. She shoved her feet into her sandals and hurried down to see if it was Aaron. But her dad was already peering out the window, frowning with disapproval.

"Who's that?" he growled.

"I think that's the manufactured home man."

"Why's he here?" he asked.

"Remember, Mom and I told you about it this morning?"

"Huh?" His face was blank. "What?"

"Mom?" Jewel called toward the kitchen. "Can you come in here?"

Mom came out with a dish towel in hand. "What is it?"

"Can you remind Dad about what's going on? Aaron is here, and I need to go walk the building site with him."

"Building?" Dad looked even more confused.

Mom nodded to Jewel. "I got this."

"Thanks." Jewel hurried out the front door, waving to Aaron as he parked his diesel pickup in front of the house. As she went over to speak to him, he pulled out a clipboard, a large measuring tape, and a bundle of wooden stakes.

"Need a hand?" she offered.

"Yeah." He handed her the stakes and a bulky hammer. "You can be my assistant."

"You got it." She squinted in the sunlight, pointing to the section of land she felt was the best spot for placing the new house. "I think it should be over there."

"I checked county records to see where your waterline and septic and electric are supposed to be." He held up some papers. "Unfortunately the house was built so long ago, we can't be sure these are right. But I got the locators coming in tomorrow."

"Locators?"

"They mark underground waterlines and things before anyone starts digging."

"When will that be?"

"Could be as soon as Friday. Or else early next week. Depending on another job I got going."

"Wow, that's fast."

"You just happened to show up at the right time." He winked. "And talked to the right guy."

"Well, I'm very grateful."

After some walking and poking around, they confirmed where the septic tank and lines were most likely located. "So placing the new house over here will probably work out great. And we'll pop the new septic tank over there, with the drain field going that way." He pointed it out.

"A new septic tank?"

"Yeah. You can't run both houses on the old one."

"Right. So another expense?"

He nodded, making a note on his clipboard. "Unless you want to use an outhouse."

"No thanks." She frowned, wondering what her bank account would look like when this was all said and done.

Before long, they were measuring and pounding in stakes and then, as she compared the site to the blueprint Aaron had brought, she changed her mind. "I want their main view to look out toward the hills," she told him.

"That makes sense."

And so they rearranged the corners and, once again, she walked around looking out the imaginary windows, until she was finally satisfied. "This looks perfect."

"Your parents will have a nice view," he agreed.

She looked back at the farmhouse behind them. "And the new house shouldn't disrupt the view from the old house too much either." Her thoughts went to the garish exterior paint. "Well, after we get it painted, anyway. Right now that horrible yellow color can probably be seen from miles away."

Aaron laughed. "Well, thanks to that ugly paint job, you got a great deal."

"For which I'm grateful."

Aaron pounded the last stake in the ground and stood. "Well, I'm starving. You ready to go try out this new restaurant?"

All day she'd been trying to think of a way to politely refuse his offer of dinner, but he looked so hopeful . . . and he'd been so helpful . . . she just couldn't reject him. "Sounds good." She looked over to his pickup. "But I can drive myself and meet you there. Save you a trip back here."

"No way. You're going with me." He tucked his hammer beneath his arm and took her hand. "Let's go. My chariot awaits."

As they walked back to his truck, she could feel someone watching. Probably Dad. Chances were he'd think she was being kidnapped. She glanced toward the house and noticed her parents standing there, so she gave a weak finger wave. She'd warned Mom that she might be trapped into dinner with Aaron. Leave it to Mom to explain things to Dad. Or not. Sometimes it seemed the more they tried to explain something, the foggier he got.

As they drove to town, Jewel asked Aaron about heat pumps. "The second floor of the farmhouse is an oven right now," she explained. "Cooper and I are using fans and opening windows at night to cool off, but it's pretty stifling."

"I bet. But it might be tricky getting a traditional heat pump with vents into that old house. There are some ductless options though. I'll hook you up with my HVAC guy."

Once again, Jewel considered her bank account, imagining it steadily shrinking. Was this crazy? How many times had she been accused of being too impulsive? Was it happening again? Would she regret all this later? And yet it seemed like a good investment.

"You seem deep in thought," Aaron said as he pulled into a parking space downtown.

"I'm sorry." She realized how quiet she'd been.

He turned off the engine. "Everything okay?"

"Yes. I was just thinking about all the expenses of placing that house and improving the farmhouse. I mean, I can imagine a really cool bed and breakfast, but will it ever repay all I've invested?"

Aaron shrugged. "Well, your property value will increase."

"I guess."

"And you and your family will be more comfortable."

"That's true. And I suppose I could get more involved in my art."

"Art?" He looked surprised. "Are you an artist?"

She shrugged. "Well, I used to be. Not so sure I still am. But I hope to take it up again."

"What kind of art?"

"Painting. Mostly landscapes. But I'm a little rusty."

His brow creased. "I guess that's okay if you enjoy it. Good hobby. But it doesn't seem like a big moneymaker to me. Not in these parts, anyway."

She wasn't sure how to respond to his wet blanket, but she forced a smile as they got out of the pickup. To be fair, he wasn't wrong. Art was not a good "moneymaker." Not that she'd been in it to get rich. Even running a gallery came with its challenges.

They were just going into the restaurant when she noticed someone waving from the open window of an old blue pickup.

Surprised to see Anna Orosco in the passenger seat, she waved back and then spotted Miguel behind the wheel. She suddenly felt awkward and embarrassed. Of course, Miguel would recognize his brother-in-law, but would he wonder why she was out with him? She glanced at Aaron but, distracted by opening the door to the restaurant, he was oblivious.

"Hope you like Italian," Aaron said as they went inside.

"Sure. Love it." She glanced around the fairly crowded restaurant. "Looks like a popular place."

"I've heard it's good. You know, we haven't had a decent Italian restaurant in this town for ages."

"Yeah, I remember Antonio's from when we were kids. Too bad it closed during the pandemic." They followed the hostess to a table by the window and sat down.

"Pizza is about as Italian as I usually get." He grinned at the hostess. "But I feel adventurous tonight."

She smiled back and handed them menus. "We've got some good specials."

After she left, Jewel perused the options. "Well, it's nice that Sweet Springs has a little more variety now. Although I've noticed there's no sushi restaurant here yet."

He frowned. "You really like all that raw fish stuff?"

"It's not all raw fish. And yes, I do like it. My daughter adores sushi."

He just laughed. "Not me. I'm mostly a steak and potatoes guy."

"And Italian?"

"Simple stuff. Like spaghetti and meatballs." He closed his menu. "Or lasagna. Beyond that, I'll pass."

"Seafood linguini." She pointed to the item on the menu. "Sounds good to me."

"To each their own." He wrinkled his nose. "Sounds like you like seafood."

"I do."

He laid down his menu. "What other kinds of things do you like?"

She assumed he meant food, but something about the twinkle

in his eyes suggested more. She was about to say how she loved Mexican cuisine and how wonderful Marta Orosco's tamales had been the other night but realized that could open a whole other can of worms. "I like all kinds of ethnic foods," she told him. "San Jose had a great assortment of restaurants. I guess I'll miss that."

"Well, you can always go into the city. Portland's not that far. And there's a lot to choose from, if you like that sort of thing. I'll admit I missed some of the perks of living in the big city when I first moved back here. But I'm surprised at how quickly I adjusted. Guess I'm just a small-town boy at heart."

"Then you're in the right place." She sighed. "It'll be an adjustment living in a small town again." She looked out the window where traffic along Main Street was moving along at a leisurely pace. "Although I'll admit Sweet Springs seems to have grown a little. And it's probably a good place to raise kids." She looked curiously at him, wondering once again what his relationship with his boys was like. "Will your sons come out to visit you?" she asked. "I mean, since it's summer?"

"Nah. My ex has them in sports camps for most of the summer."

When the server made it to their table, Jewel studied Aaron as he confidently ordered a bottle of merlot without even asking her preference. What kind of man was he, truly? And what was she doing here with him? Clearly this was a date. And perhaps even more troubling, she wasn't sure why she was so concerned about what Miguel Orosco must be thinking of her right now. Really, what difference did it make?

The wine showed up shortly after they ordered. She was not a merlot fan, especially with seafood, but she kept her opinion quiet and told herself she just had to get through this meal as graciously as possible, then make sure Aaron understood their relationship was strictly business from here on out.

"Don't you like your wine?" he asked midway through the meal.

"I'm sorry," she said, "I'm not really a red wine girl. Especially with this." She pointed to her pasta with its crab, shrimp, clams, and mussels. "But I must say this is absolutely delicious."

"Glad you like it." He refilled his own wineglass. "My lasagna is good too."

"My mom makes really good lasagna," she said absently. "I should get her to teach me how."

"You don't cook much?"

She shrugged. "I'm a bit out of practice, but I plan to hone my skills."

"My first wife was a good cook." He swirled his glass and studied the wine. "But it showed on her hips." He laughed. "Cooking was about all she had going for her."

Jewel felt unexpectedly defensive of this woman, or maybe she felt for any woman who was divorced and had children with a checked-out father. "Isn't she a good mom?"

"Devoted. She just wasn't a good wife."

"Oh?" She narrowed her eyes slightly. "You were a good husband, I suppose."

He smirked. "Okay, you're probably right. I wasn't much of a husband either."

"How about your second marriage?" She knew she was prodding too much, but she couldn't help herself. Besides, did she really care if he decided she wasn't good date material? Wasn't that her goal?

"My second marriage?" he echoed. "Well, Rita was a pretty good wife. To start with . . ." He took a sip of wine.

"Then what happened?"

He set down his glass. "I guess we just drifted apart."

She nodded. "Well, some men aren't really suited for marriage, Aaron. They do better just being bachelors. Maybe you fall into that category."

He chuckled. "You could be right, Jewel."

Relief washed over her.

"Or . . . you could be wrong." His brows arched. "Maybe I just haven't connected with the right girl yet. Or I let her get away."

Suddenly she felt extremely uncomfortable and, wanting to shift the conversation direction, she began to tell him about her dad's illness, graphically describing some of the antics she'd witnessed since moving back home. She could tell by his reaction and comments that Aaron was not familiar with any form of dementia. Lucky him. Finally, he just shook his head and asked her why they didn't have him "put away."

She nearly choked on her water, then set the glass down with a thud. "Put away?" she questioned.

"Yeah. Sounds like he's a real nutcase. Why not just lock him up? For his own good, as well as for his family's sake. That's what I'd do."

Her skin crawled at his cruelty. She clenched her jaw as she tried to hold back the harsh thoughts running through her mind. "Well, that's not what we want to do." She wiped her mouth with her napkin. "I probably gave you the wrong impression because Dad is actually really sweet too. He's always been a kind and caring man. And a good farmer. And he loves taking care of his beehives and harvesting honey. It's just that he gets confused sometimes. I've probably painted the wrong picture."

"And you call yourself an artist." Aaron snickered.

She didn't think that was funny but kept her thoughts to herself as she laid down her fork and pushed her plate away. She was done here. And hopefully done with him too. Well, after her parents' house was in place. She wasn't stupid. Based on who Aaron was revealing himself to be, she suspected she'd need to keep playing Miss Congeniality until everything was all wrapped up. She just hoped it would be worth the sacrifice!

15

Honey

CT seemed more tired than usual the next morning, but Honey suspected it was from this little heat wave they were having. It was taking its toll on her too. "You didn't eat your banana," she reminded him when she found him in his recliner watching *True Grit* for what must've been the hundredth time—this year. Of course, he didn't really "watch" it. He just let it play, taking in bits and pieces. She supposed it was comforting because the characters and scenery were somewhat familiar.

She peeled the banana and handed it to him. "It's good for you."

He just grunted but took a bite. She sat down across from him, trying to think of a conversation topic that wouldn't frustrate or confuse him. "It's gonna be hot again today."

He nodded as he chewed.

"I don't remember June being this hot before."

"June?" He frowned.

"Yes. It's June. Supposed to be in the high nineties today."

"High?" He looked at the ceiling.

"Really hot," she clarified.

"Yeah. Really hot." Suddenly his eyes grew wide. "My bees."

"They'll be running their fans," she reassured him. Back when he had all his bearings, he'd told her how the worker bees would use their wings like fans to cool the hive. Like an organic AC.

"Water." He tried to put the footrest down on his recliner but couldn't get the lever to work.

"You want a glass of water?" Honey asked.

"I can get it," Cooper offered as she came down the stairs.

"No." CT raised a shaky hand. "Bees. *Need water.*"

Cooper came over. "You water the bees, Grandpa?"

Honey thought for a moment. "Oh, I remember now. He puts out a tray of water for them on a hot day. With pebbles in it."

"Yes." He nodded eagerly, still trying to stand. "Water for bees."

"You stay here," Honey told him. "Cooper and I can get it."

He was still fumbling with the recliner as Honey led Cooper through the kitchen and onto the back porch. "I use a couple of old cookie sheets," she explained. "I think they're out here." She dug around a cabinet until she found them. "Then you line it with pebbles and fill it with water." She handed Cooper a bag of pea gravel. "But not above the tops of the pebbles."

"Why?"

"So the bees don't drown. They can land on the pebbles, get some water, then take it back into the hive." Honey could hear CT yelling at her from the house.

"Like a bee pond. Cool!" Cooper readjusted her grip on the cookie sheets and pea gravel. "I can set it up."

"Thanks. Just set them in the shade of the hives. And check on them throughout the day, if you don't mind."

"Do I need to wear the bee suit?"

"Grandpa never does. Not for just this. But if you're uneasy, I think you should."

"No, I'm fine. I like the bees. So that's all? Just put the cookie sheets out there?"

"That's it. And thank you." Honey patted her back and turned to face the house where CT was still hollering. "I better go check on your grandpa before he has a conniption fit."

By the time she got back to the living room, CT had somehow trapped himself in the recliner. With one foot stuck within the footrest and the other on the floor, he looked like he was about to topple over.

"Sit back down," she commanded him.

"I can't," he yelled at her.

"Then let's pull your foot out of there." She attempted to balance him, but he refused to extract his foot.

"Can't!" he yelped.

"Looks like you need help," Jewel said as she came into the room. "Here, let me take one side and you take the other, Mom." Together, with some tugging and pulling, they managed to free CT's foot and get him back into the chair. But he was breathing heavily with the excitement.

"Cooper is tending to your bees," Honey reassured him.

"Huh?" He looked bewildered and she realized he must've forgotten about the bee water by now.

"Never mind." Eager for a distraction, Honey pointed to the TV screen. "Hey, there's John Wayne."

"Rooster," CT corrected her.

"Oh, that's right. Rooster Cogburn." Honey exchanged looks with Jewel.

"Did you have breakfast yet, Mom?"

Honey considered this. She had fixed CT a bowl of instant oatmeal, but it hadn't appealed to her. "I had coffee."

"You need to eat something," Jewel told her.

"You're probably right." Honey followed her daughter into the kitchen. "Have you eaten?"

"I had a bowl of cold cereal," she said. "I got up early to go out and take a good look at where they're going to start excavating for the manufactured home. Just wanted to be sure we really picked the best spot yesterday."

Honey reached for the granola cereal. "I thought it seemed like a nice location. Not too far from the house but enough to feel separate. Is there a problem?"

"I don't think so. It actually looks pretty great. You're going to love the wide-open view you'll get from your front porch." Jewel poured a cup of coffee. "Guess it's just nerves."

"I didn't get a chance to ask how your date with Aaron went last night." Honey poured milk on her granola.

"First of all, it *wasn't* a date." Jewel sat down at the table. "Not in my mind, anyway."

"What about in *his* mind?" Honey carried her bowl to the table and sat across from Jewel. "Didn't you two used to date?"

"Mom used to date that guy with the pickup?" Cooper asked as she came into the kitchen.

"Good morning, Cooper." Jewel tossed Honey a warning look. "I saw you out there with the bees. They don't intimidate you?"

Cooper answered with an eye roll, then swiped an arm across her forehead as she yawned.

"You okay, sweetheart?" Honey asked her granddaughter. "Did you sleep well?"

"I guess. It was so hot up there, it took a long time to get to sleep."

"Sorry about that." Honey shook her head.

"Speaking of heat, I'm looking into getting some kind of AC," Jewel told them. "Aaron recommended a guy."

Cooper filled a cereal bowl. "Is that the dude you used to date?"

Jewel rolled her eyes. "He's just the contractor setting up Grandma and Grandpa's new house."

"You sure that's all, Mom? You guys looked pretty cozy yesterday."

Jewel seemed aggravated but simply sipped her coffee.

"Is he your new boyfriend?" Cooper's tone grew teasing.

"Mr. Hanford owns the manufactured house company," Honey told Cooper. "I doubt there's anything serious between him and your mother."

"But he took her to dinner," Cooper persisted.

"Yes, Coop, he took me to dinner," Jewel said. "I'm trying to stay in his good graces. At least until the house is in place."

"So you're manipulating him?" Cooper had a mischievous twinkle in her eyes as she poured milk on her cereal.

"No," Jewel stated firmly. "I'm just trying to keep things running smoothly. For some reason, he seems interested in renewing our friendship. Anything wrong with that?"

Cooper shrugged. "No, of course not. Just curious. Don't overreact." She held up her bowl of cereal. "I'm going to go eat this with Grandpa. He's not as touchy as some people."

Jewel made a snorting noise that made Honey laugh. "Family dynamics," Honey said quietly. "You never know quite where they're headed."

"That's for sure."

"But she makes a good point. You're not manipulating Aaron, are you? I mean, it's impressive how fast the wheels of progress are turning on this new house business, but I hate to think you're using your womanly wiles on him."

"Womanly wiles?" Jewel frowned. "Are you serious, Mom?"

"Not too serious. Just curious."

Jewel let out a long sigh. "To be honest, I had my own doubts. But I'm trying to keep everything with him aboveboard. If he takes my friendship as something more, that's his problem." She lowered her voice. "I'm curious though. Do you know anything about Miguel's deceased wife? She was Aaron's baby sister, and he seems to hold her death against Miguel. Is there a reason for that?"

Honey thought about this for a moment. "I do know there's some bad blood between them, but honestly that's all I know. And only because Marta confided to me once. Miguel never speaks of it."

"Well, I think it's a sore spot." Jewel bit her lip. "And I saw Miguel and Anna last night, you know, when I was with Aaron. And it felt sort of awkward."

Honey slowly nodded. "Well, you weren't doing anything wrong. It's too bad Aaron isn't on friendlier terms with the Oroscos. Especially for his niece's sake. Anna is such a sweet girl."

"Yes. Miguel feels bad about the estrangement too."

"Miguel told you about it?" Honey was surprised.

"Not in great detail. But he mentioned it."

"You and Miguel seem to get along pretty well." Honey peered curiously at her daughter, hoping to glean more information.

"The Oroscos are good neighbors." Jewel carried her empty

mug to the sink. "And it's so great that Anna and Cooper are becoming friends."

"Yeah, I think both girls were lonely."

"Hopefully the friendship will help Cooper get used to living here." She rinsed her coffee mug and set it in the dishwasher. "Now I'm going to check the irrigation system on the lavender field to make sure that leak is fixed. Want me to water your garden while I'm out there?"

"I already asked Cooper to take care of that." Honey sipped her coffee. "I'm afraid you girls are going to turn me into a lazy old woman."

"Fat chance of that." Jewel laughed. "We just want you all better before you start trying to run the world again."

Honey smiled. "Cooper barely let me work in my own garden yesterday. She was like a mother hen, making me sit in the shade while I told her what needed doing. She seems like a natural gardener."

"Maybe your DNA got passed down."

"I don't know. But I do think you've raised a very sweet girl, Jewel. You can be proud of her."

Jewel seemed surprised. "Really? Green hair and all?"

"I guess mothers are the last ones to know they did well, eh?" Honey lifted her coffee mug like a toast. "By the way, I'm proud of you too."

Jewel leaned over and kissed her mother's cheek. "Thanks, Mom."

As she watched Jewel head out to the field, Honey resisted the urge to get up and get busy herself. She might as well enjoy this quiet moment while she had it. Because she never knew when craziness would break out again.

16

Jewel

As Jewel wandered through the lavender field, she wondered if some farmer DNA was latently sprouting inside her. She'd never appreciated agriculture while growing up, couldn't wait to get away from this dusty, dirty place as a teenager, and despised the smell of cow manure. But something about the fresh morning air, the scent of green things growing, and the squish of cool fertile soil beneath her boots filled her with endorphins now.

Jewel wondered if this delightful new fancy, like other past interests, would last. What if this was just another whim? What if she grew weary or even bored with country living a year from now? By then, all her savings would be devoured by this wild dream. And who knew what kind of help her parents might need in the future? What if the farm became too much for them? Was she already in over her head and too naive to realize it?

Don't think about that right now. She took in a deep breath of fresh air. *Stay in the moment. Relish the here and now.* She leaned her head back, enjoying the warmth of the morning sun on her face. She paused to listen to the magpies' chatter and to inhale the lavender's soothing aroma. And she wanted to enjoy the reverberations of her mother's kind words earlier. Had Mom ever said she was proud of her before? Not that Jewel could remember. To be fair, Mom had never been profuse with praise. Her words were usually used to warn Jewel about decisions made in haste. Jewel attributed it to her being a no-nonsense school administrator with lots of problem kids to deal with. But maybe Mom had lightened up with retirement. A lot of people seemed to sweeten and mellow with age.

A chilling thought went through Jewel. What if Mom wanted to repair relationships because she wasn't long for this world? It was an unnerving thought, but Mom's short stint in the ER and her subsequent doctor visit might've instilled a new kind of perspective. She hadn't mentioned anything, but knowing Mom, she'd keep bad news to herself. Still, the hospital doctor hadn't insinuated anything too serious when she'd talked to Jewel. She'd acted like Mom should bounce right back.

Jewel bent down among the lavender plants to tug out a tall weed. Her mother had always been so strong and resilient and motivated. A bump on the head and high blood pressure wouldn't slow someone like her down. Would it? *Don't dwell on it now*, Jewel warned herself. *Stay positive and hopeful. Remain in the moment!*

Satisfied her recent fix was still watertight, Jewel headed for the barn. Already, she'd started to clear a corner to use as her studio. With a large southern window that she'd scrubbed clean, the light wasn't too bad in here. And since the barn had electricity, she might even hook up some overhead lights in case she wanted to work at night. As she swept the floor and moved a few things around, clearing even more space, she heard engine noises outside and decided to go investigate.

To her surprise, a dump truck and other trucks carrying big earth-moving machines were parading down the driveway. She assumed they must be the excavators Aaron had said would come, although he hadn't expected them today. But who was she to complain when the wheels of progress turned. She jogged toward the building site, excited and curious about what they would do to prepare for the new "temporary" dwelling. Already she'd been imagining shades of color she and Cooper would paint the small house, window boxes they might put up, perhaps even shutters to give it a cottage-ish vibe.

She was almost there when she saw Dad emerge from the front door. With his ball cap on crooked and his arms raised, he was clearly upset as he fumbled down the porch steps, yelling something unintelligible about "interlopers." What would he say when they started to dig up a corner of his alfalfa field? She'd tried to warn him of this upcoming event but like so many other things, he'd clearly forgotten.

Instead of greeting the workers like she'd intended, she detoured to cut off her father, hoping to prevent what could easily turn into a bad scene.

"Dad." She caught up and securely linked her arm into his. "Isn't it great these men are here to work?"

"Not here," he declared fiercely. "Not today. Too early for harvest."

"They're not here to harvest, Dad. They're here to work on the land." She used a forceful tone, then decided to switch to the vague route. Don't overload him with too much information. It sometimes worked. "They have to get it all ready."

"Ready?" He turned to her with a puzzled frown. "For what?"

"Ready to do *the work*. We asked them to come out here." She pointed to where bright-colored marks were spray-painted to show where electric and waterlines were running. "See, they already marked the ground. So it's safe to dig."

"Safe? Dig?" He cocked his head to one side.

"Yes. We don't want to break a waterline or get electrocuted."

"*Electrocuted?*" His eyes widened with alarm, and she remembered how he sometimes overreacted to danger or pain.

"Yes, Dad. This is very dangerous work. We better go inside. Stay safe."

"Safe?" He was completely bamboozled now.

"Yes." She steered him back toward the front porch. "We don't want to get hurt out here. Let's go inside. *Stay safe.*"

His steps grew more feeble, and he began to lean more heavily on her arm. "Yes. Stay safe."

She'd already witnessed several incidents of Dad's heightened sense of pain and danger and impending peril. It boggled her mind how a man who at one time could hammer his thumb and not even mumble would now whine like a baby if his support socks felt overly tight or he pricked his finger. She couldn't recall her father ever being frightened of anything before. Even when a sick cougar killed a calf, Dad had simply grabbed his rifle and gone hunting. FTD, she continued to learn, was a baffling disease. And not only for the sufferer. The way it twisted one's mind was mysterious to the experts too. But she'd also discovered that you could sometimes make the ailment work for you. Perhaps it was disingenuous, or maybe just opportunistic.

With her dad safely in the house, she was just closing the front door when Cooper came bounding down the stairs. Tempted to scold her daughter for leaving her grandpa to his own devices, Jewel stopped herself. That wasn't fair. A thirteen-year-old shouldn't be responsible for a befuddled man's whereabouts. Especially an escape artist like her father. He could slip out of sight in a split second. And between the three of them, he'd pulled some wild stunts.

"Did you finish watching *True Grit*?" Jewel asked her dad as she led him to his recliner.

"*True Grit*?" he repeated with interest, like he hadn't seen that movie about a hundred times . . . or more.

"Yes." She reached for the remote. "Let's see if we can find it." As she pulled up the right streaming service, she exchanged glances with Cooper, nodding toward the kitchen in a hint that she wanted a private conversation with her daughter. She increased the volume enough to camouflage the machinery noise outside, then closed the drapes on the side window. Hopefully that'd discourage him from peering out and getting all worked up over the earth-moving going on outside.

Satisfied that he was momentarily occupied, she met Cooper in the kitchen and quickly explained his fixation on the excavators. "I know he's going to create a problem if he gets the chance.

Can you ride herd on him while I'm out there? I want to be sure the excavators are doing what they're supposed to."

"I was just going over to Anna's," Cooper protested. "I was with Grandpa all morning."

"Right . . ." Jewel didn't want to rock her daughter's boat. After all, she greatly appreciated Cooper's friendship with Anna and did all she could to support it. "Well, okay, I'll figure out something. And thanks for helping with Grandpa this morning."

Cooper grabbed an apple from the fruit bowl and grinned. "I'm sure the workers know what they're doing, Mom. It's not like you're an expert or anything."

"That's true. But it'd be a mess if they tore up the wrong piece of land."

Cooper shrugged. "Yeah, I guess."

"Where's Grandma, by the way?"

"She went to her room to have a rest."

"Good. Well, have fun at Anna's." Jewel forced a smile. It wouldn't kill Jewel to sit with her dad for a while. She could sneak glimpses at the workers through the curtains when he got distracted. Cooper was right though. The excavators really should know what they were doing.

She went into the living room to be sure her dad hadn't snuck off again and was relieved to find him sound asleep and snoring. She turned down the TV's volume and sat on the couch so she could scroll through paint shade combinations for the new house on her phone. It seemed important to make the little house attractive for two reasons. One, she wanted her parents to really like their new space and, two, she wanted it to be attractive next to the old farmhouse for when they turned it into a B&B. The body of the main house was celery green with creamy white trim, her grandma's choice years ago. The color wasn't bad, but it was probably in need of a new coat of paint by now too.

Jewel decided on a deeper shade of green for the new house—a cross between moss and olive. It would be distinctly different and yet complementary to the farmhouse. Plus, the darker shade would help it to blend in with the green fields around it. For trim, she would go with an espresso brown. And she finally settled on a warm terra-cotta red, similar to their old barn, to transform the bright turquoise blue front door, as well as the flower boxes Aaron was supposed to bring by. She decided to order the paint online and pick it up the next time she went to town. That way she'd be ready to slap it on as soon as the house was put in place. Hopefully before Dad got a chance to complain about the strange shade of yellow. But before she did anything, she would seek her mom's approval on the paint colors. As for her dad, well, it probably didn't matter since what he liked today he might hate by tomorrow. Like bananas. Sometimes he loved nothing more, but just this morning he'd tossed one in the trash with only a single bite taken, claiming he never liked bananas. Go figure.

She glanced over at him, sleeping so peacefully, just quietly snoring. In moments like this, her heart softened toward him. *Dad* was still in there, but sometimes it was hard to see. She still wasn't sure how he'd deal with the Orosco barbecue tomorrow night. After his first contrary reaction to the invite, no one had mentioned it to him. But maybe it'd be like bananas, and he'd change his mind about disliking Miguel. Mom had told Jewel she'd stay home with him if he refused to go, but Jewel still wanted to encourage her to go anyway. Maybe if Mom went, Dad would give in and go. Or else he'd stay home alone and get into some new kind of trouble. That wouldn't be good. Jewel sighed. Choosing what was best for that old man was like walking through a minefield.

By the end of the day, the spot for the manufactured home had been fully excavated and filled with gravel, the new septic tank had been dropped into place, and water and power lines had been dug. Unfortunately it looked like a great big mess—especially to Dad. Jewel tried to tell him that it would all get better soon. Feeling responsible for his disgruntled state, she offered to walk him around and attempt to explain, step-by-step, what was happening.

The deep trenches for lines had been cordoned off with yellow tape, which she tried to point out. "That's to warn you not to go too close," she told him as they strolled around, keeping a safe distance from the site. "The crew will be back early next week to lay pipes and wires and then they'll refill all these holes."

He grunted. "Better refill 'em."

"Yes. They will, Dad." She pointed to the gravel rectangle. "And the new house will go right there."

"New house?" He scowled. "Whose house?"

"For you and Mom."

"We have a house." He tipped his head toward the old farmhouse.

"The new house will be better for you," she told him. "Safer. No more rickety stairs to fall down. Remember how you fell the other day?"

"I never fall." He firmly shook his head with an expression that suggested he fully believed his erroneous words.

"You probably still have bruises from falling." She pointed to his legs.

"No. No bruises."

"Well, anyway, this will be your new home."

"I have a home." He looked to the old farmhouse again. "Me and Honey. We live there." Now he frowned. "Don't we?"

"You do now. But things can change." Maybe it didn't matter if he really understood everything right now. "Well, Dad, it's going to be an awfully nice house, but if you don't want it, I guess Cooper and I will live there."

"With all those people?"

"What people?" she asked, instantly regretting it. Dad often got the idea that others lived in his house.

He pointed to her. "Do you live here too? And that green-haired girl?"

"Yes, Dad. That green-haired girl is your granddaughter, Cooper."

"Cooper?" He picked up a discarded stake with a blank expression, poking it into the ground as if to mark something. Then, noticing a few other stakes, he started picking them up and loading them in his arms like firewood. He piled them in a neat stack next to the yellow tape. Like a kid playing with blocks. Dad clearly liked having something to keep him busy, but Mom was calling now, announcing that supper was ready.

"Come on, Dad." She tugged on his arm. "You can finish this up tomorrow."

"Tomorrow"—he smiled—"is a new day."

She squeezed his hand as they walked toward the porch. "Yes, a new day."

He stopped by the flower beds alongside the porch, then stooped down to pick some of the daisies growing there. "For Honey," he said as he stood.

"She will love them." Jewel nodded. As they went inside, she thought maybe she was getting a glimpse of the man he used to be, and she was grateful.

17

Jewel

It was midmorning when a familiar black diesel truck roared up the farm's driveway. Jewel leaned the hoe she was using to weed Mom's vegetable garden against the shed and went out to greet Aaron as he strolled around the new building site.

"Whatcha doing out here?" she asked pleasantly. "Seems you'd want to be in town selling your houses on a nice sunny Saturday."

"I got somebody covering for me. Just wanted to see how things went here yesterday. Bet you were surprised to see my crew so soon."

"As a matter of fact, I was. But they seemed to have done a great job."

"Well, another job fell through, so I sent 'em straight over here. Thought you might appreciate it." He kicked a loose stone into a ditch.

"Absolutely." She beamed at him. "I'm so impressed with how quickly things are moving. Thank you, Aaron."

He tweaked one of her braids. Not wanting to waste time with hair this morning, she'd put it in pigtails just like Mom used to do. "You look like a real farm girl, Jewelie."

She bristled at the nickname. "Just cooler and easier." She tipped the brim of her frazzled straw cowboy hat back, one she'd adopted from her dad's vast collection, and narrowed her eyes in warning.

"Cute." He was oblivious to her frustration. "So I'm wondering, suppose you can clean your farm girl self up for something fun this evening?"

She grimaced, biting her tongue to keep from saying something she'd regret. After all, he was helping her with this house. She pursed her lips. "*This* evening?"

"Yeah. I got two tickets to a fundraiser over at the Stockton Ranch. Good food and drinks and old-fashioned square dancing. Thought you'd like to come with me." He reached for her hand. "Do a little do-si-do in the barn."

"That actually does sound fun, but I already made plans for tonight." She pulled her hand away. "I'm sorry." Okay, she realized she wasn't as sorry as she sounded. Mostly she was relieved to have a valid excuse.

"Plans?" He frowned. "Can't you cancel 'em?"

"No, it's with the whole family. We were all counting on it."

"So what's so special you can't get out of it?"

She resented his pushy attitude but maintained her pleasant expression. "Well, it's not that special, but I already accepted the invitation and hate to back out. Just a neighborhood barbecue. No big deal."

Aaron's countenance darkened as he glanced over to the Orosco house. "Not that many neighbors out this way."

"Which is why it's so important to maintain good relationships with the ones we have."

He was clearly disappointed, perhaps even irritated, but he smiled stiffly. "Well, okay, but you're missing out on a great time, Jewelie Girl. There'll probably be lots of folks you know there. Good way to get back in the swing of things in Sweet Springs."

"I'm sure you're right." She feigned disappointment. "Maybe another time."

"Yeah." His brow creased as he adjusted his ball cap. "Better get back to the lot. This *is* a good day for selling houses. June's always a record month. Gotta make hay while the sun shines."

"Good luck," she called out as he got into his pickup. She knew he was disappointed in her response, but what could she do? She wanted to keep their relationship on good footing. At least until they wrapped up the new house project. The sooner that was all done, the better for everyone.

Jewel returned to weeding for a bit. Then, hot and thirsty, she went inside to see if Mom needed any help with the potato salad she was making for tonight. The huge bag of potatoes on the kitchen table suggested Mom planned to feed half the county. But seeing Cooper standing at the sink, up to her elbows in potato peels, Jewel pivoted her focus and asked about her dad as she filled her water bottle.

"Last I saw, he was asleep in his chair with MeTV blaring out *The Rifleman*," Mom told her. "But you know how that can go."

"I'll check on him."

Of course, his chair was empty and the TV was blasting an obnoxious pharmaceutical commercial. Jewel called out and made sure Dad wasn't inside before heading out to look. She wasn't terribly worried since he couldn't have been gone long, but when she couldn't find him in the barn or other outbuildings, and he didn't appear to be out in a field, she grew a little concerned. She called out for him again and then walked over to the fence line between their property and the Oroscos'. Hopefully he wasn't over there creating havoc for them.

As she strolled the fence line, looking all directions, she spotted Miguel pounding in a loose fencepost alongside his cow pasture. "Have you seen my dad?" she yelled to him.

He came over, using a bandanna to wipe his brow. "I noticed him walking down your driveway earlier. I assumed he was getting mail, then I got busy here and lost track." He pointed to where he'd installed a gate and grinned. "What do you think?"

"Nice," she said absently. "But I better go find Dad. I already got the mail. Not that it would stop him. He enjoys the walk back and forth. Thanks."

"You all still coming tonight?" he asked brightly.

"That's our plan. Mom's making a mega potato salad. Of

course, you never know about Dad." She sighed. "He might not want to come."

"Well, be assured if he does come, we'll do all we can to make him comfortable here. Mama really wants to patch things up between us. More now than ever since Anna and Cooper have become friends." He grinned. "Anna thinks Cooper is the greatest thing since sliced bread."

Jewel smiled. "That's an expression my dad used to use."

"I think I picked it up from a southern sergeant in boot camp."

"Well, I better go find Dad. Thanks for the tip."

"Good luck."

As she went down the driveway toward the main road, her nerves bristled, especially when she didn't see him anywhere. What if Dad had decided to wander farther than the mailbox? Where would that even be, and how long would his wobbly legs hold out? She paused at the road, looking both ways, before she extracted her phone from her jeans pocket, called her mother, and quickly explained her AWOL dad. "Do you think he'd go anywhere down this road?" she asked.

"I don't know, but he was in a snit this morning before he fell asleep."

"What kind of snit?"

"When we told him we were making potato salad for the barbecue tonight, he threw a little fit, claiming nobody was going to the Oroscos'. Period. I told him, like you suggested, that he could stay behind. By himself. I suppose that's what made him mad." She let out a weary sigh.

"Oh, I'm sorry, Mom. I hoped it would motivate him. I should've known." Jewel looked up and down the farm road but saw no pedestrians. And no vehicles either. "Do you think that would be enough to send him off like this? Off the farm, I mean?"

"Heaven only knows."

"Well, I'll get my car to keep looking for him." Jewel turned back to the house. "Why don't you tell Cooper to do another quick search around the farm?"

"Yes. We'll both look. If we find him, I'll text you."

Jewel agreed to do the same. By the time Mom and Cooper were calling out and scouring the farm, Jewel was backing out in her SUV. Torn between anger and angst and fear, Jewel left a dust cloud behind her as she drove down the driveway. At the road, she felt like flipping a coin to determine which path her dad may have taken. Finally, she chose to head toward town because Dad had mentioned how he missed his early morning coffee with his buddies at the feed store just the other day. When she'd offered to taxi him there, her mom had quietly intervened, explaining that his friends didn't even meet there anymore. Hadn't in years. But maybe in his mixed-up mind he imagined them cheerfully waiting there and had set out to meet them.

After making it nearly to town, and feeling certain he couldn't walk this far, Jewel headed back, ready to search the other part of the old farm road. As she drove, she checked in to learn Mom still hadn't seen hide nor hair of him. "I'll keep looking," Jewel assured her. As she drove on past the farm, where properties were larger and set farther apart, she prayed that God would keep her dad safe . . . and help her find him. Half a mile from their farm, Jewel spotted a pickup truck pulled off on the side of the road. A couple stood outside, looking down at a man in the ditch. To her horror, it was Dad, leaned lifelessly against the slope of the earth, his face pale. She pulled to a fast stop, jumped out, and dashed over.

"Dad! Are you okay?" She knelt in the dried grass beside him, her heart pounding, but relieved to see he was breathing. "Are you okay?" When he didn't answer, she turned to the man. "Did you hit him with your truck?"

"No way!" he answered defensively.

"We just stopped when I noticed him lying there," the woman said.

"Probably drunk." The man shrugged with disinterest. "But the wife insisted we stop and play good Samaritan."

"Is he your father?" the woman asked with wide eyes.

Jewel ignored them and reached for her dad's hand. "*Dad?* Talk to me. Are you hurt?"

His eyes fluttered open, then closed. "Too tired," he muttered.

"You walked too far," she told him. She stood, looking at the couple. "He has dementia." She pointed to the side of her own head. "Memory stuff. You know?"

"Oh, yes, I do know," the woman said, then lowered her voice. "My uncle has Alzheimer's. I know how they can wander away sometimes."

"Can you help me get him into my car?" Jewel asked the couple.

It took all three of them to get Dad onto his feet. Then the guy helped Jewel get him into the car and the woman returned with a lukewarm bottle of water. "He might be dehydrated," she said. "It's pretty hot out."

"Thank you." Jewel wanted to hug this woman. "You *are* a good Samaritan."

"Just being neighborly." The woman smiled. "We're the Crawfords. Our farm is about ten miles down this road."

"We're the McKerrys," Jewel told them as she handed her dad the water. "This is my dad, CT."

"You should get him a medical ID bracelet," the woman advised. "My uncle has one. You know, in case he wanders and doesn't know his address and such."

"That's a great idea." Jewel glanced at her dad, who was now sipping his water in the shade of the car. He seemed fairly well recovered as he attempted to make farmer small talk with Mr. Crawford. Before long, the couple mentioned that they had perishable groceries in their car and needed to go. Jewel thanked them again and got into her SUV. "I'm glad you're okay, Dad, but you really had us worried."

"I'm fine." His tone was aggravated, almost as if she'd spoiled his fun. "People worry too much."

She wanted to scold him but bit her tongue instead.

"Took a walk," he mumbled. "Nothing to fuss about."

"Where were you walking?" she asked as she turned on the engine.

"Town."

"Uh, did you know town is the *other* way?"

"No, it's this way." He pointed the wrong way down the road. "I was almost there." He sounded even more aggravated.

She rolled her eyes. "I better call Mom and let her know you're okay."

"I'm okay. People worry."

"I know you're okay . . . *now*." Instead of calling her mom, she texted Cooper. That way her dad wouldn't have to hear the irritation in her voice. Oh, she knew he couldn't understand why they were worried. Finding him half dead from heatstroke in the ditch on a hot afternoon . . . No big deal, they worry too much, he was fine. She was still curious if his great escape had anything to do with his insistence they shouldn't go to the Oroscos' tonight, but she didn't want to ask. Why poke a hornets' nest? Instead she inquired about his bees. That was usually a safe subject.

"My bees?" His tone grew alarmed. "Need water. Too hot."

"Cooper already took care of that for you."

"Cooper?"

"The girl with the green hair."

"That girl in my house?"

"Yes. That girl is my daughter. Your granddaughter." How many times would she have to remind him of this?

"No, don't know them. They live far away."

Here we go again. She thought hard. How far gone was he today? Did his runaway experience worsen things in his brain? She wondered. "What about a wife?" she asked. "Do you have a wife?"

"I, uh, yeah. I think so."

"What's your wife's name?"

He rubbed his unshaven chin. "Honey." His tone softened. "Honey is sweet. Like honey."

"Well, Honey is worried about you, Dad."

He only said "Oh," then stayed quiet the rest of the way. But he took little sips of water and fidgeted with the label on the plastic bottle, leaving Jewel to wonder what went on inside his brain. She wished she could sneak a peek at the goings-on in there. At the same time, it would probably scare her to death.

To everyone's relief, Dad was worn out by the time he got into the house. It took all three of them to get him to bed, where he actually seemed eager to take a nap. After he was all settled in, they met in the kitchen for a little conference over some homemade lemonade. As Cooper filled glasses, Jewel explained what happened and exactly where and how she found Dad.

"I'm surprised he could even walk that far." She felt embarrassed at the judgment and irritation in her voice. But it was honest.

"Well, it sure did him in," Mom said quietly.

"Poor Grandpa." Cooper sounded genuinely sympathetic as she set three full glasses on the table. "Did he do that just because of the Orosco barbecue? If it's that big a deal to him, maybe we shouldn't go."

"No," Mom declared. "We can't let his condition rule our lives."

"Really?" Jewel wasn't so sure. "I don't see how we can help it."

Mom turned to Cooper. "You are going to the barbecue, my dear. And so is your mom."

"What about you?" Cooper asked.

"I don't know." She sipped her lemonade. "If your grandpa's having a rough time, I really don't see how I could enjoy myself."

"See, Mom," Jewel pointed out. "Dad's condition does rule your life."

"Well, I'm his wife. I have to make concessions. You and Cooper don't."

"It's not fair," Jewel declared. She knew she sounded childish, but she was feeling seriously put out by the circumstances. Sure, her dad couldn't help it . . . or could he? Sometimes she wondered. So many of his actions and statements reminded her of a four-year-old's temper tantrum. He only cared about himself and his own needs. Most of the time, it felt as if the rest of them didn't even exist.

"Life isn't fair," Mom said solemnly. "Can I tell you girls something?"

"Of course." Jewel ran a finger down the condensation on her glass. "And excuse me and my big mouth. I just got seriously frustrated with Dad today. I should read up more on his condition so I can understand him better."

Mom patted her hand. "I have some books that might help. Although they can confuse you too. Sometimes they contradict each other."

"You were going to tell us something, Grandma," Cooper reminded her.

She nodded slowly. "But I'll warn you, what I want to say will probably sound kind of odd, maybe even woo-woo." She smiled at Cooper. "Something happened a while back, shortly before your grandpa's official diagnosis. For about a year, I was noticing little things. Forgetfulness, misplacing things, losing words, tantrums. Nothing too concerning, and I tried to blame it on getting older. I mean, we all get forgetful as we age." She sighed. "Well, I could tell it was getting worse, and the doctors hinted but I was still dismissive and confident we could fix whatever was wrong with meds, nutrients, better hearing aids, whatever. Anyway, I was hanging sheets on the line on one of those beautiful spring days. It was so full of promise. And I got this distinct impression." She paused, staring out the kitchen window as if to recall that specific day perfectly. "It was actually more than just an impression. It was as if I heard God talking to me. Not audibly exactly but plain and clear just the same. Like when you know something deep within. Maybe you can't even put it into words. But this came to me in words I could hear inside of me. They were"—she paused again—"'You're going to *want* to ask *why* . . . but don't. There are no answers. Just trust me for what's coming.'"

"Interesting." Jewel nodded, realizing how many times she'd asked why this was happening to her dad.

Cooper looked doubtful. "You really believe it was *God* talking to you?"

"I do believe it. Maybe more than anything I've ever believed before."

"Did you understand what it meant?" Jewel studied her.

"Not at that time. I didn't even relate it to your father that day. But here's the truth, I have wanted to ask *why*, *why*, *why* . . . over and over again. My why questions are always about your father and the frustrating things he does. I want to ask, Why did you do that? Why did you lose that? Why did you move that? I have so many whys for God too—they're endless."

"I know exactly what you mean," Jewel admitted. "I ask Dad why all the time. Not that he answers. Just this afternoon, I asked why he ran off like that, and his answer made no sense. He was going to town but headed the wrong way."

"Well, I can't speak for you girls, but I'm learning to hold back on my why questions. For one thing, it usually just frustrates him more. And it'll frustrate you too. Even if he tries to tell you why he did something, you rarely get a right answer. Because there are none."

Cooper nodded. "Yeah, I guess that makes sense."

"Do you think those words were God forewarning you?" Jewel asked. "For what was ahead?"

"It seems that way. And I take it a step further too. It's not just about not asking CT why. I don't ask God why anymore either. I'll admit I want to ask about my husband's condition. *Why* did he get this? But I believe I won't get that answer. Not in this earthly life. And I'm okay with that." She smiled. "Well, most of the time. I'm only human, after all. I certainly have my weak moments. More than I care to admit." She took a slow sip of lemonade.

"Thanks for telling us that, Grandma." Cooper set her empty glass in the sink. "It helps. Now if no one cares, I'm going to grab a shower. By the way, Mom, Anna asked me to spend the night after the barbecue. Is that okay?"

"Sure," Jewel agreed. "Sounds fun."

"I guess." Cooper shrugged like it was no big deal, or maybe she didn't want her mother to know she might actually have a good time with her new friend. "Gets me off the funny farm for a while." She covered her mouth with a guilty look, like what she said was politically incorrect, but her mom and grandma just laughed, really laughed.

"It does feel like the funny farm some days," Mom admitted. "We all need a break from time to time." She turned to Cooper.

"I'll tend the bees while you're gone." Cooper thanked her, then scurried off.

"Okay then. You admit we need a break." Jewel pointed at her mom. "Promise me if you don't go to the Oroscos' tonight, you will get off the funny farm tomorrow. By yourself and with no worries over Dad. Because I'll be here with him. *Okay?*"

Mom looked uncertain.

"Come on, Mom." Jewel stuck out her hand. "Promise you will."

"All right." Her mom shook her hand. "Sounds like a smart idea."

Jewel squeezed Mom's hand, wishing there was more she could do, hoping just being here might be enough for now. Although if they had any more days like today, she might want a complete escape from the "funny farm" herself.

18

Honey

Honey proceeded to get ready for the neighbors' barbecue as if she was walking on eggshells. And CT was visibly on edge, like their faithful old dog Piper always was when a suitcase emerged from the attic. He actually reminded Honey of Piper as he trailed her around the house. Now he sat on the end of their bed, watching her with an expression somewhere between annoyance and confusion.

"Where are you going?" he asked for what felt like the hundredth time.

"To a barbecue." She carefully omitted the location.

"When?"

"At six." She held up six fingers, just like she'd done five minutes ago.

He frowned. "Today?"

She simply nodded as she sat down on the chair by the closet.

"Am I going?" He stood up, rubbing his grizzled gray chin as if planning to do something about the several days' growth of whiskers. She'd already reminded him over and over today he needed a shave. Not because she particularly cared that he looked unkempt. Nothing new about that. He actually looked kind of cute with some scruff. But she'd pointed it out in an effort to distract him from dogging her heels. But each time he'd walked off to the bathroom, he'd returned too quickly, clearly having forgotten why'd he'd gone in there. Sometimes he brought back a hand towel or a soap dish, like she'd asked for it.

"I'd like you to go with us," she said carefully, bending to buckle her sandal.

He nodded. "Okay."

She tipped her head toward the clean shirt she'd laid out on his side of the bed earlier that afternoon, when she'd first suggested he might shower. It was too late for that now. But CT looked down at the stained T-shirt he was wearing. "I like this shirt."

"Yes, I know." She stood to pick up the white-and-turquoise Hawaiian shirt she'd set on the bed. "But we got this in Maui," she said, inserting extra cheer into her voice. "Remember?"

His eyes lit up. "Yes."

"I'd love to see it on you."

He nodded. "Okay."

"I'll be in the kitchen." She kissed his grizzly cheek. "I'm glad you want to go with me, CT. It'll be fun."

"Fun," he echoed as he struggled to tug off his T-shirt. She resisted the urge to help him, remembering the advice she'd been given. "Let him do for himself as much as he can for as long as he can." Even so, she reached for the deodorant on his dresser. "How about some of this too?" She smiled. "Make you smell nice."

"Okay." He grinned at her, his hair tousled from removing the T-shirt.

"I'll be in the kitchen," she said again. "I need to slice some boiled eggs to put on the potato salad."

"Huh?" He looked confused again. "Egg salad?"

"Never mind." She laughed. "Just get ready for the barbecue, sweetie. We'll leave in about twenty minutes." She reminded him to use the bathroom, then left.

As she peeled the eggs she'd boiled earlier, she felt a smidgeon of guilt for being disingenuous regarding the location of the barbecue. But each time she'd mentioned the Orosco name earlier, he'd gone into a tizzy. Her plan now was to drive him around a bit, then get him peacefully next door. If she got lucky, he might not realize whose house they were at. What he might do when he did figure things out was anyone's guess. But she would just have to deal with that then.

"Is Grandpa coming?" Cooper asked as she filled a water bottle in the kitchen.

"I think so." Honey sliced an egg, then gave Cooper a closer look, smiling to see her granddaughter had dressed slightly more conservatively. Probably Anna's influence. She still had on tattered jeans like all the kids wore, but with her white Converse and plaid shirt, she looked more like the local kids. Honey considered a compliment but knew that could backfire. Instead, she focused on Cooper's feet. "I like your shoes. Takes me back to my youth."

"You wore Converse?"

"Sure. They were from the boys' department and black-and-white, but I thought they were pretty cool."

Cooper smiled. "Yeah."

"A lot of trends come back in time." She sighed nostalgically. "Like Birkenstocks."

Cooper beamed at her. "You know about Birkenstocks?"

Honey laughed. "Do I?" She spread the sliced eggs on top of the salad. "I still have an old pair that I got back when they first came out."

"Vintage Birkies?" Cooper's eyes lit.

"I guess so. I don't wear them anymore."

"What size are they?"

"Eight."

Cooper's jaw dropped. "That's my size, Grandma."

"Would you like to have them?"

"For sure." Cooper hugged her around the waist. "Thanks, Grandma."

"What are you thanking Grandma for?" Jewel asked as she came into the kitchen.

Honey filled her in, then told them both her idea for getting CT over to the barbecue with less fuss. "I thought perhaps you two could go separately." She secured plastic wrap snugly over the large bowl. "Maybe you could take the salad for me. That way I can focus entirely on your father."

"Sounds like a plan," Jewel agreed. "Ready to go, Coop?"

"I'm gonna walk over."

"Me too." Jewel picked up the salad. "We can use Miguel's new gate."

"Let them know we might be running late, please," Honey told them.

"Will do." Jewel smiled. "Good luck, Mom."

Honey sighed. "I'll need it. And no worries if we don't last long there." She forced a smile. The truth was, she wouldn't mind coming home early. After feeling like she was tiptoeing around and cajoling CT all day long, she thought she might enjoy a quiet evening here with just the two of them. She might even be willing to watch an old western with him. Just not *True Grit*—again. She knew that movie by heart!

When CT finally emerged from the bathroom, they were already fifteen minutes late, but Honey didn't mind. Although she was surprised by the strong scent of oranges that filled the air as CT walked down the hall. She kept an orange-fragranced air freshener in there, but it wasn't usually so strong she could smell it in the living room. "Are you ready?" she asked, curiously sniffing him and realizing he'd probably used the aerosol on himself. Well, at least it was organic. And his hair, all combed down slick, looked a little goofy, but it would be hidden beneath the black John Deere cap he was reaching for.

He smiled. "Ready."

"You smell like a fresh-squeezed orange." She touched his hair, then smelled her fingers, realizing that was the source of the strong aroma. Well, certainly there were worse things. "Let's go." She jingled her car keys and was unsurprised that he didn't even ask about Jewel and Cooper. Temporarily forgotten.

"Looks like a nice evening for a barbecue," she commented as they got into her SUV. "Not too warm and not too cool."

"Uh-huh."

Even though they weren't going far, she reminded him to buckle up, then started to drive, making small talk as she first went down the road, turned onto a side road, looped around, and doubled back. As she chattered at him, she pointed out a pair of red-tailed hawks, keeping him distracted as she turned down the Orosco driveway. So far, so good. As they got closer to the house, she noticed him frown.

"Where are we going?" he asked.

"The barbecue. Remember?"

"Oh, yeah. Barbecue. What's that?"

"Oh, you know. People getting together. Eating hamburgers."

"Hamburgers?" His voice grew more cheery.

She chatted on about other foods people ate at barbecues and intentionally chose to park near vehicles that CT wouldn't recognize.

"What people?" he asked as they got out.

"Well, Jewel and Cooper are here," she said lightly.

"Oh, yeah." He nodded like he understood this. She started to knock on the door, but seeing it was open, she simply led him inside. As far as she knew, CT had never set foot into the Orosco home. And since everyone was out back, she had a few more moments to help him adjust.

"Isn't this a pretty room?" she said.

"Uh-huh." He looked around with appreciation. "Nice."

Female voices were coming from the kitchen, and soon CT was being greeted by neighbors he may or may not have recognized. No matter, he seemed glad to see them. And they were friendly and kind in return. Again, so far, so good.

"Welcome," Marta Orosco warmly greeted them. "I'm so glad you came." She handed CT a napkin and held out a tempting plate of appetizers. "Please, help yourself."

"Uh-huh," CT grunted as he filled his napkin. He still seemed oblivious. But then he'd only met Marta once, and that was a few years ago.

"Others are outside," she told them as Honey took an appetizer. "And drinks too. Go visit with neighbors."

"Thank you." Honey exchanged winks with Marta. "We'll do

that." She turned to CT. "Wait until you see their garden. It's beautiful." She led him outside and around the patio, pointing out the pond and fountain and plants, pausing to greet neighbors they hadn't seen lately. Finally, feeling slightly relieved, she left CT with a group of older men. Some of the same friends he used to visit with at the feed store coffee group.

Honey spotted Jewel assisting Miguel at the barbecue. She smiled to herself. Those two looked good together! She spied Cooper and Anna sitting on a bench with their heads bent together as they focused on their phones, showing each other things that they clearly found highly amusing. So normal. So good. Things were going smoothly. Somewhat relieved, Honey returned to the kitchen to help out and perhaps catch up with some of the neighbors she hadn't seen in a year or more. She suspected most of them were aware of CT's condition, and probably just as well. That was life in a small town. She inhaled deeply as she waved to her old friend Donna Skinner. The Skinner farm was at the end of the road, and she and Donna used to walk together for exercise, catching up on all the latest news. Honey eagerly greeted Donna with a hug.

"I've missed you so much," Donna gushed. "Where have you been keeping yourself? I hear you're retired now."

"I've been home," Honey told her. "I thought retirement was supposed to feel like a break, but all I do is work." She laughed. "Still, it's nice to call my time my own." Of course, even as she said this, she questioned herself. When was her time really her own? With CT, she was on call 24/7.

"That's farm life." Donna nodded. "Always something needs doing. Do you have chickens this year? I've been looking for someone to buy eggs from."

"No." Honey sighed. "But CT keeps bees, and we have lots of honey. I've been thinking about selling that. And now that I have my daughter and granddaughter here to help, I might get chickens again."

"Oh, how nice for you! Rick had to hire help a couple years ago," Donna said as they moved to a quieter corner of the kitchen. "I wasn't sure about it, but it's allowed us to go and do more."

Suddenly she was gushing about the trips they'd taken—a cruise to Alaska and then one to the Caribbean and even a vineyard in Tuscany, the one place Honey had always longed to visit. She suppressed a wave of envy.

"How about you?" Donna asked. "Now that you're retired and have extra help, will you and CT be traveling?"

Honey sighed. "I'm guessing you haven't heard about CT's condition."

"Oh, no." Donna's eyes grew wide. "Is it cancer? So many of my friends have been diagnosed lately."

For a moment, Honey wished it was cancer. That sounded easier. "No, it's FTD."

Donna frowned. "FTD? Isn't that a florist?"

Honey couldn't help but smile. "You know, that's exactly what CT thought when he first heard it." Now she explained that FTD was early-onset dementia. She hated using that word, but sometimes it was just simpler.

"Oh, Honey." Donna hugged her again. "I'm so sorry."

"Yeah." As usual, Honey felt her emotions coming to the surface. But she really didn't want to cry. Not here tonight.

Donna released her and looked intently into her eyes. "I'm so glad you have Jewel and her girl to help you, but if you ever need anything, I hope you will call."

Honey thanked her. "What I might need sometime is to get away for a cup of coffee."

"You come on down to our place anytime, Honey. Or we can go to Starbucks if you'd like. You name it and I'll be there."

"*Mo-om?*"

Honey turned to see Jewel by the door with a slightly anxious expression. She motioned for Honey to join her, and Honey excused herself. "What is it?"

"Dad." Jewel took her by the arm. "He's, uh, making a scene."

"Oh dear." Honey let her daughter lead her out to where CT appeared to be about to get into a fight with one of the neighboring farmers. At least he wasn't about to accost Miguel. That was something.

"CT," Honey said gently as she firmly took his hand. "I want to show you something."

"Huh?" His brow furrowed with a combination of confusion and anger. "What?" he growled loudly enough to grab the attention of several neighbors.

"The fish in the pond," she said, acting as if it was the most important thing in the world. "You have to see them, CT."

"Fish?" He sounded slightly curious.

She continued to chatter at him about fish as she led him to the little pond. She was careful not to ask what had transpired back there with the men, but when she glanced back, she noticed Jewel still talking to the men gathered in a tight circle, probably explaining her father's condition. To her relief, they were nodding with what seemed understanding and perhaps a tinge of sympathy.

A little while later, Jewel brought over a plastic cup and offered it to her father. "Iced tea with sugar," she told him. "Just how you like it."

CT held the cup, then took a cautious sip.

"You look so nice tonight, Dad. I love that shirt." Jewel pulled out her phone. "Can I take a picture of both of you by the pond here?"

CT was always a good one for photos. Honey not so much. But she held to his arm, forcing a smile while Jewel took several shots. "Thanks," she told her daughter. "If they're any good, send them to me."

Honey visited a bit more with CT, talking about the fish and wondering how many lived there. Then, finally, with him somewhat calmed and comfortably seated on the bench by the pond, she considered returning to her conversation with Donna. But unsure about leaving CT unsupervised, she waved tentatively to Jewel, who gave a nod of assurance followed by a thumbs-up. Consoled that Jewel could keep an eye on CT while he was preoccupied with fish counting, Honey patted him on the shoulder, then slipped back into the house. But she had a feeling her time here, though enjoyable, was limited. Might as well make the best of it.

19

Honey

Only minutes later, Honey heard the unmistakable sound of CT making a big fuss about something. "Excuse me," she told Donna with a slight roll of her eyes. "I'm afraid I'll need to take my husband home."

"Oh, Honey." Donna patted her shoulder. "I understand." Then as Honey hurried away, Donna held up her hand like a phone and mouthed "call me."

Promising herself she would, Honey rushed outside to discover CT over by the barbecue area now. This time, he was shaking a fist at Miguel and yelling. "You thief! I won't eat poisoned food."

"Daaad!" Jewel yelled at him. "Calm down."

"I won't!" CT shouted back at her. "I won't eat poison."

"I already told you there's no poison!" Jewel shouted back. "You're imagining things."

"Poison!" he yelled loudly enough to get the attention of everyone on the property.

"CT," Honey said as calmly as she could. "Let's go."

"Yes!" He continued to glare at Miguel. "I won't eat his poison."

"Miguel isn't poisoning anything," Honey replied. "Let's go, CT. Now." She spoke louder now, even though she knew volume never helped. Her cheeks were burning with embarrassment, and she felt blood rushing up her neck. This was not good for her blood pressure. She knew it. And yet, what could she do?

CT reached for a knife and waved it threateningly.

"Put that down," she told him with all the authority she could muster. "*Now!*" Then she actually slugged him in the arm. "I mean it, CT. Put that down!"

To her relief, he set down the knife and turned to her with a gaping mouth. "Huh?"

"We're going home." She grabbed his arm and shoved him toward the side yard. "This way. Let's go now." Without giving him opportunity to respond or balk, she tugged, pulled, and shoved him through the yard and around to the driveway. But by the time they reached the car, she was boiling mad. "I can't believe you," she muttered as she got into the driver's seat.

"Huh?" He slowly got in on the other side, huffing and puffing as he maneuvered his feet inside. "Honey?"

"I'm so mad." She started the engine.

"Mad?" He looked at her with that innocent little boy expression. She knew it was genuine, that he really didn't know what he'd done wrong, but she still felt angry.

"You behaved terribly," she scolded. "Miguel would never poison anyone!"

She watched his expression change—going from the wounded boy to the angry man—and she regretted mentioning Miguel's name. "Oh, forget it," she said as she backed out. "Never mind."

"Miguel is a thief," CT growled. "He put poison in our food."

"No, he did not," she whispered, driving too fast down the driveway and feeling bad for the dust cloud she was leaving behind them. Fortunately, what little breeze was blowing pushed it away from the house.

"He did!" CT's voice grew louder. "He put poison in our food."

"Don't be ridiculous." She had just slowed down to turn onto their road when CT opened the door and started to get out.

"Stop that," she yelled, but he wasn't listening. With one foot dragging in the gravel, she knew he could fall out, so she stopped and threw her hands in the air. "Fine." She shook her head. "You want out? Get out. I don't care!"

He gave her a questioning look and then, with a defiant expression, he climbed out of the car and slammed the door shut. And truly not caring, she drove home. Their house was easily visible from here. Perhaps a walk would do him good, and it would give her time to cool off. She needed to cool off. She hated to imagine what her blood pressure might be reading right now. She could feel a throbbing sensation high in her chest, and her ears were ringing. She needed to calm down.

She parked in front of the house and practiced the deep breathing techniques her doctor had shown her as she went inside. She continued doing this as she went to the kitchen and poured a glass of cold water. Sitting at the table, feeling slightly numb, she took small sips of the water and continued breathing slowly. Inhale for four seconds, hold it there for four seconds, then exhale for four seconds followed by a sip of water. She did this again and again until the glass was empty and she finally felt a tiny bit better.

But as she sat there, she wondered if she would really care if her blood pressure went so high that it snuffed out her life. Wouldn't the next life be better than living like this? Jewel and Cooper could handle CT without her . . . or help him to get into some form of assisted care. And she would be free . . . free at last, thank God Almighty, she'd be free at last.

Of course, these thoughts were followed by a flood of tears. How had she come to this? Did she really not care about CT? The man she'd promised to love in sickness and in health, the man she'd committed to love till death did they part? She wanted to abandon him now? Like this? She reached for a paper napkin and blotted her tears and wiped her nose.

"Dear God, help me." She prayed the same words over and over between loud sobs. But she meant them as much as any other prayer she'd ever prayed. "Please, dear God, help me." She wasn't sure how long she sat there blubbering like that, sobbing and praying and going through a lot of paper napkins, but finally she wondered what had become of CT.

She hadn't heard him come into the house, but she looked around just in case. Not seeing him anywhere inside, she went out to the front porch and gazed out across the green alfalfa field where she assumed he'd cut across to get home. The sun was low in the sky, promising a pretty sunset, but CT was nowhere in sight. Had he gone onto the road and started trekking off somewhere, deciding to run away like a naughty four-year-old? She wouldn't put it past him. She called out his name, but there was no answer. Just the sound of magpies in the trees. She glanced to the Oroscos' house where she imagined the party in full swing. She hoped Jewel and Cooper weren't worried. She'd warned them that she and CT might not make it too long there. And she'd been right.

She gazed toward the barn and outbuilding. He could very likely be hiding out in one of them. She wouldn't put it past him. It was a good way to punish her. And he did that sometimes. The barn was the most likely since he'd been grumbling about Jewel's changes to his precious barn just today, as if he really used it for anything these days. Perhaps he was in there rearranging Jewel's paints and easels and things . . . again. Hopefully he wasn't making a mess of it. She set out to look around.

CT

Miguel wants to kill me. I know it. He wants my farm. He has poison. I saw it on the table. It was red. He wants to kill me. They all want to kill me. Where is my gun? I want my gun. It's in the house. I want my truck. I will get in my truck before Miguel steals it. I will get my gun and my truck. Where are my keys? *My keys!* Who took them? They're not in my pockets. Nothing in my pants pockets. Nothing! Who took my things? My wallet? Where is my wallet? Miguel took it. I know it. He is a thief. He should go to jail.

No keys in my shirt pocket. What is this shirt? Where did it come from? It's not my shirt. Who put it on me? I don't own a shirt with flowers on it. Not me. I'm a farmer. I wear farm shirts with snaps. The snaps on this shirt don't work. Why can't I work these snaps! I don't want this stupid shirt. Don't want to wear flowers. Flowers are for girls. I'm not a girl. Must get rid of this shirt. Miguel's shirt. He likes girl shirts. He is weird. He has poison.

He poisoned the food. Won't eat poison food. Why do they want to kill me? What did I do to deserve this? I am not a bad man. I want my Honey. Where is my Honey? Did she give me to Miguel? She likes Miguel. Why does she like a thief? What is wrong? What is wrong? Why is it like this? I'm not a bad man. I want my Honey.

Honey

On the edge of desperation, Honey emerged from the barn and scanned the surrounding landscape again, looking in all directions. She'd already searched every outbuilding twice, even checking the hayloft in the barn. She screened her eyes against the setting sun with her hands and yelled out his name. Her throat was raspy from calling to him so many times.

Just as she was about to give up and call for help on her phone, she noticed movement in the green field to the west. Something fluttered in the air like a flag before disappearing. Was it her imagination? She stared at the spot and called out for CT. It suddenly fluttered again, a flash of something above the tops of the knee-high alfalfa plants. She wondered if it was a pheasant or a turkey getting a last meal before the sun went down. But then it appeared again, like a flag of turquoise and white. And now she remembered CT's Hawaiian shirt with its big flowers. Was he using it to flag her attention? Perhaps he'd fallen down in the alfalfa and hurt himself. Maybe he'd broken something and was unable to stand or walk.

She ran to the field, clumsily clomping through the thick alfalfa plants while trying to reach the spot where she'd glimpsed his shirt. "CT!" she yelled again. Why had she let him walk off like that on his own? She knew better! Poor CT, he did not deserve this.

"CT," she called yet again as she trudged through the field. "I'm coming!"

There was the flapping of that shirt again. He *was* flagging her. Still calling out, she tried to run, then realized how easy it would be to trip among the thick plants. That was probably how CT had fallen.

Finally, she reached him. Flat on his back, he was shirtless and dirty, looking up at her with a lost expression and a tear-streaked face. And his jeans were wet.

"Oh, CT." She knelt at his side. "What happened?"

"I fell down," he muttered.

"Are you hurt?"

"Uh-huh." He pointed to his right leg. "My foot."

She cuffed his pant leg to examine him. His ankle was quite swollen. He winced as she checked to see if anything seemed broken. "I think you sprained it," she explained.

"Hurts."

"I'm sure it does." She looked around the sea of green, trying to decide what to do. The sky was growing dusky. She could call Jewel to bring help, but she hated to disrupt her pleasant evening. The image of Miguel and Jewel working together at the barbecue had warmed Honey's heart. "If I help you, CT, do you think you can walk?"

"I dunno." He sat up and frowned. "I think so."

"Okay then." She picked up his ball cap and stuck it on his head.

"I got wet."

"I know, sweetie." She put her arm snugly beneath his arms and then got herself into a squatting position. "It's okay. I'll help you get to your feet."

"Okay."

"Just put your weight on your left leg, okay?"

"Which leg?"

She pointed to his left leg, instructing him and hoping he could follow her directions. But it felt like a comedy of errors. It took several tries and a few loud yelps, but she finally got him up. Worried that they might both topple down again, she remained close, holding him steady as he held on to her tightly.

"Are you okay?" she asked.

"Uh-huh. Think so."

"Want to try walking?" She attempted to adjust her stance, but he wouldn't let go of his snug hold.

"Honey?"

"Yeah?" She looked up at him.

"Thank you." He gazed lovingly into her eyes. "I can't live without you."

She smiled. "I know."

"I love my Honey." He pulled her even closer.

"I know you do, CT. I love you too."

"I'm sorry . . . I messed up."

She wasn't sure which mess he meant exactly, but it didn't matter. "It's okay. You can't really help it."

"I know . . . I'm goofy."

"Yeah, sometimes." She felt her eyes filling with tears again. "I guess we're both goofy sometimes."

"I don't want to be goofy." He used his thumb to wipe one of her tears. "I'm sorry, Honey."

"I know."

"Will I be like this for . . . ever . . . always?" he asked in the most serious tone she'd heard him use in a long time. Almost like the old CT. "Will I be like this all the time?"

The lump in her throat grew painful now. It felt like her heart was breaking, and she wanted to just sob with abandon. "Like . . . what?" she asked hoarsely. Did he mean falling down, getting hurt, wetting his pants, having bad manners at the Oroscos' . . . or something else?

"My brain . . . doesn't work right. Is it broken?"

"Yes, it does have a problem."

"I want an answer, Honey."

"Okay." She braced herself.

"Will it get better?"

She hugged him tighter, then buried her head into his chest, praying for strength before looking up at him. "One way or another it will get better." Of course, she was thinking of heaven and how everyone would be made whole again, but she didn't think CT wanted to hear that just now. And she didn't think she could bring herself to say those words anyway. To speak of heaven was to speak of death. It was not a subject CT cared to talk about.

"I will get better?" He sounded hopeful.

"Yes, someday you will. But it's getting dark. We should get to the house." And with her arm supporting him around his waist and his around her shoulders, she helped him limp back to the house. By the time she got him into his recliner, they were both exhausted. Physically and emotionally. She knew what had transpired between the two of them in the alfalfa field was a genuine connection and not something she got much of anymore. It was a truly precious moment. Yet in the same moment, it felt like a dull, rusty knife had sliced through her heart. But maybe that was the reality of genuine love—hard and good just went together.

20

Jewel

The atmosphere at the barbecue was definitely more somber after Jewel's parents made their hasty departure. Her dad's cruel accusation of Miguel poisoning the food had cast a definite shadow over the party. Ashamed by her dad's lack of social graces, Jewel had tried to smooth things over, but the guests still seemed a little ill at ease. As she fought back her own anger toward Dad, she made apologies, explaining that it was simply part of his condition. Not that it made anyone feel better.

Maybe she should just call it a night too. Her poor mom could probably use some help managing Dad tonight. As Jewel considered excusing herself to run to her parents' rescue, she glanced around the backyard. Small clusters of guests milled about, talking in hushed tones, probably about her crazy family. Miguel was by himself, still minding the grill, a serious expression on his face. She'd already apologized to him, and he'd told her to forget about it. But she still felt her family had spoiled his evening.

"They'll be okay, Mom," Cooper whispered in her ear.

Jewel spun around and stared at her daughter in surprise. "You really think so?"

"Yeah. Grandma said not to worry if they left early. Remember?"

Jewel nodded. "But your grandpa was so upset and angry."

"And he's probably forgotten the whole thing by now."

Jewel sighed. "You're right."

"I bet he's in his recliner watching *True Grit* and eating a peanut butter and honey sandwich."

"Or sleeping." Jewel smiled. Cooper had him pegged. And, besides, her parents might like having a quiet house to themselves tonight.

Cooper patted her back in a consolatory way, then rejoined Anna and a couple of other teen girls who'd just shown up. Jewel tried to be discreet as she watched her daughter interact with the small group. Really, it was amazing to be at the same party as her daughter with both of them having a good time. Well, Jewel *had* been having a good time. Up until Dad's unfortunate hissy fit.

Jewel got herself a drink and then ventured back to the grill to see if Miguel needed any more help. She wouldn't keep apologizing to him, but she would do what she could to make him feel better.

"Yum," she said as she watched him set some juicy-looking burgers on a platter. "Those smell delicious." A piece of meat tumbled off a burger and she nabbed it, popping it into her mouth, then loudly smacking her lips.

"Best *poison* burgers I ever tasted," she proclaimed loudly enough for others to hear. "At least I'll die happy now." To her relief, several people started to chuckle. Then a few more jests were made, some perhaps at her dad's expense, but not untrue. Suddenly people were laughing and the party was back on good footing. She and Miguel continued to cook burgers as guests began to fill their plates. Finally, with the last burger off the grill, she and Miguel got their own food.

"I'm glad you stuck around," he told her after they found an unoccupied corner of the patio where they could sit and eat. "I was worried you were about to vamoose too."

"I felt a little guilty. You know, in case Mom needed my help. But then I realized she'd feel bad if she thought she'd ruined my evening too."

"Your mom is so good at dealing with your dad." Miguel picked up his burger and took a big bite.

"I guess she's had more practice with him." Jewel forked into her potato salad. "Dad puts her through the wringer over something or other almost every single day. I can't believe how patient she is with him. I should be taking lessons."

He nodded as he chewed then swallowed. "She's definitely patient, but it's more than just that. It's obvious how much she loves your dad. You know, despite everything. That's pretty remarkable."

"Yeah. Sometimes I want to knock Dad's block off." She laughed. "To be fair, Mom gets pretty annoyed occasionally. In fact, I was worried she might lay into him after tonight's little scene." She took a bite of her burger.

"I hope not. Like you said, he can't really help it."

"I know that in my head. And I kept telling myself that tonight. But sometimes I forget. I can get caught up in what I'm doing, and Dad can seem almost normal at times. I want to respect him as my father, but then he'll do something so out-of-the-blue weird that, well, it's like he pulls the rug right out from under me."

"Yeah, I know what that's like." He shook his head as he dipped a tortilla chip into guacamole.

"I bet you do."

"I don't even mind getting the worst of it," he admitted. "If that helps him not to go off on someone else."

"That's sweet, Miguel, but I really don't think it works like that," she said. "Like earlier today. I've been trying to get my art studio all arranged in the barn, but Dad keeps sneaking in there and changing it all around."

"He probably thinks the barn is his space."

"I guess so. But he doesn't use it for anything. Just stores a bunch of random, useless junk in there. Stuff he never uses. But he likes to move everything around all the time for no rational reason. Mom calls him the Lone Rearranger."

Miguel laughed.

"But it was beyond just rearranging today. I mean, some things were moved, but some things were just plain gone. I still can't find a tin of paint tubes. And I haven't found my favorite easel. For all I know, he's chopped it up into firewood."

"The poor guy needs something to do." Miguel wiped his mouth with a napkin. "Think about it, Jewel. He was a farmer for years. A farmer is always doing something. Now he's at loose ends. That could drive a healthy guy nuts."

"We try to find things for him to do. And sometimes he'll stick to a task for a while. But it doesn't take long before he gets distracted. Like Mom asked him to rake around her garden, and the next thing we knew, he was digging a huge hole. A hole that no one wanted and just had to be filled back in. And he was so worn out, he could barely walk into the house." She took another bite of her burger. "I mean, at least she had something to occupy him the next day. But it just goes on and on like that."

Miguel looked amused. "If he enjoys doing something, maybe it doesn't matter so much what he's doing as long as it doesn't hurt anyone."

She set down her burger, wiped her fingers, and looked into his eyes. Miguel was so sincere and kind, such a stand-up sort of guy. The word *guileless* came to mind as she nodded. "You're right. I'll try to remember that."

"So . . . how are his bees doing? Making lots of honey?"

"As far as I can tell, they're doing okay. But I have to say, as much as he loves his little buzzy-bodies, he does forget them at times. If Cooper wasn't helping, I think there would be real problems."

His dark brows arched. "She likes the bees, then?"

"She adores them." Jewel wrinkled her nose. "Me, not so much. But you should see her out there with the hives, so calm and collected. She claims the sound of the bees makes her feel at peace, if you can believe that. Although Mom told me Dad used to say the same thing."

"I have a friend who keeps bees, and he said that too."

"Coop even learned how to get into the protective suit and empty the honeycombs. She claims she'll be able to do it by herself next time."

"That's great."

"I guess. The whole business made me pretty nervous at first. I was so worried she'd get attacked and stung. You know, like Winnie the Pooh when he steals the honey."

He laughed. "I remember seeing that video when I was a kid."

"Me too. And to be honest, I've never liked bees," Jewel confessed. "I've read that they sense fear in people, so I give them their space and hope they'll leave me alone."

He nodded toward the small group of teens gathered at the far end of the yard, laughing loudly at something. "It's nice to see how Cooper seems to be fitting in here. Even with the country kids. Anna can't seem to get enough of her."

"I know Coop's here a lot. I just hope she doesn't wear out her welcome." Jewel sighed. "To be honest, her settling in here feels nothing short of miraculous."

"Yeah, I remember you telling me she was a problem child." He chuckled. "I think she's pretty cool."

"She is pretty cool. And doing far better here than she was in California."

"So do you think you'll be staying, then?" His espresso-colored eyes searched hers. "You weren't too sure about all this when you first arrived, if I recall."

"I can't deny I've had moments when I wanted to pick up and run." She shrugged. "But with Mom and Dad's new house coming next week, and the plans for the B&B, well, I guess I have to stay long enough to see how it goes." Her voice trailed off with uncertainty. She wished she was as confident as she was trying to sound, but what if her grandiose plans all flopped? There were so many ways it could all go wrong.

"So . . . if it *doesn't* go?" He continued to study her with intensity.

"I don't know, Miguel. I mean, I've sunk all my funds into this wild dream of mine. Sometimes I wake up in the middle of the night with suffocating doubts. I've even had a couple of nightmares about it. It's possible I did bite off more than I can chew. That's what Mom always used to tell me. And to be honest, my dad really scares me sometimes. He's so unpredictable. Like he could totally balk at the idea of living in the new house. He could blow up at me for even doing all this. What then?"

Miguel pursed his lips. "He never seemed to be the kind of guy who liked change."

"I know. Well, unless he's rearranging things."

Miguel smiled. "That's true."

"But you're right. I used to think he was a real stick in the mud. Every time Mom wanted to do something different, Dad would dig in his heels."

"So what's your plan if he refuses to live in the new house?" Miguel asked.

"Well, I suppose Cooper and I could live there. And, really, that would be okay. But there goes the whole B&B idea. No way could I have guests in the house with my dad living there. And I was hoping that would help to pay back my investment. Plus, it sounded like fun. I could make it look so cool, so inviting. I imagined it like an artist's retreat where I'd host small groups and even have a gallery in the barn." She sighed to imagine the dream she'd nurtured. In a perfect world, it could be so good. But theirs was not a perfect world. Not by any means.

"It does sound like a good idea, Jewel. In theory."

"In theory?" Even though she knew he was right, she didn't want to hear it.

"Well, we have dreams, but we never know what will happen in real life. I'm not saying don't dream." He waved his hand. "After all, it wasn't that long ago this place was all a dream." He sipped his drink. "But the truth is it hasn't turned out the way I'd hoped." He gazed out across the fields with a sad expression, and she suddenly remembered how he lost his wife and his father. That must've ruined some of his dreams.

"No, you're right. I guess nothing ever really does turn out exactly how we dream and plan. Not really." She felt slightly deflated now. Maybe the whole B&B plan was just an unrealistic pipe dream. Maybe she was a fool to entertain such expensive fantasies.

"I didn't mean to rain on your parade." Miguel's tone lightened. "You said the new manufactured home will be put in place by next week? That'll be exciting."

She brightened a little. "Yes. But I'll warn you, the house's exterior paint color is atrocious, and it'll be clearly visible from your property. But I promise that the first thing I'll do is paint it."

He shrugged. "Don't worry. It can't be that bad."

"Oh, yes, it can. It's this horrible bright yellow, about the same color as the stripes on the highway. For all I know, it might glow in the dark too."

He laughed.

She smiled. "But that's one reason I got such a good deal on it."

"Uh-huh?" His eyes had a knowing look. "And is the other reason Aaron Hanford?"

She felt her cheeks warm. "Well, maybe so. Aaron is an old friend. We went to school together."

"And you're on pretty good terms with him." It was part statement, part question.

"I guess. I mean, he's been very helpful. And he's really gotten things moving . . . as far as getting the house set up. He delivers what he promises. Very professional." Okay, "very professional" was a stretch, and she felt the sting of embarrassment for being so defensive of Aaron, especially since she knew Miguel had issues with his estranged brother-in-law. She wished there was a way to help the two men smooth things over. For everyone's sake. But she had no idea where to start. And now, for some unexplainable reason, she wanted to convince Miguel that Aaron meant nothing to her.

"Well, it's none of my business, but I thought maybe you and Aaron might be, uh, involved on a personal level." He toyed with the plastic cup in his hand. "Anna and I noticed you and Aaron in town last week, and she was certain you were on a date." He held up his hand as if to stop any response. "But, like I said, it's none of my business. And it's not Anna's either."

She didn't know what to say now. To deny it had been a date would sound insincere. To claim Aaron meant nothing would sound like she was protesting too much. Besides, why should she defend herself? Miguel was right. It *was* none of his business. Still, sitting there silently felt awkward. Suddenly male voices were calling out for Miguel, insisting their host join the party and come play cornhole with them.

Jewel wasn't sure if she felt relieved or disappointed as she picked up her plate and stood. "Looks like they need you."

"Eric's creaming us," a lanky guy in a straw cowboy hat told Miguel.

"Miguel's the champion," a female voice yelled from where the game was set up. "Let's make him defend his title."

Miguel excused himself as Jewel collected their empty plates, as well as a few others, busying herself by scraping the uneaten food into the trash can. She considered joining the lively cornhole crowd but decided to see if Marta needed any help in the kitchen instead.

"No, no." Marta paused from rinsing a serving dish after Jewel offered her help. "You go out. *Enjoy*."

Jewel smiled at her. "What if I enjoy being in here with you?"

Marta tipped her head to one side. "Then you stay." She handed her a dish towel. "And you dry."

As they washed and dried, Marta asked about Jewel's parents, expressing concern that Jewel's dad might someday become too difficult for them to care for. "Your poor mama. She will wear out. And your papa . . . he is a handful."

"I've had the same concern," Jewel admitted. "But Cooper and I are trying to lighten Mom's load. And like she keeps saying, we can only live one day at a time."

"Sí, sí. That is what the good Lord says too. One day is enough."

More than enough today, Jewel thought. Although tonight hadn't turned out as badly as it might have, it still felt like a letdown. She wasn't sure what she'd hoped for exactly, but the way her conversation with Miguel had ended on a sour note was disheartening. She hated to leave him thinking she was romantically involved with Aaron. But it was out of her hands . . . at least for now.

"Well, I think I'll head home to check on my parents," she told Marta as they finished up. "But thank you for everything. It was a lovely party." She winced. "Well, except for my dad's contribution. Sorry about that."

"Over and done." Marta kissed Jewel's cheek. "Forget about it."

"I'll try." Jewel hugged her. But as she walked across the field, now illuminated by the light of a half-moon, as much as she wanted to accept Marta's advice and simply "forget about it," like so many other things in life, it was easier said than done.

21

Honey

By the next morning, CT's ankle injury really did appear to be just a light sprain. Honey had administered Advil, then iced and wrapped his ankle the night before. She'd even suggested he could get it checked at urgent care, since he sometimes got worked up over physical injuries. But she was relieved when he simply waved his hand, assuring her he was okay. She hadn't really wanted to drive him into town and go through all the inevitable challenges that would follow. And CT seemed content to rest in his chair.

She'd found an old pair of crutches in the attic after she'd gotten him safely into bed, but this morning when she tried to show him how to use the crutches to get from the bedroom to the living room, it had been both frightening and frustrating for both of them.

"You should just stay in your chair." She handed him the remote as she pulled the lever to elevate his feet. "I'll bring you your breakfast."

"Peanut butter and honey," he weakly requested. She could tell their short journey to his recliner had worn him out, but it was just as well. At least he'd stay put for a while. That was something.

She went to the kitchen and was grateful to see that Jewel had already been up and had made coffee. Honey poured herself a mug, took a couple of sips, then set about putting CT's breakfast together, thanking the good Lord for peanut butter and honey!

She took out his tray, complete with his beloved sandwich, a banana, and a glass of milk. She set it on his lap, making sure it was secure, then kissed his forehead. But instead of smiling like he normally did when she kissed him, he frowned.

"Don't want this." He started to give the tray a shove, but she rescued it, catching the glass of milk just before it tottered off.

"What?" She set the tray on the coffee table and turned to look at him. "What's wrong?" she asked, trying to keep the irritation from her voice.

His brows were knit together as he glowered at her. She had no idea what was eating at him but suspected it was serious.

"CT," she said gently, "is something wrong?"

With his chin sticking out, he nodded firmly.

"Can you tell me what it is?"

He pointed a shaking finger at her. "You. Answer my question."

"Okay." She sat down on the edge of the coffee table, bracing herself for whatever was coming. "What's your question?"

His face grew even grimmer. "You made me go to that place."

"What place?"

"That place. You know. Where Miguel lives."

"Oh?" She nodded with a guilty feeling. "Yes, I took you there."

"That place. All those people. Laughing at me."

"No, CT. No one laughed at you."

"Yes! They did!"

She shook her head. "No, I never heard anyone laugh at you. I did hear you yelling at them and yelling at Miguel."

"You took me there. You made them laugh."

She was confused. "How would I make them laugh?"

"You made me go with no clothes."

"No clothes?" She felt her eyes growing wide. "What?"

"You know. You took me there. With no clothes."

"I took you there with no clothes?" she echoed.

"Yes! Just my underthings. My shorts."

"Oh no. That's not true."

"It is true. You made them laugh at me."

She was trying to process this. Why in the world would he think such a thing? But she knew she couldn't ask him. "CT, I love you. I would never, ever do anything like that to you."

"You did it. I know you did. I was there. I was embarrassed. They all laughed."

She felt as if she'd been punched in the pit of her stomach. How could he possibly imagine she would do something like that? Did he really think she was capable of being so cruel and barbaric? He'd been mixed up before, but never like this. How could his brain get so scrambled? And yet as she looked at him, she knew he believed what he was saying. How could she make him understand it was totally false?

"Hey there," Jewel called out as she came into the house.

"We're in here," Honey called back, trying to keep her voice even.

She walked into the living room. "Is this your coffee?" Jewel held out the mug Honey had filled.

"Yes, thank you." Honey took the cup with a slightly trembling hand.

"Are you okay?" Jewel frowned.

"Not exactly." Honey nodded toward CT. "Your father thinks I made him go to the Oroscos' party last night in his undershorts and nothing else."

Jewel started to laugh. "You're not serious."

Honey looked from her daughter to her husband, unsure of what to do. CT looked even more agitated now. "I am serious, Jewel." Honey inserted warning into her tone. "Your father is convinced this is true."

"Well, it's perfectly ridiculous." Jewel leaned down to peer into her dad's face. "Dad? You don't really believe that, do you?"

"I know what she did." CT glared at Honey. "She embarrassed me."

"No, you embarrassed yourself. Don't you remember?" Now Jewel paused as if she realized how ridiculous it was to ask that. "No, you don't remember, do you? I'm sorry. But I can assure you.

Mom did not take you to the barbecue in your undershorts." She stifled another laugh, then reached into her pocket to retrieve her phone. "Actually, I can prove it."

Suddenly Honey remembered the photos Jewel had taken. Bless her heart! Soon Jewel was scrolling through and showing them to her father.

"Remember the fishpond?" Jewel asked him. "You were counting the fish. I took this of you and Mom. You had on your Hawaiian shirt."

CT's brow was still creased, but he nodded almost imperceptibly. "That's me. That's my shirt."

"You were wearing it last night," Honey told him. "Remember when you fell down and used the shirt as a flag?"

CT looked cloudy again. "Flag?"

"Never mind." Honey reminded herself to keep it simple. She pointed to the photo CT was staring at. "See, that's you and me. It was taken last night. You had on clothes."

"Really?" He looked up at her with confusion. "I really did?"

"CT," she said gently, "I wouldn't lie to you. I love you."

"Why?" His voice cracked slightly. "Why do I think that?"

She pointed to her forehead like she often did when trying to explain things to him. "It's your brain, sweetheart. It's messing with you again."

"My brain?"

"You know how it's hard to remember . . . sometimes?"

"My brain is goofy?" he asked.

She shrugged. "Yeah. It's kind of goofy." She mouthed "thank you" to Jewel, hinting that perhaps she should make her exit now.

"I'll send you copies of the photos," Jewel called over her shoulder as she headed for the kitchen. "For posterity's sake."

Honey smiled as she picked up the breakfast tray. "Peanut butter and honey sandwich, anyone?"

CT nodded. "Yeah. Me. I want one."

She nestled the tray back in his lap and, once again, kissed him on the forehead. This time he did smile. Crisis averted . . . for the moment, anyway. Honey reached for the remote and turned on *True Grit*. She picked up her coffee mug, pausing to watch a scene where young Mattie gives crusty old Rooster Cogburn the what for. Too bad she couldn't take on CT like that feisty teen girl. But somehow she was pretty sure it would never fly here.

When Honey made it to the kitchen a little while later, Jewel was waiting for her, sipping on her own coffee. "What brought that on?"

"Who knows?" Honey sat down at the table. "But it sure threw me for a loop. I'm so glad you took those pictures last night."

"Me too."

"What's wrong with Dad's foot? I noticed the wrap."

Without going into all the details, Honey explained about last night. "I think he rolled it."

"Maybe that'll slow him down some." Jewel took an orange out of the fruit bowl and began peeling it. "Speaking of slowing him down . . ." She shared how CT had rearranged her studio again the day before.

"I'm sorry." Honey held up helpless hands. "But you know how he is."

"So I got to thinking. What if I put a padlock on the door?"

"Go ahead. But keep in mind that your dad will probably figure a way to break in regardless."

"I could post a Keep Out sign."

Honey looked sadly amused. "You can give it a try, but I'd be surprised if it worked."

Jewel reached across the table and took Honey's hand. "I know this is hard on you, Mom. I'm so sorry."

Sympathy always nearly undid her. And after the fiasco of last night, along with CT's wild accusations this morning, she felt particularly vulnerable. "Oh, Jewel," she muttered as she reached for a napkin. "Sometimes I just don't know how much more I can take." She poured out a bit more about last night.

Now Jewel started talking about other living situations and assisted care and memory care, and suddenly Honey felt overwhelmed. "Not now, Jewel." She held up a hand. "It's too soon to think about all that. I just needed to vent a little, but I'm done now." She wiped her eyes and nose. "I'll be okay."

"But, Mom, the time will come—"

"Not today, Jewel." Honey stood. "It's not today."

"Okay."

"I think I know where a padlock is." She went to her junk drawer and started digging through it until finally she extracted a large padlock and key. "Here. If you want to try this, it might work. Good luck."

"Thanks, Mom." Jewel gave her a little hug, took the lock, and went out the back door. Honey watched her stroll toward the barn. She looked so young and confident. Honey remembered having been like that once. And not so long ago either. Yes, Honey knew her daughter could be right. The time for seeking out more help for CT was probably coming. For all she knew, it was barreling at them like a freight train.

Just not today. Not yet. It was too soon. She sighed to remember the emotional moment they'd shared in the alfalfa field last night, both of them aching with the reality of all this . . . this hand that God and the universe dealt them. It was a lot, she knew, but she also still believed that with God's help they would manage. Somehow.

For now, though, she would go sit with CT. She was tired anyway. Both physically and emotionally. It would feel good to curl into the couch with a book in her lap while she pretended to watch the rest of *True Grit* with him. Maybe that was a good title for their life these days—*True Grit*! Yes, it did seem to fit.

22

Jewel

Life was calmer than usual the next few days, allowing Jewel to get her barn studio back in order, complete with a padlock on the door. But she knew it was just a matter of time before Dad would be back on his feet, prowling the farm, looking for something to "rearrange." Already, he was limping around the house with the help of an old cane Cooper had discovered in the attic. Naturally, Cooper was eager to have Grandpa mobile again since she loved working with the bees but still needed some coaching.

"I think it's almost time to harvest honey," Cooper told Jewel as they cleaned up the breakfast dishes. It was the second time she'd mentioned this.

"Didn't you and Grandpa just do it shortly after we got here? Is it really ready again?"

"That was spring honey, Mom. This is summer honey."

"But it was June."

"Yes, Mom." Cooper's tone was edged with impatience. "But the bees collected the pollen and made the honey in the springtime. So that honey was different than summer honey."

"Interesting. Can the bees really work fast enough to already have honey ready to harvest?" Jewel set the last plate in the dishwasher.

"Yeah. Now that the lavender is in full bloom, the bees have lots of pollen and can produce lots more honey. Better quality too."

Jewel paused to study her daughter. "How do you know all this?"

"From the book Grandpa gave me to read. Plus," she said, lowering her voice, "I took a peek at a comb yesterday, and it looked pretty full."

"Did you tell Grandpa?"

"Not yet. I was afraid he might try to hobble out there and trip over his cane and turn it into a big mess."

"Good thinking."

"But I'm not sure I should do it alone." Cooper frowned. "I don't want to do it wrong."

"Don't you think the honey can wait?"

"I guess."

"Well, I'd offer to help you, Coop, but the bees scare me. And I'm worried they'll sense my fear and get all excited."

"Grandma offered to help too. She's done it with Grandpa before. But she said her last time was last summer. And he could tell her what to do because his brain was working better then." Cooper put the milk carton away. "I feel like she's not so comfortable with it now. Although she said she'd get the honey in the jars and label them and all that, like she usually does. And maybe we can even start selling it in town."

"So does she think it's time to harvest now?"

"She said their first summer harvest was about this time last year. Plus, it's warmer than usual. That means more pollen and more honey."

Jewel appreciated her daughter's enthusiasm and knowledge, but she still felt uneasy about Cooper removing honey from the hives . . . possibly being attacked by bees. She didn't want to be a helicopter mom, but it was unnerving. "Do you think it could wait a few days? I mean, Grandpa's healing up pretty fast. He could be well in another day or two. Then he could help."

"I guess."

"Then please wait." Jewel frowned. "But tell me the truth. Did

Grandpa *really* understand what he was doing the last time? He didn't get confused or anything? I know there are a lot of steps. What if he messes one up?"

Cooper shrugged. "He seemed okay to me. And I've been reading about it and looking up videos on YouTube. I honestly think I could do it by myself, but having an extra set of hands would make it lots easier. I already asked Anna, but she's allergic to bees. Can you imagine being allergic to bees? I'd hate that."

Jewel patted Cooper's shoulder. "Well, I'm really impressed by how smart you are about all this bee biz. But I'd still appreciate it if you waited. I bet Grandpa would too. He probably enjoys harvesting honey."

Cooper nodded. "Yeah. Okay, I'll wait." She picked up the cooling tray she'd been rinsing. "Guess I'll go set this up before it gets too warm out."

Jewel was just closing the dishwasher when her mom came into the kitchen, letting out a long sigh.

"Something wrong?"

Mom gave a forced-looking smile. "Just your dad. Up to his tricks."

"What's he done now?"

"I made the mistake of organizing his dresser for him."

"Why is that a mistake?"

Mom poured herself a cup of coffee and sat down. "Probably because I labeled the drawers. I get so tired of trying to hunt down his socks and T-shirts and boxers after he rearranges everything. I thought if I labeled the drawers, it might help maintain some order. Then I put all his clean laundry in the right places. I hoped it would keep him from constantly asking me where something was."

"Seems like a good idea to me."

Mom sipped her coffee, then shook her head. "Nope."

"Why not?"

"He got mad. Told me I was treating him like a child."

Jewel laughed. "Well, he acts like a child."

"That's true. But he was insulted. He ripped off all the labels and dumped out all the drawers. Now our bedroom is a giant mess."

"Oh, Mom." Jewel patted her back. "I'm sorry."

"I told him to clean it up."

"Good."

"But I doubt he will. And if he does, who knows where he'll put things. We may never find anything again." She looked up with misty eyes. "But maybe it doesn't matter. For all I care, he can go commando."

Jewel laughed.

"Sometimes I think I should just step back, let him make his messes and live in them and suffer the consequences. I used to think that was a good way for kids to learn."

"Do you think it would work with Dad?"

Mom slowly shook her head. "No. By tomorrow he won't even remember what happened today. Consequences are meaningless to him. So it's pretty much pointless. Besides, if I let his messes remain, I have to live in them too. And I can only take so much chaos."

"It's a pickle for sure." Jewel reached for an old straw hat that no one seemed to claim. "I'm going out to water the garden before it gets too hot out. Unless you'd rather do it. In that case, I can ride herd on Dad."

Mom jumped to her feet, grabbing the old hat from Jewel. "I'll take the garden, thank you very much."

Jewel smiled. "Good choice. By the way, Aaron just texted me with exciting news. He said we can expect the delivery of the new house sometime this afternoon."

"I thought it was delayed until next week." Honey pursed her lips. "I wonder how your dad will react."

"Guess we'll find out."

"Speaking of Aaron Hanford." Mom put the straw hat on. "Did you ever get a chance to talk to Miguel about all that?"

"All that? You mean his relationship with his brother-in-law?" Jewel knew that's what Mom meant, although she sort of regretted how she'd confided in her now. She'd prefer to forget the whole thing. "I haven't seen Miguel since last night. I probably offended him."

"Well, I suspect you're making more of it than he is. I watched the way he was with you, Jewel. Something was—"

"Oh, Mom." Jewel gently but firmly nudged her mother toward the back door. "You better get to that garden before your plants are scorched. Don't want to send your lettuces into shock."

But after her mom left, Jewel let her mind wander. Should she try to square things away with Miguel? She still felt badly for the way they'd left it that night. But maybe her mom was right, maybe she was overblowing it in her head. Besides, she wasn't sure what to say. She did want him to understand there was nothing between her and Aaron, and she really hoped there was a way the two men might repair their relationship. As much for Anna's sake as anyone's. After all, Aaron was her uncle, and the Oroscos didn't have many relatives around here. Okay, she promised herself, if the opportunity arose, she would at least try to talk some sense into Aaron.

In the meantime, she knew she should check on her dad. He was clunking and thumping around in the master bedroom like something was amiss. Hopefully he hadn't tripped over his cane. As she tapped on his partially open door, she imagined him thrashing around helplessly. When he didn't answer, she tapped a little harder. "Dad?" she called. "Everything all right in here?"

"No," he growled.

Recognizing her invitation to enter, she found him sitting on the bed with clothes and empty drawers strewn all over the place. "Sounded like you were remodeling in here."

"Remodeling?" He looked up with a bewildered expression, a reminder to her that he was word challenged and took everything literally. Humor was lost on him. Well, unless it was his joke.

"What happened?" she asked lightly. "Who made this mess?"

"Honey did it."

"Oh . . . ?" She felt her brows arch. "So Mom did this?"

"Treats me like a child," he grumbled.

"Oh, right." She picked up a gray Carhartt T-shirt, folded it, and set it next to him. "Did Mom dump all these drawers out?"

He frowned with eyes downward, reminding her of a petulant child, but he remained silent.

"Do you need help putting it back together?" she asked gently.

"Together?" He looked up with bewildered eyes.

"Your clothes. Did Mom tell you to put them away?"

"Where?"

"In the drawers." She felt a wave of pity. What would it feel like to be so confused? And to imagine you were being treated like a child? What a dilemma. But how were they supposed to treat him when he acted like a child? When he threw these juvenile tantrums? She picked up another T-shirt and, folding it, placed it on the other one. While talking gently to her father, she continued gathering and folding clothes until he was sitting amid several tidy stacks.

"Should we put them back in the drawers now?"

He nodded just barely but remained seated. So she picked up a drawer and, after several tries, found its corresponding hole in the old dresser. She continued to make small talk as she tried to reinsert the other empty drawers. It was a little puzzling. No wonder he felt confused. "Now we can put your clothes back," she said cheerfully, wishing he would help. When he didn't budge, she just continued putting it all away until the bedroom was back in order. "There," she told him. "All done."

"All done," he echoed, nodding as if he'd done it himself. Then reaching for his cane, he slowly struggled to stand. "Tired."

"Did that wear you out?" She used a slightly teasing tone. But he didn't pick up sarcasm anymore.

"Yes. Need my chair."

"I'm sure you do." She took his other arm and guided him out of the bedroom and back to his recliner, where he collapsed and groaned as loudly as if he'd just plowed the back forty with a pair of old mules. "There you go, Dad. Just have a rest." She pulled the lever to lift his feet up. Sometimes he remembered how it worked but not today, it seemed. "Want the TV on?"

"Uh-huh. My movie," he mumbled. So she turned on *True Grit* and waited to see if he was satisfied with the familiar characters, if they were familiar. Sometimes she wondered. With him occupied and looking as if he was about to go to sleep, she slipped over to the side window and gazed out to where the new house would be set up later today. Hopefully without too much fuss from Dad. But like Mom kept warning her, anything and everything could go wrong when Dad was involved. Best not to get her hopes up.

23

Jewel

Although it was exciting when the new house arrived, it was also disappointing. Besides looking weird in all its newness, combined with those ghastly paint colors, the house was just generally unattractive, bordering on ugly. Especially compared to the charming old farmhouse and barn. It looked just plain out of place, and despite Jewel's eye for art, she had no confidence it could get much better. What had she been thinking?

Besides that, she was growing increasingly worried her parents would hate this new strangely bright building so prominently positioned on their farm. It just looked all wrong, and if Jewel could magically make it disappear right away, she would! It was only an eyesore, and it was embarrassing.

Fortunately, Cooper had gone to town with Anna and Marta, so Jewel was spared an adolescent opinion, at least for the day. But she could just imagine Cooper's sarcastic assessment on her mom's rash purchase. But then again, maybe not. Cooper had totally surprised her yesterday when she arranged to bring Mom's chickens back home from the Oroscos'. She'd promised everyone she would take complete responsibility for the six pretty hens. She would feed and water, gather eggs, and clean the coop. And the way Mom's eyes had lit up to see her familiar old hens pecking around the chicken yard . . . well, you'd think she'd won the lottery.

With Dad napping when the guys delivered and set up the house, Jewel had remained like a watchdog on the front porch, cringing the whole time at the thought of Dad waking in time to witness the spectacle. She couldn't imagine the fit he might throw. It was all she could do to keep herself from running out there, waving her hands like a wild woman, and demanding they take that ugly yellow house back. Somehow she had controlled herself.

Now with the movers gone, and all quiet, she walked around the exterior with a bucket of paint in hand, just surveying the awful mess she'd created. The ground all around resembled a war zone with dirt trenches and upturned soil. To Jewel's relief, Mom had simply shrugged when she saw it, wearing an expression that suggested she had bigger concerns to fret over. Or else she was just being polite. Then eventually, when Dad did wake up, he didn't even look out the window. He hadn't noticed the big, ugly yellow box yet.

She knew it was silly to start slapping on paint this late in the day, but she hoped it might bolster her spirits and hopefully encourage her parents . . . Maybe they'd all catch a vision for this place. She'd had a vision, hadn't she? She wasn't sure now.

"What're you doing?" Dad grumbled from behind her.

She jumped, then turned with a stiff smile. "Hi, Dad. I, uh, I'm painting the new house."

"Who lives there?" he demanded with a befuddled frown.

"No one lives there. Not yet." She set down her brush. "Want to see inside?"

"Uh-huh." He hobbled toward her, pausing to stab a big lump of dirt with his cane and nearly toppling over.

"Careful there." She took his arm. "It's still a work in progress."

"Progress?"

"Not done yet." She kept him balanced as he struggled on the overturned crate she'd set in place earlier as a temporary step. "A deck will be here. And a big front porch with an awning. Aaron Hanford will send his crew back later this week. We'll put some comfy chairs out here. See the great view you get? Good for sunsets."

He nodded with a blank expression, then stepped inside the house. Clearly, she was delivering too much information. Nervous about his reaction, she silently prayed he wouldn't throw a fit.

"See how spacious it is in here?" She waved a hand toward the great room with vaulted ceilings. "It's bigger than it looks from the outside."

"Uh-huh." He slowly nodded. "Nice."

She sighed in relief. "And the master bedroom is nice too. Bigger than the one you and mom share now. With an attached bath. Very handy." She led him into the master bath.

"Uh-huh," he repeated. "Nice." He tried one of the sink faucets, then frowned. "Broken?"

"Not hooked up yet. But by the end of the week, the water should work."

"Oh? Okay." He peeked at the shower. "Big."

"Yes. Very easy access too."

"Access? Uh-huh."

"Want to see the kitchen?"

"Uh-huh." He slowly followed her out, looking on with appreciation as she showed him the stainless appliances. She talked up each item and each speech was followed by his repetitive comments. But at least he wasn't criticizing the place. She wasn't sure if it was because she sounded so happy and upbeat or if he really liked it, but she wasn't complaining.

"I know it's hot in here right now." She opened a window. "But when the electricity is on, it will have AC."

"AC?" He cocked his head to one side. "CT? AC CT?"

"Yes. AC for CT." She smiled. "Good joke. We'll have to tell Mom that there's AC for CT. That should make her laugh."

He chuckled. Then she showed him the two smaller bedrooms and bath on the other side. "That's pretty much it," she told him.

"Big," he said again. And although most wouldn't describe it that way, she understood what he meant. To his confused mind, it probably did seem big. Especially since he'd never seen it before.

"Who lives here?" he asked again.

"Whoever wants to," she answered. "It's such a nice house.

Maybe Cooper and I will live here. Or you could live here, Dad. If you wanted."

"Me?" He frowned. "I don't live here."

"You *could* live here . . . if you wanted," she repeated herself, more slowly now to make sure he understood.

"Too big. Too much for me."

She shrugged. "Well, we can wait and see. You might decide you like it."

"No chairs. No bed," he proclaimed like that settled it. "Not my house."

Without saying anything, she led him to the front door, pausing to look out before she helped him down the step. "It's nice to have just one step," she told him. "And it will be bigger and sturdier soon."

He nodded with an absent look as he patted the exterior siding. "Like my bees."

"Huh?" Now she felt confused. "Your bees?"

He patted the house again. "Like bees. And honey too."

"You mean the color? The yellow?" She frowned at the bright paint. "I guess so. Yellow like bees and honey." She laughed. "Good call, Dad."

"It's a bee house."

"Well, they probably like their beehive houses better. Should we go check on the bees, Dad?" She didn't really care to get that close to the hives, but it seemed a good distraction at the moment. Keep him in good spirits.

"Uh-huh." He turned in that direction, and she linked her arm with his, walking slowly alongside him.

"It's a good house," he finally said. "Like honey too."

"Yeah, Honey likes it too," she said, uncertain as to which honey he meant.

"My Honey?" he asked.

"Yes. Mom. She likes the new house too." Okay, *like* might be a stretch since Mom had seemed more worried than pleased over this new addition to their property. But her worries had more to do with Dad than the house at the moment.

Cooper was just crossing over the field toward them, coming back from the Oroscos' house. Hopefully Dad wouldn't get worked up over that. Jewel waved at her daughter and, relieved that Cooper wanted to accompany her grandpa to the hives, Jewel stepped back.

"We need to get that honey out before it gets too messy, Grandpa," Cooper said.

"Yeah." He nodded eagerly. "Get the honey out."

"Want to do it now?" Cooper sounded hopeful. "I got the harvesting stuff all ready, but I was waiting for your ankle to get better."

"My ankle is fine." He shook his cane as if to prove this.

"Is it still warm enough?" Cooper asked him. "I mean, for the honey to flow good enough. We could get the honey out now if you want."

"Yeah. Get the honey out."

"Well, I'll leave you two experts to it," Jewel told them. "And I'll go help Mom with supper."

Dad and Cooper were already headed for the hives. Relieved to escape the perils of honey harvesting, Jewel went inside and, finding Mom at the kitchen sink, she began to report, perhaps a bit too enthusiastically, about how impressed Dad had seemed with the new house.

"That's something." Mom sliced into an early tomato. "But he could be totally opposed to it by tomorrow."

"I know, Mom." Jewel washed her hands. "But I was thinking about putting a few pieces of furniture over there. You know, to make it feel more homey. Dad seemed concerned that it was unfurnished."

Mom nodded absently. "That might help some."

"But if you're not sure"—Jewel studied her mom's furrowed brow—"Cooper and I can live there instead. It's actually growing on me, and I could start moving my stuff into it—"

"What do you really think of it?" Mom asked a bit sharply.

"Well, I'll admit I was having some second thoughts earlier. And the color is horrific. Although Dad kind of liked it." She reached for a cucumber to slice. "But I'm going to get it painted as fast as I can. And then I'll add the flower boxes and spruce up the front porch and a few more things. I think it might look like a cottage. Plus, the interior has lots of possibilities."

"You think it could look like a cottage?" Mom sounded a tiny bit hopeful. "I wouldn't mind living in a cottage."

"A comfortable cottage."

"I did like the way the Oroscos' house looked when we were there the other night. And I remember how much I disliked seeing it at first." Mom's smile looked weary. "So do your best with it, Jewel. One way or another, we'll figure things out. Excuse my lack of enthusiasm. I suppose I'm just tired."

Jewel reached for her mom's paring knife. "You go put your feet up. Let me finish getting supper ready."

"I'm not that tired—"

"Please, take a break while you can." Jewel gave her mom a gentle shove. "I insist. Dad is occupied with Cooper right now. Take advantage of it."

Mom's smile grew bigger. "I should know better than to argue with my strong-willed daughter. Who knows where that might lead."

"Good thinking." Jewel shook the knife at her. "You know me when I put my mind to something." But as her mom left, Jewel wondered how strong-willed she would be if her plan for the new house didn't go as smoothly as she hoped, or if it unraveled completely. She'd been counting on restoring the old farmhouse into a B&B. But if her parents put the kibosh on that . . . well, she and Cooper might be stuck in that bright yellow house for a while. Not exactly the artsy retreat she'd been dreaming of—and no extra income to go with it. Time would tell.

It wasn't until the following morning that Jewel discovered her dad had once again gotten into the barn. She'd already gotten a couple of early hours of painting done on the new house but, in need of more rags, she'd gone to the barn to discover the broken padlock on the door. Inside, she was dismayed to see that someone, a.k.a. her dad, had gotten into her paints. Several new tubes of oils had been emptied into a tin can and stirred around with an old paintbrush. Nearby, strokes of muddy multicolored paint were smeared across the wall like graffiti. Was this Dad's idea of art?

She heard a rattling sound in the back of the barn, near the area where she'd stored her art pieces and belongings from California. Hopefully Dad wasn't getting paint on her things. "Dad?" she called out. "Where are you?"

"Huh?"

"What're you doing?" She went around an armoire to find her father crouched down with a crowbar in hand, studying her antique trunk with a suspicious, or maybe it was devious, expression.

"Who put this here?" he growled at her.

"I did, Dad. It's mine."

"No." He shook his head, grunting as he stood upright. "Miguel did this. He snuck it in here in the night."

She stepped closer to look him squarely in the eye. "No, Dad. It was me."

"I saw him. Miguel takes my stuff. Hides my tools. Locks my barn." He shook the crowbar menacingly. "Bad, bad man."

"No, honestly, this is *my* stuff. And I locked the door."

He just stared at her now, his expression impossible to read. Confusion? Realization? Anger? It was anyone's guess.

"I locked the door because you keep getting into my stuff."

"No. Not me. Miguel did it."

She reached for the crowbar and, to her relief, he didn't resist. "You broke the lock, Dad. And you came in and messed with my paints."

"It was . . . Miguel." His tone sounded weaker. Was he questioning himself?

She pointed to the oil paint smears still moist on his hands. "That's my paint." She picked up his cane, which had been cast aside, handed it to him, then tugged him by the arm over to where he'd "decorated" the old pine plank wall. "See, Dad, that's the same paint as what's on your hands. You did that, and I know it."

"I did *that*?" He suddenly looked very forlorn. "I . . . don't remember."

"It's okay." She softened her tone. "I understand. You want to help, don't you?"

Eyes downward, he nodded glumly.

"You just want something to do. Right?"

He looked up. "Uh-huh."

"Do something helpful. Useful. Right?"

He nodded eagerly.

"Well, I need your help. I have something that needs painting."

His eyes lit up. "I can paint."

She wasn't so sure about that but wondered what harm he could do. Especially if she kept him on the backside of the new house. Only the lower half since she was using the only ladder on the other side. The few windows back there were high, and with no landscaping, Dad couldn't mess up anything on the ground. Even if he slopped the paint on haphazardly, it would get some coverage on, plus it would keep him busy.

As she helped to get him set up with paint tools, she felt a smidgeon of temporary relief. Hopefully he'd stick with it long enough to give everyone a break. The upside for her was how excited Dad had gotten about his new chore. He didn't even seem to notice that the paint was eliminating the yellow color that he thought resembled bees and honey.

With the radio tuned to a classical station, Jewel commenced painting on the front side. Already this new house was looking much better. After an hour, she went around to check on her dad and was pleasantly surprised to see he'd gotten a large patch fairly well covered. And what he'd missed, she could easily touch up later.

"That looks great, Dad," she told him. "I hope you're not wearing yourself out." She pointed to the lawn chair and water bottle she'd set up nearby. "Remember to take breaks when you need to."

"Uh-huh." He nodded without looking up, continuing to slowly brush on paint. "I'm okay."

Pleased by his fortitude, she returned to work on the front. If

Cooper came to help in the afternoon, like she'd promised, things should really speed along. Hopefully Aaron's crew would get the front deck done sometime this week. She could just imagine it with some potted plants and attractive outdoor furniture. And if Aaron delivered on the shutters he'd told her he was making in his garage, the house should be looking rather sweet in no time.

"Hello there."

She turned around to see Miguel walking toward her with paint tools in hand. "What is this?" She smiled as she went to greet him.

"Cooper is at my house, and she mentioned you're painting today."

"That's true."

"And that she was supposed to help you this afternoon?"

"Yes." Jewel nodded.

"Well, Anna was begging her to go with her to the swimming hole with some friends." He shrugged. "So I thought I could substitute." He swiped a paintbrush through the air like Zorro. "I'm not half bad as a painter."

"I would never dream of refusing free help." She grinned, then lowered her voice. "But I'll warn you, my dad is painting back there. And, well, you know how he can be."

Miguel nodded somberly. "I know. But I thought if I was helping, maybe it might get through to him that I'm not the enemy."

She thought about Dad's harsh words in the barn this morning but simply shrugged. "Guess we'll find out." She pointed to the section on the other side of the front door for him to start on. "I hope this doesn't backfire," she said quietly. "Please, forgive us if it does."

He looked reassuringly into her eyes. "No problem."

"Thank you," she whispered, suddenly worried that her dad might pop out and sling a bucket of paint at Miguel's head. But instead of fireworks, like she was prepared for, they both just painted companionably side by side, with classical music playing soothingly. She would've enjoyed making small talk with Miguel, or even offering some kind of apology for the way their conversation had digressed at the barbecue, but she didn't want to risk being overheard by Dad.

Besides, she reminded herself as she moved the ladder to the corner of the house, Miguel must not be holding any grudges if he wanted to come help today. Especially at the risk of being greeted with a shotgun by her unpredictable father. Or more realistically, a crowbar or paintbrush. At least she'd hidden the crowbar. She peeked around the side of the house to see her paint-speckled dad contentedly sitting in the lawn chair, staring up at the sky and peacefully sipping water. "Good for you, Dad," she called out with a smile and a wave. He tipped his head with a big grin. A good sign that all was well. At least for the moment. And that was good enough.

24

Jewel

The house was nearly painted and electric and water hookups completed by the time Aaron's construction crew showed up, followed by Aaron in his big black pickup. To Jewel's delight, Aaron had the shutters and flower boxes she'd requested in the back of his rig. "And I had my guy stain them for you too." Aaron held up a reddish-brown shutter. "You said mahogany, right?"

"They're perfect," she exclaimed. "Thanks so much."

"If you like, I'll put them up for you," he offered.

"That'd be fabulous." She smiled.

"And the boys should finish up with your deck and awning by the end of the day."

"I've already been putting things inside," she said. "But I can use the back door to go in and out while they're working in front." She pointed to the rear of the house. "And my dad is working back there, finishing up painting."

His brows arched. "He's able to paint?"

"Well, he's slow . . . and I have to touch-up after him. But he's loved doing it, and it's kept him busy." She didn't mention how she'd had to stop him from attempting to go inside with a can of exterior paint. After that, she'd kept the doors locked.

Aaron shook his head. "Must be a challenge, eh? Watching out for a crazy guy."

"We don't use that word around here," she told him. *Not out loud anyway*, she thought since she sometimes said that word in her head. Like when he'd "rearranged" the house-painting tools yesterday. She'd been ready to get an early start only to find everything gone. Thanks to a drippy trail of green paint, she'd soon discovered that Dad had painstakingly moved everything into her studio area in the barn, where he'd "neatly" stacked it all on her worktable.

She understood how he thought he was helping, but it was hard not to feel irritated by his "craziness." Thankfully, she'd managed to hold her tongue and simply asked him to help her take it back outside in order to finish up their project. She'd made it seem like he was helping, and he was none the wiser.

As she walked around the exterior of the house with Aaron, going over the last details and making sure they were on the same page, he stopped. His eyes were on her dad, who was painting around the water spigot.

"Hey, old man," Aaron said in a patronizing tone, "whatcha doing?"

Her dad looked up at him with a puzzled expression, then he grunted. "I'm painting. Can't you see?"

Aaron chuckled. "Yeah, I see that. But you don't need to paint that spigot."

"Spigot?" He frowned. "It's paint."

Aaron laughed. "I know it's a spigot, but it's galvanized and doesn't need to be painted. In fact, paint might make it hard to turn."

He stood up straight, looking Aaron in the eyes. "I'm painting my house."

Jewel felt pleased to hear Dad lay claim to his house. She also felt defensive. "That's right, Aaron. It's his house and he can paint it." She patted her dad on the back. "You're doing good work, Dad. Keep it up."

"But it might dry hard and be impossible to turn," Aaron told her in an irritated tone.

"Don't worry." She tugged his arm, talking quietly as she led him over to the back door where she wanted his guys to make an adjustment to the step. "I go around after him and clean things up," she whispered. "The spigot will be fine."

Aaron rolled his eyes. "Well, I guess you know what you're doing."

"We just muddle along the best we can." She turned her attention to where his crew was laying out the wood for the front deck. "It looks like you've got things under control, so I'll leave you to it." She held up her phone. "I'll be in my studio. If you have any questions, just call me."

He grinned. "You promise to answer?"

"Of course." She gave an uneasy smile, worried that last comment was about more than just business. "And please, just let my dad paint in peace. It's been a blessing to keep him busy. We all appreciate it." She forced a bigger smile. "It's wonderful to see this house coming together. I can't wait to see the deck and awning and everything all in place." She finger-waved, then scurried off to the barn. A couple hours of undisturbed creative work sounded amazing right now.

After her dad's mess with her oil paints, Jewel had decided to take up acrylics again. And, really, it made perfect sense. With acrylics' tendency to dry quickly, she had to move fast. And with stints in her studio limited, a faster work pace agreed with her. And it challenged her as an artist too. In the past she'd been guilty of overthinking her creative process, leading to stalling and procrastination. Too worried about the "perfect" outcome and the judgment of others, she'd almost paralyzed her inner artist. Being squeezed on time forced her to just jump in and do it.

But after a couple hours, which had flown by, Jewel was interrupted by the sound of loud voices and angry shouting. Suspecting her dad was involved, she dropped her brush in a jar of water and sprinted outside.

"Stop doing that right now," Aaron was yelling. "Can you hear me, old man?"

Horrified at the tone Aaron was using, Jewel ran even faster, arriving breathlessly at the new house where there appeared to be some sort of standoff. Aaron, Dad, and Miguel were standing in a triangle, with Aaron's crew watching on with what looked like amusement.

"What's going on?" Jewel demanded.

Aaron turned to her with a flushed face. "Your dad has made a big mess." He pointed down to the deck. The beautiful raw cedar boards were partially painted with the green house paint.

"Uh-oh." Jewel grimaced.

"He didn't know." Miguel stepped closer to her dad. "He thought we wanted that painted too, Jewel. But it's okay—"

"Okay?" Aaron turned to Miguel with a glowering expression. "How is it okay? And what do you mean *we*? What business is this of yours?"

"Miguel's been helping me paint." Jewel went over to stand by Miguel, grateful for the progress he'd made with her dad these past few days. They hadn't actually exchanged words, but Dad hadn't yelled at him either. He had almost seemed to appreciate Miguel's help. Baby steps maybe, but progress all the same.

"So Miguel told your dad to paint the cedar boards while we were having a break?" Aaron looked accusingly at Miguel. "Do you plan to replace that wood?"

"If it needs to be replaced." Miguel rubbed his chin. "But maybe it would make more sense to just get some good heavy-duty deck paint and cover the whole thing."

"Paint a cedar deck?" Aaron laughed. "It figures *you'd* want to do that."

Although Jewel didn't like the idea of painting the wood, she hated that Aaron was being mean even more. Both to her dad and Miguel. "That's a great idea." She nodded. "We can paint it the same color as the stained wood. And it'll probably be even more durable."

Aaron shook his head. "Won't look as good."

"What do you think, Dad?" she asked him. "Should we paint the deck?"

"Uh-huh." He nodded.

"Okay then." She smiled at him. "But I'll get a different color. And you can paint it, Dad. How about that?"

"Okay."

"Did you finish in back?"

"Uh-huh."

She took his brush and bucket. "Well, it's lunchtime, and I'm sure Mom's got something all ready for you. You better get in there."

"Uh-huh." He narrowed his eyes at Aaron. "My house. I can paint it."

She patted his back. "That's right, Dad. It is your house."

"My house," he muttered as he walked away.

"Tell Mom I'll be in later," she called, knowing full well her dad would forget by the time he got inside. Now she picked up a paint rag. "I'm going to go check on where he painted in back." As she walked away, she couldn't help thinking she was slipping away from a powder keg about to explode. Leaving Aaron and Miguel together could be a mistake, or maybe it could be a step toward healing. She could hear male voices as she headed around the house.

She silently prayed for peace as she bent down by the water spigot. Using the damp rag, she attempted to wipe off the gummy paint her dad had slapped on hours earlier. It took a little elbow grease, more water, and several turns of the faucet, but she finally got the spigot working properly. Then she touched up a few missed spots of paint and was just standing up when she heard footsteps. Hoping it was Miguel, she was dismayed to see Aaron approaching.

"Does it work?" he asked.

"Yep." She turned on the water to prove it.

He scratched the back of his neck. "You really gonna paint that deck?"

"My dad's going to paint it."

"Waste of some real pretty wood."

"Maybe not." She tossed the rag into a pile of paint things. "I got to thinking how slick a wet wooden deck can be. I think I'll look for some kind of deck paint that's not slippery. Not such a fall hazard for my parents."

He shrugged, then shoved his hands in his pockets. "So Miguel's been hanging around here?"

"He is our neighbor," she said defensively. "And my friend. In fact, his daughter Anna, who is also your niece by the way, is very good friends with my daughter. And Marta, Miguel's mother, has been a good friend to me and my mom."

"I don't have anything against my niece or even Marta." His countenance darkened. "It's Miguel who disgusts me."

"Why is that?" She stepped closer, looking him squarely in the eyes. "What did he do that's so horrible, Aaron?"

"He caused my sister's death."

"She died of cancer. How can you possibly blame Miguel for that?"

"She didn't get the treatment she needed."

"How do you know that?"

"I know."

"I don't understand how you could *know* that. Or how you could blame Miguel. It's perfectly ridiculous. It's like you've imprisoned yourself in a jail cell of unforgiveness."

"If Beth hadn't been living on that low-life Air Force base, she would've gotten better treatment. She would've survived."

"How do you know that?" she demanded.

"I just do." He looked down.

"Well, I wasn't around and don't know the details, but I don't see how your anger and hatred help anything." She placed a hand on his arm. "Look, Aaron, I'm sure you loved your sister a lot. And obviously it hurts you that she's gone. But I wonder how she would feel about how you treat Miguel. And Anna. I'd think it would break her heart."

Aaron looked at her with misty eyes and humphed. "I dunno. Maybe you're right."

"Think about what Beth would want now. For her daughter . . . at least."

He barely nodded. "Okay, I will."

She sighed, then decided to change the subject. "After all the brouhaha about the deck, I completely forgot to look at the shutters and flower boxes."

He brightened. "Well, you should come have a little look-see." He led her around to the front where the crew had gone back to finishing the deck. She stood back and admired the changes.

"I can hardly believe this is the ugly yellow house I saw on your lot a couple weeks ago. It's downright cute now."

"Not bad, if I do say so." He nodded. "How's everything inside? All the appliances and mechanicals working okay?"

"Care to check it all out?" She led him inside, where the AC was keeping it nice and cool. They walked through and gave everything a good once-over and, as far as they could see, it all worked fine.

"It's gonna be nice," he observed.

"I was so glad to hear Dad calling it *his* house. I'm still not a hundred percent sure he will want to live here with Mom, but I'm hoping."

"Do you think he even knows where he lives? I mean, no offense, but he seems pretty far gone to me. Surprised you don't want to put him in some kind of care place."

She bristled but tried not to show it. "Mom wants to keep him with us as long as possible."

"Might get to be too much."

"It might." She studied him as he looked out the window. He was probably the kind of guy who would put his own folks into assisted living without blinking an eye. And maybe that was okay. For him. But she planned to respect her parents' wishes as long as she could. And like Mom kept reminding her, they'd take things one day at a time.

25

Jewel

Jewel had gotten into the habit of strolling around the farm property in the evening. She liked to slip out right around sunset. With her parents usually on their way to bed and Cooper occupied on her phone or playing some game with Anna, this became Jewel's time of peace and quiet. A gentle regrouping after a hectic day. And today, after the disagreement over the paint mishap and the noise of the construction crew all afternoon, the serenity felt extra welcome. As she walked along the edge of the fragrant lavender field, she could breathe deeply, silence her nagging doubts, and almost imagine that everything was going to work out.

"Jewel?"

Over her shoulder, she spied Miguel walking the fence line toward her. She waved eagerly. She had been hoping to express her appreciation for how he came to Dad's defense today. She leaned against the fence with an extended hand. "Hello, neighbor."

His eyes lit up as he grasped her hand. "Hello back at ya, neighbor. Nice evening for a walk."

She smiled in amusement that he was still holding on to her hand. "Can you smell that lavender?"

"You bet. When the wind blows this way, it drifts right over to us. Nice." He gently released her fingers. "Want any company on your stroll?"

"Absolutely."

"Mind if I come over there?" He bent down, and she gladly helped to hold up the wires as he slipped through the fence.

"Welcome." She beamed at him. "I wanted to thank you for your help with Dad today. I'm not totally sure what all transpired, but I'm glad you stepped in. I think Dad was too."

"Well, I was coming over to see if you needed any more help with painting, but when I saw Aaron and his boys there, I almost headed the other way." His strides lengthened, as if he was getting worked up about it.

"But you didn't?" She quickened her pace to match his.

"Nope. Because I heard yelling, like something was wrong. I came on over and when I got there, your dad looked pretty upset so I stuck around, trying to be a peacemaker. Although to be honest, I might've made things worse. Aaron wasn't too pleased to see me."

"I'm sorry about that. Aaron can be, uh, difficult. Sounded like he was pretty rough on my dad too."

"I guess he doesn't get it." He slowed down his pace.

"He doesn't get a lot." She grimly shook her head.

"I don't think compassion comes easily to him."

That was an understatement, but Jewel didn't say so.

"So was your dad okay afterward?" He stopped walking and turned toward her with a concerned expression. "I felt so sorry for him when Aaron scolded him like that."

"I'm sure he's forgotten all about it now."

"Oh, good. I told my mother about the whole thing, and she said I should've thrashed Aaron." He chuckled.

"Well, I think your idea of painting the deck was actually really good. Thank you." She studied his face, his firm chin, straight nose, dark expressive eyes . . . so handsome. She felt an unexpected warmth rush through her and wondered if he felt anything similar. "It seems like your relationship with Dad has improved. I mean, while we were painting the last few days, he seemed to soften up toward you. And this morning probably helped too."

"Yeah, I think we're making progress. Either that or he's starting to forget his old grievances."

"Maybe both. But he did seem grateful to you for being there this morning. That was so nice to see. I really hope he can stay on good terms with you." For her sake as much as anything, but she didn't plan to say that.

"Me too." He paused for a long moment, gazing intently into her eyes until she felt like she was melting inside. Were her knees actually growing weak? Could that still happen at her age?

"I mean, since we're neighbors and all," she muttered nervously, feeling more and more like a smitten schoolgirl and embarrassed by it. Really, she was too old for this silliness. *Aren't I?*

"Yeah. Neighbors should get along," he spoke quietly.

"Yeah . . ." Despite trying to look away, she kept her gaze fixed on his dark eyes, silently wishing he'd take her in his arms and kiss her—passionately. Was there a more romantic spot for a first kiss than a lavender field at sunset? But what then? Was she really ready for this? *Was he?* She stepped back, taking in a deep breath to steady herself, to get ahold of her emotions.

Miguel stepped back too. "So, you and Aaron . . . It's none of my business, but I'm curious. Are you more than just friends?"

She thought back to their conversation at the barbecue when he'd questioned her about Aaron. "As far as I'm concerned, Aaron and I are just friends. Business acquaintances, really."

"Well, I noticed how he looked at you today." Miguel folded his arms in front of him with an intense expression. "It seemed almost territorial. Then on my way home I glanced over there again and saw you and Aaron behind the new house. I could be wrong, but it seemed, well . . . somewhat intimate."

She could tell he was uncomfortable telling her this, but she also realized how it might've looked that way. "That's because I was trying to get through to him. About forgiveness. About restoring a relationship with you and Anna. He's still so angry about his sister. I don't understand it, but he clearly blames you."

Miguel glumly shook his head. "I'm well aware of that."

"Why?" she demanded. "I just don't get it. Why can't he let it go?"

Miguel shrugged. "I honestly don't know. I've tried to talk to him in the past, but he just shuts me down. Finally, I just gave up."

"Is there any legitimate reason for him to blame you?" She knew this sounded accusatory, but she had to know. "I just don't understand why he is so convinced it's your fault Beth died. She had cancer, right? So how can he hold you responsible for that? If he wants to blame someone, why not blame the doctors?"

Miguel pulled off his cowboy hat and ran his fingers through his thick, dark hair. "Like I said, I don't know exactly why. Well, besides the fact that he's never liked me. But I've gone over and over Beth's illness and treatment plan. At the time, I believed we were doing our best."

"Not according to Aaron."

He nodded. "I have some theories about why, but I'm not totally sure. It's probably a long story. One that I don't completely understand."

"I have time."

He studied her. "Okay. How about if we go sit down and I'll try to explain it to you?"

"Sure," she agreed. "If you want to. I mean, I don't want to drag you through something that's painful for no good reason."

"I think I'd like you to know."

She pointed to the new house. "We could talk in private in there. I put a couple chairs inside."

"Sounds good." And to her delight he took her hand as they walked.

She unlocked the new house and, after Miguel sat down, she got them cold drinks from the fridge. "I've been trying to get this place more comfortable for Dad. You know, so he can get used to it. And hopefully want to live here."

"It's a nice house. But I suppose he's used to his own home. I can see how it might be a problem."

"That's what worries me." She sat down with a sigh. "But worst-case scenario, Cooper and I will move in here."

"That wouldn't be too terrible, would it?" He smiled.

"No, of course not. But we came in here to talk about you." She leaned back. "I'd really like to hear your story."

She tried to reserve judgment as Miguel explained about how he'd put his career in the Air Force at the top of his priority list, above his wife and child, admitting that he now realized that was wrong. "To be honest, I hadn't planned to marry as young as I did. But Beth was persuasive. I was still young and somewhat driven to succeed in the Air Force. I was selfish too. And I wasn't ready to have kids when Beth got pregnant with Anna that first year. Sure, I was happy to become a father, but it felt like too much too soon." He shared how Beth and Anna lived on the base in New Mexico and not always under ideal conditions. "I was too focused on work. As a result, I was probably neglectful. But I was trying to save up for our future together, you know, for when I retired from active duty. It wasn't that far off, and my dream was to farm." He sighed. "But I should've focused more on the present than the future."

"That still doesn't explain why Aaron blames you for Beth's death."

"Well, I was close to having my twenty years in . . . then Beth got sick. We both thought the Air Force had pretty good medical coverage, but Beth's family didn't agree. Particularly Aaron. Beth urged me to finish my twenty years in order to get the full benefits of retirement, and she seemed happy with her doctors in New Mexico." He shook his head. "She really played down her illness. Maybe for Anna and me. Or maybe we were all in denial. But she seemed too young and healthy to be seriously ill. Anyway, by the time we retired and came here, her cancer had really progressed and—" His voice cracked with emotion. "It was too late to do much about it."

"And that's the only reason Aaron blames you?"

"As far as I know."

"Well, I understand that he loves and misses his sister, but it seems totally unfair to hold you responsible, Miguel. You're not God."

"But saying it all out loud just now"—he leaned back and released a long sigh—"might be therapeutic, but it also makes me see how it could look like that . . . to Aaron, anyway."

Jewel considered this without replying. Maybe he was right. Or maybe Aaron was just a self-centered jerk. "I just wish you and Aaron could mend this relationship. At least for Anna's sake. It's not healthy for any of you."

"I agree." Miguel stood up. "In fact, I think I'll revisit it with him. I'll try taking more responsibility this time, and I'll really apologize for it."

"It can't hurt to try." As she got to her feet, Jewel wasn't sure Aaron would even listen, but she appreciated Miguel's willingness. "I don't know if it'd make any difference, but if having a neutral third party present would help, I'm available."

Miguel held his arms open for a hug, and she gladly went into them. As good as it felt to be there snug against his chest, she could tell it was a brotherly platonic hug, and she was determined not to make more of it than that.

"Thanks," he said as he let her go. "I needed that."

"Sure." She grinned. "Anytime."

"And thanks for listening too. I needed that as well."

"I'm grateful you would share that with me. I feel like I know you and your situation better now."

"I better get home before my mom and Anna get worried about me. They're both such little mamas sometimes." He grasped her hand with a warm squeeze, then told her good night. She remained on the front deck, watching as he trekked through the twilit alfalfa field, probably heading for the gate this time. But as he disappeared from sight, she felt a piece of her heart go with him and, although it wasn't chilly, a slight shudder rushed through her. What was she allowing herself to get into?

26

Jewel

It felt almost miraculous. Over the next few days, Dad seemed to decide the new house belonged to him. With Mom and Cooper's help, Jewel managed to move more furniture into the house, slowly sneaking in new pieces each day. But it looked homey enough that Dad enjoyed spending time in his new living room. They also took over kitchen things and some food, including Dad's beloved honey, peanut butter, and milk. Eventually they moved in his recliner and TV, and the new house became his daily go-to right after breakfast.

Finally, with Dad's "help" they moved the bed and bedroom furniture and even more household goods, and just like that, Jewel's parents were ready to spend their first night in the new house.

"We'll have a honeymoon," Dad said as the four of them stood on the front deck to say good night. "Get it?" He laughed. "Me and honey . . . our *honeymoon*."

"Oh, CT." Mom playfully swatted his arm. "You're such a romantic."

"That's a great name," Jewel said. "How about Honeymoon Cottage?"

"Yes," he agreed. "Honey and cottage . . . cheese. I'm hungry."

Mom laughed. "You're in luck. We have lots of food in our new kitchen."

"I hope you both enjoy your first night here." Jewel presented them with the bottle of champagne she'd gotten for the occasion. "I thought we should christen the house, but let's not break this on its bow. You two can enjoy it later. With your cottage cheese and honey." She winked.

"And this is for you too," Cooper handed her grandfather a bouquet of lavender and daisies she'd arranged in a mason jar. "I picked these for your new house, Grandpa."

"Uh-huh." He nodded with appreciation. "Nice."

Mom held the champagne bottle high. "I now christen this house Honeymoon Cottage."

"God bless," Jewel said.

After her parents went inside and Cooper dashed off, Jewel stepped back to admire Honeymoon Cottage. The covered front deck, recently painted with slip-proof deck paint, now looked inviting with its pair of matching Adirondack rockers and several overflowing flowerpots that Mom had planted and set into place. Mom had also filled the flower boxes with geraniums, alyssum, and ivy. It all looked so sweet and inviting that Jewel was pleased with the results.

Because she was familiar with Dad's mood swings, she understood how quickly he could change his mind about something. But if he didn't make this transition, she felt certain that she and Cooper could be quite comfortable there. With a whole lot less work than the big plans she had for transforming the farmhouse into a functioning B&B. Yet her mother was so thrilled about her new little house that Jewel hoped and prayed it would all work out. As she walked back to the farmhouse, she wondered what it would feel like to have the whole thing for just her and Cooper.

"Do you think Grandpa will make it there for a whole night?" Cooper asked as Jewel came up the porch steps. "What if he comes back here in the middle of the night? Where will he sleep?"

"Your grandma plans to give him one of his *relax* pills."

Cooper laughed. "That sounds dumb. Why not just say Xanax?"

"I know. But that's what your grandma calls them. For Grandpa's sake." Jewel remained on the front porch, leaning on the railing as she gazed out toward the new house and admired how charming it looked from here in the dusky light. Such a great transformation. "I sure hope he makes it through the night," she said quietly.

"Well, Anna and I worked hard on their bedroom." Cooper leaned against the railing too. "We took pictures of how everything was set up in their old bedroom. We tried to make their new bedroom look the same. Even the pictures on the wall. But I wonder if Grandpa will even notice."

"Well, it can't hurt. Thanks so much for your help."

"It was kinda fun."

Jewel gave Cooper a sideways hug. "I don't know what I'd do without you, Coop." With her arm still around her daughter, they went into the house.

"Mom?" Cooper closed the front door. "I keep meaning to tell you something."

"What's that?" Jewel turned with concern. Was something wrong?

"It's just that, well, I'm really glad we moved up here."

"Oh, Coop." Jewel hugged her. "I'm so glad to hear that."

"It just feels right."

She hugged her daughter more tightly. "It does to me too."

"I mean, I know it's not perfect and we'll probably still get into some fights." Cooper stepped back with a sheepish smile. "But mostly I think it's a good thing."

Jewel nodded. "Me too. Mostly."

"I wish Grandpa would get well."

Jewel felt close to tears now. "Yeah. Me too."

"But even if he doesn't . . . I'm glad we're here."

Jewel nodded. She was blinking back grateful tears, and no more words were exchanged. A good thing since Jewel was pretty sure she'd fall completely apart. But they understood each other. She knew that.

To Jewel's relief, her father didn't come storming into the farmhouse in the middle of the night. That was something. And the next morning, after giving her parents plenty of time to get up, Jewel knocked cautiously on the front door. Her mother opened it with a big smile.

"Does this mean you're doing okay?" Jewel asked quietly.

Mom pointed to where Dad was sitting in his recliner, eating a banana and watching *True Grit*. "So far, so good," she whispered.

Jewel sighed. "And you both slept okay?"

"No problems." Honey nodded toward her old house. "Maybe even better than over there."

"Do you miss it, Mom?"

She glanced at her husband, then pursed her lips. "I suppose I miss it about as much as I miss everything else nowadays . . . but I'll get used to it."

Jewel nodded somberly.

"So don't worry. Your dad is happy, and that makes me happy. Thanks again for all you did to get us in here."

"Of course. Also I had tentatively scheduled Aaron and his crew to start renovating the farmhouse next week. I guess I'll give him the green light now." Jewel glanced around the spacious living room where most of her parents' furnishings were in place. It really did look good. Not too cluttered and busy. It would be an easy room to be comfortable in. "But if things change . . . I can always pull the plug on the B&B."

"That's good to know, but I think we'll be fine here. Your dad seemed genuinely pleased with everything this morning. I think he's enchanted with Honeymoon Cottage." She actually giggled. "He thinks we're on vacation." Jewel wasn't sure if it was her imagination, but Mom actually seemed to be blushing.

"Well, I hope you can pretend you're on vacation, Mom."

She nodded. "It does sort of feel like that. And there isn't much to do as far as housework goes. Everything is so clean and new. And since you and Cooper seem to be managing everything else, well, I might just relax and hang with your dad today. Let him feel settled and at ease."

"Good plan." Jewel stepped back. "Coop and I can move in more of your things if you want. Just let us know."

"I'm thinking I'd like to become a minimalist." Mom smiled. "For a change."

"Hey, why not? If it's okay, I'll just store your other stuff in the barn or the attic."

"Makes no difference to me. I do believe less is more. Simple is better." She suddenly hugged Jewel. "Thank you so much for pushing for this, sweetie. I'll admit, I had my doubts, but it looks like you were right."

Jewel gave her a thumbs-up, then stepped away. "Enjoy!"

As Jewel walked back to the farmhouse, she replayed her mother's words. Once again, she felt taken aback by the unexpected praise. Values and expectations seemed to be changing . . . for all of them. Jewel just hoped the new house would really make life simpler for her parents. Poor Mom already had more than enough to deal with. If the new house helped, even a little, it was well worth the effort. And being part of the solution felt rewarding. Hopefully it would remain a solution.

Jewel refilled her coffee mug, then looked around the kitchen. Despite outfitting the new house's kitchen to her mother's satisfaction, this one looked barely touched. And it wasn't just from Mom's collecting over the years. Jewel knew that her parents had inherited two previous generations of stuff when they took over the farm.

Cooper came into the kitchen, stretching her arms. "How are Grandma and Grandpa doing?"

"They seem fine." Jewel watched her daughter open the fridge. Still in her oversized T-shirt and with bed head, she yawned as she removed the orange juice.

"You're up early."

"Yeah. Anna and I have a business meeting at her house this morning."

"Business meeting?" Jewel's brows shot up.

Cooper gave a half smile as she filled her glass. "It's Anna's idea that we should start a business. You know, to make money before school starts."

Jewel sipped her coffee. "What kind of business?"

"Well, Anna has all sorts of ideas. I suggested doing something with the lavender. Grandma said that was okay with her."

"That's a nice idea."

"Or maybe we could have a honey stand on the edge of town. And when it's fall, we could do pumpkins there too." She downed the last of her orange juice, then opened a yogurt container.

"Good ideas." Jewel reached up to the top of the fridge to remove a porcelain rooster cookie jar, then she used a damp dishrag to wipe away what looked like several years' worth of dust. At one time her mom had been into rooster decor in the kitchen. "Or you could manage a big yard sale right here on the farm. There's loads of stuff we need to get rid of, and I'm sure Grandma would let you keep a fair-sized portion of the proceeds."

Cooper tipped her head to one side. "That might be interesting."

"You've seen the attic and closets and how much is packed into this place. Who knows, you might even find some treasures."

"Even more interesting." She dipped her spoon into the yogurt and stirred.

"Grandma thinks it's okay to proceed with the renovations for the B&B, so I plan to start clearing things out ASAP. For the time being I'll probably store it all in the barn, but if you're not interested, I might see about hiring someone to clear it out for me."

"Okay. I'll definitely mention it to Anna at our meeting." With a banana in one hand and her yogurt in the other, Cooper made her exit. Jewel smiled as her barefoot daughter with her lime-green-tipped hair pitter-pattered away. If anyone would have told her just a few months ago that this is where they would be now, she would not have believed it. And compared to her previous life, the gorgeous downtown gallery, her swanky condo, artistic friends . . . some might say she was slumming now. And yet she was grateful and felt richer than ever.

She texted Aaron that she was ready to proceed with some remodeling projects, then she sat down to list her priorities, keeping her ever-shrinking budget in mind. Thanks to her experience renovating the gallery, she had some idea of what was involved and respected how construction costs always ran higher than initial estimates. So she was determined to keep things minimal and, hopefully, do some of the work herself.

Fortunately, the farmhouse had good bones, including hardwood floors, quality woodwork, and thanks to Mom, updated plumbing fixtures. What it really needed most was kitchen updates with industrial appliances, a good heat pump to provide adequate AC for the second floor, and a number of safety-related fixes. She also wanted to repaint both inside and out, get some new furnishings and, of course, finally add her artistic design flare in the finessing of the B&B. Hopefully, she could stretch her finances to cover it all, plus get a website built and her inn up and running by autumn. It was a lot, but she felt confident it was doable with hard work.

She'd just set her list aside when she heard Cooper screaming for help outside. Dropping her notepad, she raced for the back door, yelling for her daughter. Hearing her voice in the vicinity of the beehives, a cold fear washed over her as she raced to find Cooper, praying that she wasn't being attacked. But when she found her, there were no bees in sight. Just Cooper standing there with teary eyes.

"What is it?" Jewel asked breathlessly.

"The bees!"

"What about the bees?"

"They're gone."

"Gone?" Jewel frowned, her heart rate returning to normal. "Oh, they're probably just gathering pollen."

"No. I looked through the lavender. Not a single bee in sight. And the hives are empty. All of them. The bees are gone, Mom." Cooper pointed over her shoulder. "And Grandpa's headed over here. He'll freak."

"What is it?" Dad asked them with a puzzled expression. "Yelling? Who's yelling?" He narrowed his eyes at them, as if trying to place who they were or why they were here.

"It's nothing," Jewel answered. "Cooper just got excited."

He frowned. "Cooper?"

Jewel pointed to her daughter. "Cooper. Same name as you, Dad."

As if he knew, Dad went straight for the hives, bending down to listen. "No buzzing."

"Grandpa," Cooper said gently. "I think the bees might be gone."

"Gone?" He stood up straight. "Not all gone?"

"I was putting out fresh water trays and the hives sounded so quiet, so I looked in the lavender," she spoke quickly. "And even in the pumpkin patch. You know how they like the blossoms, but—"

"Blossoms?" He looked over his shoulder.

"But they weren't there, Grandpa. I can't find a single bee."

"Bees? Gone?" He looked panic-stricken now. "Where?"

"I don't know—" Cooper's voice cracked with emotion. "Where could they be?"

"Bees? Bees?" he called out as if he could bid them to come. "Bees?"

"Mom?" Cooper looked at Jewel with tear-filled eyes. "What should I do?"

"I have no idea." Jewel was worried. Dad would probably have a complete meltdown. "Maybe they'll come back."

Cooper got out her phone. "I'm going to google it. Maybe I can find answers." She located a website and began to read aloud a list of strange reasons bees might abandon a hive. None of them sounded particularly promising.

"Maybe they just got bored and wanted a field trip," Jewel suggested, hoping to lighten the mood. Not that it helped. Tears were streaming down Cooper's cheeks, and her dad was clearly in a state. Mumbling to himself, he slowly circled the hives, waving his arms and pathetically calling the bees as if he was calling a wayward dog to come home.

"It'll be okay, Dad. The bees will be fine." Jewel put a comforting hand on his shoulder, following him as he circled, trying to calm him and hoping his wobbly steps weren't about to make him topple over. At the same time she felt seriously irritated at the stupid bees. Why did they have to go off and leave like this? And why did anyone keep bees in the first place? She just didn't get it. If the little buzzers never came back, she thought she'd probably be glad. Well, as long as Cooper and Dad got over it. At the moment, she wasn't sure they could.

27

Jewel

Jewel was about to text Mom about this new emergency, to tell her to bring out Dad's relax pills, when she saw her mother's pale blue bathrobe flapping in the wind as she raced toward them.

"What's going on?" she asked as she joined their odd assembly by the hives.

As Jewel explained about the missing bees, her phone began to chime. "It's Miguel," she finally said. "I better answer."

"Jewel," he said a bit urgently. "Have you checked your beehives this morning?"

"As a matter of fact, the bees seem to have evacuated."

"That's because they're over here."

"What do you mean?"

"There's a gigantic swarm on the old oak tree behind my house. My poor mama is so terrified for Anna that she's locked them both in the bathroom."

"Oh no. What should we do?"

"I already called my friend Walter. He's an expert beekeeper. He's on his way, but he lives on the other side of town."

"Oh, good. Thank you."

"But before Walter gets here, I wanted to check to see if they were your dad's bees. You know, before he hauls them away."

"Hauls them away?" She blinked. "How do you haul bees away?"

"I'm not too sure myself, but Walter seems to know what to do. And he's got whatever it takes on his truck to do it with."

"That's wonderful. Thank you so much. I'll tell Dad. He's very upset."

"I don't know how long it'll take," Miguel said, "but I'll keep you posted."

She thanked him again and hung up. "Dad," she called out. "We found the bees!"

"The bees?" His eyes grew wide. "Found?"

"Miguel has found the bees." She spoke slowly to be sure he understood.

"Miguel found the bees?" Cooper asked eagerly. "Where?"

Jewel explained about the swarm in the oak tree. "Miguel and his friend will bring the bees back here."

"Miguel? Has my bees?" CT's brow furrowed.

"Your bees are in Miguel's tree, but he will bring them home for you."

"Miguel?" Dad sounded more hopeful. "Bees coming home?"

"Yes!" She nodded eagerly, realizing this was another opportunity for Miguel to score points with her dad. "Miguel has worked it all out. He will get your bees back here today."

"Today?"

"Yes. But it might take a while."

Mom took Dad by the arm now. "Enough time for you to eat breakfast."

"Breakfast? I ate breakfast."

"No. It's still in the kitchen. Waiting for you. Come on." Mom steered him away from the hives, gently guiding him back to the new house.

"I know you were supposed to meet with Anna," Jewel told Cooper. "But because of her bee allergy, she is locked in the bathroom."

"Locked in the bathroom?" Cooper rolled her eyes. "Sounds like overkill."

"It was Marta's idea. Trying to protect Anna, I guess."

"Poor Anna." Cooper's mouth twisted to one side as she studied her phone. "But I still wonder why the bees left. Do you think I did something wrong, Mom? I hope the hive doesn't have a disease. And I don't think it's lack of water. I give them water every day." Her tears were gone, but her eyes were still troubled.

"I have absolutely no idea what went wrong, Coop, but Miguel's friend Walter is an expert. Maybe you can ask him."

She nodded. "Yeah. I do want to talk to him. I'm going over to the Oroscos' right now. Even if Anna's locked up, I can still go out and see the swarm. Maybe take pictures. I bet it's big."

"Okay." Jewel cringed inwardly to imagine an aggravated bee swarm. "But please, be careful."

"Don't worry, the bees know me." Cooper was already sprinting toward the alfalfa field.

Jewel took a deep breath and silently prayed that all of them would remain safe from the swarm of bees. It was one thing for Dad and Cooper to act so casual around the hives where the bees were mostly contained, but a loose swarm of agitated bees sounded terrifying. What if they were angry about something?

Honey

By the time Honey got CT back to the new house, he was still fully aware of his missing bees but had already forgotten that Miguel was working to get them back.

"My bees," he lamented. "Where are my bees?"

Honey attempted to explain again. Then directing him to their old kitchen table, she pointed at his breakfast of scrambled eggs and peanut butter toast and helped him sit down. She knew the eggs would be cold by now, but she also knew CT probably wouldn't notice that. She refilled her coffee mug, then sat down across from him, but seeing how upset he still was, she decided to get one of his relax pills. Thankfully, he never protested taking one. Maybe he thought it was one of the many vitamins she was always shoving at him.

She returned with orange juice and the pill, waiting for him to take it. "Looks like a nice day," she said as she sat back down.

"Why did they leave?" he asked as he chewed on a bite of toast.

"The bees?"

"Uh-huh. Why?"

"Like Jewel said, they wanted a field trip."

"In my field?"

"I guess they got lost," she added. "But they are all together."

"Together?"

"Yes. You know how bees stay together?"

"Uh-huh." He nodded as if this made sense.

"And Miguel is bringing them home."

"Now?" He started to stand.

"No." She put a hand on his arm to stop him. "Later. I'll tell you when."

"Okay." His hand trembled as he picked up his fork. "Okay."

They ate breakfast in silence now. Not unusual for them these days, but for some reason Honey missed the friendly little chats they used to have more than usual today. Maybe it was the new house. Honeymoon Cottage. The sweet name seemed to hold so much promise. Promise that it could never deliver. Yet CT had been in such good spirits last night that she'd almost imagined they were their old selves again and actually on a real vacation. Drinking champagne to music that she had put on, playing a game of cards where she let CT win, and going to bed happy and enjoying the old familiar snuggles that CT never seemed to forget.

But in the light of day, the stressful upset over the missing bees and eating a cold breakfast, well, it was a letdown. Not that she would tell anyone. CT obviously wouldn't understand, and she didn't want to hurt Jewel's feelings. And really, it seemed silly to even feel this way. So trivial. After all, she was here in a new house. With fewer responsibilities than before. She should be grateful. And she was. But still . . . She glanced across the table where CT was sitting with his mouth hanging open, like it so often did nowadays. His plate was mostly empty, and it looked like his relax pill was working. That was something. She stood up and smiled.

"You know, CT, I bet if you watch *True Grit*, the bees will be back before you even know it."

"Huh?" CT looked confused, and she realized that she'd used too many words. That and he'd probably temporarily forgotten the bees.

She picked up their empty plates and tried again. "You can watch your movie." She stopped herself from adding that he should rest until his bees came home. Let sleeping dogs lie.

"Oh, yeah." He slowly shoved himself to his feet. "My movie."

Honey guided him to his recliner. Everything in the new house felt closer and easier. Fewer rooms for CT to get lost in. And somehow the smaller house didn't feel crowded. Really, it was a good thing they'd made this move. Honey would get used to it, eventually. And fortunately, despite their rocky start to the day, CT hadn't mentioned that anything was different even once. Maybe he'd already forgotten the old farmhouse. How long until he forgot her? He seemed to get confused while looking at her sometimes, and she knew the day would come when he wouldn't know her at all. She felt a lump in her throat when she considered the inevitable. But what would she do about it then? She inhaled a deep, soothing breath. She didn't need to think about that now.

As she took her time to clean up the breakfast things, putting the tidy little kitchen back into apple-pie order, Honey remembered her old friend Donna and how they'd reconnected at the barbecue, even discussing a follow-up coffee date. Of course, after CT's outburst against their poor host, Honey had been too embarrassed to call Donna for a coffee date later that week. And then she blamed her procrastination on her demanding life and too many distractions. But maybe she'd give Donna a call and invite her to meet up once the missing bees debacle was settled. Because Honey knew she needed someone to talk to. Someone outside of her family. More than ever lately.

Whether it was right or wrong, Honey had acquired the habit

of putting up a strong front for Jewel and Cooper. Sometimes she felt like a phony, but not wanting to trouble them with her problems, she kept her ever-growing concerns to herself . . . and to God. She knew the girls had their own struggles. Raising a sometimes-willful adolescent wasn't easy for anyone. Add to that Jewel's big B&B plans and setting up Honeymoon Cottage, well, it was enough to deal with. And young Cooper, still getting used to everything here, was building new friendships, meeting neighbors, and just being a confused teenager . . . that was a lot.

So grateful for their help, Honey didn't want to upset things with her heartaches and fears. And the truth was CT did frighten her at times. There were those moments when he was so disoriented he didn't even recognize her. And more than once he'd accused her of being in cahoots with Miguel and even being romantically involved with the young man. That was worse than ridiculous but very real to him.

Then there were mornings when he was so disoriented he thought he was in his childhood home and she was his mother. Sometimes he got so confused and agitated over the imaginings, she couldn't predict what he'd do. And she was equally unsure of what she should do if something went seriously sideways. And she knew that it could. And it probably would . . . eventually. She just didn't know when "eventually" would arrive.

The dementia books she'd read and reread described this behavior as the final stages of FTD. And for the last stages, when a patient became too difficult, the only option the experts recommended was supervision in a full-time memory care facility.

Honey hated the idea of this. She knew that CT would hate it even more. At least the old CT would. That can-do CT. The man's man who'd farmed and hunted, driven and repaired farm trucks and tractors, been king of his outdoor world—that man would rather be six feet under than locked down in some bleak nursing home reeking of urine and disinfectant. And who could blame him? If she were in his shoes, she'd feel the same.

She could still remember the conversation they'd had after his father had been put in an institution like that. His dad had been diagnosed with early-onset Alzheimer's, but now Honey suspected it had been FTD as well. Concerned for his dad, CT and Honey had flown to Phoenix to visit him in his care facility. But they'd been appalled at the nursing home. CT had been so upset, he'd gotten into a full-blown argument with his stepmom, Dorothy, criticizing the poor woman for allowing such a travesty.

Honey glanced over to see that CT was now asleep in his chair, his familiar movie playing loudly. She sighed and refilled her coffee mug, then sat down at the kitchen table. She ran her hand over the familiar worn wood. She was afraid the old-fashioned farm table and chairs would look out of place in their new, modern house, but it actually seemed to lend some sweet charm to the place.

Maybe CT, like his dad, would be so impaired by the final stages, he wouldn't know the difference if he needed to be in a nursing home. Tears began to flow at the thought of this. She'd been crying more and more lately. Not when anyone was watching, of course, because it only seemed to stress others out. But in her quiet moments alone, she'd been trying to let her tears flow freely. She'd read that her pent-up emotions could raise her blood pressure, and she sure didn't need more of that!

Honey tore off a paper towel strip and used it to blot her eyes and blow her nose, then taking a deep breath, she looked out the kitchen window. Taking a few more slow, deep breaths, she gazed across the rich green alfalfa field. So peaceful, so calming. And then she began to relax, realizing she really did feel a bit better after a short cry.

She whispered her favorite prayer a few times and was grateful for its soothing. "Let go and let God." Sometimes it was all she could muster in the form of faith.

She tossed her damp paper towel in the trash, then turned back to check on CT. Not to her surprise, he was gone. His favorite disappearing act. Just vanish without a word. That man! Despite his awkward shuffling walk, he could still slip away unnoticed when he wanted. She checked the master bedroom and bath. Finding both empty, she knew he'd gone outside. Probably in search of his beloved bees.

28

Jewel

To distract herself from obsessing over Cooper and the missing bees, Jewel got serious about emptying out the kitchen cabinets, removing everything except the essentials needed for her and Cooper to fix basic meals. Then she packed all the odds and ends, some that probably hadn't seen the light of day in decades, into the recycled moving boxes she'd stashed in the barn for just this purpose.

Finally it was past noon and she'd received no word from her daughter, so she shot her a text. In return, Cooper sent back a couple of disturbing photos of a huge living ball of honeybees clinging to the trunk of a big tree. Did Coop think that was reassuring?

Still, determined not to worry, Jewel picked up one of the heavy boxes to take out to the barn. She was barely down the back porch steps when a familiar pickup drove a bit too fast up the driveway. What was Aaron doing here now? He pulled right up to the porch, then jumped out and insisted on taking the box from her. Relieved for the help, she gladly handed it over.

"It's heavy." He huffed as he took it.

"It's full of old cast iron." She walked beside him.

"Throwing it out?"

"No, I think it was my great-grandma's. I plan to have some

kind of sale. There's so much old stuff to get rid of. I'm hoping Cooper will help."

"Might be some valuable pieces," he said as she opened the barn door for him.

"Maybe." She pointed to a stack of boxes. "Thank you."

"No problem." He grinned as he set the new box on top.

"So, what are you doing here?" she asked.

"I came to give you an estimate. You texted that you were ready to move forward, and I wasn't busy."

"Oh, wow." She smiled. "Thanks. That'd be great. Come on into the house and look around. It's kind of a mess since we were in the midst of getting my parents moved into the new house."

"How's that going?"

"So far, so good. Well, except for Dad's bees."

"His bees?"

As they went inside, she explained about the AWOL bees, and he just laughed. "Maybe it's a good thing. Somebody like your dad probably shouldn't be working with bees in the first place."

She bristled at his judgment but held her tongue. "Well, Cooper's been helping him a lot. She's becoming quite the expert. And it would probably break both of their hearts not to get the bees back." To change the subject, she got out her list and began to go over what she wanted done in the kitchen, waiting as Aaron made his notes.

She walked him through the house, pointing out a few other things she thought might need attention and then down to the cellar to talk about the duct system for the new heat pump.

He grimly shook his head. "Might need to replace it all."

"Really?"

"Well, I'll let my HVAC guy decide. But I wouldn't be surprised." He closed his notepad. "Are you sure you want to make all these renovations?"

She blinked. "Yes, of course. Why shouldn't I?"

"It's a lot to invest."

"Like I told you, I want to create a B&B," she reminded him. "I hope to generate some income and—"

"Well, if you really want to generate income, you should just sell the whole place."

"Sell the whole place?" She couldn't hide her aggravation now. "This is my parents' farm, Aaron. I can't very well sell it. And even if I could, why would I?"

"Because it would make a good development."

"A development?"

"Yeah. You could put in thirty to forty building lots here. Do you realize how much you could make on a deal like that? And I could help you—"

"Aaron"—she held warning in her tone—"this is my parents' property, and I have no plans to—"

"It's really your mom's property," he interrupted. "Your dad is too far gone to have an opinion—"

"Oh, don't fool yourself, my dad still has opinions." She didn't care to mention some of his opinions were a little offbeat. "And as for my mom, I'm sure she has no intention to sell."

"Maybe not today. But when your dad is gone . . . well, she might be ready to move on. Selling this property would give her the freedom to live anywhere, do anything."

Jewel hadn't really considered this and wasn't sure she even wanted to.

"Look, I'm not trying to be a downer, Jewel. But you should face facts."

She reached for the stair railing then looked him straight in the eyes. "You're right, this is my mom's property. In fact, it was her family that left it to her. And my mom loves this farm and the countryside. I seriously doubt she will ever want to sell it."

He held up his hands defensively. "Hey, I wasn't trying to step on toes. I just thought it was something you might want to consider. For everyone's best interest. Your mom's not getting any younger. And running a B&B and maintaining this property, well, it could turn into a real money pit. Ya know?"

She did know. But she wasn't about to admit it as she trudged up the stairs. Back in the kitchen, she folded her arms in front of her and cocked her head to one side, narrowing her eyes into an I-mean-business look. "So, Aaron, I guess I'll look for another contractor to handle my renovations. Obviously your heart's not into it if you think we should just sell the whole place." She strode toward the living room and, as a clue their conversation was over, opened the front door. "I appreciate your expertise, but I think it's time to part ways." Instead of waiting for his response, she went onto the front porch, eager to send him packing.

When he joined her out there, he looked slightly crushed. Or were those crocodile tears? She didn't really care. She just wanted him gone. She leaned against the porch railing with a no-nonsense expression, arms folded in front. But instead of leaving, he planted himself in front of her.

"Oh, Jewelie, don't overreact when someone gives you some friendly advice. It might be hard to hear, but someone needs to say it. Can't you see I care about you and am just trying to look out for your welfare? For you and your daughter and your mom. Three women out here alone . . . with your dad going downhill so fast. A B&B might seem fun at first, but things break down, weather can get rough in winter, a roof can leak, a pipe can break. It gets expensive. And before you spend one more penny on this place, well, it just seems responsible for me to point out another option."

He stepped even closer to her, planting his hands on the porch railing on either side of her and looking tenderly into her eyes. "You're a beautiful woman. A talented artist. An intelligent businesswoman. Do you really want to be tied down to an old run-down farm? You could sell and reinvest in a comfortable, new, low-maintenance home for you and your daughter and mom. You might enjoy living in town with neighbors next door. And you could start up a new art gallery, like the one you used to own. It could be handily located right downtown where folks can get to it and enjoy it. Think about all the traffic you'd never get out here in the country. And you could be a real asset to the community. Join the chamber and get involved . . ."

She couldn't deny there was an appeal to all he was saying . . . and yet, as she glanced over her shoulder to where the pumpkin patch was coming on strong, then over to where the lavender field was in full bloom, she felt a tug on her heart. She'd enjoyed years of city life but, to her surprise, she hardly even missed it now.

"I get what you're saying," she said stiffly. "I appreciate you caring enough to speak your mind." Uncomfortable being boxed in against the railing, she decided to just buck up and speak her piece. At least she had his full attention. "It might seem foolish to you, but I need to pursue this dream. Mom and Dad are happy as clams in the new house, Cooper is actually happy here—she likes the country life—and I have a real vision for this farmhouse. It'll take work and perhaps have some big challenges, but I think it could be a profitable B&B, and I can imagine a really cool gallery in the barn. It won't be open every day, but for special exhibits by invitation only. And I want to run artist retreats and maybe even make this into a venue for music festivals or weddings or who knows?" She shrugged. "I just can't give it all up. Not yet, anyway. If you don't want to help me renovate this money pit, as you call it, please, just say so, and I'll find someone who—"

"Okay, I'll do it," he said quickly. "And I'll do it for less than any other contractor in town. Under one condition."

She felt cautiously curious. She narrowed her eyes. "What's that?"

"If it becomes too much for you, and things don't go like you planned . . . and if you decide to utilize my idea to create a division on this property, then you will let me handle it for you. Can you agree to that?"

"My mother would have to agree first," she pointed out.

He nodded. "I know. But if you reach that place, can you agree?"

She considered his condition. In her heart, she seriously doubted she'd ever want to see this property subdivided and developed in the way he'd described. So she wasn't really worried about making that concession. "Okay, I can agree to that."

He stuck out his hand. "Shake on it?"

"Yes." She extended her hand. "You have my word."

He beamed as he clung to her hand. And now she noticed the

sound of wheels coming down the driveway. She looked over to see a pair of pickups. One was unfamiliar but had a load of some white boxes in back, but the second one looked like Miguel's, and both were driving slowly. She noticed Cooper in the passenger seat of Miguel's pickup, waving eagerly and pointing at the truck leading the way.

"The bees," Jewel said suddenly. "That must be Miguel's beekeeper friend. They're bringing the bees back." She nudged Aaron aside. "I'm going inside. I don't want my bad vibes to upset the bees." She scurried into the house and, to her dismay, Aaron was at her heels. As she closed the front door, she realized how easy it would be for Miguel to misconstrue what he'd just witnessed on the porch. And she had no doubts he'd been looking. So just like Desi would say to Lucy on Jewel's favorite old sitcom, she'd have some 'splaining to do.

Honey

It'd taken about twenty minutes of searching before Honey found CT. She couldn't help but smile to herself when she'd discovered him tinkering with his old farm truck. With the hood up, he was leaning over the engine, talking to himself and acting like he was about to make it start. He didn't even notice the wires that she'd had Miguel disconnect to ensure the pickup stayed in place. With the temptation of a peanut butter and honey sandwich, she'd lured him back into the house. And swinging wide of the hives, she'd managed to distract him from noticing how quiet they had been today.

Once they were at the house, she realized how worn out he was from that little excursion. He could barely make it up the single porch step, and she had to help him inside and into his chair. He collapsed into it with a grunt, then looked around. "Where is this?"

"Honeymoon Cottage. Home," she said as she reached to pull

the lever to elevate his feet. Then to make sure he didn't wander off again, she gently removed his shoes and set them out of sight in the bedroom. She smiled as she came out. "Remember Honeymoon Cottage?" she said cheerfully. "Our vacation home."

He brightened then nodded as if he remembered, although by the blank look in his eyes, she felt fairly certain he didn't have a clue what she was talking about. Just the same, she continued playing the game. "How about a mimosa?" she said lightly as she opened the fridge, removing the leftover champagne and some orange juice. She poured their beverages into goblets and then brought them over to him. "We'll make a toast."

"Toast?" His brow furrowed. "Peanut butter and honey?"

"Yes. But first this." She clinked her glass to his, making him smile. "Here's to us, CT. And to Honeymoon Cottage."

His eyes twinkled as he clinked his glass against hers for a second time. She held hers up and took a sip, and he imitated her. "Now I'll go make that peanut butter and honey sandwich," she said. "I'm sure you worked up an appetite."

"Uh-huh," he muttered. "Honey."

She hummed as she fixed his lunch. Despite their rocky start, she wanted to make their first full day in Honeymoon Cottage as pleasant as possible. Just as she set his plate on his eating tray, she got a text. She set down his milk and pulled out her phone. It was Cooper, saying the beekeeper was rounding up the bees and that they would be bringing them home within the hour. She also warned that Walter wanted them to keep things peaceful and quiet when they arrived. In other words, keep CT inside.

Honey considered informing CT of the good news but realized that would simply agitate him all over again. She'd let it go for now. When the bees were safely returned, he could go visit them. Thank goodness Miguel had stepped in. Hopefully CT would appreciate his neighbor's help in this bee rescue. She would make a point of reminding CT of this and of what good friends they had in the Oroscos.

CT had barely finished chewing his last bite of sandwich when his head tipped back. By the time Honey stealthily removed the tray, he was snoring like a chainsaw. Even as a pair of pickups drove slowly up the driveway, CT didn't flinch. While Honey tidied up the kitchen, she kept one eye on her husband, knowing how easily he could slip away. Then she sat down on the sofa, opened a deck of cards, and proceeded to play solitaire on the coffee table. Determined to keep him inside, she would stay at her post until she was certain the bees were safely in place.

Finally, she heard an engine and got up to see one of the pickups gone and just Miguel and Cooper out in front of the farmhouse. Since CT was still sleeping, and she assumed the bees were back, she decided to go investigate. Knowing she would need to reimburse Miguel's friend for this help, she grabbed her checkbook.

"How did it go?" she asked Cooper and Miguel when she was within earshot.

"It was exciting," Cooper told her. "Walter knew just what to do." She pointed to some new hives. "He's loaning us those hives since that's what he used to help move them. And he checked our hives and thinks they're still okay. Hopefully the bees will relocate later in the day."

Honey held up her checkbook. "Well, I should pay Walter for his trouble."

"I gave him your phone number," Miguel told her. "He'll call in a couple of days to see if you guys need to keep his hives."

"Did he say why the bees left?" she asked.

Cooper shrugged. "He wasn't sure. He said the conditions here looked okay, but maybe something upset them."

Honey couldn't imagine what would upset bees like that, but she was watching Miguel. He looked troubled, and his eyes were fixed on the house. That's when Honey noticed Aaron Hanford's pickup parked over by the barn. "Looks like Aaron came by," she said.

"Yeah." Miguel just nodded. "I should be getting back."

Cooper exchanged a glance with Honey. Then they both thanked Miguel for his help and watched him get into his pickup and pull around.

"He seems upset," Honey said quietly.

"He saw Mom and Aaron on the porch," Cooper told her.

"So?"

"So, it looked like they were, uh, kind of embracing or something."

"Really?" Honey couldn't believe it. That didn't sound like Jewel.

"Yeah. Miguel got real quiet after that."

"Oh." Honey didn't know what to say. "Well, I'm sure it was nothing."

"Miguel really likes Mom." Cooper bit her lower lip. "And I thought Mom liked him too."

"How do you feel about that?"

Cooper shrugged. "Miguel is a good guy. I like him. Lots better than Aaron Hanford." She made a face. "Even if he is Anna's uncle, he kinda creeps me out."

Honey smiled. "Well, I'm sure your mom can straighten whatever happened out." She peered toward the house. "What's she doing, anyway?"

"I told her to stay inside. Walter said not to let anyone or anything upset the bees." She pointed to the new house, where CT was standing on the front deck, looking their way. "That probably goes for Grandpa too. Can you keep him occupied?"

"Why don't you come talk to him," Honey suggested. "That might distract him." She put an arm around Cooper's shoulders. "I bet you haven't had any lunch."

"Yeah, I'm starving."

As they walked toward the new house, Honey thought how comforting it was to have a sweet granddaughter like Cooper around, green hair and all. She stopped herself and stared at Cooper, shocked to see no more lime green. "What happened to your hair?" she asked. "The green is gone."

Cooper shrugged. "I had Anna trim it. Think Grandpa will notice?"

Honey laughed. "Who knows?" She playfully tugged the thick ponytail. "I used to have thick, dark hair just like this before it started turning gray."

"Mom says I look like you." Cooper smiled. "And I saw those photos in your bedroom. I think maybe I do too."

"Well, I'll take that as a high compliment." Honey felt a youthful spring in her step as they stepped onto the deck. Granddaughters were good medicine! After fixing Cooper some lunch and seeing her situated with CT while they watched some goofy animal videos that Cooper pulled up on YouTube, Honey slipped out the back door and called Donna.

"Hello," Donna answered cheerfully. "Is this Honey?"

"Yes, how did you know?"

"I still have your number saved in my contacts."

"That's nice. Thanks. So I was wondering if you'd like to meet for coffee this week?"

"I'd love to, except I'm in Alaska."

"Alaska?" Honey walked around to the front deck.

"Yes. I got a great deal on a cruise, and we decided to just go for it."

"Oh, that sounds fun." She sat on a rocker, trying not to feel jealous.

"It's delightful. Perfect weather. Beautiful scenery. Fabulous food. Oceanside suite with a balcony. You and CT should take an Alaskan cruise, Honey."

"Oh, I don't think CT would be up for that." She shuddered to imagine the trouble her husband might get into on a cruise ship. Trying to tinker with the engine room or losing his balance and toppling overboard.

"There are some older couples here. Some with dementia challenges too."

"And they feel safe?"

"Seems like it. Might be a good break for you. You could just relax while someone else does the cooking and makes the bed."

"It does sound lovely, but I'm not sure how relaxing it would be if I was worried about CT. But I'll think about it." Of course, Honey didn't think she'd ever take CT on a cruise like that. Just getting to the boat dock sounded ominous. And, although he might not remember it, CT had always claimed he wasn't a cruise person.

"Well, let's get together when I get back, Honey. I'd love to see you."

"You give me a call when you're back home and all settled." Honey tried to sound brighter than she felt. They said goodbye, and Honey hung up. With a sigh, she leaned back in the rocker, looking out over the alfalfa field. With a slight breeze wafting over the top of the alfalfa, it felt kind of like being on a big green ocean. She could imagine it was. And she could pretend Honeymoon Cottage was their fancy oceanside suite with a balcony, just missing the cute umbrella drinks.

But she couldn't dream away her husband's dementia. Not while she was awake, anyway. Sometimes she had happy dreams of the way things used to be. Too bad she hadn't realized back then that they were actually living out the good old days. Of course, that brought the old Carly Simon song to mind. Amused, she started to hum the tune as she rocked, singing the lyrics aloud. "These are the good ol' days." And suddenly she realized these really were the good old days *still*. And life on this side of heaven wouldn't last forever, so she better enjoy what's here while it's here—and perhaps practice a little more gratitude along the way.

29

Jewel

Miguel had been distant for the past couple of weeks. Jewel knew he was busy with farming, and since she was in the middle of her farmhouse renovations, she decided it was probably for the best. Things had been warming up a little too quickly between them. As much as she liked Miguel, she wasn't sure she was ready for a serious relationship. And that's where it felt like they were headed. Not only that, but she worried what would happen if they got involved and it fell apart? How would that impact being good neighbors, or even Cooper's friendship with Anna?

For the time being, Jewel felt more comfortable maintaining a little distance. So, nose to the grindstone, she'd been clearing things out and painting. To keep it simple, and because she thought it looked classic and would provide a good backdrop to all the art she planned to display in the house, she'd decided to paint most of the downstairs, as well as the guest bedrooms, a linen shade of white. The bathrooms were painted a very pale aqua, with white woodwork.

She was painting kitchen cabinets today. Keeping in the spirit of the original green paint, she'd gone a few shades darker, and the contrast against the linen color was perfect. Aaron had tried to talk her into replacing them altogether, but when she went over the options, and how long it would take to get something new, plus the price tag, she decided the old cabinets were fine. With a fresh coat of paint and some new farmhouse-style hardware to replace the chipped and worn wooden knobs, they would be perfect.

By now she and Cooper had cleared the house of the accumulations of past generations. To Jewel's surprise, she'd found some keepers too, furniture items she could reuse or repurpose to outfit the B&B, which would not only look great but would also save her money down the line.

Cooper and Anna had the task of sorting and pricing everything out in the barn. The plan was to hold a big barn sale this upcoming weekend. Jewel had encouraged her parents to oversee the sifting process in the barn. She didn't want to get rid of anything without their approval, but so far Mom had only salvaged a few items of sentimental value, claiming she'd become a true minimalist. And Dad didn't seem to recognize or even care about much of anything out there.

The one interesting thing Dad had salvaged was a teddy bear with a red-and-green Christmas vest. The plush toy had been Jewel's at one time. But her dad held it protectively to his chest as if he'd just rescued it from sure destruction. Now he kept the stuffed bear by his chair in the new house. According to her mother, he sometimes held and stroked it to soothe himself.

Jewel knew this whole business of moving things from his old home and piling boxes in his beloved barn could agitate him or make him feel more displaced than usual, and no one wanted that.

To that end, she'd decided to ask him to help paint the farmhouse's exterior. But she hadn't chosen the colors yet. She wanted it to feel friendly and inviting and had several sample palettes laid out on the front porch, but so far none seemed just right.

She heard footsteps coming into the house and, not expecting any of the construction crew today, went to investigate. "Dad," she said cheerfully as he walked through the nearly empty living room. "You came to visit."

"Who lives here?" he asked with a frown. This was his usual

question when he came into the house. It was something she'd have to figure out when the day came to open the B&B, but she'd let that go for now.

"Cooper and I live here, Dad."

"Huh?" He went into the kitchen. "What're you doing?"

"I'm painting." She nudged him away from the cabinets' wet paint.

"Oh?" His eyes lit up.

"Maybe you can paint too," she said.

"Uh-huh." He nodded. "I can paint." He reached for the brush she'd laid on the edge of the can.

"But not in here." She led him toward the back porch. "Outside. Come on, Dad." Wanting to get him out of harm's way, she led him to the back door. As they walked past the big red cabinet that held his honey supply, he paused to open it, reverently appraising the numerous amber jars.

"Honey," he said with a pleased expression.

"Yes. That's your honey, Dad. Pretty, isn't it?"

"Uh-huh." He reached in to take a jar. She knew Mom already had stocked quite a few jars in the new house, but whenever Dad passed through here, he usually got one to take with him. Although the porch stairs had been rebuilt by one of Aaron's guys, she took his arm to help him down. Then she led him out in front and turned him around, pointing up at the two-story house.

"I'm trying to decide what color to paint," she said absently.

"Uh-huh."

"I like the green, but I'm not sure." She studied the house's lines and roof color, trying to imagine what would look best. "And it really needs fresh paint. So maybe it's time for a change. You know, to make it more inviting for guests." She knew she was using too many words, but her dad seemed to enjoy the attention.

"Uh-huh." He nodded with a blank expression.

"And I'm trying to think of a name," she continued.

"Name?"

"For the B&B."

"Bees and bees?" His forehead creased just like it always did when she mentioned the B&B. "My bees?"

"For the bed and breakfast, Dad. It's called a B&B."

"Honey bees and bees?" He held up his golden jar of honey. "Lots of bees."

She decided to humor him. "Sure, honey bee and bee." And then it hit her. Why not? "Maybe we should call it the Honey Bee and Bee. You know, like bees. Buzz buzz."

His eyes lit up. "Yeah, buzz buzz."

"The Honey Bee and Bee," she repeated. "Buzz buzz."

"Bees and bees, buzz buzz. And honey."

"That's it, Dad! That's our name. The Honey Bee and Bee. Like honey bees. I like it."

"Honey. Buzz-buzz bees. I like it," he echoed happily.

She began to imagine cute honey and bee logos that could go with the name. And she'd find recipes involving honey for breakfast items. And they could sell jars of honey too. Maybe open a little gift shop in the barn. So many ways to utilize what was literally under their noses. It was perfect!

She peered at the house again. "So you helped me name it, Dad. What color should we paint it?"

He squinted up at the house. "Honey."

"Honey?" She turned to him.

"Like this." He held his jar toward the house. "Honey."

"The color of honey?" She considered the golden amber in his jar. She hadn't included any shades of yellow in her color palette choices. Probably a reaction from the new house's original color. "It could be friendly."

"Friendly honey." He grinned. "I'm hungry."

"Okay, Dad." She firmly nodded. "I think you're right. The Honey Bee and Bee will be painted the color of honey. And you will help me paint it. And now you should go get your Honey to make you a sandwich." She wasn't exactly sure what shade of yellow she'd choose but definitely nothing like that screaming bright yellow the new house had been painted. She imagined a subtle golden yellow. She'd have to check out the honey jars in the cabinet for inspiration. She knew various seasons produced different colors of honey. Hopefully one shade would be right. Anyway, it was an interesting idea.

By the end of the day, she'd decided the color of the siding would be a rich warm hue of amber. Like autumn honey. Not too bright, but not too muted either. She even mixed up the color herself, using her acrylic paints. Finally, she held up the cardboard sample to the house, studying it in varying light. She would paint the farmhouse trim and shutters olive green, to complement Honeymoon Cottage. And the doors would be a rich rusty red to match the weathered barn. She held up her new paint samples near the barn and new house, concluding they would be sweetly compatible.

The next morning, she told her mom about the Honey Bee and Bee name, then showed her the paint color selection. After getting Mom's approval, Jewel headed to town for the paint. As fate would have it, she ran into Aaron at the hardware store. Although she wanted to maintain a congenial working relationship with him, he always seemed to assume it should lead to more. Apparently today was no different.

"Come on, Jewel. You *have* to eat lunch," he urged for the third time.

"It's a little early for me." She pointed to where the young man behind the paint counter was mixing the first five-gallon bucket of paint. "And I want to get started on painting today."

"More reason to grab a quick bite now," he insisted. He called out to the paint guy. "How long is that mixing going to take?"

"The whole order?" The guy looked upward as if the ceiling held the answer. "Twenty minutes. Maybe more if I get busy with other orders."

"Come on." Aaron tugged her elbow. "The deli has their gyro special today, and they're really good."

Embarrassed to be drawing attention, she reluctantly agreed, and before long they were eating some pretty tasty gyros. But aware of the time, and her dining companion, she ate as quickly as politely possible, listening while Aaron went on about what a good sales season he was having at Hanford Homes.

"I'm happy for you." She took a fast sip of her iced tea.

"And good news." He looked at his phone. "Your farmhouse sink and quartz countertops will be ready for install tomorrow. You all set for that?"

"I just finished painting the kitchen cabinets."

"Great. And my HVAC guys have scheduled your new heat pump to be installed early next week."

"That's great," she said as she finished off the last bite of her gyro.

"I think those were the last things on your list, but I haven't had time to come by to check on the progress. How's it looking to you so far?"

"Just fine. Your guys do good work. I might need a couple of tweaks. Minor things. I'll text you a list later." She wiped her mouth with her napkin and then stood. "Thank you for lunch, Aaron. You're right, the gyros were good. But I need to get going. Make hay while the sun shines." She forced a smile as she headed for the exit. At the door, she was surprised to see Marta Orosco and another woman seated nearby.

She greeted Marta but was met with a somewhat questioning look along with a stiff little wave. Flustered and wanting to explain that meeting with Aaron was just business, which may not have been completely true, she simply waved back and hurried out. Small towns! She never knew who she might run into. Of course, that was also the beauty of a close community—something she looked forward to enjoying more. But she hated to give Miguel's mother the wrong impression.

Honey

After Jewel had left for town, CT was fixated on painting and kept asking when he would get to do it, even after Honey had told him a dozen times, "Not until Jewel says so." She wished Jewel hadn't mentioned it. Jewel and Cooper still sometimes imagined it brightened CT's world to talk about things to come. But CT's time span was all about here and now. Like an anxious three-year-old, he didn't know how to wait.

So when CT went AWOL shortly after Jewel left, Honey wasn't too surprised and suspected he might be getting into Jewel's art materials again. She set down the banana she'd brought for his midmorning snack and hurried outside, calling for him as she went to check the barn. But when she found him, he was inside the farmhouse kitchen, trying to pry open a bucket of paint with a dinner fork.

"CT," she said, trying not to scold. "This is Jewel's project. She's been working on it." She glanced around the room that barely resembled her old kitchen. "Jewel needs your help outside."

He looked up from the can, fork still in hand. "Outside?"

"Yes. She went to get house paint. We have to wait for her to come home."

"Home? To paint?" He set the fork on the floor. "Okay."

"You need to save your energy so you can help her this afternoon." She took his hand. "You know how you get tired."

"I know."

"And there's a banana waiting for you."

He smiled. "You take care of us."

"That's right." She led him to the back porch, waiting as he paused by the red honey cabinet. As usual, he removed a jar of honey. She didn't bother to tell him they were overly stocked. "Can't have too much honey," she said as they went outside.

"Too much honey?" He scowled. "No."

"No, not too much. We have enough honey." She waited for him to navigate the steps. "Honey is one thing we always have plenty of."

He pointed at her. "Always have you, Honey."

She smiled. "That's right."

"Always together," he said as they walked. "How many years?"

"Forty-seven in August."

"How old am I?"

"How old do you think you are?" This was a question she asked him from time to time just to see if he could remember. Sometimes he got close.

"Forty-seven," he proclaimed.

She almost wished he was forty-seven again. If she could turn back the clock, maybe she'd do things differently. Perhaps retire sooner, or go traveling while it was possible. And yet the very idea of all that just made her tired right now. "You'll be *seventy* in the fall," she said as they strolled. As soon as the words were out, she instantly regretted them. Maybe CT felt better imagining he was only forty-seven. But more than likely, the numbers were lost on him.

"Seventy?" He sounded impressed. "That's a lot."

"It's enough. For now."

"Here we are," he declared as they stepped onto the front deck. But then he turned to her with uncertainty. "Who lives here?"

"We do, CT. This is Honeymoon Cottage." She usually said this before they went inside because that name seemed to make him happy. And just like always, he added, "Home sweet home." She closed the door and pointed to his chair. "Look, there's a banana just waiting for you."

As CT shakily lowered himself into his chair, she tried to repress the sensation that they were both living in an old folks' home for couples, a slow-moving place where people just sat around eating bananas, playing checkers, and watching TV all day. Really, this was a pleasant and efficient house, and so much better than any sort of assisted living facility, like someone had suggested to her last year. This smaller house really did suit their needs. Still, it wasn't the beloved old farmhouse that she'd known for her entire life. Honeymoon Cottage was a blessing, but it wasn't the same. Nothing was the same. And never would be again. C'est la vie.

30

Jewel

By the end of her third painting day, Jewel had made very little progress on the house. This was partly due to her dad's need for help and direction as he worked on the backside of the house, and partly because where she was painting in front got more sunshine and weather and consequently needed more attention. So she'd mostly been sanding, scraping, and priming to get it ready for paint. Despite her eagerness to get the honey-gold paint on the front, she'd heeded the paint guy's advice to do the prep work first. But at this rate, with just her and Dad, it was going to take forever. Mom had offered to help today, but the whole point of engaging Dad was to give Mom some time to herself. And, not surprisingly, Dad was working at a snail's pace and spending most of his time in his lawn chair.

As Jewel washed brushes in the laundry sink on the back porch, Cooper came out. "Hey, Mom, whatcha up to?" she asked pleasantly.

Jewel's first response was to act like a martyr and growl at her daughter, who'd been occupied with sorting the barn sale the past few days. Then she and Anna had taken today off to go swimming. "Got the painting started." Jewel stood straight with a weary sigh. "It's a little more involved than I expected."

"Is Grandpa helping?"

"Helping?" Jewel rolled her eyes. "Yeah."

"Cool. And guess what Miguel wants to help with?"

Jewel looked up from shaking the wet brush. "What?"

"He wants to build us a produce stand. Grandma said we can sell stuff from her garden and fruit trees since she doesn't want to do any canning. And we can do eggs and honey too. And later on, we can sell pumpkins. We'll be rich."

"I doubt you'll get rich, but it does sound fun."

"I told Miguel I might get you to draw up a design for the stand. You know, since you're the artiste." Cooper smirked.

"I could do that."

"Tomorrow, Anna and I will be making barn sale signs and getting everything set for the big sale. But when that's done, I'll help paint."

Jewel felt like crying. "Oh, thank you, Cooper. I wanted to ask, but you've already been doing so much already."

"I could ask Anna to help too," Cooper suggested.

"Wonderful."

"I bet Miguel could too. He's a really good painter."

"Oh, I doubt he'll have time." Or that he'd want to see Jewel after their last misunderstanding over Aaron. "But do tell Anna I'll pay you girls for your work."

"Cool." Cooper pulled out her phone. "I'll text her right now."

"Thanks." Jewel felt a small flicker of hope as she rinsed the last brush. She hadn't been too eager to get up on a tall ladder, which would be necessary for some parts of the house, but those two agile teens might enjoy the challenge. She laid the brushes on paper towels, then kicked off her paint-speckled Converse and went into her fully remodeled kitchen, pausing to admire how pretty and efficient it now looked with its upgraded appliances, recently installed gray quartz countertops, and gleaming-white farmhouse apron sink. She'd replaced her mom's old dining set with a hefty harvest table she'd found in a local antiques mall and placed a couple of stools around it. It not only looked perfect but was handy for extra food prep space.

She'd considered doing yellow and black in there, to make it compatible to the whole bee theme, but not wanting to get too juvenile, she stuck with her original linen walls and green cabinets, adding in a few more classic touches of her own style, including some original paintings that felt appropriate to a farmy but sophisticated kitchen. Country meets art. It had only been finished for a couple of days now but still made her happy just to look at it.

Despite being tired, she decided that instead of ordering pizza like she'd planned, she would fix a homemade meal for her and Cooper tonight. She actually enjoyed cooking when she had the time and ingredients. And cooking in this lovely kitchen would be a reward in itself. Before long, she had chicken breasts on the industrial stove's big grill, making enough for leftovers tomorrow. And with her favorite jazz station playing on her XM radio, she was partly dancing and partly working on a generous green salad with the abundant produce she'd gathered from the garden this morning when she heard someone tapping on the back screen door.

"Come in," she yelled, thinking it was one of her parents, although they usually were relaxing after their own early dinner by now.

"Hey there."

She looked up from slicing a cucumber to see Miguel coming inside, dressed in faded jeans and a pale gray T-shirt. His straw cowboy hat was in hand as he stood in the doorway. "Oh, Miguel." She laid down her knife and waved him in. "Welcome. Come see my new kitchen."

"Nice." He stepped in, pausing to look around with what seemed genuine appreciation. "Very nice."

"Thanks." She wiped her hands on a dish towel. "It actually inspires me to cook."

"Even better." He sniffed. "Smells good."

"There's plenty if you want to join us." She smiled brightly.

"Well, I mostly came over to talk." He sounded uneasy.

"I've been wanting to talk to you too." She opened the new wine cooler, then removed a bottle of an Oregon rosé and held it up. "Interested? I was just wishing for a grown-up to share a celebratory glass with me."

"Sounds good." He pulled a stool up to the harvest table and sat. "I see you started painting the house. Looks like you've got your work cut out for you."

She tugged to remove the cork. "I guess so."

"Anna just told me that she's going to help you."

"Oh, good. Coop said she was going to ask. I hope that's okay with you. I know Anna's been doing a lot over here, but I plan to pay her."

"No, that's fine. I just thought maybe I could lend a hand too."

She poured a glass. "Do you have time? I mean, I know how busy farming can get in August."

"Well, it's really kind of in between seasons right now. It's not harvest time yet, and I just moved the cattle yesterday. Other than daily chores, I'm not that busy."

She took the glasses to the table, then sat across from him and lifted her glass. "Toast with me over my new kitchen?"

"Here's to a beautiful kitchen that will prepare beautiful food for all who visit this house." He scooted her flower arrangement of lavender, poppies, and daisies aside to clink his glass against hers.

"Thank you." She smiled as they both took a sip. It was so good to see him. She'd almost forgotten how handsome he was, or how just being with him sent a schoolgirl sort of thrill through her.

"So I wanted to talk to you about my, uh, brother-in-law."

"Aaron." She nodded as she set down her glass.

"Yes. Well, I took your advice and tried to reach out to him again." He frowned. "But I got a pretty chilly response."

"I'm sorry."

He shrugged. "I guess I'm not that surprised."

"Well, at least you tried." She got up to check on the chicken. Flipping the pieces over, she turned down the flame. "I wanted to talk to you about Aaron too," she said with her back still turned.

"Yeah?"

She tried to remember how she'd planned to explain, but her mind was blank as she sat back down across from him. "Well, that day, when you helped with the escaped bees—"

"How are they?"

"Oh, just fine. Walter helped Cooper get them back into their original hives, told her a few things she should be doing, you know, since Dad forgets."

"That's good." He sipped his wine. "So is this. Thanks."

"Uh-huh. Anyway, I know you saw Aaron sort of putting a move on me on the front porch. I only wanted to talk business, but he always seems to want to push things further. But I, uh, I just wanted you to understand that there is absolutely nothing between him and me. In fact, I will be so relieved when the heat pump gets installed next week. Then I'll be all finished with Aaron." She sighed and took another sip of her wine.

"All finished?" Miguel eyed her curiously.

"All finished," she assured him. "Well, mostly . . ." She told him about the agreement she'd made with Aaron. "I told Mom all about it, and we both agree we have no intention of turning this into a building lot. Ever."

Miguel gave a slightly knowing nod. "That doesn't surprise me."

"That we would never sell?"

"No, that Aaron had something like that in mind."

"Well, it surprised me." She heard footsteps and turned to see Cooper coming down the stairs. "Dinner will be ready in about fifteen, okay?"

Cooper looked from Miguel to her mom and then bit her lip. "Well, I was just going to tell you I wanted to go over to Anna's. I didn't know you were fixing dinner here, Mom. Marta made enchiladas."

"They did smell good," Miguel said.

"Well, if that's what you want, Coop." Jewel concealed her disappointment. "Miguel probably wants to go back too."

"Oh, I can have enchiladas anytime," he said casually. "I'd rather stay here and celebrate the grand opening of the Honey Bee and Bee kitchen." He tipped the salad bowl toward him. "And my mom's idea of green salad is iceberg lettuce and tomatoes. This looks great."

"Okay then." Cooper grinned. "See ya later."

After Cooper left, they both sat quietly at the table, and Jewel couldn't quite remember what they'd been talking about, so she improvised. "Well, I'd really appreciate your help with painting, Miguel. You're such a good painter. But please know I'd understand if you get too busy. Your farm has to come first."

"Right. But with you and me and the girls all working, I bet we can get this house done in no time. Hopefully before the fair."

"Fair?"

"The county fair," he told her. "4-H."

"Oh, yeah. I hear Anna has a calf to show."

"Yeah. So we have to take time out for that. She's been selling one every year, building up her college fund."

"That's wonderful. I wish Cooper could get interested in something like that."

"She already is. She wants to go to the fair with us. I just haven't, uh, had the chance to ask you if she could join yet. If she likes it, maybe she'll have a calf of her own next year."

"That would be something." Jewel shook her head in wonder. "Living here has been so good for Cooper. I don't think I'll ever regret making this move. Even if the B&B flops, my barn gallery is a bust, and I never sell another piece of art, I would be willing to flip burgers at Dairy King just to stay on here."

He laughed. "Well, I can't imagine it'll come to that." He sniffed. "If this chicken tastes as good as it smells, you might consider the restaurant business."

"Speaking of which, dinner must be about done." She got up to check, turned off the grill, and gathered up two place settings. "We'll have to eat in here because I'm still waiting for the dining set I ordered a few weeks ago."

"Why wouldn't we eat in here? We're celebrating the kitchen's grand opening." He stood up. "Can I help you with anything?"

"No, there's really not much to do."

"Then do you mind if I look around? I'm curious to see all your improvements in the house."

"Sure. Make yourself at home. Mostly it's just been paint and clearing things out, bringing a few sparse pieces in, and hanging some of my paintings."

As he went to check out the stripped-down house, Jewel puttered around happily in her new kitchen. It was like playing house. To the sounds of smooth jazz, she artfully arranged the new placemats and napkins, the flower arrangement in the center, her pretty salad on one side, and the wine bottle on the other. Picture-perfect. Which reminded her, she'd need to start getting photos for the website she'd already started to build.

"I can't believe how changed it all looks," Miguel said as he rejoined her. "Anna said you'd taken everything out, but it's like a totally different house now."

"Pretty spartan, eh?"

"Room to breathe. I wouldn't criticize your parents' taste, but it seemed a bit cluttered before. My mom is the same way. If there's a space to put something, she likes to fill it up."

"Well, my mom inherited a lot from her grandparents. I guess it was hard to let it go."

"And the paintings you've hung all around—wow, they're really good. Who is J. Benedict?"

"That's me. I did those paintings when I was still married to Cooper's dad." She set the plate of chicken on the table. "I only switched back to McKerry last year."

"Well, they're beautiful. I had no idea you were so talented."

She smiled and sat. "Why, thank you."

He reached for her hand. "Mind if I ask a blessing?"

"Not in the least." She bowed her head and, instead of enjoying the warm rush of his hand holding hers, tried to concentrate on his words.

"Dear heavenly Father, please bless this delicious-looking food. But even more than that, bless this house. Bless Jewel and Cooper as they create new lives here. Bless all who grace their doorstep. Bring your sweet goodness to this lovely place. Amen."

She opened her eyes and looked at him. "Thank you for that. That was beautiful."

He still held her hand. "And so are you."

She felt herself blushing as his fingers slipped from hers, and he reached for the wine. "Care for more?"

"We are celebrating, aren't we?" She picked up her napkin with a festive wave. "Of course!"

And there, sitting in the new farmhouse kitchen, she and Miguel enjoyed a simple meal and each other's company. Just like old friends. And perhaps a little something more someday. She hoped so.

31

Honey

Seeing the old farmhouse getting painted that rich golden-yellow left Honey with mixed feelings. She liked the color selection well enough. And she was extremely grateful CT seemed to adore it and highly amused over how he believed he'd picked the "honey paint" all by himself. But seeing the farmhouse go from green to a harvest sort of gold was like saying goodbye to an old friend. Or maybe it was the shock of seeing summer on its way to becoming autumn, sort of like how her life felt. These things happened so fast.

Her grandmother had chosen the pale green back when Honey was a small child and sent to live with her grandparents while her parents followed her dad's military career overseas. Honey couldn't remember what color the house had been before that because it had always seemed to be pale green. Just like her old cabinets in the kitchen, which were now a lovely olive. But all these changes were hard to swallow. Not that she ever voiced her disgruntlement. It would hurt Jewel's feelings too much, and her old confidant CT just plain wouldn't get it.

Perhaps that was something she missed more than anything. The sad truth that CT, her best friend, could no longer understand her petty little grievances like he used to. She remembered how easily she could dump on him after a difficult day at school.

He had always been a sympathetic listener and a great encourager, and he often had words of wisdom for her. But those days were long gone now.

Feeling guilty for her secret resentments regarding the farmhouse changes, she reminded herself it must be a bit like the way CT had felt when he'd been forced to give up driving and guns and even farming. She also reminded herself that the changes Jewel was instigating would allow her daughter and granddaughter to make a living and remain here on the farm indefinitely. That was no small reward and well worth her temporary inner discomfort.

But at the same time she felt sad to see this last change as she stood outside watching the last of the exterior paint being applied by Jewel and Miguel, who were now painting the dark green trim color in front. Cooper and Anna were applying a second coat to the sides, and poor old CT was still puttering away on the backside or sitting in his lawn chair. Already, the farmhouse interior was so different. She felt almost discombobulated when she went inside, but she had to admit it looked surprisingly beautiful. Far beyond anything she ever could've imagined for the space. Like making a silk purse out of a sow's ear, as her grandma used to say—it was impossible. But Jewel, with her artistic vision, had done it.

While Jewel was occupied the other day, Honey had snuck in to really snoop around. And the transformation had been startling. The light-colored walls, all painted the same color for the first time ever, made the house feel larger, cleaner, fresher. It reminded her of how she used to feel on the first warm day of the season, opening all the windows to air out the house. Now the AC cooled them off without lifting a finger.

And her daughter's artwork, so perfectly displayed, made the house feel like much more than a countrified farmhouse but almost like a gallery, only friendlier. The old oak floors, which Jewel had gotten refinished, now gleamed with a golden patina that only years of living could achieve. And the gently revamped bathrooms, in that lovely pale shade of blue, with fluffy white towels and lavender-scented accoutrements, felt clean and new.

Although the fixtures were still the plain white ones she'd had installed when Jewel was a girl, back in the eighties, they looked just fine. But it was the kitchen that still took her breath away each time she entered. It could've been featured in a design magazine. Or at least *Country Living*.

Any guests who visited the Honey Bee and Bee would not be disappointed. Yet Honey still had mixed feelings. To be honest, these changes and renovations were something that Honey would've liked for her and CT at one time. Back when they were younger and able to enjoy the place. But having a career had taken priority over home improvement for Honey. And there were lean years when they could've lost the farm if not for her income. But even during summer months, when she'd imagined doing some big fixes on the house during her time off, she'd get herself busy with outdoor projects . . . like chickens and cows or the landscape, the garden, the greenhouse, the lavender fields, or just walking the fields with whatever dog they'd had at the time.

Something had always beckoned her outdoors on those warm days, so she'd been painfully aware of how the farmhouse had been way overdue for attention. Sometimes it had even kept her awake at night. But she'd promised herself she'd catch up with all these projects after retirement. And then CT got worse, and her focus switched to him and all the appointments they needed to go to, chasing answers that didn't exist. And, well, there you go. Honey knew she should just be pleased that Jewel had cared enough, and had enough vision to actually do it.

"So what do you think, Mom?" Jewel stepped down from the porch, using a bandanna to wipe her olive-green paint-smeared hands. "You haven't said much yet about much of anything over here. I hope you're not having second thoughts."

Honey set down the cooler of drinks that she'd just refreshed with ice and slowly shook her head in wonder. "Oh, Jewel, I was just thinking about everything you've done here. Honestly, I can hardly believe it. And in such a short time." She looked into her daughter's eyes. "It's truly amazing. Just gorgeous. Inside and out. You're a real wonder-worker."

"Really? You like it?"

"It's all just beautiful." Honey beamed at her. "I'm so very proud of you, sweetie. And you know what my favorite part is?"

"The kitchen?"

"It's pretty gorgeous, but, no, it's your artwork throughout the house. I knew you were talented, but I always got the impression from your website that you only did modern or abstract art. I had no idea you'd been doing landscape and still life."

Jewel laughed. "Well, those paintings didn't do too well in California. Too urbane and cliché. So I just stored them in the back room of my gallery. Now I'm glad I saved them. I think they fit a farmhouse motif."

"Well, I just love them." Honey shook her finger. "In my opinion, they're neither urbane nor cliché. They're like real life . . . only better. They're beautiful."

"I have more paintings if you'd like any for your house," Jewel said.

"I'd love a few pieces."

"They're in the barn. I'll show you when we both have time." She took another step off the porch. "Marta is bringing over dinner," Jewel told her. "I hope you and Dad will join us."

"If your dad feels up to it, I'd love to."

"I think he's finally gotten over his trouble with Miguel. In fact, he seems to really like him."

"It's about time." Honey smiled. "That's quite an accomplishment. In a way, bringing people together and healing relationships, well, that's probably more valuable than all the renovations you've done here. More amazing too."

Jewel's nod was somber. "I agree."

"Anyway, I won't distract you any more. Looks like you're closing in on the end. And the exterior of the Honey Bee and Bee really does look grand. It's a color I never would've picked and yet it feels right."

"It's actually historically correct for this house. I looked it up."

"Well, it's very rich and inviting." She patted Jewel's back. "Nicely done. I'm going to check on your dad and then my old friend Donna is coming for a little visit."

"Good for you, Mom. It's about time you started having a social life again."

As Honey walked around to check on CT, her feelings were a little less mixed, and she didn't feel disingenuous either, because everything she'd said to Jewel was true. She just hadn't described all her feelings, because there was no point. Plus, she was certain that she would get over it in time. Change was supposed to be good. And even if it wasn't good, it was inevitable. So she might as well move on!

After finding CT sitting in his lawn chair, in the shade, she gave him a fresh bottle of water, kissed him on the forehead, and reminded him not to overdo it. Then she headed back to Honeymoon Cottage just in time to see Donna's little electric car pulling into the driveway. That Donna, always cutting-edge. Honey waved, directing her friend toward the graveled parking area right next to the new house.

"Come and see my new digs," she said as they embraced. "I even baked cookies."

"This is cute." Donna paused to look around. "Really, really cute."

"You can attribute the cuteness to Jewel. She's so gifted at these things." Honey pointed to the old farmhouse. "After we have a good visit, I'll give you the full tour of all the amazing changes she's made over there." As they went onto the covered front deck, Honey explained about the B&B that was "coming soon."

Donna laughed when she heard the name. "That's perfect." She looked around, taking in the potted plants and rockers. "This is so charming, Honey."

"Thanks. It makes me happy." Honey pointed to the field. "And the wide-open view. It's my peaceful place." She opened the front door. "Welcome to Honeymoon Cottage." She giggled. "CT and Jewel came up with that, but I like it." She gave Donna a short tour of the small house, and Donna thought it was all just wonderful.

"I'm so happy for you. This place really is perfect for you and CT. Low maintenance and one level. It was a brilliant plan. Well done."

"Again, I have to give credit to Jewel. Her idea." They sat down at the kitchen table where Honey had laid out refreshments. "To be honest, I had my doubts at first."

"Was it hard to let go of your old house?"

Honey explained how she'd just been feeling. "But CT and I are both having to let go of so many things . . . it's just one more."

"Well, having this sweet cottage is a pretty nice swap." Donna pursed her lips. "But I'm guessing you can't keep CT here indefinitely. Have you looked into any of those places I texted to you?"

"I haven't really had time." Honey frowned. "Truthfully, I just haven't wanted to do that yet. I know the time will probably come . . . but I hate to rush it. For CT's sake. He still enjoys the farm." She explained how he was "helping" to paint and how he liked to rearrange things and feel occupied. "And needed. He wants to feel necessary."

"I totally understand." Donna nodded. "But how about the resources I gave you for help in your home, you know, to give you a break? Have you looked into those?"

"I've made a list. But I'm hoping once all the renovating is done around here, I can count on Jewel and Cooper to step in sometimes. They're both willing."

"That's good. But you might want some kind of nurse's aide eventually."

"I know. And like I said, I've made a list. Thanks so much for sending me those references. It's reassuring to know they're out there, especially in our small community."

"Well, after all my years in social services, I know a few people." She winked. "Now, tell me what you're doing for yourself."

Honey held up her hands. "I don't really know. Like I said, I guess I'm waiting for the renovations to get done. And the light's at the end of the tunnel."

"I just know that caregivers usually put self-care at the bottom of their to-do list. I don't want to see you do that, Honey. You've always been so involved. And you have a lot of friends. I know I plan to start calling you up more often."

"I hope you will." Honey pointed to Donna's phone. "Got any Alaska pictures there?"

"Are you kidding?"

"I'd love to see them."

Donna scooted her chair closer, and Honey put on her reading glasses and listened with real interest as Donna described their recent trip and gushed over the fabulous photos. Finally, it was getting late and Honey reinvited her to tour the old farmhouse.

"You don't have to ask me twice." Donna stood. "I love remodeling projects. I keep watching HGTV and thinking we'll do something with our old place. But it's lots easier said than done." She waved a hand. "We don't even have AC yet. You must be absolutely loving this."

"It's been pretty nice. Not sure how we did without it for so long. Jewel put it in the farmhouse too."

Honey felt very nearly happy as she led Donna through the farmhouse. Of course, Donna had nothing but praise for every bit of it. Finally, they were on the back porch where Jewel was washing brushes, and Donna got a chance to gush at her. "It's just brilliantly beautiful. Everything is absolutely perfect. When can you do my house?" Donna asked.

Jewel laughed and thanked her. "It's been a fun project."

"Your mother must be so proud of you."

"You got that right." Honey eagerly nodded. "My Jewel *is* a jewel."

"Thanks, Mom." Jewel's smile looked a little weary. "And we're all done with the exterior. Other than some touch-ups in back. But I'll do that when Dad's not around to, uh, *supervise*." She rolled her eyes and they all laughed. As Honey walked Donna back to her car, she decided that all in all it had been a very good day. And everyone needed a very good day from time to time!

32

Honey

Despite the drizzly, cloudy morning, Honey felt energetic and happy as she cleaned up the kitchen. CT had eaten a good breakfast and seemed in good spirits, albeit a bit worn out from a restless night. But she hoped his low energy, combined with the weather, might keep him housebound today since, with no more painting to occupy him, he'd taken to wandering the property again.

She heard CT's slow steps shuffle up behind her. "The rain," he said in a worried tone. "Not good. Hurts my grain."

"We don't have any grain this year."

"Oh?" He peered out the kitchen window.

"The pumpkins and alfalfa and lavender like the rain."

"My bees?"

"Oh, they'll love it. Cools things off."

"Oh?"

"Tell you what." She smiled brightly. "As soon as I'm done here, we can play cards."

"Cards?" His eyes lit up.

"Yeah. That's fun on a rainy day."

"Uh-huh."

"You go find the cards while I finish here." Although the decks and scorepads were in the same coffee table drawer as always, she knew this search would challenge him. Plus, the hunt would keep him busy. CT had always loved playing cards. Of course, they'd been forced to work down from their usual gin rummy. A couple years back they'd switched to a simpler rummy. Then to crazy eights. Now they were down to go fish. And CT would get so confused that playing cards was just that—playing as in play-acting. At least for her. CT sincerely believed his eights matched threes, and sixes paired nicely with nines, and unless she was feeling feisty, she almost always let him win.

But her heart felt light as she turned on the dishwasher. Almost as if she could see a light at the end of the tunnel, although that wasn't the right metaphor since she knew CT's situation wouldn't improve. It was what it was. But with so many things completed on the farm, she felt like this could be a new era. Honey had less responsibility, and Jewel and Cooper would now have extra time to step in to help. Caring for CT would become more manageable. Even if the girls got busy again, Cooper with school, which would start in a couple weeks, and Jewel with her B&B plans, Honey would simply take Donna's advice and engage some outside caregivers to assist. Hopefully that wouldn't be too expensive. Who knew, after Donna's encouragement about cruises, and how lots of challenged passengers enjoyed it, Honey might even take CT to Alaska.

She rinsed her dishcloth and then refilled her coffee cup and turned around to see that CT was gone. Probably searching for the cards in the bedroom. Or using the bathroom. She got out the cards and pad, then moved the small table they used next to his chair, bringing in a dining chair for herself before she called out for him. When he didn't answer, she went to see if he was in the bathroom. She knew his habits and sometimes he could be in there for a while. But the bathroom was empty.

"CT?" she called out again as she went to the other side of the house. Opening the door to the bedroom she'd set up as her office, then the bathroom, and finally the guest room—also known as a place she could slip off to when CT's snoring kept her awake, she found no one. CT was clearly gone.

It only took a minute or two to kick off her slippers, tug on boots, then fish a jacket from the big walk-in closet. She grabbed a cowboy hat from the hooks by the door and set out to find him. But she was barely down the front step when she heard a female voice calling for help. She couldn't tell if it was Jewel or Cooper, but it seemed to be coming from the barn. Her walk turned to a run until she reached the barn where the door was open. Cooper was kneeling by CT, who was splayed out on the barn floor and groaning in pain. It took only seconds to figure out what had happened. Someone, probably CT, had set up a ladder next to the loft.

"CT." Honey knelt beside him too. "What happened?"

"Fell down," he muttered. "Hurt."

"What hurts?" she asked as she pulled out her phone, ready to call 911.

"His leg," Cooper told her.

Honey ignored the comment for the moment and felt around CT's head. "How about your head? Did you hit it?" He looked puzzled, but since she found no lumps, she decided it was okay. "How about your back?"

"Uh-huh," he said. Tears were now coming down his cheeks. But that wasn't so unusual for him these days. "Hurts."

Honey looked at Cooper, but the poor girl looked so stricken, she was afraid she was about to go into shock. "Go get your mom," Honey told her.

After Cooper left, Honey tried to evaluate CT's condition. It was pointless to ask if anything was broken or if he could walk. Finally she just called 911 and, while holding CT's hand, explained the situation. By the time she answered the normal questions about breathing and consciousness, Jewel and Cooper were back, both trying to console CT. And Jewel, bless her heart, had brought a pretty Pendleton blanket from her house to spread over her father.

"I'm sure he needs to go to the hospital," Honey told the 911 woman. "But I'm not sure if we can get him there, or if he can even get to the car. Especially since he says his back hurts." It didn't take long for the woman to convince Honey that he probably needed a transport and Honey agreed. The woman promised that EMTs were on their way, and finally the call ended and Honey just sat there on the barn floor, holding CT's hand.

"You should probably ride with him," Jewel said.

Honey just nodded.

"Coop and I will follow. Okay?"

Honey felt tears in her eyes. "Thank you."

"I need to go turn off my oven," Jewel said. "Thanks to this weather I decided to make blueberry muffins this morning."

"Sorry." Honey sighed to realize how quickly plans could change.

"It's okay. I'm just starting to practice up for the B&B." Jewel's smile looked nervous. "Coop can keep you company, okay?" She looked at her daughter.

"Duh, Mom." Cooper rolled her eyes, and Jewel headed out.

"How you doing, CT?" Honey asked since his eyes were closed.

"Hurts." He groaned. "Hurts a lot."

"Help is coming," she assured him. "Try to relax."

"Hurts," he said again.

"Want me to pray for you?" she offered.

"Yeah. Pray." He closed his eyes again and she did too.

She had never been comfortable praying aloud in front of others, but sensing CT's need for soothing, and hoping for some divine intervention, she started to pray. It was nothing fancy or wordy, just her letting God know they needed some help and asking for CT to be okay. As she prayed he seemed to relax. Finally she had no more words so she opened her eyes and was pleasantly surprised to see that Cooper's eyes were closed and her head was bowed too. "Amen," Honey said quietly.

"Amen," CT echoed.

It seemed to take forever for the paramedics to arrive, but Honey felt peaceful as they all waited in the barn. When Jewel rejoined them, she still looked shaken, and Honey suspected she was blaming herself for not locking the barn door.

"It's not your fault," Honey told her. "This stuff just happens. I could feel guilty for being preoccupied while he was fretting over the rain. I told him we'd play cards and then turned my back." She snapped the fingers on her free hand. "Just like that he takes off." She looked down to see if he was listening, but his eyes were still closed and, judging by his looser grip on her hand, he was more relaxed now, only letting out a quiet groan from time to time.

"I wonder how high he got up the ladder before falling?" Jewel asked.

"Who knows?" Honey said.

"I was so worried about that ladder while we were painting," Jewel admitted. "So I always hid it out of sight at the end of the day. I can't believe he found it."

"Well, he's sneaky," Honey said quietly. "And surprisingly fast when he wants to be. I've considered getting wildlife cams to see what he's up to."

Jewel almost smiled. "It would be amusing."

"I wonder *why*—I mean, what did he think was up there?" Cooper looked up at the loft.

"God only knows." Honey shook her head.

"It's mostly just boxes of old photos, farm records, and memorabilia," Jewel told them. "Things I thought we should hold on to, to sort out when we have more time. But Dad couldn't have known about that stuff."

"Just one more why question we won't be able to answer." Honey sighed, then listened. "Is that a siren I hear?"

Sure enough, it was, and it was getting closer. Honey sent Cooper out to tell the paramedics where to find them and, before long, a team of three EMTs were tending to CT. Despite his pain, he seemed to enjoy the attention as they took his vitals, then poked and prodded his legs and back. Honey quietly explained CT's mental condition. "So I should probably ride with him, if that's okay."

"Absolutely." The woman made some notes on her tablet and before long, CT was being carefully lifted onto a gurney and then they were on their way. Ambulances always made Honey nervous, and she was sure her blood pressure was elevated, but remembering her deep breath routine, she continued to hold

CT's hand and pray silently for him to be okay . . . then counted the seconds in her head until they finally arrived at the hospital.

Jewel

As she and Cooper drove to the hospital, Jewel knew it wasn't really her fault, but she still felt guilty about her dad's fall. "I should never have left the barn door unlocked," she confessed as they pulled into the ER parking area.

"Oh, Mom." Cooper sounded exasperated. "Don't blame yourself. You know Grandpa. He gets into mischief no matter how hard we try to keep him out of it."

Jewel snagged a spot close to the door. "I know."

"Even if you'd locked the door, Grandpa knows how to break locks."

"I know," she said again. "But I still feel bad."

"Well, maybe he's fine. You know how Grandpa can think he's dying from a sliver in his finger."

Jewel smiled as she got out. "Yeah, underneath his whining and crying, he's a tough old bird."

"And how many times have we seen him fall down and heal up and be just fine?"

"That's true." Jewel pulled her hood up, and they both jogged through the rain to the entrance. "I'm sure Grandma is with him," she said as they found seats in the nearly empty waiting area. "In fact, we probably didn't need to hurry over here so fast."

"Sure, you could be home doing something really important, like baking muffins." Cooper's tone was sarcastic.

"Thanks." Jewel smirked at her.

"Now I'm hungry. I never had breakfast." Cooper glanced around. "Think we can find something decent to eat around here?"

"I know my way to the cafeteria, but I can't promise much as far as the food goes." Jewel texted Mom their whereabouts, then stood.

The cafeteria, like the waiting room, was fairly quiet too, but they discovered some good-looking bagels. And Cooper got yogurt and fruit as well. They were just finishing up when Mom texted Jewel back. She read the short message, then shook her head. "Sounds like Grandpa broke some bones."

"Uh-oh." Cooper stuffed her banana peel into the yogurt container.

"His ankle for sure and probably his hip too." She frowned. "And not on the same leg."

"So he can't even use crutches to walk."

"Sounds like it. Grandma says she'll be here awhile, and Grandpa might have to stay overnight. They'll give him some more tests and might schedule surgery on his ankle. She says we should just go home." Jewel finished her coffee.

"Think that's all that's wrong?" Cooper asked as she dumped the trash.

"I hope so. Guess we'll find out."

As Jewel drove them home, Cooper was focused on her phone, and Jewel began to feel even more guilty. If only she'd locked that door. Maybe Dad would be okay right now. She also felt sharp disappointment. Just when things had seemed to lighten up . . . for everyone . . . and now this. Ah, life!

Jewel kept her phone handy as she puttered about the house, fussing over things that didn't need fussing over. Cooper had gone over to Anna's to tell her the news. Although Jewel suspected she was just trying to escape her mother's pacing and fretting. Finally, remembering that Dad loved blueberry muffins, she decided it was better to keep busy than worry. But by the time the last tray of muffins was cooling, it had been nearly two hours since they'd left the hospital, with no new messages. Maybe it was time to check in. After all, Mom had her blood pressure to consider. She might need moral support by now.

When Mom didn't text back, Jewel grew even more concerned, but she busied herself with cleaning up the baking mess. Then her phone finally chimed. Jewel hoped it was Mom but was surprised to see a text from Miguel, offering to take her to the hospital and even to sit with her. She sent an eager "yes!" in reply.

As he drove her to the hospital, she confessed how she was on pins and needles, worried about both her parents. "I realize it's not really my fault, but I wish I'd locked that door last night."

"You can't blame yourself," he said. "You know how your dad is."

"I *do* know how he is. But that's even more reason to protect him."

"But what if you can't?" He stopped for a traffic light. "I mean, sometimes we just have to let some things go and admit we're human and make mistakes." He turned to look at her. "And then forgive ourselves . . . I think someone lectured me on this recently."

"The light's green." She knew he was referring to when she'd talked about rebuilding bridges with Aaron.

He grinned. "You can't control everything, Jewel."

She grimaced. "I can't control *anything*."

"That's probably true. Think about it, what can you really control?"

"Good point. I certainly can't control anyone in my family. Good grief, I can't even control myself sometimes." Now she confessed how many blueberry muffins she'd consumed while baking today, and they both laughed. Not for the first time she thought Miguel was good medicine. Especially for her.

33

Honey

By the time Honey drove CT home from the hospital several days after his accident, she knew that he'd suffered a broken hip, shattered an ankle, and had an injured knee, which would be looked into more later. She also knew that CT, probably thanks to pain pills and sedatives, did surprisingly well in the hospital by himself. She'd spent the first night with him, but seeing that he'd slept pretty soundly, she only stayed through the surgery the following morning, then went home that afternoon, exhausted.

While CT had been undergoing surgery to put some pins into his ankle, a hospital social worker named Barb met with Honey. After answering some routine albeit intrusive questions about CT's living conditions and whether it was a safe environment, which Honey could neither confirm nor deny, Barb began to talk about his recovery. Her first recommendation was nursing home care. Naturally Honey balked at the idea, and Barb switched gears ever so slightly. Showing more concern for Honey's health and well-being, she described various options for CT's care . . . later on. Things like home nurses and physical therapists who made home visits and finally hospice for those last days. Honey pretended she was listening, then reassured Barb that they'd all know when they were ready for that. Not that she ever would be . . .

Once again, Barb had changed routes, suggesting some practical ways to make CT's home recovery easier for everyone. From that point on, Honey wrote down everything Barb told her, then texted the list to Jewel, asking her to round these things up. But the last nugget of wisdom the social worker had shared, Honey had written down for herself. Barb said to practice *detached amusement*. At first Honey was confused. What did that mean? Barb reminded her that little could be done to change the outcome for CT. He would continue to decline, doing the unexplainable, getting lost and confused, probably falling more. But if Honey could step back and see the humor in it, perhaps even laugh, it would be easier on everyone. She remembered times they had laughed.

Just last week, they'd laughed uncontrollably in bed after she'd made the simple remark that the wind wasn't blowing. It'd been blustery all day, and the nighttime peace and quiet was lovely. But with his hearing aids out and his mind scrambled, CT kept mishearing her. "Not snowing?" he asked. "Need mowing? Sowing?" After several repeats, she was shouting at him—so much for peace and quiet—and finally she told him never mind. Of course, he misheard that too and more tries only made it worse until his guesses were so nutty, she cracked up laughing, and he did too. Sure, he didn't know why he was laughing. Maybe she didn't either, but it lightened the moment. Detached amusement.

It seemed miraculous, but somehow Jewel had gotten Barb's recommended supply list together. Just last night, Jewel had assured Honey the equipment would be delivered and in place before Honey and CT got home from the hospital today. Not only that, but Miguel had built a ramp on the front deck. Did this mean caring for CT would be easy? She doubted it, but with Jewel and Cooper's promised help, she wasn't too worried. And the prescribed tranquilizers and pain pills they'd picked up at the hospital pharmacy on their way out would probably help too.

"Have you missed home?" she asked CT as she turned into the driveway, pausing a moment to text Jewel they were here.

"Home?" He was clearly confused. Earlier today, he hadn't even recognized her. Probably due to all the medical workers that had been in and out to assist him. He thought she was his nurse. But after some conversation, and a kiss, he got it. She was his Honey.

"Home is Honeymoon Cottage," she said cheerfully.

"Home . . . Honeymoon Cottage," he echoed in a pleasant tone.

She spotted Jewel and Cooper in front of the cottage, waving a warm welcome. "Look, it's Jewel and Cooper."

"Huh?"

She suspected he didn't recognize those names at the moment, but it didn't matter. As she parked as close as she could get to the house, Jewel pushed out a wheelchair and then, like a three-ring circus, they attempted to get CT into the chair, over the gravel, and up into the house. Fortunately, probably thanks to the pain pills, he didn't complain too much. And when he saw the welcome home sign and balloons, he was as delighted as could be.

"Birthday?" He clapped his hands.

"Sure, why not," Jewel said, and she broke into the happy birthday song, with Cooper and Honey joining in. "Come see your room," Jewel said to her dad. "It's all fixed up for you."

Honey had been a little worried that CT would resent being in a hospital bed in the spare room, instead of with her in their big bed, but to her relief, he seemed oblivious as Jewel showed him everything. She'd done all she could to make the room attractive and homey, and CT seemed pleased. Or else he was just enjoying the attention of three females catering to him. Eventually, with all three of them helping, they got him into the bed without dumping him on the floor.

"A nurse's aide is coming tomorrow," Honey told them. "To remove his catheter and give us some tips for how to safely care for him." She tucked the blanket up around him and smiled. "Ready for that peanut butter and honey sandwich I promised you?"

His eyes lit up, and he nodded. Whether it was silly or not, Honey thought this might not be as hard as the social worker had described. And if it was, at least she wasn't alone. The three of them clustered in the kitchen while Honey made CT's sandwich.

"I can't believe how you pulled this all together," Honey told Jewel. "Getting all those medical supplies here before we got home."

"He seemed to like the room," Jewel said.

"Does he need someone in there with him all the time?" Cooper asked. "I mean, I can go sit with him if you think I should."

"I think having that bedrail, plus his injuries, should keep him in place for a while." Honey poured a glass of milk. "But you know your grandpa."

"For all we know, he might be crawling out on his belly to check on his bees by now." Jewel laughed, then glanced over to the spare room door.

But CT was still in the bed and glad to see his lunch being wheeled in front of him. He hadn't been a fan of the hospital's peanut butter sandwiches from the kids' menu since they didn't have honey, but he smiled after his first bite, proclaiming it good!

Jewel

Helping Dad recover at home took more time and energy than any of them expected, but after a few days, they established a routine of sorts, sharing shifts and being on call in case he fell down. Thankfully, that'd only happened a few times, and thanks to the helpful tips from the nurse's aide, they knew how to get him up with just two people, but that meant two people needed to remain on duty. Not in the house together, but within running distance with a phone handy. Thanks to this schedule, no one felt particularly put upon. And they all enjoyed breaks of time without any caregiving responsibilities. Mostly, Jewel was grateful that Mom didn't seem too overwhelmed.

Of course, their happy routine came to a screeching halt when Cooper begged to go with Anna to the fair for a few days. Apparently, 4-H families exhibiting livestock enjoyed camping at the fairgrounds. It was a social thing, and Cooper was dying to go with the Oroscos and experience life at the fair. Jewel wanted her to go, but that meant she and Mom would now split CT duty two ways instead of three.

With her dad feeling better and more energetic, instead of sketching and painting like Jewel had been doing on her regular morning shift, she was now wheeling him around the farm, checking on the pumpkins and the bees and whatever else suited his fancy. He called it his exercise, but she was the one who got sweaty. They were just embarking on a morning stroll when Miguel strolled over. "Can I help?"

"Sure." She gladly surrendered the wheelchair. Then, walking beside him, she asked how the county fair was going.

"Anna won a blue ribbon," he said proudly.

"Wow. Good for her."

"It's not the highest award, but it's the best she's ever done in the four years she's been showing."

"What's higher than a blue ribbon?"

"A purple ribbon. It's like the grand prize. I'm sort of glad she didn't get it though. It gives her something to keep working toward. Anyway, her calf gets auctioned tomorrow morning. I'll bring them all home after that's done."

"I'm so glad Cooper got to go and experience all this. Thanks so much for including her."

"She seems to have really enjoyed it. And it sounds like she's pretty serious about raising her own calf next year."

"That's so amazing. But I doubt I'll be much help. Even though Dad had cattle when I was a kid, I didn't join 4-H or get very involved."

"Don't worry. We'll help her."

"Dad will probably like being included." She leaned down to tell CT that Cooper might raise a calf next year, then instantly regretted it since he immediately asked to see the calf, like it was out in the barn right now. Hopefully he'd forget soon.

"I wondered if you'd like to go with me back to the fair this afternoon," Miguel asked as they turned back toward the house. "My mom even offered to come over and hang with your mom while you're gone. I mean, if you want to go. We thought that might help free you up."

"That's so sweet, but I hate to ask her to leave the fair if she's enjoying it."

He chuckled. "I actually think she'd like a good excuse to get out of there. It's fun at first, but after a couple of days, it can wear on you."

"Well, I'd love to go to the fair." And as incredible as it sounded, and something she would've laughed off a year ago, she truly would love it. Partly for a chance to get off the farm, partly because it just sounded fun . . . and mostly because she'd be with Miguel. "I haven't been to a county fair since I was about Cooper's age."

"All right. And if you want an authentic taste of being a real 4-H family, you can even spend the night with us."

She blinked. "Spend the night?"

"Sure. In the camp trailer with the girls and me. You and Cooper can have the bedroom in back, and Anna and I will bunk in front. There's plenty of room."

She considered this. "That actually sounds like fun, but I have to be on call with my mom at night." She lowered her voice and nodded toward her dad. "You know, in case he should fall or anything."

"What if *my* mom is on call?" he suggested. "I'm sure she wouldn't mind spending the night over here if necessary."

"Really? Or she could sleep in the farmhouse and just keep her phone handy," Jewel suggested. "Then she could pop over if needed."

"What do you think?" he asked hopefully.

"I think that sounds wonderful." She actually clapped her hands like a little kid and then, feeling embarrassed, she laughed. "Does the fair still have a Ferris wheel?"

He laughed too. "You bet. And if you're a good girl and don't make yourself sick on cotton candy and elephant ears, I'll take you up on it."

"Okay. I'll do my best." She felt her cheeks warm, suddenly imagining a romantic moonlit ride on the Ferris wheel with Miguel.

"Then it's a date." He wheeled her dad's chair up the deck ramp, then bent down to shake his hand and tell him goodbye. "I need to go tend my cows," he told him, then stood up and looked at Jewel. "So I'll let Mom know she's needed here. She's got her car there so she can leave and be back here before we even head for the fairgrounds. I've got some chores to do, but I expect to be done by midafternoon. Can I pick you up around two?"

"I'll be ready," she assured him, still feeling slightly giddy. She was going to the fair with Miguel! What could be more fun?

Both girls seemed happy that Jewel was joining them, but as quickly as they said hello, they said goodbye. Apparently they had big plans for the afternoon, but they promised to meet back at the trailer for dinner around six.

"Not that they'll be hungry," Miguel said after the girls scurried off. "My poor mama had all these meals planned, but the girls have been so full of fair food by dinnertime each night." He grinned. "She's made some generous donations to the pigs."

Jewel laughed. "Well, if you like, I could fix our dinner tonight."

"Nope. On the last fair night, we usually go out to eat at the barbecued rib place. It's not fancy, but it's sure good."

"No arguments here." She looked around his camp trailer. She'd noticed it on his property before, but it was bigger than she'd imagined. "This is a cute camper," she told him.

"Thanks." He explained how the couch and dining area transformed into beds for him and Anna. "Let me show you to your suite, ma'am." He picked up her bag, then opened a door beyond the kitchenette. "Here you go." He set her bag on the neatly made queen-size bed. "Unfortunately, we have no room service."

"Aw, too bad. But I guess I can rough it for one night," she teased back.

"So, how would you like a tour of the livestock barns to start out with? It's cool and shady in there during the heat of the day."

"Cool sounds good." She was glad she'd worn a sleeveless snap shirt, one she'd borrowed from Mom in the hopes she'd look more like a farm girl today. And to complete her look, she had on blue jeans with a rodeo belt she'd borrowed from her dad's younger, skinnier cowboy days, plus a straw cowboy hat that no one ever seemed to lay claim to. As they walked toward the barns, she tried not to wrinkle her nose at the strong smells that she associated with the livestock barns—smells she used to make fun of as a teenager. But to her surprise, other than the manure pile out back, the barn smell was not that bad. And having Miguel as her tour guide with all the animals made the whole thing fun and interesting.

When they were done, he checked his watch. "There's a pretty good concert in a few minutes. I already got tickets, so if you happen to like country music." His brows arched as he studied her.

"I pretty much like all kinds of music. Well, not heavy metal so much." She didn't mention that country would be near the bottom of her "like" list.

"Then let's see how you like the Flannigan Family Band. They're a local group. Sort of country meets bluegrass."

As it turned out, she did like the Flannigans. A dad with six sons, between the ages of twelve and twenty, with more musical talent than seemed fair for just one family to share. "That was delightful," she told Miguel as they were leaving. "Thank you."

"It's almost time to meet the girls at the trailer and then we'll go to dinner, assuming they have appetites. Can you smell that?"

She sniffed and nodded. "The barbecued ribs?"

"Yep. I didn't have lunch, so I'm starving."

The girls were already in the back room changing their clothes when Miguel and Jewel returned. When they emerged looking more fashionable and cleaner than earlier, Anna explained that they wanted to go to an evening concert geared for teens. "So, we'll just eat here if that's okay, Dad." Anna ran a brush through her hair. "Abuela left lots of food."

"Abuela?" Jewel asked.

"Spanish for *grandma*," Cooper told her.

Jewel gave an amused nod, enjoying how Coop was trying to fit into Anna's world. So delightfully different from Coop's old friends in San Jose. The girls chattered to themselves as they foraged through the small but well-stocked fridge. Miguel turned to Jewel. "Need to freshen up before we go? You might want something warmer if we decide to walk around after dinner."

"Good thinking." She went to the back room and opened her overnight bag. She'd packed a lightweight cotton cardigan and impulsively slipped in a sundress as well. But she suddenly felt silly at the thought of dressing up for a county fair. She shook out the pretty dress. It was white rayon with a Navajo-inspired border around the hem of the full skirt and looked perfect with the turquoise-and-silver necklace Mom had given her during their recent sort-and-move process. She knew the dress looked good on her, but if everyone else was walking around in blue jeans and shorts, would she look out of place? Did she even care?

She brushed her hair and refreshed her lip gloss. When she emerged, wearing the pretty sundress with the cardigan looped over one arm, the girls were gone, and Miguel's eyes widened. "Sorry to keep you waiting," she told him.

"No problem." He set down the soda he'd been drinking and stood. "You look . . . beautiful."

She smiled and thanked him. As he took her hand to lead her down the trailer steps, she felt her cheeks warming. Hopefully she didn't appear too presumptuous, but after all, he'd been the one to say they had a "date." Still, as they strolled through the fairgrounds, quieter now that the crowd had thinned, she was glad she'd gone to the extra effort. "It's cooling off nicely," she told him as they got in line for the barbecue place.

Before long, they were seated at a table covered in a red gingham tablecloth. And then a waiter who looked to be about Cooper's age appeared to take their order from the very limited menu on the table. Fortunately, plenty of napkins and several moist towelettes were provided with the ribs, and somehow Jewel managed to keep herself from looking too messy by the time they were done. "You're right, Miguel," she told him as they left. "Their ribs are amazing."

After dinner, they wandered around the fairgrounds, looking at quilts, art exhibits, and food stands. Finally they came to the hall that displayed the "latest" products—goofy items that Jewel couldn't imagine anyone would really want, as well as the old standbys of "new and improved" cookware, nutrients promising ageless youthfulness, "time-saving" appliances, and a few items whose purpose they couldn't even figure out. "Well, that was educational," she said as they left the exhibit hall.

"Now how about the Ferris wheel ride?" Miguel asked as they strolled past another food stand. "Unless you'd rather have some dessert first." His brows arched. "Because before we're done tonight, I plan to indulge in an elephant ear."

"Ferris wheel first," she told him. "I don't want you eating so much that you toss your cookies up there."

"No worries." He laughed and, linking his arm in hers, led her through the carnival area. While he bought tickets, she just looked around. It was all so festive in the twilight. There were colorful balloons and flags and graphic signs, with a background of cheerful music and the sound of hawkers trying to lure unsuspecting folks to their booths. It was like a real time warp, and Jewel was so grateful to get to experience it.

"I'd like to paint something that captures all this," she told Miguel as they got into the surprisingly short Ferris wheel line. She noticed the younger crowd stood in long lines for the wilder rides. "It's all so magical."

"It is." Miguel greeted the muscular young ticket taker who motioned them forward, and then, ever the gentleman, Miguel helped her get into the Ferris wheel car. She felt a rush of childlike excitement as the young man locked them in, and soon they were going around and around.

"It's like a giant living kaleidoscope," she said as she looked at the colorfully lit fairgrounds whirling around down below them.

"I hate acting like a tourist with my phone, but would you mind if I took a couple pics? You know, to inspire me for painting later?"

"No, of course not." He chuckled. "I'm used to Anna taking photos of everything, including her food sometimes."

"Well, I try not to be addicted to taking pictures." She reached in her small shoulder bag, slipping out her phone and even doing a quick check to make sure neither Mom nor Coop had texted. Then she took a few pics of the wonderland below from several angles. And when Miguel wasn't looking, she snatched a couple of him. As she leaned forward to slip her phone back into her bag, she felt Miguel's arm slide around her shoulders. She smiled happily as she zipped her bag closed, then leaned back. "This is all so perfectly beautiful," she said quietly.

"It sure is." He turned to her. "All of it. Including you."

That warm, nervous rush went through her again, and now they were stopped at the very top of the wheel, the car just rocking gently back and forth with the motion, as new passengers boarded below. Jewel felt slightly breathless as they continued to look at each other, and then Miguel leaned forward and gently kissed her. Looking almost surprised at himself, he leaned away. "I, uh, I hope that was okay with you."

Jewel felt dizzy, and it wasn't from the height of the Ferris wheel. "No, Miguel, that was not okay." She firmly shook her head, holding back a smile. "It was way better than okay." She laughed and he kissed her again!

34

Jewel

After a surprisingly good night's sleep sharing the bed with her daughter, Jewel awoke refreshed and eager for the day. Cooper was still sleeping and the trailer was quiet in front as Jewel got ready for the day. Tiptoeing out, she saw the blinds remained down, but only Anna was curled up in the dinette bed. The sofa bed was tidied up and empty. Knowing Miguel wouldn't be far away, she decided to hunt him down. Right after she found a good cup of coffee.

As it turned out, she found both. After standing in a coffee line for a few minutes, where other early morning farmers were waiting, she found Miguel, who reminded her that he hadn't gotten an elephant ear last night.

"Care to join me for one?" he asked her as they walked with their coffees.

"That sounds delightful," she said. "They're kind of like donuts."

It was strange strolling across the quiet fairgrounds. Several maintenance workers were out and about, sweeping debris up from the previous night, and a few food booths were open, including the one that sold elephant ears. Several others were already waiting.

"Looks like you're not the only one who appreciates elephant ears for breakfast," she told him as they got in line.

"Good taste." He winked.

Eventually, they got their pastries and took their "fair fare" to a picnic table by the coffee kiosk to dine. Their conversation felt a little awkward at first, probably because Jewel kept thinking about the Ferris wheel kiss the night before, but it slowly returned to normal as he told her about this morning's 4-H livestock auction.

"They usually have it earlier in the fair, but our auctioneer got a summer cold, so the whole thing got postponed until today." He explained how that put more pressure on the livestock owners, having to keep their animals clean and healthy and looking tip-top before the auction.

"And today is the big day."

"Yes." He checked his watch. "Hopefully Anna is tending Barney by now."

"Barney?"

"Short for Barnabas."

"Of course." She smiled. "Both the girls were still asleep when I snuck out, but that's been almost an hour now."

He reached for his phone, then put it back. "I'd remind her but letting her do this on her own is part of growing up."

"When does the auction start?"

"Ten. But prospective buyers start checking out the livestock at nine, so you want them at their best."

Now Jewel felt nervous for Anna's sake. But she understood what Miguel was saying about the girl learning responsibility. Still, she pulled out her phone. "I think I'll check how Mom is getting along." She sent a quick text and was reassured that all was fine and that Marta had actually spent the night in Honeymoon Cottage.

Jewel laughed as she relayed the text. "She said they had a slumber party." And there's a text from Cooper too, saying they're with Barney.

Miguel looked relieved. "I could use another cup of coffee. How about you?"

"You're reading my mind." She watched as he went for more coffees. He looked so handsome in his blue-and-white plaid snap shirt, Wranglers, and a sharp black felt hat. As he talked to the older woman in the booth, her eyes lit up, and Jewel could tell he was saying something pleasant. He was always so polite to everyone.

They were just finishing their second coffees and getting ready to check on the girls and the calf when a couple of fellow farmers came over to chat with Miguel about harvest time and whose crops would be ready first.

"I'll go check on the girls in the barn." She gathered their empty cups. She knew this harvest talk was important since neighboring farms shared combines and bailers and other machinery to allow them to use state-of-the-art equipment for a fraction of the cost.

"Meet ya in there," he told her.

She dropped the empty cups in the trash barrel, then headed toward the stall area where Miguel had pointed out Anna's calf yesterday. She didn't see Cooper around, but she spotted Anna. Like her dad, she had on a crisp blue-and-white shirt and Wranglers, and her hair was pulled back in a neat ponytail. She was talking to a tall man whose back was to Jewel. Hopefully an interested bidder.

"Mom," Cooper hissed in Jewel's ear, making her jump. "Come this way."

"Huh?" Jewel was confused. "What's—"

"That's Anna's uncle," Cooper whispered as she led Jewel out the back door.

Jewel blinked. "Aaron? Seriously?"

"Yeah. He just showed up and started asking about her calf, and I thought maybe I should disappear."

"Interesting." Jewel glanced at the nearby manure heap. "Can we go someplace else to wait?"

"Oh, Mom, don't be a wimp." Just the same, Cooper led her around to the side where some benches were set up.

"So he was asking about her calf?" Jewel prodded. "Is he going to bid?"

"I don't think that's why he came." Cooper sat down, crossing her arms in front of her with a wrinkled forehead.

"Was he being nice to Anna?"

"I guess. I mean, he wasn't being rude or anything. But it was sort of weird. And I could tell Anna was pretty shocked to see him."

"I can imagine." Suddenly she remembered she'd told Miguel she'd meet him there and felt concerned. Despite Miguel's resolve to forgive his brother-in-law, she knew that Aaron could be a real piece of work. What if he said something and the two men got into an argument?

"I, uh, think I'll check on Miguel," she told Cooper. "He might be caught off guard to see Aaron here. I'll give him a heads-up."

"Good thinking. That could be awkward."

Jewel hurried back to the coffee kiosk, but Miguel wasn't there. So she headed back to the barn in time to see Aaron and Miguel in what looked like a conversation that could become heated, with Anna standing by with a slightly helpless expression. Feeling protective of Miguel, she hurried over and, linking her arm into his, looked at Aaron.

"What are you doing here?" Aaron asked with a furrowed brow.

"I'm here with Miguel," she told him. "Everything okay?" She glanced at Miguel and could tell by his tight jaw that something was up.

"I was just telling Miguel that I might want to buy Anna's calf," Aaron said.

"And I was just telling him to come to the auction," Miguel explained.

"But I was going to offer a fair price right here," Aaron said. "But he is refusing."

Jewel looked at Anna. "Well, it's your calf, Anna, shouldn't you have the last word?"

Her brown eyes were wide. The poor girl was clearly too nervous to deal with this.

"I'm sure she wants to participate in the auction," Miguel said firmly. "Right, Anna?"

She nodded eagerly.

"Sounds like you're doing her thinking for her." Aaron narrowed his eyes. "Kind of like you did with her mother."

"Aaron Hanford," Jewel scolded him. "That's untrue and unfair, and you really should apologize."

Aaron shrugged. "Well, you might be right. That wasn't necessary." He cleared his throat. "Sorry."

Jewel looked from one man to the other, and since no one was speaking up, she decided to just continue. "So, Miguel was just telling me more about the auction, and I can understand why it's important for Anna to participate. She's spent all this time raising her calf and hoping to win a blue ribbon. Why would you, her very own uncle, rob her of the opportunity to see how Barney does in the auction?" She pointed to Aaron. "Why can't you just join in and bid with the others? Or are you above that?"

"No, I'm not above that."

"Then are you trying to take unfair advantage of your own niece to get a better price?"

"No, that's not it," he said quickly. "I just, uh, wanted to—"

"Then why not stick to the program?" she challenged. "Don't you realize the price Anna gets will go to her college education?"

"That's right!" Cooper declared. Jewel hadn't even noticed her daughter standing right next to her.

"And, Aaron, even if you should be outbid"—she eyed him curiously, knowing she was taking a poke at his pride now—"at least you'll help to get her price up there. Isn't that what a loving uncle would do?"

He took in a slow breath, then nodded. "Yeah, of course. I just thought I could simplify matters. But now that you've explained it better . . . Sure, I'll wait. I'll bid with the others. Might even be fun." He gave a crooked smile, then tipped his hat and left.

"I think he got the hint," Anna told Jewel. "Thanks."

"Yeah." Miguel nodded. "Thanks."

"That was great, Mom."

When it was time for Barney and Anna to take their place

on the auction block, the bidding was solid, but in the end, Aaron Hanford won the bid. And when he went up to shake Anna's hand, they were both smiling. And back behind the crowd of chattering bidders, Miguel and Cooper and Jewel were all smiling too.

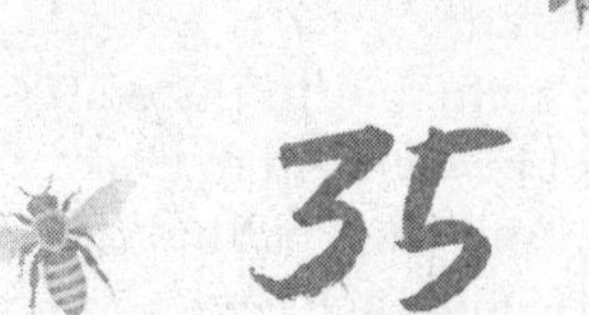

35

Honey

The crisp autumn air always filled Honey with a sense of wistful hope. It wasn't that she didn't like summertime, but when it was time for that season to end, she was never sad to say goodbye. This year was no different. As she and CT took their usual morning stroll, slowly but surely due to his cane and his limp, she shook her head at her worn-out vegetable garden. Okay, that always made her a bit sad. But then again, that was life. In the spring, all was fresh and green and new. The world was young and alive, full of promise.

But now, as usual, her garden looked faded and picked over. The leaves were shriveled and brown, and her sunflowers hung limply, waiting for winter birds to come foraging. A few brave tomatoes and some hearty squashes still hung on, but it was like the writing on the wall for the end of the growing season. For the first year in memory, Honey had taken a pass on canning, other than putting up a few jars of peaches from their favorite peach tree. Maybe next year, if summer wasn't too jam-packed with activity like this summer had been.

The consolation was that most of her garden's yield had been sold at Cooper's and Anna's roadside produce stand. The structure, designed by Jewel and constructed by Miguel, with CT's "help," had been operating on the edge of town for a couple of months now. Jewel had created handsome signs for the stand, and the whole thing was so attractive, she'd even made a charming painting of it. The piece was so loved by everyone that she'd had it reproduced into prints, which they also sold at the stand.

She and CT paused by the lavender now. Faded and worn and draped in the gray morning fog, the field reminded her of sweet-smelling Gladys Price, an elderly woman who attended their church. Like Honey, the lavender plants were ready to hunker down for winter. Their aromatic purple blooms had been cropped and bundled into thick bunches and tied with twine by the enterprising girls. Some of the fragrant bunches still hung from the roof of the little produce stand, but they'd probably be sold out before long.

They continued along slowly, but CT eventually stopped walking and asked to rest on the bench that Honey and Jewel had set next to the pumpkin patch. Littered cheerfully with colorful pumpkins, this field still had some life left in it. They hoped some of the remaining pumpkins would grow jack-o'-lantern size in time for the church's annual harvest party. The other somewhat deformed ones, nibbled by deer, would remain to provide seed for next year's crop.

The previously harvested pumpkins were attractively lined up all around the produce stand at the moment. They left them there throughout the week, and their numbers decreased daily. But they didn't worry too much about theft in these parts. If someone needed a pumpkin that bad, they might as well take one. Sometimes they even found cash tucked under the big rock they kept on the produce stand. Their form of the honor system when someone wanted to make a purchase when no one was around. Honey, their most valuable item, had been transported back and forth in a wooden crate, like gold. Until they ran out.

Honey sat down next to CT, pulling her wool collar higher to keep her neck warm. She made a mental note to take some stadium blankets to the stand this afternoon. Since it was Friday, she and CT would mind the stand. The girls had some school activity that evening, and the stand still had regulars who liked to stop before the weekend. Besides grabbing blankets, Honey would try to remember to gather up those straggling tomatoes and squashes before leaving. And if she got around to it, maybe a loaf or two of pumpkin bread. She didn't tell the customers, but the pumpkin came from a can.

She smiled to herself, still musing over the success of the girls' charming harvest stand and how popular it had grown with the locals. She felt a little sad to think their stand, like the rest of things getting ready for the change of seasons, would close in a few weeks. Still, it had been a prosperous venture for the girls.

CT made a huffing noise, and she turned to him, patting the knee of his "good" leg. "It's our day to work the produce stand," she reminded him, and he smiled. He loved chatting with customers as he repeated the same stories and got befuddled over making change. No one seemed to mind. Instead, they praised the produce and his farming abilities, and he acted as if he'd personally grown and harvested every single item there. And no one corrected him.

After all, he'd been the one to plant the pumpkins last spring—at least some of them—and the lavender, at Honey's request several years before that. Well, with help. It was no surprise that the bestseller of all had been CT's honey. Every time he'd sold a jar, he beamed with pride. It hadn't taken long to run out of the jars they'd allotted for the stand. The rest of the honey, held in reserves, was for CT's personal use, and for the Honey Bee and Bee, which—thanks to Jewel's diligent work and inviting website—was soon to have its very first guests.

Jewel was excited about the prospects, and Honey was proud of her for pursuing her dreams. It hadn't been easy. Summer had been filled with ups and downs for all of them, but somehow it seemed they were stronger and better for it. Even CT, although fading daily, seemed contented and happy in his own way. She thought of all the times she wanted to ask why. Why had CT, of all people, been allotted this illness? Why had their last years of life together been turned upside down like this? But she knew those answers were for another life. In the meantime, she realized that CT's illness was what had brought their little family together. It was exactly what Jewel and Cooper had needed to restart their lives, to give them purpose, to bring them home, to make them all into a family. And it's what Honey had needed too. Not only that, but she suspected their family would soon grow to include the Oroscos before long. She'd seen the look in her daughter's eyes and observed Miguel's tenderness toward her. And if that happened, the farm property that had been divided could be stitched back together again. Reunited, just like all their hearts over the past few months.

"We had a good summer," Honey said to CT.

"Uh-huh." He adjusted the brim of his cap. "Real good."

"Looks like everything is getting ready to rest now." She sighed with contentment.

"Uh-huh. Rest." He shivered. "That's good."

"Ready to go inside?" He nodded, and she stood, holding her hand out to him. He took it and, steadying himself between her and his cane, stood shakily.

"Can you make it okay?" she asked. Sometimes at this stage of their walk she'd been forced to run back for the wheelchair.

"With my Honey . . . I can. I can make it." He smiled and together, hand in hand, they slowly walked home.

A Note from the Author

Dear Reader,

First of all, thank you for reading *Welcome to the Honey B&B*. Unless you get my newsletter or follow me on Facebook, you might not know my husband Chris (like CT in my book) suffers from FTD. So, as you may suspect, much of the details about the illness described in the book are extracted from real life. I suppose it was as much therapeutic for me as it was meant to help inform readers about this lesser-known form of early-onset dementia. It is a cruel and confusing ailment that impacts a whole family in a myriad of ways.

On my own journey with my husband, I've tried to become better informed in order to better care for him as well as myself. I am Chris's main caregiver and will continue to do so in our home as long as it's doable and safe for both of us. I recently hired some part-time in-home help and am currently navigating that. None of this matches what we'd planned for our happy golden years. But life is like that. Like I often tell Chris, "We do our best and trust God for the rest." What else can you do?

Anyway, I thought perhaps readers who may be dealing with similar challenges of a loved one with dementia might benefit from some of the resources that have helped me. Below is a list of books that I continue to reread, hoping to glean more information and keep some useful coping tools handy. I'm sure there are many more resources I've yet to discover, but here's my little list. I wish you and yours health and happiness and peace—and appreciate any prayers for me and my family.

Blessings!
Melody Carlson

— To Learn More —

Books:

- *Understanding the Changing Brain: A Positive Approach to Dementia Care* by Teepa Snow (Positive Approach, LLC, 2021)
- *Dementia Caregiving: A Family Guide to Embracing Dementia: 8 Easy Steps to Daily Care and Enhanced Communication* by Malcolm Oppenheimer (HSN Publishing Ventures LLC, 2023)
- *Caring for Carol by Caring for Me: A Journey with Dementia and Self-Discovery* by Anthony P. Mauro Sr. (Luminare Press, 2024)
- *Defeat Your Anxiety: Practical Tools from a Christian Therapist to Transform Your Thinking* by Jeffrey Sumpolec, MA, LPCC (Sycamore Media Group, 2024)

Resources:

- Association for Frontal Temporal Degeneration (TheAFTD.org)
- Frontotemporal Dementia, Johns Hopkins Medicine (https://www.hopkinsmedicine.org/health/conditions-and-diseases/dementia/frontotemporal-dementia)
- "What Are Frontotemporal Disorders? Causes, Symptoms, and Treatment," National Institutes of Health (https://www.nia.nih.gov/health/frontotemporal-disorders/what-are-frontotemporal-disorders-causes-symptoms-and-treatment)

Turn the page for a sneak peek at

Just for the Summer

one

Hotel Jackson, Seattle

Ginny Masters rarely blew her temper. Today could prove the exception. She silently counted to ten while studying her boss's frosty expression. Diana Jackson, owner of Hotel Jackson Seattle, had to be one of the most difficult people on the planet. And working in the high end of the hospitality industry, where most guests at this boutique hotel acted overly entitled, Ginny had met more than her fair share of thorny people.

"I *know* I already informed you of that reception, *Genevieve*." Diana's nostrils actually flared. "I'm absolutely certain of it."

"If you *had* told me, I would've scheduled it accordingly." Ginny fingered the edges of her tablet, standing her ground, but knowing full well that Diana would win. Never mind that Diana had totally blanked on her best friend's daughter's last-minute wedding reception. It made no difference now. Ginny would receive the brunt of the blame for Diana's blunder—and be forced to pick up the pieces.

"Oh, I'll admit it was short notice when I told you." Diana's voice softened ever so slightly as she placed a placating hand on Ginny's shoulder. A familiar gesture when Diana was about to manipulate the opposition to her advantage. "Poor Vivian was so distraught that her dear Rebecca planned to elope, I promised her the Skylight Room as a way to coax Rebecca back to sanity. After all, they are a very influential family in Seattle." Diana paused to stare up at the chandelier, rubbing her chin as if deep in thought or perhaps inspecting for dust.

Ginny decided to try empathy. "I can understand you wanting to help your friend out, but I—"

"I am certain Vivian booked this in early April. Maybe even March. And I told you about it the same day." Diana's softness turned brittle as she locked eyes with Ginny. "Rebecca's reception will be held right here. On Saturday night." Her hand slipped from Ginny's shoulder. "I will try to overlook your negligence to schedule it as you were instructed. It's not the first time you've let me down. *Now fix this!*"

"But the Bremmers' fiftieth wedding anniversary is booked here on Saturday night. It's been locked in since early February." Ginny tapped her tablet, pointing at the date.

"Then *unlock* it." Diana stepped back with a stony expression. "I don't care how you do it, just straighten out your mess!"

Ginny watched as Diana briskly crossed the ballroom, her clicking heels echoing up to the high ornate ceiling. To argue was pointless, but Ginny's heart went out to the Bremmers. The sweet couple attended her church. She'd known them for years. The most undemanding folks, always helping others. And although the Bremmer children had planned this wingding, she knew how much the elder Bremmers were looking forward to it. She also knew they'd be completely gracious about this double-booking. But their children . . . not so much.

As she hurried back to her office, she formulated a plan to "fix this" as Diana had commanded. And since Diana had said she didn't care how it was done, Ginny did what she often did. She took the matter completely into her own hands. By the end of the day, she had convinced the oldest son, Thomas Bremmer, to accept the Skylight Room, gratis, for a rescheduled early afternoon celebration. To sweeten the deal, she promised if their festivities wrapped up by five o'clock, hotel drinks and hors d'oeuvres would be on the house as well. Knowing this was mostly a church crowd, she wasn't too worried about the bar bill, which is where most tabs ballooned.

"And the wedding reception flowers will be delivered Saturday morning," she told Thomas before hanging up. "So your party can have the enjoyment of those as well. I can assure you they will be gorgeous." And expensive, she thought, as she looked at the name of the florist in charge.

"Well, that's an offer that's hard to refuse," Thomas admitted. "I'll let my younger sister handle the task of notifying the guests."

"I'm truly sorry for this inconvenience. Thank you for understanding."

"Mom and Dad and their older friends will probably appreciate the earlier time anyway. No night owls in that crowd." He chuckled. "I hope you'll be able to join us, Ginny. I know my parents would love to see you there."

"I'll do my best," she said. "But that'll be a busy day for me." She closed her tablet. Thomas Bremmer was a nice enough guy and a successful CPA with his own firm. She'd even dated him a couple of times a few years ago. But he just wasn't her type. As she thanked him again and hung up, she vaguely wondered . . . What exactly was her type? Even if she found her type, would she ever have time for a real romance? Not as long as she was managing Hotel Jackson for its cantankerous owner. Diana Jackson assumed that Ginny was gratefully married to this job. Always treating her like it was such a privilege to be the head manager here. Maybe it was at first. But that was more than ten years ago.

"Ginny?" Adrian Jackson poked his head through her cracked open door. "Busy?"

"No more than usual," she told him.

He grimaced. "So Mom told you about Rebecca's wedding reception?"

She nodded grimly.

He entered her small, cluttered office and, leaning against the edge of her console table, folded his arms in front of him in a totally Adrian pose. “So you’re okay, then? I mean, I tried to warn Mom you already had something booked. I even had it on my schedule.” He shrugged with a furrowed brow. “But she seemed pretty determined. Sorry.”

“It’s all worked out now, Adrian. Don’t worry about it.”

“Oh, good. I figured you’d handle it, Ginny. You usually do.” He brightened. “I don’t know how you do it though, and I’m sure I could use some customer service lessons from you.” He chuckled. “But I’m just the bean counter here. I don’t have to be nice. Especially when it’s time to shake someone down.”

She couldn’t help but smile. Adrian wasn’t the type to shake anyone down. Sure, he was a reliable CFO for the hotel, but not highly motivated. Growing up rich probably hadn’t helped him in that department. Although she suspected even if he’d grown up like she had, his lackadaisical nature would still be laid-back. In a way, it was probably one of his best qualities. He was always calm. Sometimes irritatingly so.

“Any dinner plans tonight?” He stood up straight. “I know you’re supposed to get off at seven. I could probably get us into Le—”

“No thank you, Adrian.” She checked her watch. “I, uh, I already have a date tonight.”

“You do?” He looked just as crestfallen as he usually did when she turned him down. Wouldn’t he have gotten used to it by now? “Who with?”

“My bathtub.” She shoved her notepad into her bag.

“Aw, come on, Ginny. When was the last time you did something *just for fun*?”

She considered this. Of course, he was right, but she didn’t plan to let him know that. “I’m exhausted, Adrian. It’s been a long day, and I have to come in early tomorrow.”

“How about a rain check, then?” He grinned. “It even goes with the weather.”

“Oh, I don’t think—”

“But my buddy Jean Pierre is managing Le Jardin now. I can make reservations for—”

"No, please, *don't*."

"Okay, how about this? I'll give you a ride home," he offered. "Then I'll call Ono's for takeout."

As tempting as that sounded, she knew she had to decline. For Adrian's sake. "No thanks."

"I don't get you, Ginny. Honestly, you're the worst workaholic I've ever known. Don't you remember what happens when you're all work and no play?"

"Yeah. Ginny's a dull girl." She forced a smile. "So you've told me before. Thanks."

He brightened. "So I can make us a reservation for, say, next week? I know you're going to love what Jean's done to the menu."

"As lovely as that sounds, please, let me think about it." She wouldn't have to think too long but didn't want to let him down too hard all at once . . . again.

"Okay, fine. If you don't want to go out tonight, why can't I bring sushi by your place?"

"No thanks, Adrian." She gave him her sternest look.

"Is this because of Mom?" His lower lip protruded slightly. "Has she said something to you recently?"

"No . . . I'm just really tired."

"Then just let me get you sushi." He reached for his phone. "I'll call it in now. I can still drive you home, and then I'll bring it back to you. I won't even stay to eat with—"

"No thanks." She grimaced and grimly shook her head.

"I know this is because of Mom."

"I'm just really tired," she tried again. "Sorry to be such a party pooper."

"Oh, Ginny." He leaned forward, peering into her eyes. "Why do you let Mom keep you under her thumb like this?"

How many times had she told Adrian she liked him but wanted only his friendship? Yet he continued to blame Ginny's coolness on his mother. To be fair, he wasn't entirely wrong. Diana vehemently opposed Ginny dating her only son. Not that Ginny had ever wanted to seriously date Adrian. She simply tried to be politely friendly with him. "Look, Adrian," she kept her tone gentle. "You know as well as I do that your mother doesn't approve of—"

"What Mom doesn't know won't hurt her."

"But it might hurt us." Ginny felt relief when her phone rang. Waving Adrian away, she answered it. "This is Genevieve Masters," she said in her usual courteous but efficient tone. Naturally, it was housekeeping again. Still complaining that the laundry was extra slow today. "I know they're shorthanded, Rosaria. There's a flu bug going around down there," she told her head housekeeper. "I'll speak to Lindsey again, but *please* try to make do in the meantime."

"In the meantime, we're nearly out of towels and pillowcases."

"Right . . ." Ginny paused to think. "Hey, can you spare a couple of housekeepers? Ones who'd be willing to go down there and lend a hand for a day or two? I'll even offer a little bonus."

"That might tempt the Johnson twins. They're always scrabbling for money."

"Great. I'll call down to the laundry to arrange it and get back to you ASAP."

Several phone calls and a little job juggling later, the linen problem was being resolved and everyone was moderately happy. But this was only Tuesday. As Ginny removed her heeled pumps and pulled on her walking Keds, she realized the hotel would get busier by the end of the week, and even more so with graduations and weddings around the corner. It was just life in a popular boutique hotel in the heart of Seattle. But sometimes it felt exhausting and never-ending.

Not that Ginny was complaining. Managing Hotel Jackson more than ten years was pretty impressive for someone without a hospitality management degree. Something Diana regularly reminded Ginny of—usually right before job review time. Ginny's educational status always provided Diana with her standard excuse for denying more than a minimal cost of living raise. Ginny knew that managers of similar hotels made more. Much more.

But it wasn't just about the money. After all, Ginny had learned frugality as a child. Before becoming manager, she'd gotten lots of pinching-pennies practice working her way through the ranks in the hotel. But those experiences in the laundry, housekeeping, and restaurant all proved valuable to her later on. She understood the ins and outs of hotel management personally. And attaining the top management position here was no small deal for a girl with only two years of college.

At least it had felt that way when she was still in her twenties. Sometimes, especially of late, she wasn't so sure. Diana was notorious for pulling a fast one like she'd done today. Almost as if she derived pleasure from watching Ginny squirm and then scramble to pull a rabbit from her hat. Sure, the challenges could be fun . . . sometimes. Especially when she succeeded.

But the stress was starting to catch up with her. And the demands of an unpredictable work schedule had taken their toll on her personal life. She laughed out loud as she pulled on her trench coat. *What personal life?* Adrian was right . . . Ginny didn't know how to have fun. Had she ever?

Slipping out the rear employee exit, she frowned to see the deluge increasing the already oversized puddles on the sidewalk. Why hadn't she worn her rain boots this morning? Wet weather wasn't unusual for Seattle in spring, but the low clouds loitering atop the Sound looked gray and dreary . . . and gloomy and cold.

She was almost to her apartment complex when her cell phone chimed. Seeing it was her baby sister, she eagerly answered. Gillian was Ginny's only flesh-and-blood relative in this world. And although Gillie was ten years younger, they had always been close. Even more so after their single mother died when Gillie was only eleven. That's why Ginny quit college and went to work full-time. It was the only way to take guardianship of her kid sister. But it had all been worth it. Especially now that Gillian was just finishing her last year of med school. The light at the end of their long, dark tunnel.

"What's up, sis?"

"Best news ever," Gillian gushed. "You're not going to believe it, Ginny!"

"Tell me!" Had Gillie already gotten a job?

"I've been invited to work at the Howard Institute."

"The Howard Institute?" Ginny stepped under an awning to avoid the rain and hear better. "A real job? Already?"

"Yes! The Howard Institute is this amazing cancer research clinic."

"That's awesome, Gillie! Congratulations!" Ginny was suddenly imagining the two of them moving into nicer housing outside of the noisy city.

"But one thing, Ginny. The institute is in Boston."

"Boston . . . really?" Ginny tried to keep the disappointment out of her voice.

"I know it's a long way off, Ginny, but this is a huge opportunity for me. The Howard Institute is renowned for its cutting-edge research."

"I know you've always wanted to specialize in oncology."

"And Dr. Billings is one of the most respected oncologists in the country."

Ginny took in a deep breath, willing enthusiasm as she stepped out from the protection of the awning. Feeling the cold runoff water going straight down the back of her neck, she hurried toward her apartment building just a couple doors down. "Then even more congratulations are in order, Gillian. I'm so happy for you. You go, girl!"

"*Go girl*—across the country? So you're really okay with this, Ginny? I mean, we always talked about getting a house together after I finished—"

"Oh, those were kid dreams. The new dream is for you to go to Boston. Become a world-famous oncologist. And save lots of lives. We can always get a house together when we're old women with nothing better to do." Ginny forced a tinny laugh as she hopped past a mud puddle. Stopping by her apartment building, she ducked under its frayed canvas awning.

"I'm so glad you're okay with it, Gin. I promised to give them my answer by the end of the week. They want me to start right after graduation. This summer I'll be a research doctor!" She let out a happy squeal. "I'm so excited."

"I'm really, really proud of you."

"You know I never could've done it without you. As soon as I'm in a place where I can, I plan to pay you back for all—"

"Don't be silly. The way you pay me back is by succeeding. And I get bragging rights. I can tell everyone my baby sister is a famous oncologist."

Gillian laughed. "I'm so relieved you're okay with this. I have to go now. I'm on night shift at eight."

Ginny told her goodbye and went into her building. The cold lobby, damp with rain, smelled mustier than usual. One of the light fixtures appeared to be burned out, and the other flickered as if it were about to join it. As she removed and shook out her soaked trench coat, she tried not to think of how eagerly she'd been waiting to escape this dreary place. They'd moved here after Mom died. Mostly because of the proximity of Ginny's job. Plus, it was cheap.

Ginny would never tell Gillian, but she'd been perusing real estate websites lately. Printing a few photos out, filing them in a folder . . . and dreaming of the starter house they would buy together as soon as Gillian started to practice medicine. Ginny had even managed to accrue a meager savings account to contribute to a down payment. She knew they'd have to start small. But she'd hoped for a little house with a big view, a cook's kitchen, and a real wood-burning fireplace. Well, that dream, like the rest of her life, would have to remain on hold for now.

two

Frederickson's Fishing Lodge, Idaho

Jacqueline Potter was fed up. Seriously! What was Grandpa Jack thinking? That she was his indentured servant or personal slave . . . or just an overworked, underpaid employee? She dumped his dirty clothes from the basket onto the laundry room floor and growled. She checked the fitness tracker on her smartwatch. Already, she'd put in more than six thousand steps and it was after five o'clock. Quitting time! Except Grandpa wouldn't be satisfied until his favorite Carhartt shirt was washed and ready for tomorrow.

If it wasn't bad enough to be stuck managing Grandpa's decrepit fishing lodge for the past six years, he now expected her to do his stinking laundry too? She held her breath as she shoved his old fishing shirt, which smelled like rotten sardines, into the washer, followed by a few other ripe items. She tossed in a soap pod, then slammed the door, pressing the electronic button so hard that the stupid machine refused to cooperate.

"Okay, fine," she told the stubborn washer—the same modern model she'd insisted the lodge needed last year. "See if I care." She kicked the empty laundry basket across the room, then, feeling a smidgen of guilt, tried the On button again. A little more gently, and this time it worked.

Oh, sure, she knew she had a bad attitude. And she should feel sorry for Grandpa. Laid up with a swollen ankle and bruised elbow. But that's what you get when you go traipsing around in the river at his age. Good grief, the man was in his seventies! Why on earth hadn't he retired by now? Maybe this was the perfect time—while he was limping around—to urge him to sell this run-down old lodge and move into some sensible senior living place where he could enjoy the rest of his golden years in pampered leisure. Maybe meet a nice old lady.

"Anyone in there?" Margie the cook called from the nearby hallway.

"Just me," Jacqueline grumbled back. "The new laundress."

Margie came into the laundry room with arched brows. "I didn't realize you knew how to do laundry, Jackie."

Jacqueline tossed her a look as she pushed a loose lock of hair behind her ear. "Who do you think washes *my* clothes?"

"Your French maid?" Margie smirked. "Well, that's real nice you want to help out with the laundry. But I need—"

"I don't *want* to help out. I'm only doing Grandpa's clothes because Cassie seems to have disappeared from the planet, and his *favorite* flannel was dirty. He has dozens, of course, but do you think he can live one whole day without his favorite shirt? Apparently not."

"Well, if you're done in here, I could use a hand in the kitchen. The Brower party is coming in earlier than I expected and now I—"

"*What?*" Jacqueline demanded. "They weren't supposed to arrive until tomorrow afternoon."

"Not according to Kent Brower. He and his buddies are outside right now, checking out the dock and the boats, and they're hungry for supper."

"You're kidding." Jacqueline planted her fists on her hips. "I'll send them packing!"

"Mr. Brower said you booked him to arrive *today*."

"No way. I booked them for tomorrow through Sunday."

"Yeah, you might wanna double-check that." Margie picked some soiled towels from the floor, tossing them into the empty basket. "When I couldn't find you, I took a little peek at your reservation book. Turns out Mr. Brower was right."

"Well, that book isn't always up-to-date. I keep reservations on my iPad too."

"Maybe so, but the Brower party is here now. I'm just glad they didn't get here before lunchtime. That would've been slim pickin's. Anyway, those fellas are hungry, and I need help getting supper ready." Margie pointed at Jacqueline. "That means you."

"Oh, Margie." Jacqueline let loose with a loud moan. "I'm done for the day."

"No you aren't." Margie gave her a gentle but firm shove toward the door. "Come on, Princess. You know this is men's week at the lodge. Seems like they eat twice as much with no women around. Anyway, I got a pile of potatoes that need peeling. And then there's—"

"Can't you get someone else—"

"Ain't nobody here but you and me, girlfriend. You can just thank your lucky stars the Riverside Cabin was vacated and that Cassie got it all cleaned and ready, or you'd really be scrambling."

"Why can't Cassie help you with supper?"

"She already went home. Some kind of birthday party or something."

"I wish I'd already gone home," Jacqueline mumbled as she shuffled toward the kitchen.

"You *are* home, honey." Margie laughed. "Welcome."

"I mean home in my own cabin." Jacqueline had planned to start streaming a new series about British royals tonight. Anything to escape the reality of her own pathetic life.

"I know where you live, darlin'." Margie handed her an apron.

"This is so not fair. Being forced into menial labor. That is not in my job description."

"Send your complaints to the management."

"I *am* the management!" Jacqueline sputtered as she tied the apron.

Margie pointed to a large bag of potatoes next to the sink. "I want that whole bag peeled—pronto!"

"Potatoes? Seriously? Why do I have to do—"

"Less talk, more work, *Cinderella*."

"Yeah, where are those helpful little mice when you need them?" Jacqueline picked up a big potato, glaring into the spud's eyes. "This is going to ruin my manicure."

Margie's laugh was not sympathetic. As Jacqueline peeled the potato, she wondered why she'd ever accepted this job in the first place. Sure, it had sounded fun . . . in the beginning. And sometimes it was kind of fun. Most of the visitors here were fishermen, and she'd enjoyed all the attention she'd get from them. But, like most of the guests, it had grown old. And the fun had steadily deteriorated over the years. Even with a new season ahead, she didn't feel the least bit hopeful that life would improve for her. Let alone offer any sort of fun. She couldn't even remember the last time she'd had any real fun. Would she ever have fun again?

Melody Carlson is the award-winning author of more than 250 books with sales of more than 7.5 million, including many bestselling Christmas novellas, young adult titles, and contemporary romances. She received a *Romantic Times* Career Achievement Award, her novel *All Summer Long* has been made into a Hallmark movie, and the movie based on her novel *The Happy Camper* premiered on UPtv in 2023. She and her husband live in central Oregon. Learn more at MelodyCarlson.com.

A Note from the Publisher

Dear Reader,

Thank you for selecting a Revell novel! We're so happy to be part of your reading life through this work. Our mission here at Revell is to publish stories that reach the heart. Through friendship, romance, suspense, or a travel back in time, we bring stories that will entertain, inspire, and encourage you. We believe in the power of stories to change our lives and are grateful for the privilege of sharing these stories with you.

We believe in building lasting relationships with readers, and we'd love to get to know you better. If you have any feedback, questions, or just want to chat about your experience reading this book, please email us directly at publisher@revellbooks.com. Your insights are incredibly important to us, and it would be our pleasure to hear how we can better serve you.

We look forward to hearing from you and having the chance to enhance your experience with Revell Books.

The Publishing Team at Revell Books

A Division of Baker Publishing Group
publisher@revellbooks.com